GRUNT HERO

First published 2017 by Solaris
an imprint of Rebellion Publishing Ltd,
Riverside House, Osney Mead,
Oxford, OX2 0ES, UK

www.solarisbooks.com

ISBN: 978 1 78108 515 8

10 9 8 7 6 5 4 3 2 1

A CIP catalogue record for this book is available
from the British Library.

Designed & typeset by Rebellion Publishing

Printed in Denmark by Nørhaven

WESTON OCHSE

GRUNT HERO

A TASK FORCE OMBRA NOVEL

SOLARIS

For My Grandfather,
James David Estes,
My First Hero

From this distant vantage point, the Earth might not seem of any particular interest. But for us, it's different. Consider again that dot. That's here, that's home, that's us. On it everyone you love, everyone you know, everyone you ever heard of, every human being who ever was, lived out their lives. The aggregate of our joy and suffering, thousands of confident religions, ideologies, and economic doctrines, every hunter and forager, every hero and coward, every creator and destroyer of civilization, every king and peasant, every young couple in love, every mother and father, hopeful child, inventor and explorer, every teacher of morals, every corrupt politician, every 'superstar,' every 'supreme leader,' every saint and sinner in the history of our species lived there—on the mote of dust suspended in a sunbeam.

Carl Sagan, speaking of what
Earth looks like from space

People are giving up not just hope, but their lives. Reports of suicides are streaming in. Today's zeitgeist is why even try? So is that it? Have the aliens won? Have they supplanted us as a species on this, our once great planet, Earth? Is it time to just roll over, kiss our asses goodbye, and take what they give us? Or do we fight? Someone once said that he won by merely surviving. Is that our only goal now? Just to survive? It doesn't seem like enough, does it? We'd achieved a Golden Age here on Earth. Whatever we wanted we could find at the click of a button. If we wanted it sooner, we could have gone to a big box store. Foods from all over the world were at our disposal. We could watch movies, listen to music, and live... really live. There are those who would see a return to that. Then there are those who, like Henry David Thoreau, would see us achieve a simpler kind of life. I'm not sure which one is the loftier ideal, but I am certain that either one is better than dying. The Old Bard said it best when he said, *To Be or Not To Be*. So you ask me, good listeners, which one will you be? Someone who wants to die? Or someone who wants to live?

Conspiracy Theory Talk Radio,
Night Stalker Monologue #1721

PART ONE

War was always here. Before man was, war waited for him. The ultimate trade awaiting its ultimate practitioner.

Cormac McCarthy,
Blood Meridian, or
The Evening Redness in the West

CHAPTER ONE

NOT EVEN THE cold burn of the frigid ocean spray could scour away my sins. Yet I still embraced it, leaning into the bow of the umiak as it bucked on three foot seas, letting the water splash and sizzle against my bare skin. Summer was almost over and the warm days were already skidding into another Bering Strait winter, so this would be our last hunt until next spring. We were searching for polar bear and hunting with traditional weapons. I was invited to the expedition to learn the old ways so I could become closer with my new tribe. I stretched out my arms to embrace the moment, wind searing my face, the spray of water soothing the newest of my tattoos. I closed my eyes and let the faces of each of the men's and women's names I'd put on me flash past, the wind and surf washing them clean of the dirt and grime of their deaths, leaving only the inked letters.

Mike 1 and Mike 2 killed in Iraq.

Olivares killed in Vegas.

McKenzie killed at Kilimanjaro.

Macabre killed in Los Angeles.

And the others.

So many, too many for one person to be able to handle. I'd barely been able to deal with my own existence, much less bear the responsibility for so many dead. Mother knew this when she sent me here. I'd come to a new understanding about death. Death didn't have to be the end. Death could be the beginning as well. I'd come trying to forget, trying to exorcise the knowledge from my psyche so I could heal. But forgetting had been the absolute wrong thing to do. I should have been remembering the lives they'd lived, the sacrifices they'd made, the moments of pure joy that we'd shared. And it took coming to this snow-blasted corner of the world for me to figure that out.

The Yupik people of St. Lawrence Island believe in reincarnation. Whether it be a person or an animal, they revered people who died or animals they had to put down for food, careful not to destroy the spirit with the flesh. They did this because the end wasn't the end. It was merely a transition into another state of being.

That had been my problem for so long. I'd thought only of their shattered bodies. Their deaths had become the symbol for their lives. Mother had called it synecdoche. She'd said that my brain had created a symbol for them and I had to find a way to change the symbol. She'd told me to remember each one for something different, then think about those moments until they were imprinted upon my psyche. She'd also realized that I'd spent so much time trying to save my flesh that I'd neglected my own spirit. She'd seen that even in her collective, I was still too close to the blades that had wounded me. So she'd sent me north to the farthest length of her reach—an island north of the Bearing Strait, as close to Russia as it was Alaska.

Merlin Apassingok laughed behind me from where he sat and steered the outboard motor. "You look like that girl from that movie about the ship and the iceberg," he said.

"*Titanic*," I yelled back. "The movie was *Titanic*."

Truth be told, I felt like the girl from *Titanic*. The feeling of freedom was almost pure enough to make me think I was flying. The frigid winter and the warm friendship of Merlin's family had nurtured the idealist young man I'd once been, causing him to return. There'd been a time before all the wars when I'd enjoyed the simple things in life. I'd had aspirations instead of obligations. Everything had seemed fresh and new and wasn't shadowed by the things I'd done.

"Look there," Merlin said.

I opened my eyes to where he was pointing. An immense bull walrus swam even with the boat. Behind it came an orca, a natural predator.

"Hang on."

I immediately sat and grabbed the gunnels of the small traditional whaling boat.

Merlin shoved the engine rudder hard, causing the umiak to curl behind the walrus. He killed the engine, grabbed a weapon and rose like a hunter of old. He'd left the harpoon in the bottom of the boat. He wasn't about to kill the Orca. Instead, he chose the aangruyak, a lance meant to dispatch a dying walrus. Holding it with both hands, he waited until the orca rushed beneath the umiak, then slammed the lance into the water, thumping the side of the whale.

The whale bucked in pain, lashing the hull of the umiak with its tail.

Merlin fought for balance, then sat down and kicked

the motor to life. The umiak was soon parallel with the walrus. He handed the lance to me and I stood, facing the rear, ready to deter the orca again if it got too close.

The Yupik had been hunting walrus since before recorded time. Their favorite method was to do it by kayak, but as often as not, they'd use the umiak, especially since the advent of the outboard engine. The walrus's only natural predators were man, orca, and polar bears. The bears had been coming more and more since the water was warming, sending the walruses even farther north. To have a big bull on the island was no small thing. If it could make landfall, it would draw others, helping to enlarge and protect the ugly of walruses already on Savoonga. To protect it on its journey was the right thing to do. To protect the walrus meant to protect a way of life.

The umiak suddenly lurched, sending me flying into the air. When I slammed into the water, the impact and the cold shocked me. I was unable to move for a few precious seconds. Somehow I'd kept my grip on the lance. When I opened my eyes, I saw the orca was only a few meters from me, roaring through the water like a black and white shark, its toothy mouth open and ready to bite. I pushed the point of the lance towards it, ocean water causing the wooden shaft to move so ponderously, the point barely arriving in time to spear the end of the nose. My legs suddenly began to work and I kicked out and shoved the lance with everything I had. But it wasn't enough. I'd bloodied the whale, but it still came on. I barely managed to kick a leg free when it bit down in the space I had just been. A microsecond later, a harpoon split the surface of the water and sliced into the killer whale's right eye, sinking through it until the barbed point pierced the inside of the mouth.

The orca stopped thrashing as it died, blood gushing from inside the mouth and from where the harpoon rended the eye.

I didn't have time to consider anything other than I was out of air. I wanted desperately to gasp, but to do so would be to breathe in sea water. The surface looked to be a few feet above me. I kicked, realizing that I was only a few seconds away from drowning. But as hard as I kicked, I couldn't gain traction. My insulated seal-skin boots and walrus-skin pants weighed too much.

Then I felt a nudge at my back. I remembered that orcas usually hunt in packs. I couldn't imagine a more terrible death than to be eaten alive. I fought the urge to scream as I reached upwards, trying to pull myself to safety. Then another nudge, this one pushing me towards daylight. I gasped as my face broke the surface, reveling as the cold, clear air filled my lungs. Hands grabbed me from above. I scrambled to grab the side of the boat. Within moments, Merlin had me back in the umiak.

I glanced down at the water and saw the bull walrus. Its scarred hide. Its forearm-sized tusks. White whiskers. The bull regarded me with a liquid eye for a few long moments, then it slowly turned and was once again surging towards Savoonga.

Merlin grabbed me and began to rip my shirt free. My feet and pants were dry, but the cold of the water was already turning my hands blue from exposure. Although the wind bit through me, it also served to dry my skin and hair. Merlin handed me a walrus-skin blanket from the boat's stores and I draped it around my shoulders, suddenly warm for what it seemed like the first time in an eternity, although it had been less than thirty seconds.

I sat there shaking for a few moments, before I realized that the boat wasn't moving. I looked around. Merlin stood at the stern, doing something I couldn't see. I got to my feet and joined him, careful to keep the balance of the umiak right.

Tears flowed from his eyes as he tied the tail of the dead whale to a rope affixed to the back of the boat. Then I remembered. We'd only been trying to divert the whale. It was forbidden by the Yupik to kill an orca whale. They were revered and, along with the raven and the wolf, were never to be killed. The orca was believed to watch over hunters and fishermen. Now Merlin had killed one. Would it matter that he did so to save my life? The part of me that understood the traditions knew immediately that it wouldn't matter. There'd be a price to pay, and for Merlin's sake, I hoped it wasn't too high.

I put a hand on his shoulder and could feel the tremor in his body from his half-surpressed sobs. He spoke low in the singing language of the Yupik. I knew then that he wasn't crying for himself, he was crying for the orca. He was already mourning the soul of the fish, serenading it, explaining to it that he had to kill it to save me. I couldn't speak the language, but I understood this at a deeper level, because it's what I would have done in his place.

One warrior-hunter to the other.

The past is never dead, it is not even past.
William Faulkner

CHAPTER TWO

I HAD NEITHER seen nor heard from OMBRA in the eight months since I blew up the master in the Hollywood Hive. So when I saw the man in uniform standing on the dock waiting for me, it actually came as no surprise. I'd been expecting Mr. Pink to ask me back into the fold for several months now. That said, I had little use for OMBRA at the moment. Yet even as we docked, he came running, calling my name and fumbling a salute. I ignored him, my only care in the world for my new brother, Merlin. Coming back so early from our bear hunt, the other members of the tribe knew something had gone wrong and had already begun to gather. When they saw the orca tied by its tail to the stern, their collective countenance changed from curious to anxious. They didn't have the story yet, and when they did, the worry would marshal straight to anger.

Merlin's father, Sebastian, was the first of the group to approach. He took a long look at me, noting that I was wearing a blanket instead of the heavy wool shirt. He looked far older than his fifty years, but his physique was well defined—shoulders and arms rock hard. He was clearly Merlin's father. The family resemblance was unmistakable. They shared the same long black hair, his tied back with carved pieces of ivory, and the same wide open faces. Like all the Yupiak, their skin was swarthy and their epicanthic folds were slight.

Sebastian placed a hand on my shoulder and I lowered my head. I felt shame for putting Merlin in the position where he'd had to choose between the orca and me. If I'd been more careful, none of this would have happened. I just wasn't as well-balanced as the Yupik when it came to small boats.

Merlin untied the orca, and brought it alongside the boat. The beast was half again as long as the vessel and would have grown larger still had it lived. Sebastian and Merlin exchanged words in Yupik. I decided to let them have their space and walked off the dock and over to where Merlin's sister stood.

"What happened?" she asked.

As I told her, her face grew troubled.

"What's going to happen?" I asked.

She stared at the ground. "This won't end well."

"Is it that serious?" I asked, knowing immediately I shouldn't have even opened my mouth. Instead of responding, she walked over to a group of women and began whispering. By the way they looked at me, I could tell she was telling them what I'd told her. I sighed. Soon this would be all over the small village.

An OMBRA soldier edged up to me. A young black kid, he wore an urban camouflage uniform in blues, grays and black. Atop his head was a maroon beret with the OMBRA flash. "Is now a good time, sir?"

I glanced at his nametape—NANCE. I couldn't see any indication of rank, but that didn't mean anything. He could be a private or a general for all I cared. Nance was fresh and clean. I doubted he'd been in any service before the Cray came down and EMP'd us back to the Stone Age. He'd definitely not battled a hive like the one we'd broken our teeth on at Kilimanjaro. Nor had he been part of any of our deadly forays into Los Angeles. I doubted OMBRA would send a REMF or Fobbit, as they'd become called, but one never knew. Perhaps this poor young man had just drawn the short straw.

"Who sent you?" I held up a hand, "Wait. Let me guess? Mr. Pink sent you."

Nance didn't bat an eye. "No sir, actually it was Captain Ohirra."

Captain, now. I remembered when I'd first met her in the old missile complex under the Wyoming plains, before the invasion. Back then we didn't know what we didn't know; all we did was suck up OMBRA's training, wondering why the curriculum concentrated on alien invasion science fiction books and movies. Ohirra had seemed so small and unassuming. Little did we know she was whip smart, dedicated, and could tie someone into knots with her small circle jujitsu mastery. "How did you find me?"

Nance grinned. "Now that took a while. We tracked you to a place in Northern California near Mount Shasta."

Ahh. Memories of Mother flooded in. She'd worked so hard to help me regain some of my humanity. She'd almost done it too, but then Suzie had killed herself and it sent me over the edge. *"I have a place we send those who need to find a definition for themselves that doesn't include their past."* At the time I had no idea what she'd meant. But I'd been working on it and thought that I might have actually figured it out.

"I was there for a few months," I said.

"Real crazy forests. Tallest trees I've ever seen. Met a woman who went only by Mother."

"What'd you have to trade for her to tell you where I was?"

He grinned. "Two pallets of medicine for her people."

"Fair trade, I suppose," I said, watching as two fisherman marched out to the dock and led Merlin away. As he passed by the group of men, they all turned away from him. Merlin's eyes were fixed on the ground, or perhaps to a place where he hadn't been forced to kill an orca to save me.

"What's going on?" the soldier asked, his eyes wide.

"The orca is sacred to them and Merlin killed one."

"Why'd he kill one if it's sacred?"

"To save my life." I saw him glance at me, confusion in his eyes. "You see, it's like this. They have these beliefs that certain creatures should be worshipped. To kill them puts the tribe at risk. Just because I was fool enough to fall in the water isn't a good enough reason to break this belief. Merlin should have let nature take its course."

"But then you'd be dead."

I gave him a stony look. "I've spent a good portion of my adult life trying to kill myself. It's nothing new to me."

This took him aback.

"How'd you get here?" I asked.

"By plane. We have a crew waiting for us."

"Then they'll be waiting for a long time, because I'm not coming."

Nance nodded and handed over a CD in a plastic holder. "Captain Ohirra said you'd say that. She asked me to give this to you."

I took the CD, then gave Nance a long look. "I have some things to do. If I need to talk to you, I'll be in touch."

Nance came to attention and saluted.

I looked at him. My reflex was to salute back, but that single motion could change my life, so I merely nodded.

Then I turned and walked back to the boat. I grabbed my shirt and pack from where we'd stowed them, then headed towards my hooch. When I'd first arrived, they'd given me an abandoned tent next to the ugly. At the time it had been the start of winter, so the tent had been covered in walrus hide with plank floors, walls, and ceiling. Now that it was summer, most of the wall planks were on the roof, letting the hides be either down, or rolled to let air through. I usually kept them down. That close to the ugly, I often received unwanted attention, whether it be from a curious walrus pup, or from a big bull who didn't understand why the walrus hides wouldn't respond to his rubbing. Later on, once they'd accepted me, they'd invited me to stay in a tent further from the raucous noise and action, but I'd declined. I'd never had trouble sleeping, and the constant sounds of the walruses barking and groaning in the ugly had become something I looked forward to. Now was no different. The noise rose as I approached. The cacophony might have daunted some, but it had been far more soothing than the noise I'd had in my brain when I'd arrived.

The interior was Spartan. I had a simple bed made of walrus hide, rope and wood. Really nothing more than a hammock suspended just above the floor. The only other furniture was a small wooden table and wooden chair, except for a shelf which held a dozen books I'd borrowed from the Savoonga lending library. I'd read them all before, but wanted to see how reading them now compared to when I'd been in training at OMBRA. I was currently re-reading Joe Haldeman's *The Forever War*. On the first read through, I'd concentrated more on the battles with the Taurans and the tactics humans used against them. I remember, even as I was locked in the cell and made to study, being fascinated by how they'd been forced to use medieval weapons to fight the aliens.

Now, rereading it, I was attuned to something different. Early in the book, soldiers returning from the initial run-ins with the Taurans rejoined the military after coming home because nothing was like it had been when they'd left. In the book, it was because hundreds of years had passed, but here on the real Earth it was because of the way people looked at things. It was one of the reasons I kept re-enlisting. Whether it be Kosovo, or my second and third tours in Iraq, I remember promising myself that this would be it, that I'd go back to the Land of the Big PX and never deploy again. Then I'd come home and watch my fellow man entranced by reality television and the daily lives of housewives from New Jersey or bearded men who make duck whistles. I'd see the blank looks in their eyes when I tried to describe how alive I'd felt while deployed, how the fear refined me. I'd try and explain how it felt to accidently kill a kid or watch one of your men evaporate from an IED or get told that the town you took from the bad guys at tremendous loss of life was now back in the hands of those same bad guys. Instead of trying to understand, they labeled me, then returned to watching adult cartoons about yellow people and anything at all having to do with the

Kardashians. It was like they were the aliens and we'd already been invaded. I just couldn't stand it.

But when I'd first read *The Forever War*, I'd been a far simpler man. I'd yet to strap into an Electromagnetic Faraday Xeno-combat suit. I'd yet to see an alien, much less kill one. I couldn't help laugh as I thought that the alien Cray—the giant flying mantis-looking beings that could pulse EMP and destroy everything with a circuit board—were the only aliens attacking. They were just the warm up. An image popped into my head—me, standing naked except for a diaper in a cage in the middle of a room, mindless, my brain controlled by the fungus *ophiocordyceps invasionalis*, which had turned me into an alien-created zombie keen to infect anyone who wasn't like me. But instead of biting as the locus of infection, there were ascocarps growing on my neck and chest which would explode with fungus spore in the proximity of a human. I'd gone from being the Hero of the Mound to the Lieutenant Who Pooped in His Pants.

I tossed the disk on the table and sat down hard on a chair. I rubbed my face with my right hand, trying to wipe the images away. This unwanted trip down memory lane had probably been the result of Nance arriving in uniform. That he had a message from Ohirra made it worse. She'd been with me at Kilimanjaro. She'd been with me in L.A. She was the only one of my first squad to have survived—and Thompson didn't count, damn it.

I closed my eyes and listened to the ugly.

Like the battering of the waves, or the whistling of the wind through the trees, it lessened the mental load and allowed me to drift through the past, slip-sliding down memory lane until finally sleep found me.

Every man has his secret sorrows which the world knows not; and often times we call a man cold when he is only sad.

Henry Wadsworth Longfellow

CHAPTER THREE

TWO HOURS LATER, I searched and found Merlin on a rocky outcropping overlooking the harbor. The weather was about forty-two degrees Fahrenheit without the wind. I wore a thick sweater with a T-shirt beneath. I'd acclimatized fairly well, but would never be the native Merlin was. He wore the same insulated pants and boots he'd worn on the boat, but now wore a Patagonia sleeveless parka over a Guns N' Roses Appetite for Destruction Tour T-shirt. His normally braided hair was loose and moved gently in the onshore breeze. He chewed bear jerky as he stared out at the small sprawl of Savoonga where it reached right up to the rocky shore, the dun-colored sand, the froth of the surf, then the slate of the Arctic Ocean. The town held about three hundred Yupik, a few Russian fishermen from the Chukotka Peninsula, and several gringos like me. I'd met the others, and they'd traveled with all haste to get away from the Cray. I couldn't blame them. When they'd asked me why I was here, I said the same; it was easier than trying to explain that I came here trying to get away from myself. Which was what Merlin seemed to be doing.

I shivered as a gust of wind tore through me, wishing I'd dressed a little more warmly.

I sat down beside Merlin. I looked for the library, then the men's traditional long house where they were probably meeting and talking about Merlin, then found my place, closest to the ugly, the place where interlopers were housed.

Without anything else to say, I stuck with the traditional. "Sorry, Merlin."

"Nothing to be sorry for." He bit down and chewed for a moment. "I made the choice."

"Still…" What was there to say? I reached out a hand and Merlin passed me the piece of jerky. I bit into it and wrenched a piece free, chewing on the gamey meat. I passed the rest back. I watched as a Russian fishing trawler pulled into the harbor with a fresh catch. So far the leviathans hadn't affected fishing this far north. Then again, there was no more commercial fishing so we really couldn't know.

Finally Merlin said, "I saw a soldier waiting for you."

"He had a message for me."

"What did the message say?"

I shrugged. "Dunno. Didn't listen."

He turned his head and regarded me. "He came all this way and you didn't listen?"

"I already knew what he was going to say. They want me back."

Merlin grunted. He nodded to the men's long house. "I know what they're going to say, too. They're going to ask me to leave."

Coming and going. Either way you leave a place. "Where are you going to go?"

"Tradition is for me to take my stake, load up my

quyak, and strike out maybe one hundred, two hundred kilometers. Either Chukotka or Alaska, it doesn't matter as long as I'm far away from here."

"And then what? Is it forever?"

"Depends on the fishing and hunting. If they don't get worse, then I can come back in two or three seasons. If I come back and they're worse, then I'm banished forever."

I exhaled explosively. "Jesus, Merlin."

He shrugged. "Such is our way."

For a moment I felt sorry for myself, ashamed of what I'd done, just like when I'd been in charge and one of my men had died. Then I fought against it as the face of Mother imposed itself upon my psyche. She'd always looked like that actress Kathy Bates, maternal and serious. She'd told me what I'd told myself for years. She'd reiterated the same thing a squad of PTSD counselors had said to me. I'd heard it all before, but somehow, coming from her, it had made a lot more sense.

"You can't blame yourself for the decisions of others. Everyone has a choice. If they choose to do something that ends up getting them killed, then it's their fault."

I remembered sitting like a school kid, staring into her eyes, and asking, "But what if they died because of something I did, because of an order I gave them?"

Her stare had been that of generations of mothers who'd stared at their children, knowing that the child had the answer but just needed to hear it aloud. *"They chose. Humans always have a choice. Even when ordered to do something, they have a choice. You cannot blame yourself for the results of another's choice."*

I could hear her voice in my head as if she were sitting beside me. And it helped. It really did. But it didn't ameliorate the feelings I had for Merlin. He was about to lose everything he held dear.

I watched him as he stared at the only home he'd ever known. Old Woman Black Hands' tattoos inked on his arms showed his history. Walrus and bear hunting scenes merged with scenes of fishing, flat halibut and muscular salmon, cavorting from the water, dancing in air. I'd seen his back as well. The centerpiece was an orca, swimming dead on forward, the tattooist creating a point of view that seemed as if the orca was swimming into Merlin's back, becoming him, guiding him.

Far different from the tattoos Old Woman Black Hands had given me. Among the unit insignias and waving flag I'd had done before the invasion were the names of every person who'd ever died because of me. I didn't have fish or bears or walruses. I had war and invasion as my past. At times, Merlin and I could be so similar, but then we were so very different. You only had to examine our tattoos to see the difference. But here and now, on the small bluff overlooking Savoonga, we were just two men, looking out on what represented peace and civilization, knowing that they'd have to leave it behind and not knowing if they'd ever be able to return.

Merlin pointed east. "What is that?"

I turned my head and searched the sky. At first I didn't see anything. Then I saw three dark dots.

"Too small to be a plane," he said.

We watched as the dots approached, getting larger and larger. They moved irregularly, gaining and losing altitude. They certainly weren't planes, nor were they helicopters. In fact, I seriously doubted that they were even mechanical. Instead, they looked like larger birds or...

I shot to my feet.

Cray!

They'd never been this far north. Damn!

I began running down the hill. I had to warn the town.

Merlin fell in beside me and as I ran, asked, "Those things the aliens you fought?"

"We have to warn everyone. We have to find weapons."

"There's an armory in the long house. I'll go there."

Merlin peeled off to the left and I continued on to the center of town, which as I tracked their flight, was where the Cray seemed to be heading. Thankfully, I didn't have far to run. The bluff was less than half a mile. I ran between two homes, then across a yard. Howard Makepeace was loading crab traps into the back of his truck. He saw me running, then looked to where I was looking in the sky. Out of the corner of my eye, I saw him grab a rifle from the inside of the truck and head after me. I ran across Tumbaloo Road, then across another yard filled with three Big Wheels and a crocket set, then I crossed Post Office Road.

I was about a hundred yards away when the first multi-winged, jagged-clawed alien Cray crash-landed in front of the General Store. Sadie and Peter Savinga stood near the entrance, their mouths agape. A Yupik I knew only as Ernest and a Russian named Pavel smoked cigarettes near the corner of the building.

"Get inside!" I bellowed. "Get inside and lock the doors!"

Ernest and Pavel stared at the alien beast as its chest heaved and its wings fluttered, but other than that, the Cray wasn't moving. Thankfully, I believed it was probably exhausted from the flight from the mainland, which was more than a hundred and fifty miles away. I'd never seen one fly so far. Usually they stayed around the hive, the drones protecting it and the queen inside from attack. For it to fly this far either meant it was terribly off course, or it was searching for something.

I thought of how I'd set the tactical nuke in front of the master in the machine interface device in the bowels of the Hollywood Hive, then mind-jacked one of the Cray to help me escape. Had they been looking for me all this time? Is that what this was? Revenge?

I glanced up and saw the other two were inbound. One would land in about thirty seconds. The other was flagging and might not even make landfall.

I made it to the General Store and held out my arms. "Easy, big fella," I said, realizing at that very moment that I'd rushed into combat without any armor or any weapons. The talons on the ends of the hand-like appendages were matched in sharpness by the spikes that sprung from each of the Cray's joints. It had three sets of wings. Two sets hung limp on its back while the highest set twitched like antennae at every sound. Its triangular, mantis-like head regarded me as it tried to get to its feet.

I balled my fists as I searched around for something to use as a weapon. Without one, I'd most assuredly die. Humans needed EXOs to fight the Cray.

Makepeace skidded to a stop beside me, his eyes wide and his lips white. He held the rifle to his shoulder, the barrel trembling. "What should I do, Mason?"

"Shoot the damn thing," I said.

Makepeace took aim and let off three shots from his .306 hunting rifle. Two impacted the alien's chest, while one missed entirely.

I remembered how many rounds they could absorb.

We'd need a lot more than a single rifle.

"Go for the eyes," I said. "Take your—"

The Cray suddenly rose up on its hind legs, rising seven, eight, nine feet tall.

Someone screamed.

Then all hell broke loose as everyone who had a weapon pulled it and began to fire. One thing about an Arctic subsistence hunting society was that everyone had guns. I clenched and unclenched my fists as I realized not quite everyone. Not this schmuck.

The Cray lashed out towards me.

I threw myself to the ground.

Makepeace continued to fire.

The Cray grabbed him by the head, lifted him up, then slammed him into the ground with a sickening sound of bones crunching.

Makepeace's rifle skidded free.

I dove for it. I managed to grab it, then crab-walked out of the path of a Cray claw.

The Cray went down on one leg as everyone continued to fire. It lashed out with a claw, ripping Pavel's thorax wide open. I watched as his eyes shot wide and his body emptied into his hands before he fell face first to the ground.

I put the rifle into my shoulder and tried to fire, but the trigger wouldn't move. I glanced at the trigger housing and saw where the side had been caved in. I grabbed the barrel and heaved it at the alien, catching it on the side of the face. It suddenly jerked its head my way. I stumbled backwards, onto my ass. It began to follow me, unconcerned about anything else. Above its head I saw as the second Cray landed on the roof of the General Store.

Bob Schmoosh skidded to a stop in his old Ford Bronco, one of the few vehicles on the island, blue and red lights flashing.

The Cray pulsed, sending an EMP surge directly at the vehicle, killing it and the lights.

The other Cray, on the roof of the General Store, pulsed too, killing all the power to the building below, which did more harm than it knew. All of the frozen goods were stored there, without which many of the Yupik would die. But I had more immediate things to worry about than food for the coming winter. I was still back-pedalling as the Cray pulled itself after me, intent on doing to me what a little boy might do with an insect.

I felt the earth shudder, followed by the sound of something mechanical. I looked up and saw a white machine above. I couldn't make out what it was until it stepped past me, reached out and grabbed the Cray's face with one hand, while the other hand grabbed the alien's arm.

An EXO! For a moment I wondered how it had gotten here, then I remembered that an OMBRA plane was waiting for me. Who knew how many EXOs it might contain? I watched with delight as the nine-foot tall white EXO multitasked, opening up on the Cray atop the roof with its shoulder-mounted XM214 rotary-barreled machine gun while it ripped the head from the other Cray.

The alien on the roof took a dozen rounds before it tumbled off the other side of the roof.

Gotta love the XM214. Pulled out of mothballs at Aberdeen Proving Ground before the invasion, it was the EXO's primary attack armament, comprised of a six-barreled rotating mini-gun fed from a backpack ammo supply through an ammo feed arm. TF OMBRA modified the original 1970s General Electric design, giving the system three backpack-mounted 500-round ammo boxes linked together, for a total of 1500 rounds. The original 1970s electronic controls, which could modify the rate of fire on the fly, were micronized, hardened against EMP and incorporated into the ammo boxes, giving the system triple redundancy and protecting the electronics. The servo that spun the barrels only engaged when the automatic harness system that pulled the weapon back out of the way was released.

Two more EXOs ran past, heading for the other side of the store.

I finally pulled myself to my feet.

Battle sounded from behind the building. Those who'd survived the surprise appearance of the Cray ran behind the Bronco.

The EXO nearest me turned around.

Nance.

Maybe he wasn't the wet-behind-the-ears soldier I'd mistaken him for.

I began to notice some differences on his EXO from the types of suit that I had worn— minor modifications and some streamlining. Some I could figure out, but other improvements left me wondering.

But as the third and final Cray crash landed into the walruses' ugly, I had little time to concern myself with mechanical improvements to a battle machine. There was something much more important; we had to save the walruses.

I began to run in the direction of the screams of dying pinnipeds.

Nance passed me as if I was standing still.

The other two EXOs followed close behind.

I ran another hundred meters, then stopped and watched from afar as they joined on the Cray and dispatched it in mere moments.

Just then, the men from the long house came running. Many carried rifles, but others carried more traditional weapons like the lance I'd used on the whale. Sebastian led the way with his son, Merlin, beside him.

They stopped when they came upon me.

"Those some of the aliens you fought?" Sebastian asked.

I nodded. "These were bigger."

"Did they come looking for you?"

I thought of the way the Cray had regarded me, then chased after me. Could they have been sent after me? It didn't fit their behavior. Neither the Cray nor the Hypocrealiacs had ever demonstrated the desire for revenge. In fact, the human race had been shown such disregard, it was as if we didn't really matter.

But I didn't have time to answer. One of the other men of the long house, Oberon, pointed at Merlin and shouted, "No, it was this one who brought them here." He turned to his fellow Yupik elders. "Don't you see? No sooner did he kill the sacred whale than the aliens descended."

Angry voices began to murmur in the crowd.

Sebastian stared at the ground.

Merlin stared at me, sorrow bleeding from his eyes.

> Whether or not we believe in survival of
> consciousness after death, reincarnation,
> and karma, it has very serious implications
> for our behavior.
>
> Stanislav Grof

CHAPTER FOUR

THE DYING CRAY had killed seventeen walruses and wounded nine others. While the Yupik women treated the wounded walruses, the men of the tribe removed the dead, then harvested the meat from their bodies. With the power out in the General Store, they had to put the meat in the earth, using the old ways, letting the frozen tundra act as nature's own freezers. Nothing could be wasted.

Merlin had not been invited to join them and watched from his place on the rocky outcropping where I'd found him previously.

I gave him a wide berth and headed towards the airfield. It wasn't much. Two hangars, a control building, and a single runway. One of the hangars was open and empty, so it was pretty easy to figure out where OMBRA had set up shop. Inside sat a gray C-130, its ramp down, the interior filled with boxes of ammunition and supplies. Five white EXOs were parked against one wall. The pilot, co-pilot and crew chief glanced at me from where they'd set up near the front of the plane. I gave the pilot a nod and he returned it. He didn't look thrilled to be here.

When Nance saw me, he ran up and saluted. I still refused to return it and merely nodded instead. He introduced me to the other three OMBRA soldiers and we sat around a fire barrel on hard plastic chairs, chatting. They wore the same urban fatigues Nance was wearing. Two couldn't have been more than teenagers and the third considerably older, probably in his forties. He'd removed the top and wore only a black T-shirt. His big arms held a history I couldn't yet divine; tattoos with swords, spears, and daggers, and a lot of French. His name was Private First Class Charlemagne, whose real name was Didier Bourdon. He'd spent time in the French Foreign Legion before the invasion and had joined TF OMBRA's Europe in Bruges.

It seemed that in the last six months EXO drivers, as they'd come to be called, had taken on a certain notoriety. Because of this new-found fame, Mr. Pink, forever my genius nemesis, had decided to allow EXO drivers to use call signs, which were then posted on public forums and tracked for numbers of kills. There were fan sites and fan clubs for the drivers.

Nance went by the call sign Inglewood and had seventy-two kills.

Charlemagne had thirty-nine kills.

The other two EXO drivers refused to give out their names, but their call signs were Obelix and Asterix, which I vaguely recalled might have been from a French or German comic. They each had thirty confirmed kills and always fought together, regardless. They barely looked eighteen. Obelix was a boy and Asterix was a girl and they appeared to be twins.

I sort of thought the whole thing was ridiculous. Call signs and confirmed kills. Next thing you knew and we'd be sponsored by whatever businesses were still around. I could see it now—*This battle is sponsored by End of the World Wheaties.* Maybe the EXOs would start wearing advertisements, like soccer players had before the invasion. I don't know why Mr. Pink felt that morale was such that this sort of absurdity was necessary, but I somehow knew that I'd be having a personal conversation with him about it soon.

"So everyone has a call sign?" I asked.

"Only drivers," Charlemagne answered.

I glanced sideways at Nance. "Please tell me that I don't have a call sign."

Charlemagne grinned with something like hero worship on the other side of the burn barrel.

Nance regarded me flatly. "Okay fine. You don't have a call sign."

I stared at him for a long moment. "But I really do, don't I?"

He nodded.

I sighed and could only wonder what I'd been saddled with. "What is it?"

"Hero Prime."

Oh dear God. Mr. Pink had gone off and made me a poster boy for his war effort... again.

I looked from one EXO driver to the other and all regarded me with reverent stares. Even the twins, who I still had to figure out, gave me a look as if they'd like to eat me in order to become me.

"That's a little over the top, don't you think?"

Charlemagne shook his bald head. "Not at all. We've seen the video feeds from Kilimanjaro. Your tactics are part of the curriculum. I've studied your moves backwards and forwards. They called you—"

"Hero of the Mound," I said, finishing the appellation. That name was the first time Mr. Pink had used me as an inspiration to fight.

"Then there was the Battle for L.A.," Asterix said.

"You discovered the vector for the zombie fungus. You blew up the hive," Obelix added.

"Then, of course, there's the number of your kills," Nance said, beaming.

I'd never really considered counting the number of aliens I'd killed. It just seemed like a waste of time. To think that OMBRA had somehow kept track made me wonder what other things they'd kept track of.

"Don't you want to know how many Cray you've killed?" Nance asked.

"Not really."

"Seriously," Nance added, as if it were some magic word like *abracadabra*.

"None of that shit means anything. How many aliens someone killed means nothing if someone dies on a mission. This is the fate of the planet we're talking about, not some rack and stack ranking system meant to make the last few survivors feel good about themselves."

"Easy for you to say," Obelix said.

"Yeah, easy for you to say," Asterix mimicked.

I glared at them until they looked away. Snarky fucking teenagers. That's exactly what they were and the last thing I needed at the end of the world. Frankly, I wanted to punch them in their faces. Instead, I changed the subject.

"What do you think brought the Cray here? There can't be a hive within a thousand miles."

"You should really listen to Captain Ohirra's briefing," Nance said.

I nodded. "Lay it out for me. Tell me what you know."

Nance glanced at the others, then began speaking. "OMBRA tracked communications from the Russian Spetsnaz using some sort of high altitude UAVs. Several ships have fallen from the sky over their country. Initial reports were that the ships were some kind of advanced space craft. But what intrigued OMBRA most were the references to the *human aliens*."

"Human aliens? That's odd."

Nance nodded. "Exactly. We thought the same thing."

"So what are you doing here?" I asked.

"The easternmost crash site is less than five hundred miles from here on the Chukotka Peninsula. It's literally in the middle of nowhere. As of this moment, the Russians haven't made it there. Our mission is to swoop and scoop. Too easy."

I shook my head and laughed. "Nothing is ever that easy. I left the CD with the briefing back in my hooch."

"That's okay, we have another master copy." Nance asked, "Are you ready for the briefing?"

I shifted uncomfortably in my chair. "Sure."

Nance went over to his pack and rifled inside of it until he came out with a tablet. He dialed up the briefing and handed it to me. I grabbed my plastic chair and took it inside the aircraft so I could be alone. I put the chair down, sat facing the OMBRA crew who were all watching me, and pressed play.

Ohirra's stern face appeared on the screen. It had been less than a year, but it looked as if she'd aged ten years. I remembered when we'd both been young, living in the shadow of our own dead, long before Earth had been invaded.

"Mason, I'm not going to mince words. We need you.

I need you. Things are happening fast and I don't have the right people in the right places to handle the things that need handling. If what we heard from the Russians is right, it's a major game changer. Bottom line is that high altitude surveillance drones intercepted some Russian coms, reporting that several spacecraft had crashed in their area with человека инопланетяне aboard, which was translated to mean 'human aliens.' We can't be sure what that means, but my intelligence staff and Mr. Pink believes it might be the other shoe dropping. We've always wondered about the Hypocrealiacs. We've known they've had purpose-made alien species taking our planet. From the Cray to the Leviathans to the kudzu to the zombie fungus, they've been systematically taking away our planet. What we never knew was why. We'd surmised it was because of some intergalactic war, but we could never be sure. Now with actual spacecraft littering the landscape, we can maybe see who's been doing the fighting.

"I know you've been on a much-needed sabbatical. I totally get why you needed it. I was there, remember? I was on the L.A. mission and at Kilimanjaro. I've been with you since the beginning." She paused and I couldn't help but feel a little selfish. She was right. She'd been through most everything I'd been through. She deserved the same break I'd had. "But now I need you back. I've sent Corporal Gordon Nance and his team to your location. My intention had been to leave you alone, but then this happened. We need you to go and investigate the Chukotka crash site. We need you to retrieve bodies so we can take DNA samples. And of course bring back as much technology as you can.

"This is probably the most important mission you

will ever have. If we fail to get to the site in time we'll be in the dark, a place we can't afford to be. We need to find out who was piloting the craft and figure out if they are the good guys or the bad guys... or both. Like always, we don't know what we don't know, and we need you to tell us what that is."

She leaned in close to the screen.

"Mason, for this last bit, if someone is listening to you right now, get them out of there. This is for your ears only." She waited ten seconds. "Okay. I know the team I sent you is a mixed bag, but they are the only ones I can guarantee have no agenda. Pink has had more and more closed door meetings lately. Something is going on. You'd think their senior intelligence officer might be a part of those meetings, but they're blacking me out. We've always known that he's known more than he lets on. It's only getting worse.

"I had techs put a special black box in your EXO. Not only has it got a special crypto that will allow me to contact you as long as we have high-altitude drones in the vicinity, but it will also let you tap into the Global HMID Network. I know that's the last thing you want to do, but there might come a time when you need to. If so, don't let the lives of your team rest on the hatred of the process... or of Thompson.

"That's it. Trust Nance, he's good. And get what we need. It just might save us all."

Then she pressed a button I couldn't see, and the screen went blank.

I leaned back. Realizing I'd been holding my breath, I released it in a slow, steady stream.

I wasn't surprised at all that Mr. Pink was up to his old shenanigans. Although his name was Wilson, I'd been calling him Mr. Pink ever since we met because of his uncanny resemblance to Steve Buscemi's character in *Reservoir Dogs*. In fact, I'd known the moment that I'd seen the alien HMID in the bowels of the Hollywood Hive that he'd known so much more than he let on. That our HMIDs so closely resembled the alien's communications box meant they'd somehow captured one shortly before or after the invasion, and then succeeded in reverse-engineering it.

I closed my eyes as an image of Michelle slid past my defenses. It was from Kilimanjaro, when we'd found a private moment behind the generators before the big battle. The way her eyes shone in the light, both of us full of wonder and terrified because of our love. Then the image dissolved, only to be replaced by the image of her the last time I'd seen her, right before I'd killed her.

"I'M SO TIRED of it now." Her voice was tiny and breathless.

"Even heroes need the chance to rest," I told her.

She'd smiled. "Is that what I am? A hero?"

"Of course you are."

"I'm not a monster?"

I ached at her even having to ask the question. "Never. You did what none of us would do. You're far braver than I ever was."

She smiled. "But you're the Hero of the Mound."

I stroked her head. I felt a thin layer of fuzz beneath my hands. "And you are the hero of us all."

She closed her eyes and sighed, finally holding me with her withered, useless arms.

I closed my eyes.

I wasn't sure how long we held each other, but when I finally noticed the others trying to get in the room, I knew we didn't have much time.

"I'm really quite crazy," Michelle said suddenly.

I couldn't help but laugh. "Yes, you are. But then so are we all."

"What now?" she asked.

"I came to take you home."

Her eyes snapped open. "Thank you. Oh, thank you."

I fought back emotion as I saw my hand reach down her body and pull out each hose until the only thing that connected her to the infernal machine was the cable attached to her neck. I folded her into my arms, so that her hips were over one arm and the other held the back of her neck. I leaned down, she opened her eyes and we had a final kiss, even as her fluids drained away.

She looked me in the eyes. She tried to speak but she couldn't, but I heard her words in my mind.

"I love you, too," I said. Then I pulled the main cable out of the back of her neck.

Her eyes snapped shut.

Her breathing hitched.

And sometime in the next few seconds she died.

I KEPT THE image of that moment in my mind for a minute, then swallowed it away along with my tears. And to think that Ohirra wanted me to communicate to the—what did she call it—the Global HMID Network? That was never going to happen. Fucking HMIDs were the worst thing we humans had ever invented. An image of Michelle's ravaged body spiked through my head, causing an instant migraine.

I got up, walked down the ramp, and handed the tablet to Nance.

"You listen to it?" he asked.

I nodded.

"You going to come with us?"

"Probably."

I headed toward the exit. Halfway there, I stopped. "Just out of curiosity," I asked Nance, "how many kills do I have?"

"Four thousand, seven hundred and sixty-six."

I nodded again. "Must have been a busy man," I said, then walked into the cold Arctic night.

Anyone else worried about this New United States of North America? I hear they're conscripting anyone and everyone, but for what reason? They've cleared all of their major cities of Cray. They've all but pruned away the vines. Hell, the skies are black with the smoke from their great pyres. So it begs the question, if they're creating a force, then what is this force for? Trust me, I'm not a fan of complete and utter chaos... a little order is a good thing. But a return to an iron-fisted government, over taxation, and government lackeys peeking into my everyday business is not what we need. This was supposed to be a reboot. This was supposed to be a chance to do it better than before. So why, I ask you, is the New United States of North America building an army instead of rebuilding the infrastructure?

Conspiracy Theory Talk Radio,
Night Stalker Monologue #1742

CHAPTER FIVE

MY SENSES WERE heightened. My skin sizzled in the cold wind. My eyeballs were on fire and took in everything and nothing, hyper-aware of my surroundings. I hadn't felt this wired since the day I'd arrived. Part of me reveled in it, the part that forgot how absolutely tiring it was to be switched on all the time. Another part of me hated the hyper aware state PTSD encouraged. I'd been so relaxed the last few months I'd actually let my guard down, and in doing so, had found myself enjoying life and those around me. I wasn't constantly establishing various threat levels for everyone I came in contact with. I hadn't been seeking out and logging the best avenues of egress every place I found myself. I hadn't been developing A, B and C plans for operations upon contact.

I'd actually been living.

I'd actually been *normal*.

I hadn't even realized how much I'd been changed by being away from everything until the appearance of the Cray in the village and Ohirra's briefing. Then it was like I snapped back into place. Where I'd looked out upon the world before and admired its beauty, now I examined it, searching for whatever threats it might present. I don't know which *me* I liked better.

The one who didn't know or the one who cared too much?

It had gotten colder while I was in the hangar. I shoved my hands in my pockets and lowered my chin to my chest. I headed down the bluff into town. Several dozen men and women worked near the ugly. The women harvested meat while the men dragged the Cray aside. I wondered what they were going to do with it. I knew that if they decided to break it down for meat I'd never in a million years let a piece past my lips. In fact, I shuddered as I thought about it.

Another group was gathered at the pier. There weren't any Yupik due in, so I didn't know...

I broke into a sprint, running faster than I'd run when the Cray had attacked. I threw myself down the hill, knowing that any slip or stumble would send me falling face first into the scrabble-covered tundra. But I didn't care. Once again, someone was getting bullied. Not by a person or a group, but by a belief. I might not be able to stop the bullying, but I could stand by my friend and brother.

By the time I got there and pushed my way through the gathering crowd of silent men, Merlin was shoving a seal skin duffel bag into the nose of a long, walrus skin kayak. A trio of harpoons and a .306 rifle lay next to a smaller bag that he was still packing. His father, Sebastian, stood with his arms crossed, watching him pack in silence. As did the other men, their arms crossed, faces creased with dogmatic superiority.

I spared them a single look, a fire hose of disdain. I searched around and saw what I was looking for. I pushed back through the men, grabbed a kayak and a paddle, then drug it through them none-to-gently. I set it down next to Merlin's.

"What do you think you're doing?" he asked, his eyes down, embarrassed, devastated.

"Going with you."

"Don't be ridiculous." He looked at my newly acquired kayak. "You don't even have any supplies."

"Will you wait for me until I go back to my hooch and grab some?"

He shook his head.

"Benjamin, you should stay out of this," Sebastian said.

"He's my brother, Sebastian."

The old man sighed. "If he was your brother, you shouldn't have put him in this position."

I whirled around. "No. You don't get to do that. How many people have you killed, Sebastian? How many deaths do you have on your head?" I searched his eyes, but he wouldn't meet mine. "Yet you'd have a death on the conscience of your son." I ripped my shirt off, ignoring the growing cold. I felt my skin pimple in the wind.

Several of the men backed away from me. They didn't know my true history, now tattooed on my body by Old Woman Black Hands, her technique that of the old ones. The pain had been excruciating as she pulled the bone needle through my skin, bringing the graphite and soot coated seal intestine through after it. More of a stitching than tattooing, it rendered the same effect.

Now they beheld me.

Black letters on white skin.

Names of the dead.

My dead.

My responsibility.

Each one a cross to bear.

For me and the whole wide world to know.

"Do you want to know what the weight of a dead man is? Look at me. Look at the dead I carry. Remember how fucked in the head I was when I arrived? Look," I said, pointing at a name. "This one was killed by a sniper doing something I told him to do. And see this one? He was killed by an IED, his body evaporating in a pink cloud of patriotic nonsense."

I felt a hand on my shoulder. "Enough brother," Merlin said.

I shrugged off his hand. "No. This is my decision," I said picking up my shirt and putting it back on. "Sebastian and the others don't understand how death can change a man."

"They never will, brother," Merlin said. "You should know by now that we think of death not as the end, but as a beginning."

I scoffed and pointed towards the men in the crowd. "Do you all really believe in the great raven and the idea of Skyland? You, who are a Moravian. And you who are Russian Orthodox? And you, who are Mormon—what do you believe in? An afterlife where you are one with nature, or one where there's a heaven or hell?"

A man named Simon growled, "You don't know your place, boy."

"It's because I don't have a place," I snapped.

John Sey pointed a crooked finger at Merlin. "He brought those monsters that killed Pavel. It was his doing by killing the orca."

I shook my head. "He didn't bring those things. They were sent to find me." I wasn't sure until I voiced it that it was the truth, but once the words found freedom, there was no argument. "They were sent to hunt me down and kill me." I glowered at them all.

But it was the Black Hand Woman who pushed her way through the men, who addressed me next. "If you had died, then they never would have come."

I stared at her. I loved her for the pain she'd simultaneously given and taken away from me, but at that moment I wanted to hate her. But I couldn't. Because she spoke the truth in a certain way. Her logic was only marred by time. After all, even if I would have died, the Cray still would have arrived. Or would they? I thought about OMBRA's Global HMID Network and how they could communicate across the globe. I knew then that the Hypocrealiacs could do the same. How long had they known I was here and not acted? It made me wonder why they decided to ask.

I stared at the Black Hand Woman. Publically, I couldn't argue. I was loathe to disrespect her. So instead, I turned to my brother. "You about ready?"

"You are not going with me."

"No, brother, I *am* going with you."

"You're crazy."

"What does that have to do with anything?"

"There's nothing to be said," Merlin whispered coarsely. "I have to leave for a time to make the spirits happy."

"And I do as well." When Merlin glanced irritably at me, I added, "Since the Cray were coming to get me, Pavel's and Howard Makepeace's deaths were on my head as well." And then I tipped the kayak over the edge of the doc and into the water. I climbed in and paddled out fifty yards before turning around. "You coming or not?"

He looked at me, shook his head and laughed, then put his kayak in the water and joined me.

When he came abreast, I asked, "So where to, Captain Merlin?"

He stared at me with wide eyes. "You know you're going to die without supplies, right?"

I shrugged and grinned at him. I'd been to Kosovo and Iraq and Afghanistan and Mali and Kilimanjaro and L.A. I'd fought armies and terrorists and aliens and alien-made zombies. I had the unreasonable temerity to believe that I wouldn't die... that I *couldn't* die. Still, it didn't matter. Maybe it was time to die. Maybe I'd give my hundred and seventy-five pounds of flesh to the frigid waters of the Arctic. It just didn't matter. What mattered was that I needed to be here, now, with my brother.

We paddled in silence for a few moments, the only sound the lapping of the waves, the occasional bull call from the ugly, and a pair of greenshanks flying overhead, perhaps curious why two men would sail the ocean in the skin of a walrus. I'm sure the incongruity of it all baffled them to no end.

A mile out the seas began to rise. We'd gone from two foot seas to four foot seas, our kayaks rising and falling, disappearing from each other as we found our own troughs, only to rise up again, cresting together on different waves. I felt like Santiago being pulled by the great marlin, out of control, yet reveling in the ride. Any second I might die and the thought of it thrilled me.

Finally Merlin yelled, "Turn back. Go with the soldiers that came for you."

"Not without you."

"But I'm exiled."

"Not from us." A wave hit me at an angle and threatened to swamp me. I fought to keep myself afloat. I didn't care at all about dying, but I did want to get my point across, to make Merlin understand what it was that I was offering. When I was once again sure I wasn't going to drown, I added, "We need you. We need your help."

He glanced over at me with confusion.

I barely noted it, struggling to keep the waves from sending me over.

"You don't need me. You have so much more than I can offer."

Cresting the top of a wave, I dropped hard to the trough, the impact winding me. I paddled furiously to make it to the next crest. The sea gave me a break as the distance between crests increased. As I sloughed into the trough, I screamed, "You have no idea what I need. Trust me, brother, when I say I need you, I really need you!"

We paddled a few more minutes. I fought to keep him in sight. Then, out of the corner of my eye, I saw him curse, and make a wide turn, heading back to shore.

I prayed to the Old Man and the Sea, Santiago himself, and turned to follow.

Soon we were angling back to St. Lawrence Island. But instead of the pier, we headed to the ugly. Half an hour later we made landfall. After I pulled myself onto the shore, I realized that I could barely feel my arms. Had Merlin taken longer to decide, I never would have made it back.

Once we were both ashore, our kayaks clear of the water, Merlin turned to me.

"So where is it we are going?"

I managed to lift an arm and point northwest. "There."

His eyes narrowed. "The sea?"

I shook my head.

"Russia?"

I nodded, then added, "More specifically, Chukotka."

"What's there?" he asked.

"We're going to find that out." I put a hand on his shoulder. "You ready?"

He turned to look back at his village. From the ugly you could see the town pier where the Yupik men stood watching us. Behind them and off along the shore stood the Yupik woman, also watching. Merlin had braided his hair into a long black pony tail. But several wisps of hair had snuck free and caught the wind. They danced in the breeze as walrus pups mewled and bulls grunted.

Merlin had never been a man of many words, which is what drew me to him in the first place. During my healing period, he'd been the proverbial rock I'd tied my bow to. It's funny, even though I'd grown up on the ocean in San Pedro, California, I'd never been much into boat culture. But for the subsistence-living Yupik, who the rest of the world borrowed the word kayak from, without boats, they'd cease to exist. Not only was I taking Merlin away from his island, I was taking him away from a way of life.

"I knew this was going to happen," he said, his stentorian words slow and measured.

I watched and waited for him to continue.

"When you came, you were so eager to learn, but so uncomfortable on the water. I thought we'd lose you to the ocean last winter. But then you learned, and you tried your best to become Yupik. You even made the men of the long house feel bad, because they'd put you in the crazy house by the ugly and you refused to move." He dragged his gaze away from his people and regarded me. "When I saw the orca, I knew there was going to be some great change. I wasn't sure what form that change would take, but I felt it, as sure as one can feel that first winter wind slither through one's soul." He turned back to stare at his people. "This was always meant to be, I think. The Raven long ago set me on this path. I feel there's something I must do with you. Something important."

I sought for something to say, but was unable to voice what I was thinking.

"I will go with you, Ben Mason. I will be your brother. Like you, I will try my best to be useful, no matter how uncomfortable I feel. But you must promise me one thing."

I swallowed back emotion and nodded.

"When we are finished with this thing, whatever it is and wherever it takes us, you must promise to let me go home once more. For these are still my people. They are my life. I must pay for what I did, but it was never meant to be a life sentence. Merely a time where I must put myself into danger, allow the great Raven to test me, and then see who I might become after I am changed by whatever the Raven is about to do."

I swallowed again, critically aware of the importance of the moment. "Yes, my friend, my brother. I will bring you back to your people. That I promise."

He nodded once, then we both turned our backs on his village.

Show me a man with a tattoo and I'll show
you a man with an interesting past.
Jack London

CHAPTER SIX

WE ENTERED THE hangar together, carrying Merlin's gear.
I'd thought of grabbing things from my hooch, but
there was nothing I really wanted. I'd come here with
nothing and I was going to leave with nothing. Scratch
that… I was leaving with a brother.

Charlemagne clapped and laughed when he saw me.
He went to Obelix and held out his hand. The other
frowned, reached into his side pouch and pulled out
a can of Coke. It had been a long time since I'd seen
one and could just about imagine the taste. Obelix
passed the can to Charlemagne, who held it like a baby,
then found his seat again. Asterix barely noticed we'd
arrived; she seemed busy with something on her tablet.

I stared at them for a moment. I was going to have
to do something about those call signs. They were
dehumanizing and I didn't like that at all.

Nance, on the other hand, was all smiles as he
greeted us.

"Are we on mission?"

I nodded. "We have one more passenger."

Nance's eyes shot me a question.

"He's Yupik. So are the people where we're going. If

we need to negotiate cultural sensitivities, Merlin can be the one to do that. I recommend we take him with us."

"I guess so," Nance said, glancing at the line of EXOs.

I knew immediately what he was thinking. "Listen, kid. If we go in shooting everything in sight without regard to the local's lives, then we're as bad as the Cray. They came in and took our planet by force. Do you think we're going to do the same to the people we're going to see?"

"Uh, I don't think so," he said.

I put a hand on his shoulder. "Good plan."

"This planet's dead anyway," Asterix said. "The problem is that no one has told it so it doesn't know to roll over."

I held up a fist in sarcastic solidarity. "That's the fighting spirit." To Nance I said, "So here's the deal. I'm a civilian, so I'm not in charge. You're the boss. We're just along for the ride. What's the plan?"

I watched his furrowed brows dance in confusion for a few moments. "Let's start getting everything on board and cinched down. I'm going to talk to the pilot to see how fast we can be wheels up."

Over the next hour, with the help of the loadmaster and crew chief, the EXOs were lined up against both sides of the airframe and locked into place. All the rest of the gear was affixed to a palate attached to the floor. I'd spoken with the pilot, who was less than thrilled to be flying near Bingo fuel in the Arctic to find debris we didn't have an exact location for. He had enough fuel for sixteen hundred nautical miles of flying, which didn't count the need to find a landing site next to wherever the crash had occurred.

Chukotka Autonomous Okrug was a region of Russia

that had very little governmental oversight. It was literally on the edge of nowhere. The population was about 27 percent Russian, but those densities resided in a handful of coastal towns. The interior, where the crash was supposed to have occurred, was occupied by the Reindeer Chukchi and the Siberian Yupik. There was a lot of shared language between the Chukchi and the Yupik, so Merlin felt he could translate if need be. Being late July, the temperature was the same relatively balmy fifty degrees Fahrenheit that St. Lawrence Island was.

The pilot noted that a storm was brewing in the Gulf of Anadyr and wanted to keep his eye on it. The region had the highest number of hurricanes in Russia, and we didn't want to become a victim.

When we cranked open both the front and back hangar doors, the men of Savoonga waited. I saw them, but ignored them. We'd said all we needed to say to each other. Merlin remained onboard. I helped the crew chief latch the last few items in place, then settled into my own harness seat and strapped myself in like everyone else.

Asterix was still doing something on her tablet.

Obelix leaned back, his eyes closed, listening to music on headphones.

Charlemagne sat next to Merlin. He asked Merlin if he wanted to play cards, but the Yupik shook his head.

Nance sat beside me.

We remained silent as the C-130 was wheels up, nose pointed towards the sky at a forty-five degree angle, our bodies pressed back in the seats. Once it leveled out, everyone relaxed a bit. Charlemagne undid his harnesses and began to stretch in an open area near the palette. I watched as he went through a series of moves in slow motion, before recognizing it as a martial art, only I couldn't place the actual name of it.

I got up and went to him. After a few moments of watching, I asked, "Is it Japanese?"

He shook his head and grinned. "Indonesian. Pencak Silat."

I nodded and watched him for several minutes. He was doing the same form, only approaching an invisible target from different angles. Try as I might, I couldn't figure out what he was actually doing.

"Balance disruption," he explained, seeing my confusion. "Stand in a fighting stance and face me."

I did, holding my hands up, fists tight, shoulders loose.

"Now watch what I do." He stepped just past me, turned and pushed. I found myself on my butt, wondering how the hell I got there.

"I found your hole and stepped into it."

I raised an eyebrow, not knowing what he meant.

He reached down and pulled me up. His hand felt like a brick. He positioned me like I'd been, then explained. "Look how you're arrayed on an axis." He pointed to my front and back feet. "You're balanced from front to back. Now see this?" he said, pointing to the space between my feet. "That is your hole. Listen, imagine a triangle. Your front foot is at one corner, your back foot's at the other corner, and my entry point into your hole is the other corner."

I saw the genius of it. "That's for front and back, yes?"

His eyes took on a playfulness. "Pretty much, but..."

"What's the catch?

"Let's try it and see. But this time, keep me from going into your hole."

I got back into position and so did he. I waited, loose on my feet. I'd had my share of fights and had an impressive set of wins. But that was because I couldn't quit. I watched Charlemagne bounce on his feet. I noted the scars on his face and head, as well as the ones along his knuckles.

He feinted towards my front hole, and I turned to the right, blocking it. He backed away, bouncing back and forth on his feet like a prize fighter. Then he feinted towards my front hole again. I barely managed to turn when he launched towards my exposed back. I spun back, realizing when I presented my front hole to him how he'd tricked me. He stepped in and pushed me over with a finger.

Pretty much, but...

Yeah, now I saw it.

I laughed as he pulled me back up.

"Do you do that in the EXO, too?"

His eyes brightened. "The Cray are no different. They each have holes to exploit."

"You know that sounds gross, right?" Asterix said, watching us with his arms crossed.

His sister punched him in the shoulder. "Grow up."

I ignored them and invited Merlin to join us. Soon we'd worked up a sweat, practicing stepping into each other's holes—balance disruption, where have you been all my life. Everything was going well until Nance was called to the cockpit by the crew chief. He spent a few moments in there, then I felt the aircraft turn in a wide circle. I desperately wanted to know what was going on, but I even more desperately didn't want to be in the military anymore. I let Charlemagne school Merlin while I watched and waited. Finally Nance came out of the cockpit. He gestured for me to come forward and join him.

When I got to him I asked, "What's going on?"

Worry shone in his eyes. Sweat beaded his brow. "Come and take a look."

He led me into the cockpit. It was tight, but there was enough room for both of us to bend down and look out the windscreen.

Leviathan. Bigger than any aircraft carrier—more like the size of five city blocks. Slightly oblong, it had a front—if that was the front—like a manta ray and the rear was rounded. I'd never seen one before, but had heard of their existence. One of the Yupik men had told a story in the warmth of the long house about seeing one a hundred miles north of Savoonga. He'd said that a family of polar bears lived on it. I noted that the surface was mostly dry, probably because it hovered above the water by several feet. This one didn't have a family of polar bears. It had much, much worse.

"Are they what I think they are?"

The pilot nodded. "Cray. We've counted thirty-seven."

If one of the Cray got close enough to the C-130, its EMP burst would turn us into a flying rock.

The co-pilot seemed to understand this, and kept glancing worriedly at the pilot.

"Which way is it heading?"

"Same as us," the pilot said.

Which meant that the Cray that had attacked the village had most likely not been coming for me, instead trying to make it to the Leviathan.

"How far are we from Savoonga?"

"Two hundred nautical miles."

"And how fast is the Leviathan traveling?"

"Our radar tracks it at thirty-three knots."

"That fast?" I asked.

"That fast," the pilot replied.

A warning light flashed. The co-pilot pointed to the radar.

"One, two, three Cray are airborne."

"That's it then," said the pilot. "Back on course.

He pulled the C-130 out of its racetrack, and put it on a heading back towards Chukotka.

I watched for a moment as the three red dots began to recede, only they weren't receding as fast as I would have imagined.

Finally, I asked, "How fast are we going?"

"Four hundred twenty miles an hour," said the co-pilot.

"And how fast are they going?"

"One hundred and fifty miles an hour."

My jaw dropped. I'd never known a Cray to achieve even half that speed. I'd noted back on Savoonga that the ones which had attacked had seemed larger. Now I knew why. These weren't drones. These were something else entirely. These were reconnaissance Cray or worse... hunter-killers.

Show me a hero and I'll write you a tragedy.
F. Scott Fitzgerald

CHAPTER SEVEN

ONCE BACK IN the hold, Nance pulled me aside. "Listen, sir. You should really be the one in charge."

I shook my head. "No reason to be. You're doing just fine."

"But this doesn't make any sense and it feels weird. You outrank me."

"I used to," I said, smiling. "Now I'm a civilian. I don't outrank anyone."

Nance was about to say something else, but stopped. I could see him arguing with himself about whether or not to keep going. My curiosity was piqued.

"Out with it."

I saw the way he looked at me.

"Seriously," I said. "Say what you want to say."

"Captain Ohirra said that you might be reluctant because of everything that's happened."

I grinned, but there was no joy in it. *Everything that's happened.* Code for you've killed far too many of your own people. I swallowed back a retort and said, "Here's how I look at it. We're both fighting for the same thing— the survival of the team and the survival of our planet. I'm doing it as a citizen, much like those American farmers and settlers did during the Revolutionary War.

You're doing it as soldier, recruited, trained, and readied for war. If I was alone I'd be in charge of myself. But now that I'm with you, I fall under military edict. You're the senior military person on the team so you're in charge. Me, I just happen to be an expert in killing things."

Yeah. Both Cray and my own men and women.

"It's been a long day. We have about four hours and I need some shut-eye. So if you don't mind, Corporal…"

He stared at me a moment, and then sighed. "Carry on," he said, playing the game.

I found a spot on top of the pallet. Charlemagne was pointing out different things on the EXO to Merlin. Asterix and Obelix were still practicing the sullen teenager routine. Nance went to his own EXO and began to PMCS it. And I was already fucking tired of it all. I laid back and rewound the conversation I'd had with the young corporal. I'd made all that shit up on the fly. Ohirra had me dead to rights. I didn't want someone else to die, at least not under my watch. Not that I was going to let anyone else realize my reasoning.

I slipped into a fitful sleep.

My dead lived on in my dreams. Of all things, they played poker. Except instead of being themselves, they were dogs. More specifically, the velvet dogs playing poker painting come to life.

Thompson was the bulldog.

Michelle was the Lassie dog.

Olivares was the German Shepherd.

Mikey was the hound.

Stranz was the Doberman.

And McKenzie, fittingly, was the Scottie.

I watched like a fly on the wall as they played, talking about me.

"He gave us a St. Crispin's Day speech," Stranz said. "It made me want to die even faster."

"He was always good as speechifying," Mikey said... the same Mikey who'd evaporated in a cloud of mist. "In fact, you know you're going to die when he starts talking."

"Happens every time," McKenzie said.

"Oh shit," Thompson said, "He's watching."

All eyes turned to me. I felt an uncomfortable shiver as they regarded me, the canine eyes suddenly alien and intrusive. Their gaze held me in their grasp until finally Olivares said, "Go fish." Then they all laughed uproariously, returning to their game and playing some odd version of poker, Go Fish, and old maid.

They talked about the best places to pee and the best cuts of meat. They talked about chasing balls, and then Michelle waxed long about the sheer joy of chasing cars: barking at them, then running towards them only to have them flee in utter terror of her. When she was done, she broke into song, singing *killmekillmekillme* to the tune of Culture Club's Karma Chameleon.

I forced myself awake. I must have been sleeping deeply, because my mouth felt like twelve miles of hot desert road. For a moment, I forgot where I was. Staring at the ceiling of the hold in the back of a C-130, I didn't know if I was going to Iraq or Afghanistan. Was I a sergeant or a lieutenant? What was my mission? I couldn't remember any of it. My mind was as empty as a wide, flat plain.

I let my eyes slip closed once more, then awoke with a start.

Olivares stood over me.

"You going to sleep all day, troop?" he asked.

Jet black hair cut into a high and tight. Pock-marked cheeks like Tommy Lee Jones and a switchblade smile. He'd always been a better soldier than I was. The only thing I'd ever done better than him was that Michelle had chosen to be with me.

I yawned and stretched. "Man. I was having one hell of a dream," I said. Sitting up, I noted I was in my old army fatigues. I glanced beneath me and saw that I'd been sleeping on a pallet of MREs. I tried to describe the dream, but it was fleeting, on spider silk. Something about walruses and the sea. I remembered an orca whale and almost being eaten. I shook my head to clear it and when I did, the dream went away entirely.

"Where are we?" I asked Olivares as I stood and shook the sleep from my legs.

"Somewhere over Texas."

I nodded, then noticed that other than the pallet of MREs, there was nothing else in the hold. Not even any other soldiers. That couldn't be right.

Then I stared at Olivares. We hadn't met until OMBRA recruited us. The first time I'd laid eyes on him was in the underground training facility in Wyoming. The last time was at Fort Irwin, right before he'd taken a squad to Las Vegas to—

"What's going on?" I asked.

Olivares smiled. "I was wondering when you were going to ask."

"Am I still asleep?"

"Like a babe in the womb."

"Who is this? You can't be Olivares."

"What, you don't believe in coming back from the dead?"

"Seriously, what is this shit?"

Olivares, or whoever the hell it was pretending to be Olivares in my dreams, stared at me for a moment. Then he said, "It's been a long time since we talked, Mason."

Then it hit me—*Thompson*. I'd first met the boy when he'd become part of our team back in Alaska, after the invasion but before Kilimanjaro. He'd been a drummer in the army band before they'd turned him into a stone cold EXO killer. Then he'd volunteered to be a Human Machine Interface Device or HMID. After I'd become a *fungee*, then been cured, my brain had somehow rewired so that I could mentally communicate with the HMIDs. In fact, it had been Michelle who had been in my head helping me understand, right up until the point I'd killed her. They'd believed the hypocrealiacs had intentionally programmed the *ophiocordyceps invasionus* fungus to not only infect other species, but to allow their brains to be used and controlled by another alien species— whatever had been in the HMID-like black box beneath the Hollywood Hive.

"I thought I told you to fuck off, Thompson."

He made the Olivares simulacrum grin again. "Long time no brain invade."

Thompson had a way of eavesdropping, then forcing his communications through my brain. In fact, that he and Mr. Pink had used me to kill the supposed 'master' beneath the hive was what cinched my decision to leave OMBRA far behind. Not that I didn't mind killing aliens, but it was the being used against my will part that I couldn't ignore.

"What is it you want?"

"Nothing now, but later... I'm going to have something for you."

"How are you communicating?" A terrible thought came across. "Have you been with me the entire time?"

Olivares shook his head. "You were pretty isolated there."

"That was my plan."

"I'm bouncing this signal through the ship's communication array as well as three UAVs."

"Why now? Is it because you missed me so much?"

Olivares gave me a strange look, almost like disappointment, but tinged with something I couldn't figure. "You might be surprised how much you've been missed."

"Oh, I suppose Mr. Pink has been pining away for me all this time."

"Something like that." He paused, then asked, "Do you remember when we were together in the metro tunnel beneath the hive?"

"You mean when you were in my head and I was in the tunnel being sniffed at by a guard dog Cray? Yeah, I remember that."

"Do you remember what you asked me then? The question I didn't answer?"

I threw myself back in time. All I could recall was how terrified I'd felt carrying the nuke into the back door of the hive like I was delivering a pizza. "No, I don't."

Olivares nodded. "Think about it then. See if you can remember what it was I wouldn't answer."

"Why not just come out and say it?"

Olivares shook his head again. "Once I say it, it can't be unspoken."

Now I was really confused. "That pretty much sums up everything someone says."

"Not if you really think about it." He depressed a button and the ramp began to lower. The interior of the hold was now filled with the sounds of rushing air. He walked to the edge of the ramp and pointed down. "This is where the magic happens."

Down below? Where'd he say we were—Texas? I was about to ask him what he meant, when he said one last thing.

"Watch out for the Russians. They're close."

Then he jumped. Instead of falling, he landed on a cloud, then found another and leapfrogged out of sight.

Fucking dreams.

Now how was I going to wake the fuck up?

If you kill enough of them, they stop fighting.

Curtis LeMay

CHAPTER EIGHT

TURNS OUT, I didn't have to figure it out. Nance shook my shoulder and I snapped awake.

"What is it?" I asked, sitting up and making sure that this was the real C-130 and not the dream version.

"We're an hour out. Need to give a mission brief."

I wiped my face with my left hand and started to stand, but he put a hand in the middle of my chest and wouldn't let me. For a brief moment, I felt heat bloom in my face, then I relaxed as I saw the concern in his eyes.

"What is it?"

"You were mumbling when you slept."

I wiped my face again. "Dreams. They never stop, you know?"

He looked me in the eyes, then said, "You were saying 'killmekillmekillme'."

I frowned as the image of Michelle dying in my arms slapped me across the face. I couldn't help but close my eyes, but the image stayed. I blinked hard, trying to see something else, but the image remained superimposed over Nance's concerned face. I'd thought I'd gotten over it. I'd barely thought about her or anyone else in the last few months. Diving into the subsistence life of the

Yupik had occupied every waking breath. Now look at me.

"That wasn't me saying it," I said, my voice suddenly raspy.

"But it was you. I heard it."

"No, I mean it was my—" What should I call her? We hadn't really been boyfriend and girlfriend. We'd only been with each other once, but our love ran bone deep. "She was the woman I loved. She asked me to kill her and I did." Seeing the look of shock and confusion in his eyes, I added, "She became one of the first HMIDs. She was miserable."

Nance's reply was stony silence. He stared hard at me for what must have been a full minute. "Have you talked about this with anyone?"

I shook my head. "Who's there to talk to? We all have problems."

"We don't all have the *same* problems. There's always someone to talk to."

I grinned. "Sounds easy."

"It could be. Worked for me."

Now it was my turn to look hard at him. What was it in his past that haunted him? We all had something now that we'd been planet-jacked. But more and more it wasn't something we did, but something that we saw, or something we were unable to do... like save our families and our loved ones from the destruction of the Cray and the fungees.

"Do you know how the original member of TF OMBRA were selected?"

He shook his head.

"Unlike now, where they take anyone with a heartbeat, back before the invasion they were looking for extra special soldiers. Mr. Pink tracked me down on the Vincent Thomas Bridge. I was trying to commit suicide like that film director, Tony Scott."

"I've met a lot of people who tried to commit suicide."

"I have as well. But we're not talking about a lot of people. We're talking about all of us. Every one. The whole damned unit. Imagine a unit where every member has done and seen such terrible things that we all tried to off ourselves. That was us. That's who we were. And why did they do it? OMBRA claimed that there was something in our brain chemistry that made us better against the invaders."

"But you eventually succeeded. You were the Hero of the Mound."

I shook my head. "Like Hero Prime, that's all propaganda. My point is that I'm so fucked up in the head I might be a handicap to the mission."

He lowered his eyes, then climbed up on the palette beside me. He held his hands out before him and stared at them. "You're no different than any one of us now. Maybe before, but not now." I was about to argue, but he continued, his voice barely above a whisper. "I killed my mother two years ago."

My heart skipped a beat.

"She was visiting her cousin in Stockton when the invasion hit. I was assigned to Fort Irwin and went AWOL immediately. Hell, most of us left, more concerned for our families than protecting a red, white and blue idea. America doesn't even exist anymore. This New United States of North America is just some old guys trying to grasp onto a failed experiment. Now there's only OMBRA. For good or bad, OMBRA is all that means anything."

He breathed through his nose, his lips tight.

"Your mother," I nudged.

"Yeah, Moms was visiting Latricia in Stockton. I managed to make it there in three days. You were in training and didn't see it, but the world went straight back to the Dark Ages. There was no law, there was no civilization. People charged head first into their basic instincts. When I found the house, Latricia lay face down in the kitchen. I could tell she'd been repeatedly raped. She had blood all over her." He wiped a tear away. "She was dead. Took me two more days to find my Moms. A group of teenaged boys had rounded up all the older women and were using them as sex slaves. My mom was one of them, kept with the others in an old slaughterhouse.

"I was barely twenty then, so I looked a lot like them. I infiltrated their group. To keep up appearances, I had to be part of the raping of three women." He suddenly looked me in the eyes. "Know what's worse than raping a woman and hearing her scream? Raping a woman and not hearing her scream. All three of them just took it. Those boys had fucked the humanity right of them." He looked back at his hands. "That night I killed nine of the boys. Stabbed seven of them in their sleep, and fought the other two. They thought they were tough, but they weren't. Just fucking teenagers at the end of the world thinking their life had become a video game. Fucking *Grand Theft Auto*.

"They were trained to win first person shooters. The difference was that I *was* a first person shooter. 11B. Infantry. I hunted the rest down and shot them all. By the time I was done, it was sunrise. When I went to free the women... when I opened the gates that were keeping them in, guess what they did?" He looked at me.

I shook my head.

"They did nothing. They just stood there and waited. They thought I was just another rapist coming to rape them some more. It never once crossed their mind that I'd come there to free them. So I grabbed my Moms and left." He closed his eyes. "Moms was broken—in her mind and body. She couldn't speak and she could barely walk. But I didn't even care about that. I just wanted to get as far away from Stockton as possible. I forced her to walk with me. The roads were clogged with vehicles that had run out of gas. If it had been just me, I'd have used a motorcycle like I'd done to get there. But my Moms was in no condition to ride. In fact, she was in no condition to walk. The morning of day three she began puking blood. It was then I noticed her entire torso was layered with purple and green bruises. She had internal bleeding.

"You see, had I stayed in Stockton and taken her to a competent medical authority, she might have lived. But I'd force marched her seventy miles away into the middle of nowhere. She died that night. I buried her the next morning near mile marker 391 on Interstate 5."

I let the silence gather around us before I spoke. "There was nothing you could do."

"I know. I've heard it all before. Even if I'd found someone willing to take care of her, chances are she would have died anyway. I know it." He poked hard at his head with his forefinger. "But up here doesn't get that. It keeps telling me that there was something I should have done differently. My brain won't let go of the idea that it was me who killed her instead of those damned boys." Then he turned to me. "Just like your brain won't let you forget. The more you try and hide it, the more it finds ways to remind you."

He slid off the pallet and stood, facing away from me. "It's holding it inside that kills you. You don't hold cancer inside. You ball it up and throw it the fuck away. Bad memories are worse in shadow. Let the light in. Confront them. It's the only fucking way." He turned his head slightly. "We have mission brief in five minutes. I expect you there, Hero Prime." Then he walked forward and sat down, stone faced, staring at a map that was rolled out on the floor.

> Luck is what happens when preparation meets opportunity.
>
> Seneca

CHAPTER NINE

I SPENT THAT five minutes thinking about Olivares, probably the best soldier I knew, and the one I'd hated most. I was actually sorry he'd died in Las Vegas. He had a way of bringing out the best in me. More than once he'd called me a *shit soldier* or a *shit non-commissioned officer,* and he'd been right each time. Once I got over being angry about the comment, I'd pulled myself up and corrected whatever it was I was doing.

I watched Charlemagne, Merlin, Asterix, and Obelisk as they each sat apart, lost in their own realities. This was no unit. This was a group of individuals brought together for a common goal. As a unit they might survive. As individuals they wouldn't stand a chance. I had no faith in any of them and no surety that if I was in a firefight and against the odds any of them would come to my aid. And they could say the same about me.

A lot of the problem had to do with those damned call signs. Hero Prime, two cartoon characters and a medieval French hero. They were playing characters rather than being themselves. Mr. Pink, in his effort to motivate, had inadvertently created EXO fighters who fought using persona. I thought back to pro-wrestling and fighters like Cena and Hulk Hogan and The Undertaker. Each of them had signature moves. Was that what EXO fighting had come to? Was that who they were now? I'd been in the shit. I'd fought an entire hive and knew that I never had time for a signature move. My signature move was surviving. Whatever. If they wanted Hero Prime, I might just give it to them.

I let my gaze stray to the EXOs. I hadn't paid them much attention because I hadn't really been into the mission, but now I noticed they were a slightly larger and a lot sleeker than versions one and two. The Hydra anti-air missile system was the same, as was the rotating machine gun. Each EXO also had a meter-long harmonic blade attached to a scabbard in the back. My guess was that the larger size had more to do with extra power and extra battery life. I'd have to be familiarized before we hit the mission... something I should have done already.

Olivares again.

You're a shit soldier.

I watched Nance studying the map and realized for the first time how far out of his element he was. The guy was a corporal. Sure, he was an eleven bang, but that didn't mean he could lead. Even with the best of intentions, he'd failed to create a cohesive crew. My gaze shifted... and I'd brought Merlin into the center of it.

I stood and walked over to where Nance sat. I noted that the map had little geographical features which indicated a flat plain. No way to hide us there. Not only would the drone of the C-130 give us away, but the sight of EXOs marching across the tundra would be unmistakable. There would be no element of surprise.

We'd need to be on point and on mission.

Nance glanced at me and I said, "I'll take it from here, son."

His eyes narrowed for a moment, then opened wide as he realized that I'd finally come on board. *About time, you shit soldier.*

Nance's face washed with relief. I nodded, sat on a seat beside him, then called the others over.

Charlemagne and Merlin came first, both eager and bright-eyed. The brother and sister took their time. I counted to forty-five before they were actually sitting in place. If Nance noticed, it didn't seem to bother him. But it sure as hell bothered me. I knew I'd have to address it, but also understood that I couldn't make enemies of them right before the mission.

"Okay, here's the deal. Captain Ohirra has sent us to find and retrieve any salvage we can from a spacecraft that crash landed. This is our first real chance to gain some insight into what sort of spacecraft the aliens have been using. As to which aliens they belong to, that's yet to be determined. Curiously, OMBRA intercepted a Russian report of bodies. When translated, the report indicated that the remains of 'human aliens' were present. We're not sure what that means, but we definitely need to see if we can get our hands on the remains so OMBRA can learn as much about them as they can before we have to face them. These could be the next enemy and we need to be prepared."

I paused to see if everyone was understanding what I was saying.

Asterix raised her hand as if she were in school.

I noted the behavior then nodded for her to proceed.

"I thought Corporal Nance was in charge?"

I shook my head. "You're wrong. Lieutenant Mason is in charge."

Her eyes widened in surprise. Then she said dramatically, "I stand corrected."

"Yes, you do." I gestured to the map on the floor. "Somewhere out in that nothing is our target. We can't be sure whether the crash is contained or over a wide area. There might be debris for miles."

"What about the Russians?" Charlemagne asked.

"Yeah. What about them?" asked Obelix.

I glanced at Nance, who said, "The pilot is scanning frequencies. If the Russians are anywhere near, we'll be able to pinpoint them. The problem is if they are near and they have radar, then we'll have been made."

I nodded. "Right. We have to hope they're either willing to share or don't have any ground-to-air missile capabilities. Now, when we get on the ground we're going to do things my way. We're also changing designations."

Obelix frowned. "Changing designations?"

"Your call signs for one. They're not only ridiculous, but they're too hard to say."

Charlemagne narrowed his eyes and looked to Nance for input. But Nance was equally surprised. The two French cartoons, however, were simmering, verging on outrage.

"But our fans…" Asterix began.

"Yeah, what about our fans?" Obelix said.

I pinned them with my eyes. "Fans? The world is ending and you're concerned about a loss of popularity?"

"But you don't understand—" she began.

"What don't I understand? That the alien Cray came and sent us back to the Dark Ages? Or is it that I don't understand that the planet is being terraformed? After all, I probably forgot that I spent time in my own personal hell as a fungee'd zombie."

Merlin put his hand on my arm. "Easy, friend."

I shook off his touch and pointed at the pair. "Unless your fans are willing to come on this mission for you, they are no concern of mine or yours." I scowled and said, "Fans," like it was toxic.

But Asterix wasn't having it. She shook her head hard enough to make her brown hair sway across her eyes, reminding me of that weird girl in *The Breakfast Club*. "You don't understand. Our scores are tied to our call signs. Without the call signs, it will mess up the entire record keeping system. Without the call signs, we can't achieve the higher levels."

Dear God! Mr. Pink had turned our survival into a video game. I felt my blood begin to rise and tried to calm myself. But try as I might, the very idea behind what had been done was an insult to everyone who'd died.

"Scores?" I spat the word. "You have targets and you have kills. Jesus, what the hell happened in the nine months I was away? Was killing the Cray becoming so easy that you had to make a game of it?"

"Cray not so hard." Obelix smiled. "We pick them off one by one. Easy."

"One by one. You've never been against a hive, have you? Try a thousand Cray coming at you and all you have is the trust of your squad."

Obelisk rolled his eyes. "Whatever, man."

My ideas of not making enemies vanished under a wave of rage. I was on him faster than he could smirk, riding him down onto the unforgiving metal deck of the plane. One hand was wrapped around his throat and the other balled into a fist, my finger pointing at his face. "If you fucking roll your eyes at me one more time, I'm going to chew them out of your face." I felt a hand on me, and yelled, "Get off!"

Out of the corner of my eye, I saw Merlin pull out his knife and hold it out. "Not one of you touch him," he said.

Obelix wasn't smirking. He wasn't sneering. He wasn't rolling his eyes. All of his attention was on the tip of my finger.

"Leave my brother alone!" Asterix screamed.

"This is a goddamn military unit, not high school," I said to both of them, but particularly to the snot under my hand. "I'm the ranking officer. I say, you do. No comments. No facial expressions. I say, you do. Now say it."

Obelix still couldn't take his eyes off my finger. So I slapped him. "Say it."

"I—I say, you d—d—do."

"The rest of you, say it."

All of them did, including Merlin and a grudging Asterix.

I released Obelix neck and sat back, but didn't stand. "What's your name? Your real name."

"Earl," he said, fear leaving him as he realized I wasn't going to punch him. "Earl Stone."

I nodded. "What's her name?"

"Pearl. We're Earl and Pearl Stone."

"Earl and Pearl. Cute. You are now Hero Three and she is Hero Four."

I got to my feet and pointed at Charlemagne. "You are Hero Two and Nance, you are Hero One."

"Who are you?" Charlemagne asked.

"Hero Prime. Just like you said. Or you can just call me Prime."

Merlin, who was still standing with the knife in his hand, cleared his throat. "Uh, what should I be called?"

I grinned. "Put the knife down, brother. You're Merlin. Merlin's a great name." I turned towards the team, then reached down and helped Earl to his feet. "Now, you all want to be heroes? We can do that. We're Hero Squad. Not one of us is more or less of a hero than the other. Your number of kills is irrelevant. I don't want to hear them mentioned, unless it has something to do with helping each other out. Any questions?"

Obelix stared at the ground, his fists balled. I knew the stance. I knew what he wanted.

"You want to hit me, Hero Three?"

Although he shook his head, his fists were balled.

"Yes, you do. You want to hit me hard. What if I said I'd let you hit me?"

He looked up, clearly not believing me.

"Here's the deal. You have every right to be mad. I shouldn't have jumped you. I let my temper get the best of me. You want to hit me, I'll let you."

I saw the fist coming from a hundred miles away. I could have easily dodged it, but I let it score me on the side of my face. Although the kid had put everything he had in it, the punch was no more powerful than the slap I'd given him. But he had to do it. I had to empower him. So I let my head roll with the punch.

When I again looked at him, his head was held a little higher and he was ready for me.

"That was a good one."

Then I surprised him by offering my hand.

He accepted it with a soft grip.

Pearl stared at her brother a mix of awe and fear on her face.

"That the first time you've hit anyone?" I asked.

"In real life?"

I nodded.

"Yeah."

"Not even in an EXO?"

He shook his head.

Hadn't he just said not in real—then it hit me—all of it—what Mr. Pink had done.

"You've never been in the military have you?" I asked, looking from the boy to the girl and back. They both shook their heads. I noted a spark of pride in the girl's eyes. She had an impressive number of kills for someone without any military experience, as did the boy. And to think that all of their experience came from video games. Ender Wiggin proved it by destroying the *buggers*. Alex Rogan proved it by being the last starfighter and defending the frontier from the Ko-Dan Armada. Where before I'd thought Mr. Pink had been insane for setting up the new program, now I saw its genius.

"Where'd you two come from?" I asked.

"Salt Lake City," she said.

There'd been a hive there. I wondered how they'd missed it.

Sensing my question, she answered, "We were spending a week in Park City when everything happened. After a few days, my father went back to SLC and my mother took us deeper into the mountains. It wasn't until she got sick that we came out, but by then it was too late."

I nodded. Without modern medicine a simple flu could prove deadly.

Earl spoke softly. "We heard on the radio that OMBRA

was taking all comers. All of our friends, my father, everyone was killed. We just wanted to fight back. Turned out we were really good at it."

"What video games did you play?" I asked.

Earl snorted.

Pearl grinned. "All of them." Then seeing my doubt, she added, "No, seriously. It takes us about a day to finish one."

"Hero level," Earl said.

"Always at hero level," she added. "First Person Shooters are my favorite because they give me the instant gratification I need, but that one likes leveling," she said pointing at her brother.

He grinned, "Loot."

"Well, there's no loot to be had fighting with the EXOs," I said.

"What about the alien tech?" Pearl asked.

"And the remains?" Earl added.

I couldn't help but grin. "Okay, let me correct that. There's loot this mission. Just remember that we're working together. This isn't a competition."

Nance cleared his throat, a thin smile on his face. He was probably thrilled to be in an actual military unit again. "You mentioned when we're on the ground we're going to be doing things your way?"

"Right. Take your seats." I waited until everyone was seated, then continued. "Formation X-ray is Hero One and Two in bounding over watch on my left and Hero Three and Four in bounding over watch on my right. This will be our basic tactical formation." I noted that Earl and Pearl looked confused. "We're going to have to explain *bounding overwatch,* aren't we?'

She nodded.

"What's been your strategy for killing Cray?" I asked.

"Run at them as fast as we can, get there first, and shoot to kill," Earl said.

"We're not going to be doing that," I said. "That's video game strategy." Before the invasion, I'd watched as my friends and fellow soldiers would play *World of Warcraft*, swarming through caves and dungeons in search of loot. Even though every one of them knew military tactics, they'd push and shove, trying to be the first one to the loot cast off by dead creatures, other characters, and boss rooms. No, we were definitely not doing that. "Nance, I expect you to ensure the rest of Hero Squad understands military tactics." To Charlemagne, I added, "I'm sure I don't have to explain tactical formations to you, now do I?" The reason his numbers had been lower than these two young gamers was because he'd remained at Nance's side while they'd sprinted forward. I wasn't going to have that.

"No, sir."

I grinned. Ohirra would be happy. Maybe even Olivares would stop giving me eternal shit if he could have seen how I'd turned the group around.

Suddenly the C-130 bucked, then took a sharp left. I barely managed to get ahold of webbing to keep me from hitting the far wall, which was now below me.

Merlin and Charlemagne tumbled into the row of EXOs. Nance had grabbed hold as well.

Somehow Earl and Pearl had managed to stay in their seats. They were busy buckling up, as was I, when a voice came over the speaker.

"We've been hit. We're going down."

All I could think at that moment was that I hoped we were over land.

That which does not kill us, makes us stronger.

Friedrich Nietzsche

CHAPTER TEN

THE SHEER TERROR of being in a plane that's crashing is unmatched by anything. The absolute lack of control one feels, especially in the essentially windowless hold of a C-130, is barely mitigated by the idea that I didn't want to see us careening into the ground. I held onto the netting with a death grip as I wondered if I wanted to survive. Would it even be reasonable if we crashed and I was able to crawl out of the smoking ruin—maybe paralyzed or worse? Perhaps now was the chance for the universe to decide if I really deserved to live or die, a judgment for everything I'd done. As we spiraled downward, I ignored the cries of Hero Squad, instead listening for the punch line for the intergalactic joke.

Suddenly the plane leveled.

It was in this moment of calm that I realized I'd been holding onto something that I should have long ago let go. It came as an ice pick through whatever reality I'd constructed and shone as a truth I never should have failed to notice. Bottom line was that I wanted to be me. The problem was that I'd been trying to be who I'd been—to find that wet-under-the-nose kid who'd joined the military so long ago. I'd been trying to be that person who hadn't witnessed innumerable deaths, mass burials, and my soldiers—no, my friends—explode in plain sight. I wanted to be the kid who thought the worst that could happen was to get shot in the arm or the leg and then return home, like what happened to the Duke in all the best John Wayne movies. But I could never go back. I could never be that kid. Why I even wanted to be him was a failsafe my brain had sought for too long. I was the sum of my actions. I'd been molded in combat and forged by what I'd seen. I could never be that kid again, and in reality, I didn't want to be him again. To do so meant to forget the glorious lives and the terrible deaths of too many friends. It would be an insult to those I'd lead into combat.

This realization was more than stunning—it was life changing. My PTSD had always been magnified through the lens of who I once was compared to who I was now. But finally I realized that this never needed to happen. Why would I have assume that I could return to being that pristine pure kid who chased his friends and shot invisible bullets from finger guns? Was that it? Was the heart of my PTSD that I'd been trying to be a person who'd never done or seen anything bad? A boy in a plastic bubble?

Even as Charlemagne and Merlin scrambled to their feet and buckled themselves in, I laughed, the sound loud and intrusive in the suddenly chaos-free space.

Was the solution that simple? If I embraced who I'd become—if I accepted it as the continuing version of me—would that make everything easier?

I thought of who I'd become:

An itinerant lieutenant in the only real western block military unit who'd been asked to lead a group of soldiers to recover alien debris.

A man who'd loved and been forced to do the right thing, even if it had been the hardest thing.

A soldier who could be counted on to accomplish a mission.

I glanced at my squad, now nervously looking around, strapped to a suspect airframe, and realized something. Each of them had already accepted their deaths. They'd thought about it, checked the block beside the possibility and moved on. Damned if I wouldn't do everything in my power to keep them from dying, but if they did, it wasn't on me. I let out an explosive breath of air and felt a lightness of being I hadn't felt in an age.

"Jesus, Lieutenant, why are you so happy?" Nance asked. "We almost died."

"Almost only counts in horseshoes, sex, and hand grenades." I couldn't stop grinning. "Hero Squad, repeat after me." All eyes were on me. Pearl clearly thought I was insane. "Whatever doesn't kill me makes me stronger."

No one said a word.

My eyes narrowed. "That's an order." I repeated. "Whatever doesn't kill me makes me stronger."

Charlemagne and Merlin mumbled a repeat.

"Everyone. Whatever doesn't kill me makes me stronger."

They all sort of said it.

I shouted it again and they said it with a little more energy.

I shouted it again and they matched it.

I shouted it again and they drowned me out.

Soon, we were shouting the line and laughing, over and over and over, trying to voice our joy of life and laugh at death so that the world could hear it. We continued shouting, everyone smiling, everyone finally one team, until the pilot interrupted.

"Corporal Nance, we need you up front."

Nance glanced at me and I smiled. He in turn gave me a worried look.

I unstrapped and went to the access door to the cockpit. I knocked once, then it opened.

I crouched down and looked out the windscreen. We were low. Probably less than five hundred feet. Beneath us, tundra with a few splotches of snow whizzed by.

"What's going on?" I asked.

The pilot glanced at me, eyes narrowed. "You finally in charge, Mason?"

I nodded. The intricacies of the relationship with me and my warriors weren't his business. He was a bus driver, pure and simple. But I knew to be polite. "We took a hit?"

"Surface-to-air missile. Left engine. We're going to have to set down."

"Were you able to identify the attacker?" I asked.

"SA-7 Grail. Old school Soviet tech."

"You weren't able to avoid it?"

"Santa and his reindeer have more jukes and moves than this old rust bucket," the co-pilot said. "We're lucky to still be in the air." He glanced at the pilot with barely concealed admiration.

"You getting anything on the frequency scanner?" I asked.

The co-pilot shook his head. "Only some native gibberish. Low end coms. Walkies really. Nothing we can confirm. Nothing Russian."

That got me thinking. I stuck my head back in the hold. "Merlin, put on a headset," I said pointing towards where a pair of them hung, plugged into the plane. Had I been on my game, I would have been wearing them to keep track of what was going on.

Merlin complied and after I asked the co-pilot to pump in the feed, Merlin began to listen. It only took him a few minutes to get excited. He began to summarize what he was hearing. "Two reindeer herders complaining because they lost two of their herd to soldiers. Seems last night they poached two deer and cooked them."

"Can you get a location?" I asked.

"Can I ask them?"

I glanced at the pilot who had the ultimate decision about the safety of the aircraft. He shrugged, and I said, "Sure. Why not?"

Merlin spoke into the headset. I could only pick out a few words, but I did know he repeated himself three times. It seemed like the Yupik on the peninsula hadn't been expecting to talk to a cousin from St. Lawrence Island and began by asking about the fishing and how much winter stores had been packed. Within moments, Merlin reported the location of a Russian contingent numbering thirty-three soldiers who were on the move to a crash site. The good news was that we were closer to the crash site than the Russians. In fact, if the herders were to be believed, it was only fifteen clicks away. The bad news was that they'd probably been the ones to fire on us as we passed over them and they knew we were here.

"Can you land this thing near the crash site?" I asked.

"I can land this baby on a desert island. That's not our problem," said the pilot. "Once we land, we're not going to be able to take off again." The co-pilot plugged in the new coordinates. "Or at least we shouldn't."

I saw the problem right away. "We don't have enough fuel to get back."

The pilot shook his head. "Not even halfway. By the time we crossed the coast, we'd be nothing more than a flying brick."

"Do we have any radio coms with anyone?" I asked, remembering how Thompson had communicated with me. "I think there are some UAVs within range that can retrans your signal."

The co-pilot looked at me. "How do you know about the drones?"

I shrugged. "Seems like the obvious solution."

"Well, we've been sending a continuous SOS, but have no way of knowing if it's getting through," the pilot said. "We're going to keep sending it along with coordinates until we land. Once we're down, it's cross your fingers time."

"Been there done that," I said. "Let's worry about what we can change. You get us down and we'll conduct the mission. We just have to hope that the cavalry arrives in time. What's the projected ETA of the Russians?"

"Eighty minutes," said the co-pilot.

"Looks like we'll be fighting them regardless." I grinned. It was about to be grunt time. "You get us down and let me handle things from there."

Both the pilot and co-pilot acknowledged. I let them do what they had to do to keep us in one piece and headed back to the hold. I explained the situation to the squad, then strapped in. We had about seven minutes until landing. I spent that entire seven minutes sending my own mental SOS to Thompson. As much as I hated the fact he could peek into my brain anytime he wanted, now was the moment when I hoped he was doing just that. Because if he wasn't, we were either going to freeze or face odds I wasn't too confident we could survive.

The debris field was seventeen miles long. As the pilot sought a landing strip level enough not to rip the wheels off the old rust bucket, he described the scene a mere two hundred feet below.

"...must have been immense. Pieces of what... fuselage... metal or some material littering the tundra... are those... impossible... bodies..."

"But they can't be," said the co-pilot. "The proportions are all wrong."

By now we all wore headsets and were listening to their ruminations. I felt, then saw, the others staring at me as if I had the answers. I just stared back. We'd find out soon enough. It was ironic, really. Before the invasion we'd have relied on satellite imagery to find the crash site, but now, after we'd been ass-kicked back into the Dark Ages, we'd had to rely on the complaints of a pair of reindeer herders to pinpoint the exact location of the alien ship.

Amidst the bewildered half-descriptions came a sudden harried command from the pilot. "Everyone hold on."

The aircraft slewed left, then right. I held on, staring blankly at the fuselage, imagining the ground coming up to meet the plane, even though it was really the other way around. A low singing came to my attention. I glanced over at Merlin, whose eyes were tight shut. He had a white-knuckled grip on the netting he was sitting on. It was at that moment that I realized that Merlin had probably never been on a plane. He looked terrified, which was such an atypical emotion for him. I'd seen him stand toe-to-claw with a polar bear, holding it off with a lance until the other men of the tribe could bring it down. I'd seen him on partially frozen seas, blocks of ice capable of caving in his kayak at any second. I'd even seen him stand unfazed as a grizzly bore down on him, rifle in his shoulder, knowing that he only had one shot and confident in his ability that he would bring it down.

I'd love to be able to tell him that this was nothing. That a C-130 could probably land sideways and never get a scratch. The old battle hound of airborne divisions was made to be tough. I'd been on enough spiral combat landings and take-offs that they seemed normal to me.

Then the earth came up to meet us with a bone-jarring slam.

All we know is that, at times, fighting the Russians, we had to remove the piles of enemy bodies from before our trenches, so as to get a clear field of fire against new waves of assault.

Paul von Hindenburg

CHAPTER ELEVEN

WE WERE UNSTRAPPING before the C-130 came to a stop. The first thing I did after they let the ramp down was have Charlemagne suit up and then deploy him outside the aircraft. Inside his EXO he towered over me. I led him down the ramp. The air was crisp but not cold. The ground had a softness to it. Not muddy. A foot or two of the tundra had melted.

"Head two kilometers in that direction," I ordered, pointing to where the Russians were coming. "Burst your radar for three seconds every five minutes, then switch off. Got it?"

The EXO head nodded, making me feel as if I'd just been talking to a robot. Good thing it was on my side.

When I turned to go back in, I noted the crew chief and his assistant were busily erecting two large tripods, one on either side of the ramp. Once they slid the M2 50 caliber machine gun on one and began to rack an ammo belt into the side of it, I immediately felt better. Knowing there were two of them made me feel almost hopeful that we'd survive this mess.

Inside, Nance had just finished explaining bounding over watch to the kids, telling them they had to coordinate their movements with himself and Hero Two. I ordered them into their suits and had them standby.

As it turned out, Nance had brought a box of goodies. Good thing, too. Out here on the edge of the world with Russians heading toward us, I felt sort of nervous. I reminded myself that a modern EXO had the firepower of a Vietnam War-era battalion. It wasn't as if we were powerless. The problem was I'd never gone up against traditional forces, unless you count the treachery of Dewhurst, who'd tried to sell us out so that Sebring could have an EXO to reverse engineer. Luckily the M63 tank hadn't been able to fire because I seriously doubted I would have been able to withstand a round from a 105mm main gun. It probably would have left a hole in me the size of a basketball, then keep on going for a few more miles. Not knowing what we faced with the Russians worried me. Knowing what arms and armor they had could let me better plan. As of this moment, we were completely blind.

But that was about to change.

Nance showed me the gear.

Two things immediately intrigued me.

The first was a small V-winged UAV with a downward looking camera. It was slick, black, and had a four foot wingspan.

"We can control this through our suits. Your command module can allocate control to any one of us. The feeds are also available to us, depending on your information sharing setting. This other one here," he said, pointing to a quadcopter, "is for battlefield management. It goes on station directly above us, and moves based on our movement, providing us with a flat representation of the battlefield."

I quickly reimagined how helpful it was going to be, allowing me to deploy forces to points under direct contact. Both were necessary and needed.

I suited up. When I pulled on my helmet, I could have sworn it had that new EXO smell. I switched on the internal electronic grid which made the suit impervious to a Cray EMP burst. I remember back when the Faraday Suit was first revealed. Its invention had been a logical response to the threat of the Cray. We'd all read Scalzi and Steakley and knew how they'd portrayed power armor and powered exoskeletons. Borrowed from Heinlein's *Starship Troopers*, which were in turn borrowed from E. E. Doc Smith's Lensman novels, it wasn't as if there was a copyright on the idea. When mere humans were forced to fight creatures so much larger than themselves, they needed mechanical assistance to survive, which was why the Electromagnetic Faraday Xeno-combat suit, or EXO, was invented by OMBRA technicians.

The suits initially had problems with external communication. Just as an EMP burst couldn't get in, transmissions couldn't get out. Fortunately, OMBRA had been able to beg, borrow, and steal the best technicians on the planet, who devised a method using Extremely Low Frequencies (ELF) with a ground dipole antenna established through the soles of the EXO's feet. Since the majority of EMP energy is seen in the microwave frequencies, the system was capable of operating on a battlefield in which EMPs had been brought into play. Advanced digital modulation techniques allowed them to compress data on the signal, allowing real-time feeds between team members and back to base. A backup, transmit-only communications system resided in an armored blister atop the helmet. Called the Rotating Burst Transmission Module (RBTM), it was comprised of a one-inch rotating sphere inside of the blister with its own battery power. One side of the sphere was able to pick up a packet of data when rotated 'inside' the Faraday cage of the EXO; when rotated 'outside' this protection, it transmitted the packet as a burst.

While the exterior of my new EXO was brash white, the interior was red and lined with better cushioning than I remembered. The outer covering alternated layers of Kevlar and titanium, bonded together to protect both the wearer and the grounding web. Internally the suit had hardened electronics for video feeds, voice communication, targeting, night vision, sound amplification/dampening and vital sign monitoring, along with heating, cooling and an air rebreather system with CO_2 scrubbers, all powered by extremely light, high-energy rechargeable batteries. And I was right about the extra size. Technicians had managed to double the battery life, allowing the suit to keep engaged for forty-eight hours.

All systems were controlled by eye movements, through an internal HUD system with Gaze technology, or remotely from base as a backup. I gaze-flicked the status of all the other EXOs and was pleased with how quickly the information was at hand. Then I brought up Charlemagne's feed and checked real time what he could see in the visual spectrum as well as radar. Other than debris along the ground, there was nothing within miles.

I returned attention to my own suit as I assessed the weapons suite.

Each EXO had three primary weapon systems.

The integral rocket launcher (IRL) was mounted over the left shoulder on rails, so as to rotate it back out of the way or bring it forward to firing position when needed. The standard payload was thirty Hydra rockets with air-burst warheads set to detonate at a range determined before launch by the suit's internal targeting system. Missiles were free-flight after launch, with a hardened internal timer for detonation. This system was designed to engage alien drones at maximum to medium targeting range. If need be, it would engage the Russians in much the same way.

The XM214 was the EXO's primary attack armament. The new model had 500 more rounds and these were all white phosphorous.

Of course, not every situation caused for a range weapon. There'd been more than one occasion where I'd felt the need or the situation had necessitated me going medieval on their asses. For that I used the harmonic blade. A meter long and sixteen centimeters wide, TF OMBRA's harmonic blade vibrated at ultrasonic frequencies, making it thousands of times more effective at slicing through armored opponents than a normal blade. The weapon was made from Stellite to help withstand the vibrational forces as well as any environmental extremes an OMBRA grunt might encounter, and the vibration was generated in the hilt by an electrically isolated system powered by a high energy battery.

Yeah, being an EXO driver didn't suck. I'd last worn one in Dodger Stadium, on my way to the Hollywood Hive. I'd forgotten how I felt while wearing the suit. The power and protection, the servos allowing full range of motion, and more. I flexed the missile launcher, then brought forward the machine gun. Being in an EXO was like being a tank with two legs instead of tread. I wanted to shoot something. I wanted to break something. I stood there for a few seconds grinning like an idiot.

Then I saw Merlin trying to get my attention.

I turned to him and he backed up several feet. I realized my weapon's systems were deployed and retracted them. Now instead of looking like some sort of robotic dreadnaught, I was merely an imposing nine foot tall mechanized warrior. Merlin, who was actually a few inches taller than me, seemed like a child beside me.

"What am I supposed to do? Come along?" he asked, eyeing me speculatively.

I toggled the public address system. "Get on the radio and see if you can find places where we might hole up in case we lose this position." Then another thought hit me. "You might also ask if any of the Yupik here might have taken any *souvenirs* from the wreckage. Might make our job easier."

He nodded and went back inside.

I could tell he wanted to be part of the action, but without an EXO he'd be more of a liability than anything else.

Two minutes later, the four of us were standing outside the plane.

Nance launched the winged UAV and sent it south at an elevation of two thousand feet. I flick-gazed the feed into my window, then reduced it so I could later access it with ease. Then I shot the quad-copter straight up five hundred feet and set it to center above my EXO. I checked the feed and saw the four of us, the plane, and the crew chief and his assistant manning the 50 cal machine guns. I was intrigued by my ability to see them through my visor as well as through the feed. I wondered how I was going to be able to manage it.

I spoke briefly with the pilot, then had Hero Team go four abreast with thirty meters of spacing between each of us. Then we broke into a loping run towards the debris field. The plan was to get in and find as much loot as we could prior to contact with the Russians. We had roughly thirty minutes before they were in contact range of our missiles. It was hardly enough time, but it would have to do.

Nance was to my left and the twins were to my right. We stayed in line as we entered the debris field. If OMBRA wanted pieces of spacecraft, there'd be no problem. It was as if there'd been a sub-orbital party, because confetti-sized pieces of space craft were all around us. I doubted that OMBRA wanted us to get out a dustpan, so we continued inward, searching for something larger. And we were gradually rewarded.

We stopped at an odd piece roughly the size of a Volkswagen, but shaped like it had been torn from a larger piece. I had the team stop and we gathered around it. What I'd found curious in the smaller pieces was magnified in this piece. There was a liquid quality about the metal. Even in the flat grey sun of the Arctic, multiple hues of color could be seen in the wreckage. I reached down and touched a section with the gloved forefinger of the EXO and gasped as the colors converged on the point where I'd touched it. I jerked my hand back and the colors disseminated again. Then I touched it in another place and watched the colors come together.

"What do you make of this?" Nance asked.

"Not up on my alien space craft engineering skills," I responded. "To me this is pure science fiction."

"More like science fact," Pearl said. "It's right here in front of you."

I nodded but couldn't help but recognize the surrealness of the situation. Two years ago I had been in Afghanistan fighting Taliban and thinking how surreal that was, and how I'd never imagined being in that situation when I was going to high school in San Pedro where my biggest fear was being jumped by members of the 8th Street Angels. Now, standing in the Arctic Circle and staring at pieces of an alien aircraft while both Russians and Cray were bearing down on us, I felt that it was an honest thing to say that I wouldn't be surprised if I saw Santa Claus in the next few minutes, feeding his reindeer and pushing his elves to make more wooden toys for the good kids of the world.

I looked around. The debris field was miles long. Searching it this way would take hours.

I checked in with Charlemagne. He was still on station, but reported visual contact from the UAV. I toggled the image and saw for the first time the Russians who were coming for us. And what I saw wasn't at all what I'd expected.

A T-80 tank led the convoy. A covered truck carrying soldiers took up the rear. But what held my attention were the three middle trucks. All three were flatbeds carrying three odd red and black metallic shapes. It took a moment for me to realize what I was looking at because they looked like giant metallic spiders with their legs tucked beneath them; legs folded under a two-sectioned body. The larger back section had wide ventilation slats while the smaller front section sported a reflective blister.

"Bots," Pearl said. "Those are giant spider bots. I saw them in *Escape to the Stars* a few years ago."

I turned to her, not understanding the reference, and she laughed. "It's a game where Earth is destroyed by nuclear war and the survivors must got into space to survive. One of the options is to travel to Alpha Centauri which is controlled by an alien race that uses spider bots as not only a mode of transportation, but also to combat giant roly polys that spit acid."

I gaze-flicked back to the UAV feed and nodded. "So these are the Russian equivalent of EXOs. Charlemagne, keep your eyes on the feed and see if you can discern any armaments."

"Do you mean besides the eight metal arms?" he asked.

"Yeah, besides the eight metal arms."

"WILCO."

Seeing the UAV feed gave me an idea. I gaze-flicked to the quadcopter's controls. It wasn't much help to us now, so I sent it in front of us at alternating forty five degree angles, trying to cover as much area and as quickly as possible. I estimated that the convoy was only ten minutes from Charlemagne's position. I couldn't let him sit out there alone, but as a first strike option, I liked having him there.

We continued forward, this time at full speed, which was thirty-seven miles an hour—nearly double the speed of an average sprinter. Using the quadcopter to search instead of our own faculties, all we did was follow behind.

The deeper into the field we went, the larger pieces we saw. I began seeing what could only be body parts. They weren't identifiable, but I'd been to enough IED explosions to recognize what a piece of organic tissue looked like.

Just then Nance went down beside me.

I halted and spun, my radar searching for a target. But the sky and the ground were empty. Then what had taken him down?

Nance groaned through the intercom as he slowly pulled himself to his feet.

"What happened?" I asked.

I saw the embarrassment on his face and knew even before he said it.

"Tripped. Was watching dual feeds instead of where I was going."

I checked his vitals and the EXO system. Everything seemed to be one hundred percent.

"Then let's go."

I turned and was soon at a sprint again. The twins hadn't bothered to stop and were far ahead, but they weren't moving. Nance and I both slowed, then stopped. What I saw there left me stunned. It wasn't exactly human, but it had human-like features. It was missing an arm and part of a leg, but was otherwise mostly intact. It wore a silvery, form-fitting suit with some sort of insignia over the left breast. It had five fingers on its remaining hand. Its remaining foot was encased in a form-fitting boot, but if the hand had five fingers I presumed that the foot would have five toes. In fact, it looked very human except for the length. Nearly the size of an EXO in height, it was as though a normal human body had been stretched impossibly long. The face had the requisite human features, but wasn't anywhere near the symmetry one would expect. An eye was missing, replaced by some sort of mechanical gadget. I also noted a piece of metal sticking out of the side of its neck at an odd angle. Probably killed it before it ever hit the ground.

"Nance, take this and RTB," I said, meaning return to base.

He knelt down and stared at it, but made no move to touch it.

"What's wrong?"

"It's just that—this is the first alien I've ever seen that looks human. I thought they'd be different."

"I'm no scientist," I said, "But look at the Cray. They're bipedal just like we are."

"But don't they also have wings?" Earl said.

"They do, but so do birds. My point is that there's probably a similarity in alien body structure based on the sort of planets they were created on." I tried to channel Spock, who I knew would be talking about star classes, planet classes, and carbon-based life forms, but I'd maxed out my science knowledge. "All I know is that we're supposed to bring the remains back to HQ, and here we have some remains."

Nance gently lifted the corpse and got to his feet. He glanced at me, then turned and ran back towards our base, the C-130.

I looked out over the plain and saw more bodies. The twins and I jogged past several until we came to one that was definitely a human male. His proportions were exact, plus one arm had a tattoo of the United States Marine Corps Globe and Anchor.

"That's not something you see every day," Pearl said.

"I think we now know what they meant by *human aliens*," I said. "How do you think he got up there?"

"Maybe he was captured," Earl said. "Could have been a test subject."

I didn't think that was the case, but kept my speculations to myself. Although he wasn't wearing the skin-tight silver suit the long man was wearing, he wasn't wearing a uniform I recognized. Black pants ended in a hem cinched above black laceless boots. His top had been mostly ripped away, but it seemed to be some sort of black, form-fitting antiballistic armor, accentuating the pectoral muscles. A black metal band circled his neck, reminding me of an old original *Star Trek* episode called *The Gamesters of Triskelion* that had thralls competing against each other in a gladiatorial arena. I only remembered it because of the character of Shahna who had long green hair and had a skimpy silver bikini. Is that what this marine was? A thrall? We needed to be sure to examine the metal around his neck.

"Let's take this one, too. Hero Four, you can do the honors."

Earl gave a half-assed salute, then picked up the body using one hand. He threw it over a shoulder. "Now what."

"RTB."

He turned and sprinted back.

"What now?" Pearl asked.

At that moment, Charlemagne broke into the feed. He sounded unusually happy. "Here they come." Then came the sound of his rockets and machine gun firing.

> The proper function of man is to live, not
> to exist. I shall not waste my days in trying
> to prolong them. I shall use my time.
>
> Jack London

CHAPTER TWELVE

HERO THREE AND I grabbed the biggest pieces of debris we could get our hands on and headed back towards base with all haste. Although I kept my focus on my path ahead of me, I gaze-flicked to the circling UAV and watched as a flood of rockets left Charlemagne and arched into the convoy.

He'd sent most of them against the tank. Because of the T-80's reactive Chobham armor, he'd sent only a third of the Hydra rockets against the turret. What we really needed were Sabot rounds; then again, the EXOs were designed to fight aliens, not fellow humans. I watched as each exploded, but they did little damage to the tank. But the remaining ten were targeting the tank's tracks and exploded upon impact, sending pieces of tread flying in all directions. The tank listed, then slewed to the left as a track wheel disintegrated.

"Get out of there!" I roared. Although I hadn't ordered him to attack, he'd made the right decision. But now that he'd gotten their attention, he'd be in a heap of trouble the moment they recovered from the shock and awe of his initial attack.

"Just a little more," he murmured, his voice as calm as if he were baking chocolate chip cookies rather than single-handedly taking on a Russian convoy carrying spidertanks.

I felt a tickle in the back of my mind, both familiar and strange. I instantly thought it might be Thompson and reached out. *Is that you? Thompson?* But there was no reply and the tickle was gone.

I continued to run, watching Charlemagne's white EXO and how it stood out against the gray and green of the flat tundra. He began to traverse backwards as another six rockets fired from his shoulder. Then he began to lay down machine gun fire in clean ten round bursts towards the rear vehicle.

My gaze tore from him to the spidertanks, which were all coming to terrible life, their black legs uncurling, their red segmented bodies raising. But then all three on the first flatbed exploded as the six missiles ate into them. Leg pieces flew in all directions, many three or more meters long. I watched as several of these pierced the earth like giant spears.

Of the six remaining spider bots, three tore off the rear flatbed and towards the back of the convoy, while the other three tore towards Charlemagne, moving impossibly fast, their eight legs manipulating in perfect arachnid precision.

He fired six more rockets at the oncoming bots.

Suddenly the tank fired. Although heeled over and off track, it must have been able to get its barrel to traverse enough to get a firing solution on Charlemagne. He juked left and the 125mm round soared past and disappeared in the distant tundra.

I gaze-flicked to his point of view and almost wished

I hadn't because it looked for all the world like giant spiders were bearing down on me... him. Suddenly round discs unfolded from the front of each spider, very similar to a dish antenna. I couldn't discern what they were, but within seconds, every rocket exploded in midair. The bots were momentarily hidden by the explosions, then they were rushing through smoke and fire.

My point of view spun dizzyingly as Charlemagne turned and began running for his life.

I flick-gazed to the UAV and watched as the bots gave chase. Luckily, the EXOs seemed to be a fraction faster than the bots because Charlemagne was increasing the distance between them.

A full squad of twelve Russian Special Forces had piled out of the rear vehicle and gathered behind the three remaining spider bots. They were hunched down and seemed to be waiting to move out. Several of them looked into the air, spotting the UAV. Soon, all of them opened fire. My viewpoint lasted three more seconds before the UAV exploded, ending whatever reconnaissance advantage I had.

The C-130 began to grow in the distance. "Hero One. Deploy three hundred meters at ninety degrees and get down. Remain there until ordered."

I saw an EXO peel away from the plane and move towards my right.

"WILCO," Nance said.

"Hero Four. Deploy three hundred meters at one hundred and eighty degrees and get down. Remain there until ordered."

"You mean you want me to lay down?" Earl asked.

I fought the urge to scream at him, reminding myself

that he wasn't military. Just a punk kid with video game mastery. "Yes, I mean lay down."

"Oh, okay. Why didn't you just say that?"

We were seriously going to have to work on military commands. While I ran the last kilometer, I sent the quad-copter forward to replace the UAV. I definitely wanted to have eyes on the Special Forces.

I gaze-flicked the radio. "Merlin, you have enemy inbound. Get the 50 cals pointed the right way and get them cranking."

"Which way is that?"

"Look for the EXO with giant spiders chasing it and you'll figure it out."

"What do you—Oh *shit*."

"Yeah, that."

Twenty seconds later Hero Three and I arrived at the C-130.

The side of the plane with the damaged engine was away from the oncoming action. The pilot and co-pilot were making good use of their skills, trying to fix it as best they could. The pilot glanced at me as I arrived, a look of frustration carving his otherwise smooth features.

The crew chief and his assistant were laying down grazing fire to each side of Charlemagne.

These were matched by barrels that had appeared in the front of each spider bot and began to fire. Charlemagne was hit with several rounds in the back. He staggered, but kept coming.

The crew chief went down with rounds through the face.

Merlin didn't hesitate. He jumped over the body and was soon laying down fire with the M2.

I gaze-flicked Heroes One's and Three's IRL and selected three rockets from each of them to fire, targeting each of the onrushing spider bots, then let them fire. If what I thought had happened before, the rockets should find their home easily. I watched as the six rockets streaked towards their targets. One of the bots stopped and turned to its left. Just as before, a round disc unfolded and within seconds two of the three rockets heading towards it exploded in midair. The third rocket hit the central bot, just as the other three hit it. The middle bot exploded, pieces of spider legs shooting in every direction. One impaled the side of the aircraft. The end bots both scored one hit.

"Hero One and Three, attack."

The EXOs leaped to their feet and ran at the wounded bots.

"Go for the blister on top. I bet you'll find the driver there."

As the spiders turned towards their new opponents, I made my move and began sprinting towards Charlemagne. Although his vitals were in the green, I had to see for myself. When I got to him, I spun him around. The EXO armor was scored, but no rounds had made it through. He grinned at me through his faceplate.

With Pearl now at my side, the three of us joined the fray.

Nance fired point blank at his spidertank, unloading a hundred rumbling rounds at the already smoking machine. His EXO was half as tall as the bot, and as I saw the tank raise five meter spider legs into the air, their battle looked straight of a Ray Harryhausen film. In *Jason and the Argonauts, The 7th Voyage of Sinbad,* and *Clash of the Titans* the stop-action animator had pitted humans against titans, dinosaurs, a giant octopus, and an immense Cyclops. Seeing Nance's battle, it was hard for me not to relive the wonder I'd felt when I'd first seen those movies. But that awe only lasted a second as Charlemagne joined me and we rushed to help Nance.

We had to dispatch these two spidertanks before the other three appeared with ground troops or we'd be quickly overwhelmed.

Then my blood went cold as one of the legs pierced Nance's EXO and pinned him to the ground.

I screamed and let loose with a missile aimed right at the blister. I didn't dare do more with Nance so close by. I chose to target the blister, believing that if there wasn't a driver beneath, it was at least the brain of the bot.

Charlemagne roared past me, his harmonic blade in hand, swinging it like a Highlander.

The spidertank tried to turn and face the oncoming missile to bring to bear its mysterious disc, but by impaling Nance to the earth, it had also pinned itself in place. The missile struck true, exploding the blister. The bot immediately folded on itself, legs dead and loose, rattling to the ground.

"Hero Two, get to the other bot," I shouted.

Charlemagne wheeled right, and joined the twins, who had already ripped the blister free and were holding an angry Russian high above the tundra.

But all my concern was for Nance. I gaze-flicked to a private channel. "Nance, you okay?" Checking his vitals, I could see he was quickly declining. His blood pressure was dangerously low, telling me he was probably bleeding out.

Labored breathing and a cough answered my question.

I skidded to a stop and fell to my knees. The leg had punctured the very center of the EXO. Lance's eyes were wide. He'd already coughed blood onto the inside of his visor. The tip of the leg that had pierced his suit was made of polished metal. I glared at one of the others and noted that it came to a vicious tip.

"Hey, kid. How you feeling?"

Nance's eyes opened and he stared at me with wide, fear-filled eyes. He knew the truth of it, just as I knew the truth of it. Even if we were able to get him free of the leg, there wasn't any critical care medical facilities within a thousand miles.

"How—how—the others?" he asked, barely able to speak.

"The others are fine. You led them well, son."

"But I—you are the—"

I shook my head. "It was you who brought them here. It was you they followed."

He coughed more blood against the visor. His body shuddered and his vitals, which had been flashing red, stayed solid red. The kid was gone.

Heroes aren't born. They are made through actions that are witnessed and lauded. Shannon Alder took it further and said: *Heroes are not made. They are born out of circumstances and rise to the occasion when their spirit can no longer coexist with the hypocrisy of injustice to others.* Pretty speak, but basically it says that a regular person can only take so much before they are forced into action. Why am I lathering on about heroes? Because I think it's time we had one. The Greeks had Achilles, the Norse had Beowulf, the Mesopotamians had Gilgamesh, and the British had King Arthur. So where are the heroes now? When will they rise? Have you seen one?

Conspiracy Theory Talk Radio,
Night Stalker Monologue #1803

CHAPTER THIRTEEN

WE HAD JUST enough time to and reload and make some barebones plans before the rest of the Russian forces crested the horizon. Merlin and the crew chief had been able to recover the remaining workable spidertank and had driven it to a place behind the C-130. The driver's instrument panel was pretty straight forward and allowed them to move it, but everything else was a mystery. The crew chief postulated that the disc was some sort of acoustic weapon similar to the Short Range Acoustic Device, or SRAD, that had been deployed around airfields in Afghanistan to defeat shoulder-fired Taliban anti-aircraft missiles, but he couldn't be sure. We'd figure it out later.

I deployed Heroes Three and Four both left and right a kilometer and had them go to ground. I wanted them to be in a position to get behind the ground forces if possible. I also left Nance in place. As much as it sickened us to treat his body that way, he was far more useful to us where he was than if we'd retrieved the body. He had almost a full magazine and most of his rockets. Although he was dead, I still had access to his suit and could use it as a possible Trojan horse. Charlemagne and I would remain at the plane, making it a large target for the incoming enemy forces who would hopefully not be able to determine the locations of Three and Four until it was too late.

I felt the tingling in my head once more. I queried it, seeing if Thompson was trying to contact me. One of the side-effects of the weaponized zombie fungus was that my brain had been rewired and I now had access to previously unavailable theta waves. The Hypocrealiacs never made anything for a single purpose. The fungus had not only been a way to be rid of humans, but it also allowed humans to be their eyes and ears, controlling the *fungees* with a single transmitted thought. I'd been cured of the effects of the fungus, but what lingered was the ability to communicate remotely with HMIDs. But I'd always wondered if I couldn't also communicate with the Hypocrealiacs. Since they'd purposely developed the fungus for communication, couldn't it work both ways?

Was that what the tingling was about? Were there live aliens about?

"Thousand meters out and closing," Charlemagne said.

I gaze-flicked to the quad-copter's UAV feed. The Russian spidertanks were one line with thirty meters separating each of them. The machine gun and SRAD were deployed and ready. Behind each bot were four Special Forces soldiers kitted identically. One carried an RPG while the other three carried some variant of the Kalashnikov. Both weapon's systems were old as hell, but were as reliable as they were deadly.

"Merlin, you guys figured out that bot yet?" I asked through the suit's radio.

"Nuh uh. Lots of buttons. Don't know want to press the wrong one and go boom."

I grinned as I glanced at the pissed-off Russian we had tied to one of the pallets in the hold. "Boom would definitely be bad and I don't think the bot driver is going to want to be forthcoming."

"Even if I asked nicely?"

"Do you know how to ask nicely in Russian?"

"Как вы водите это?"

I laughed. Of course he knew Russian. With all the fisherman docked in Savoonga basic competency in the language would be something easy to obtain. "Then maybe after this is done you'll get a chance to ask him. Until then, do what you can without going boom, okay?"

I resumed my vigil. The enemy was now even with Heroes Three and Four. Once they moved forward three hundred meters, I'd let them attack, taking out the bots from behind first, then the soldiers. But the

Russian forces stopped. I saw each of the Special Forces soldiers huddling behind their spidertanks. Did they really think they could go up against OMBRAs EXOs? It was a shame really. The Faraday suit was designed to defeat the Cray. Using it on fellow humans seemed wrong.

The Russians continued to remain in place. What were they doing? Suddenly my coms crackled and I heard in heavily accented Russian, "American forces. Stand down. Do not try to attack again. We request parlay."

Interesting on many levels.

I contacted my squad. "Prepare for action on my mark only." Then I gaze-flicked to the radio. "To whom am I speaking?"

"Commander Putrachev, formerly of the 24th Special Purpose Brigade, Mother Russia. Now of the 1st Special Purpose Company, Yukos Prime."

Wary of delaying tactics, I was ready to launch an attack within seconds. But my curiosity needed sated. "What is Yukos Prime?"

"Was oil company. Had technology. Now in charge."

Like OMBRA. I thought about my reply for a moment then said, "Lieutenant Mason, formerly of the 173rd Infantry Brigade Combat Team, America, now with OMBRA."

Silence ruled for a tense thirty seconds, then came the reply. "Hero of the Mound Mason?"

Seriously? How could they know unless... but of course. Mr. Pink had probably used me as a recruiting tool across the globe. Join OMBRA and watch all of your friends die around you. We kill more of your friends before 9 AM than most organizations do all day.

"What do you want?" I asked, tired of being infamous.

"Why did your combat machine attack us?"

Combat machine? Oh, he meant the EXO. I thought about how to respond and realized that we'd fired the first salvo of this conflict and maybe we hadn't needed to. At the time, I'd felt that Charlemagne's actions were logical and spot on. But in retrospect, we never allowed the Russians the opportunity to explain their presence or desires. We'd spent so much time fighting the Cray that we'd forgotten the time honored tradition of parlay. Even the French at Agincourt sent a messenger to King Henry prior to the battle in an attempt to stop the conflict. Ultimately the English forces, heavily overmatched and outnumbered, had won, but that was because of superior technology. Much like the situation we faced here.

"Why did you fire on our aircraft?"

He didn't answer.

So I asked, "What are your intentions, Putrachev?"

"Hand over your man in combat machine."

"That's never going to happen," I said. Then asked, "What were your intentions prior to attack?"

"Investigate crash. Recover technology."

"Same as ours."

"But this is not your land. This is Russian land."

I checked radar, then the UAV to see if there was any movement, but I detected nothing.

"I thought you said you worked for Yukos. Like America, there is no Russian."

A few seconds of silence was followed by, "Russia is in the heart."

Interesting. I'd lost my patriotism long ago. Given the opportunity to join the New United States of North

America I'd turned them down. I was tired of belong to things. Then again, I realized that I was still within OMBRA's grasp, but that was of my own doing. I'd consciously decided to rejoin and conduct this mission. I could understand when he said Russia was in his heart. But I didn't feel the same. America wasn't in my heart. She hadn't earned the right to be. But my friends were, both living and dead.

"Cease your combat operations, Putrachev. You are outnumbered."

"You destroyed six of my combat machines and killed six of my men."

"I have dead as well."

"All the blood is on your hands, Mason."

I sighed. "Isn't it always? This is one thing I can be sure of, Putrachev. If you continue you will die."

"Then we die. We must continue to fight. It is who we are."

I felt the urge to punch something. Halfway through the conversation I'd decided that I no longer wanted to fight the Russians. But here they were insisting that they die. Why couldn't we unite against the alien forces? Why couldn't we fight together instead of against each other?

"Putrachev, listen. Give us twenty-four hours and we will depart this location. The debris field is immense. You will find what you were looking for, I am sure."

A moment of silence was followed by the Russian's voice, now low and filled with sadness. "You do not understand. My men have been killed. They must be avenged."

"Fight for the living, Putrachev, not for the dead."

"I do not understand this concept," he said.

"You are not alone, comrade. Very few do. It is an idea that one must come to realize through great agony."

"I have yet to have this agony," he said.

I sighed. "Give it time."

I waited five minutes. As each minute ticked down, I became evermore hopeful. But then the Russians began to move forward.

"Stand by, Heroes," I said. Then an alarm went off on my radar. A fast moving object was heading directly towards us. I stepped out of the back of the C-130 to get a visual. My jaw dropped as I observed my first space ship plummeting towards me. At first it was a silvery object, then it became bigger and bigger as it came closer. I noted that the Russians were still moving. The last thing I needed was to be in combat with an alien space craft incoming. "Putrachev, stop! Incoming space craft!"

The Russians halted and we all stared as the space craft dropped to within fifty feet of the ground and hovered. It was easily the size of a house. It was donut-shaped with a hollow center. The skin of the space craft seemed to be moving in circles around the circumference of the machine. I chewed my lip, wondering if I should shoot it or greet it.

The tickling returned in the back of my mind. Was it coming from the space craft? Were these the Hypocrealiacs, and if so, what sort of weapons systems could they bring to bear? I was thinking I should instigate actions when another alarm went off. Multiple unidentified flying objects were coming in from the south. I counted more than a hundred of them.

Damn.

I wondered what could they be, then realized.

Cray!

The space craft suddenly lowered to the ground over the top of Nance and the spidertank that had killed him. They disappeared from sight. Seconds later, the craft rose straight up. Nance and the bot were now in the donut-hole of the ship, held in place by metallic arms. Then it raced south. When I lost visual on it, I continued following it with my radar as it intersected the Cray. The icons indicating incoming Cray began to wink out one after the other, which could only mean that the space craft was somehow taking them out of the equation. It couldn't be the Hypocrealiacs. So if it wasn't them, then who?

I was so entranced watching the Cray being killed that I failed to notice the Russian's movement.

"Hero Prime, the Russians are withdrawing."

I turned my attention back to the situation at hand.

The Russians were indeed pulling back. They held formation and were backing towards the road.

"Commander Putrachev, what are your intentions?" I asked.

"Today we will not fight." Then he paused, "But tomorrow is not today."

I nodded to myself. "I understand," I said.

I waited until they were two kilometers distant, then ordered Heroes Three and Four to RTB. I ordered Charlemagne to keep an eye on them. Then I let out a sigh of relief. It seemed as if no one was going to die in the next twenty-four hours. Small victory, but victory nonetheless.

Assuming there are one hundred advanced intelligences in our own galaxy and that they are evenly spread throughout the galaxy, the nearest one would be about 10,000 light-years away. To cover that distance by any means we know of would take at least 10,000 years and very likely much longer. Why should anyone want to make such long journeys just to poke around curiously?

Isaac Asimov

CHAPTER FOURTEEN

I HAD TO put the alien space craft or UFO out of my mind for now, even though I wanted to do nothing more than talk about it. It's one thing to fight aliens, but another altogether to see their ships. Up until now all of the technology had been organic—the hives, the Cray, the fungus, the kudzu, the leviathans, et cetera. We'd sort of forgotten that there were other alien races, that there was a war somewhere out there.

Back before I blew up the Hollywood Hive, Ohirra had explained it perfectly.

"As it turns out, there *are* no invading aliens," she'd said. "Remember what we postulated back in Africa? It's true. The species we've encountered so far have specific tasks. The Cray, the Sirens, the needlers, the alien vine, even the spore; purpose-made, purpose-sent. But the master alien race, the one controlling them, whatever the hell they are, have no intention of coming here. They want to mine us. They want our iron. They want our sodium. They want our silicon. They want our water. They're in the middle of a war and we're just a convenient planet to harvest. We're a supply depot for someone else's conflict."

What that also meant was that we had no target, no way to stop them. No way to convince them to stop. As soon as we figured out how to defeat one alien, they'd just send something else. But by the way it acted, the alien space craft was a major game changer. It hadn't killed us. And it had taken out the Cray for us. Sure, it took Nance and the bot, but my guess was that they wanted them to study—the same way we took samples of their dead and tech.

What was it Sun Tzu said? The enemy of my enemy is my friend. We might have just caught the first glance at our brand new friends... ones who were going to let us finally get our pound of flesh from the damned intergalactic bullies who had jacked our planet.

But for now, I had to get my squad and the flight crew to safety.

I approached the pilot and asked, "How soon can we get out of here?"

He and the co-pilot were standing on the wing talking to each other. The cowl of the engine was still open. He took a moment and wiped sweat from his brow. Wrinkles had gathered around his eyes. He was my age, but right now he looked far older.

"We've done all we can. I can get her airborne, but I don't know how far I can fly until I know our weight." He nodded towards the spidertank, which was in perfect working order except for the missing blister. "You intend on bringing that with us?"

"I was hoping we could."

"It still doesn't solve the problem of fuel," he said.

"I'm working on that. Merlin, can you find us some fuel?"

"What kind?" he asked from where he sat with his headset on.

I looked to the pilot for the answer.

"Jet-A or JP-8," he said. "Our other problem is that we lost two of the integral wing fuel cells on this wing. One was ruptured, and I had to shut the other one down. That's an initial loss of two fuel cells. So on this wing I have one fuel cell with a capacity of 1,483 gallons JP-8. At 6.74 lbs per gallon that equals 9,997 pounds... so let's call it 10,000 pounds. The other wing cells are fine, but for balance and structural reasons, especially if I'm carrying max payload, I need them to be the same, so I can only have one of the cells full, which is no problem, because each is a third full." He pointed to each wing. "So with a total of 2,966 gallons, and with a full load, I average 3.7 gallons per mile. According to my calculations, we're 842 miles from Savoonga and 950 miles from Nome. Both locations have fuel, although Nome would be better for repairs. To get to Savoonga I'd need 3,159 gallons. To get to Nome I'd need 3,555."

"So you can't even get us there if we were refueled."

He pointed at the wing he was standing on. "And that's if we have 2,966 gallons, or the equivalent of two fuel cells. Remember that the other wing's cells were one third full. So were these. Because we lost two fuel cells, this wing currently only holds 493 gallons, one third of the other, which means we really have 1,976 gallons of fuel."

My face fell.

"And, we're only operating on three engines."

"Wouldn't that use less fuel?" I asked.

He nodded. "But those three are going to have to work harder. Bottom line is, the lighter we can get, then the further we can fly. If we were empty, we could make it with a couple hundred gallons to spare. But I'm going to confer with the crew chief before I say anything more." He stared at me for a moment, then returned to conversation with the co-pilot.

I met the others at the rear of the plane.

To Merlin I said, "Any luck?"

He shook his head and continued conversing to someone in Yupik. He seemed to be arguing. Then he signed off and shook his head. "Redneck Yupik up here want to help, but before they'll even start they want to trade in seal skins." Merlin shook his head. "The fate of the world is at hand and they're worried about seal skins."

I nodded, because I knew exactly how he felt.

I noted that Earl and Pearl were speaking on a private channel. For a brief second, I thought of eavesdropping, but then I decided against it. They'd given me no reason to doubt their loyalty to me, so it was only fair to give them trust in return.

"Any movement?" I asked Charlemagne.

"They've established an OP at the tank. The rest of them have pulled back. A smaller group comprised of one bot and eight soldiers headed to the debris field."

"Well, there's sure enough for everyone. Since I have no orders to keep anyone else from getting their hands on the remains and tech, there's no mandate to stop them."

Pearl requested a private channel.

I accepted. "Why didn't we just attack?" she asked. "I mean, we had the Russians outnumbered."

"Because our war isn't with them. Our war is with the Hypocrealiacs."

"But the Russians attacked us first."

"They did," I acknowledged.

"So that means we can kill them," she said defiantly.

I shook my head. "No it doesn't mean we have permission to kill them. There is no requirement to shoot back. That's a choice I make as your commander."

I could see in her eyes that she was trying to work through my response. "But they killed Nance."

Again I shook my head. "Nance was a soldier fighting in combat. He died in combat. He chose to fight. Circumstances killed Nance. He was merely a participant, just as the bot driver was."

She stared at me for a long moment. I expected her to continue arguing, but she surprised me by nodding finally. "I hear you. Let me process that." Then she shut down the private channel.

I decided it was time to get out of the EXO. I parked the suit, then climbed out. I stood in the slightly chill hold in Kevlar shorts and toe shoes. I grabbed a bottle of water and downed it. Then I found an MRE and started picking through it, eating the cheese and crackers first, then the entrée—chicken pesto pasta—which tasted like chicken pesto ass. Even so, I'd expended enough energy that I needed to replenish. Earl and Pearl saw me and decided to park their EXOs as well. Once Earl finished, he relieved Charlemagne. Never once did we speak. We didn't have to. We all knew what everyone was thinking. We all had questions. We just didn't have answers, so it wasn't worth talking about.

Finally Charlemagne broke the silence. "Was that really a fucking spaceship?"

I nodded. "Did you notice it took out the Cray?" I asked.

"Like a mower. Buzzed right through them," he said. "Think they're on our side."

I hated to say it out loud, but if it was true, then it was a major game changer. "I think so," I said. "Or at least, not against us."

I stood, grabbed my trash, and stuffed it in the bag.

"You and Pearl run full checks on the EXOs. Let's get them charging and ammo'd up."

Then I went to clean up, taking a whore's bath at the end of the ramp by using a bottle of water and a small piece of soap. Wearing nothing but my shorts and the toe shoes, I was chilled by the time I'd finished. When I was done, I sent Merlin to get food and water. He grumbled about redneck Yupik, which told me that we probably weren't going to get help from them.

Ten minutes later the crew chief and the pilot approached me. Dressed in fatigues and covered in sweat, they each gave me exhausted looks before addressing me.

"We have two options," the pilot said. "We can fly due east to Lorino. There's a major airfield there. Or we can fly to Savoonga."

"Why do I feel like there's a major *but* you're leaving out."

The pilot nodded. "My loadmaster thinks we can make it. We'd be flying on fumes and a prayer, but the winds are favorable to us and the lack of fuel by weight has opened the window of possibility."

"What's at Lorino?" I asked.

"We had a report of a buildup of Russian military units there as part of our pre-flight intelligence report. We might be able to get in and out of the airfield before anything happens or—"

"Or we could get shot at by another SA-7." I shook my head. "I'd rather take my chances with a wing and a prayer than going to a place where you know we'll be in danger. What's your opinion?"

The pilot frowned. "I don't like either option but they're what we have. Given the dangers posed by an attempted landing and takeoff in Lorino, I think trying for Savoonga is our best bet."

I turned to the crew chief, "Then let's get everything strapped down and ready for flight. Whatever help you need from me and my squad, just ask. We work for you now."

The next two hours were filled with getting the EXOs in place and strapping the spidertank down. I'd fought with myself about keeping it. Getting rid of it would definitely get us a few more miles. But I wanted to make sure we could investigate the technology used to make it, especially the acoustic weapon. I'd also noted that Merlin had been getting acquainted with the controls. If he was going to be a part of our team, perhaps this could be the way.

The very last thing we did before the pilot swung the ungainly beast around was to let our Russian bot-driver go. He wasn't too happy we were taking his bot with us, but he'd have to get over it. We waited until he was well clear, then strapped in, raised the ramp, and began to pray to the fickle universe that we deserved to make it back to Savoonga in one piece.

The tragedy of life is in what dies inside a man while he lives—the death of genuine feeling, the death of inspired response, the awareness that makes it possible to feel the pain or the glory of other men in yourself.

Norman Cousins

CHAPTER FIFTEEN

WE HAD TO shut down two engines but we made it back to St. Lawrence Island with just enough fuel left to run to the store for a case of good beer. The cheer that went up was unmatched. Joyous embraces and high fives brought us a bonding moment even I couldn't choreograph. But the feeling was short-lived.

Before the pilot lowered the ramp, he called me forward and gave me a headset. It was then I learned two things. The first was that another C-130 was on site. This one was an AC-130 Spectre Gunship—basically the weaponized version of the one we were on with two Vulcan 20mm cannons, one 40mm Bofors cannon, and a 105 Howitzer. It had been in battle recently against a battalion-strength group of Cray and had managed to stay far enough away from their EMPs to butcher them all. The other thing I learned was that the battle had taken place in Savoonga. The city was all but destroyed. There were few survivors.

I knew that once I told Merlin he'd blame himself.

But the truth was that OMBRA had intercepted communications and had known the Cray were on their way to destroy the debris from the spacecraft, thus the reason OMBRA sent the C-130 in the first place and convinced me to lead the mission. What they hadn't told me was they'd known the Cray were coming. Had I known that there were going to be significantly more than the first three, I would have marshaled the EXOs to protect the city. That was probably why OMBRA had left out that bit. And why I'd leave it out as well when I broke the news to Merlin.

I'd always been one to pull the scab off quickly, so when I went back into the hold, I let everyone know. Merlin stared at me for a long moment, then began to wail, singing a Yupik funeral dirge I'd heard twice before. But those had been for two people. This was for an entire tribe and held enough emotion and pain to bring tears to my eyes.

I had the pilot lower the ramp. Merlin took off at a run. I sent Charlemagne after him with the command, "Don't let him do anything stupid."

After both of them departed, I told the twins to move the EXOs and the spidertank to the AC-130, then went around the corner and found a spot to be alone.

Thompson had been pinging me ever since I came within fifty miles of Savoonga, probably leapfrogging off the Spectre's coms. But I'd held him off. First because I was more concerned about us landing, and second because I had to relay the sad news to Merlin. Now that we were both landed and Merlin was informed, it was time to see what the HMID version of the kid I liked wanted.

After I gave him an EXSUM mission brief, he let me

know that the strange donut-shaped alien spacecraft had been seen everywhere. He also pointed out that the communication transmissions intercepted from the aircraft weren't Hypocrealiac in origin, which made OMBRA enthusiastic in believing that these might actually be representatives of who the invading aliens were fighting.

Have they seen them engage yet? I asked.

There have been no reports of engagement, but the space frames have been removing pieces of our technology to study.

Like Nance's EXO and the Russian spidertank.

The actions inform the hypothesis that they are newly arrived and trying to ascertain our level of technological advancement.

But they haven't been in contact yet?

Negative.

I thought about the last time he'd intruded into my dreams, then asked, *What were you trying to tell me last time? Something about Texas and 'this is where the magic happens.'*

I can't speak to that right now but soon.

Come on, Thompson. Enough with the mysteriousness. Just tell me.

Really, Mason. I am not allowed.

Mr. Pink?

He can release the information. If you want to know, you need to speak with him.

Oh, I'll speak with him all right. He's going to get an earful.

That's been anticipated.

I bet it has. Then I thought of another question. *Were you trying to get in touch with me when I was on mission? I felt a tingling much like when you contact me.*

Did you lose any time? he asked.

Not that I know of. I thought about it for a moment, then answered, *No. Definitely not.*

If you lose time following that tingling sensation you must report it at once.

Why? What is it, Thompson? What will it be?

Do you remember the alien you came face-to-face with beneath the Hollywood Hive?

It had been a large rectangular structure made from some sort of black substrate. The surface had undulated and I had got a glimpse of something impossibly large; somewhere deep inside lights had made storm clouds.

What we called the Master? The one who made me attack my team and sever Stranz's arm with my blade? That alien?

The Master had even blocked my emotions during the tragic event, which is why the sheer shame of it now seemed so fresh. I moaned as the scene replayed in my mind—the shocked look on my sergeant's face as I drove my blade first through his minigun, then the upward swing that severed his arm.

I see you remember, Thompson said. *I've attempted to shore up your defenses so that doesn't happen again, but it's not a foolproof solution.*

I absolutely, positively never want that to happen again. I imaged Charlemagne's ever-present smile wiped off his face by my harmonic blade. *How can I keep it from happening?*

You can't. The fungus rewired your brain for better or for worse, making it a two lane highway. We originally called these aliens Masters and we weren't far off. Our

Global HMID grid has been battling them constantly. These Masters are spaced throughout the globe and have a footprint similar to ours. They appear to not only be directing activities, but are also communicating with unknown space-based forces.

Which is why you knew the Cray were coming to Savoonga. You hacked their signal.

A momentary pause. We'd hoped they'd bypass the village. The Masters had staged several leviathans offshore and we believed the Cray were bound for them.

You were mistaken. I breathed deeply, then let out the air. These Masters, are they the Hypocrealiacs?

Meaning are they the ones who task organized and purpose sent all the other alien species to our planet? We don't think so. We believe these Masters are like all the others in that they have been purpose sent, with the exception that they are the only race who communicates to all of the various alien races.

So who really is the Master species?

We just don't have data for that. Think of these Masters as the J staffs for the commander or 'Crealiacs. They work for a commander and ensure all of the logistics, operations, communications, and intelligence is performed.

Intelligence? I asked.

Don't forget they can see through every species that has been infected with the fungus spores… even those very few who have been cured of it. They literally have eyes and ears everywhere.

Except north and south of the 45th parallel.

The planet is warming. They'll soon be able to project even there. What is it you like to call it?

Planet-jacked!

Yes. That's good. So your orders are to bring back the remains and debris back to OMBRA HQ at Fort Irwin. Then we're going to have a reconnaissance mission for your team.

So there are still things you don't know.

In all seriousness, Mason, there are places on the planet that are completely dark to us. It's as if they're letting us see what they don't care about but hiding what's most important.

Is that where you're sending us? To a place like that?

Most definitely. Specifically, Odessa, Texas.

And you have no idea what's there?

None at all, but we think it might be a beachhead for the new aliens. And you know what Sun Tzu said.

The enemy of my enemy is my friend. I'd already thought about that but am trying not to build hope.

Come on, Mason. Can't you cultivate a little hope?

Not after everything I've seen. There is no hope. Only opportunity seized.

Then think of the opportunity you can seize.

There is that.

Oh, and one more thing.

And that is?

We have a surprise for you when you get back.

I groaned. I fucking hate surprises. And I told him so, then signed off.

A moment later, Charlemagne came running up. "Boss, Merlin's in a bad spot."

"What's he done now?"

"Taken things into his own hands."

"What does that mean?"

"You have to see it to believe it."

My heart sank as I began to run. I should have been

with him instead of speaking with Thompson. What had I been thinking? His family might possibly... scratch that... probably were dead. I owed him my life and I repaid it in death.

I poured on the speed, churning my legs through the tundra grass as fast as they could go.

Without a family, man, alone in the world, trembles with the cold.

Andre Maurois

CHAPTER SIXTEEN

MERLIN HAD DOUSED himself with gasoline and stood in the middle of the old wooden dock. Maybe two dozen Yupik remained and stood watching, their faces carved with a tired mixture of exhaustion and anger. Merlin's sister was among them. Her thoughts were hidden behind dead eyes. What struck me raw was that the scene was in total silence. The only sounds I could hear were the whistling of the wind, the lapping of the waves against the dock's pylons, and the occasional walrus song from the ugly.

Any other place, any other people, and they'd be trying to get the person to stop.

But not these people.

Not here.

And it made me furious.

I slid to a stop ten feet away from Merlin, surrounded in a half circle by the surviving Yupik. "Merlin, stop!"

He held a red plastic fuel can, hugging it to his chest. He stared at the ground, his shoulders almost imperceptivity moving to silent sobs.

I spun towards the crowd just as Charlemagne and the twins ran up behind them.

"How can you let him do this? He is one of you!"

Black Hand Woman stared through me, then turned her back on me. At that moment I wanted to rip every tattoo she'd given me and throw them back in her face. The others saw her move and joined her, one by one— every surviving member of the tribe turning their back on Merlin. Finally it was only his sister. She stood, her head held high, chin jutting, staring at her brother.

"Is this what you want, Heavenly? For Merlin to kill himself? Is this what you think is proper?" I shouted. "Is the entire invasion to be blamed on Merlin? I don't want to fucking belittle your belief systems, but the aliens don't care a fuck about your beliefs. They didn't care about the Christian beliefs or the Muslim beliefs or even Buddhist beliefs. They just fucking came and no Jesus or Allah or Buddha or even your Raven appeared to stop them.

"Merlin is not only fighting for the survival of Savoonga and the Yupik here, but also for the whole of mankind. Do you really think that Merlin killing the orca caused the Cray to come and attack? If you do, then you're a lot more stupid than I took you for. The Cray were coming long before that. They were coming to destroy the debris from an alien space craft. And how do I know this? Because OMBRA intercepted their communications and found out about it."

A few Yupik began to turn and listen to me, including the Chiklak brothers. I called to them.

"George... Sam... Merlin is your blood brother. You played as children. You hunted bear together using the old ways. And now you're going to blame Merlin for something the aliens had planned long ago?"

"How do we know what you say is true?" Sam asked.

"Do you think I lie? What advantage would I have to lie?"

Now everyone had turned around. I felt the gaze of dozens of eyes.

"Because you want Merlin to live," said Black Hands Woman. "I know your history. I etched it on your skin. You lie because you don't want another name recorded there. You lie because you don't want to feel the guilt of their deaths."

My rage fell momentarily away as I laughed. "Black Hands Woman, even after all of this you don't understand. Before I came here, when I was broken, I was that man who felt sorry for himself, who was afraid to lose. I was the man who thought he'd sent soldiers to their deaths. But my time here has changed me. Time away from death has let me understand it better. I've always known that grunts like me don't fight for flags or lofty ideals or a commander's speech. We're grunts. We do as we're told. We fight for the grunt in the proverbial foxhole on either side of us. We fight for ourselves. I'd forgotten that all of my grunts had the same belief. All of them, from Mikey all the way to Nance, who died a few hours ago—every last one of them laid down their life so that I might live. And now I should feel sorry about it?"How dare I feel sorry for myself for that! Their deaths were a gift and I'd been disrespecting it. Living with you made me realize the importance of life and the gift of death... how you take creatures from the sea and land and honor their deaths by letting them live on as objects to be used and cared for."

I turned to Black Hands Woman and ripped my shirt off, pointing to the names she'd inked on me. "These names... these grunts all died so that I might live. That I was their leader had nothing to do with it. Whether we were on mission or ambushed or just unlucky had nothing to do with it. They chose to fight. They chose to let me lead them. They fucking *chose* to be in the circumstance that killed them. Did they want to die? No. But they did and I'm going to honor them. Each of these names is a memory of someone great. Each of these names has a history that I want to remember. Each of these names is a hero... a grunt hero. Every last fucking one of them. So when you tell me that I don't want to feel guilt about their deaths," I laughed hoarsely. "You are dead wrong. Just as you have been dead wrong about a lot of things." I waved my hands at the crowd. "Now away with you. Go find someone else to blame about the invasion. I'm going to concentrate on my brother."

I turned to Merlin, who was now staring at me wide-eyed. "Brother." I shook my head and walked toward him with my arms out. "Brother, trust in me. This isn't you. This is the aliens. This is all about them. Killing an orca had nothing to do with this." I walked up to him, grabbed half full gasoline can from him and tossed it aside. Then I embraced him, my arms encircling him, his face shoved into the crook of my neck. The smell of gasoline stung my eyes. "I'm sorry the Cray attacked, my brother, but they've been attacking everyone since they landed. Savoonga is just the latest casualty in a long war."

He sobbed. I held him fast. Eventually I noted a presence beside me. I turned my head slightly and saw that it was Heavenly, her eyes now filled with emotion.

"Merlin, I have been where you are. I watched the Cray destroy my hometown. I watched them kill my friends. But we aren't helpless. We can kill them. We can get back at them. We can go to them and show them what violence is really about." Then I lowered my voice so only he could hear. "And we go to them so that you can kill, because through their deaths comes the cleansing necessary for your soul."

"What you're talking about is revenge," he whispered.

"It's a good a reason as any to fight. Entire nations have risen and fallen because of revenge. If there's no other reason to fight, revenge has always been a suitable option."

I released him and stepped back.

Heavenly moved slowly forward, then reached out a tentative hand. She gently touched Merlin on the arm.

He looked at her, his eyes full of tears.

Then they embraced.

I watched for a moment then turned, giving them privacy. When I did, I saw that no one had left. They were all staring at me. Standing there without my shirt I felt oddly naked.

Black Hands Woman brought me a blanket and I wrapped it around my shoulders, shivering a little. I stared into her ancient, deeply creased face.

"I understand now," she said, then walked away.

The crowd began to disperse, Yupik going their separate ways. Sam Chiklak stayed where he was. When he was sure he had my attention, he nodded, then moved off.

Peal and her brother approached with Charlemagne closely behind.

"Didn't know you could speechify," Pearl said.

"Is that what it was?" I shrugged. "I was just pissed off."

"We says the same thing in *Légion Etrangère*," Charlemagne said. "Iz article deux of our *Code d'honneur du legionnaire*. It says, *Chaque légionnaire est*

ton frère d'armes, quelle que soit sa nationalité, sa race ou sa religion. Tu lui manifestes toujours la solidarité étroite qui doit unir les membres d'une même famille."
He grinned. "Each legionnaire is your brother in arms whatever his nationality, his race or his religion might be. You show him the same close solidarity that links the members of the same family." He put his arms around Earl and Pearl, suprising them both. *"Vous etes mon famille!"*

I saw Earl staring at the names inked to my body. His mouth hung slightly open as his gaze wandered my personal graveyard.

"You want to play the kill game, Earl?" I asked as his eyes met mine. "You go out there and kill enough, you'll have your own litany of dead friends and fellow grunts. This is what it looks like when you have four thousand seven hundred and sixty-six kills."

"Is that what I am, a grunt?" he asked.

"Didn't you get the memo? Who'd you think you were, some kid playing at war, never going to die, never going to get hurt? This ain't a video game. This shit is real. Good people get killed, life sucks, and then you die. The only thing you can control is what happens in between." I placed a hand on his shoulder. "Welcome to grunt life."

He swallowed, as if realizing for the first time that there was a penalty to be paid greater than death. Sometimes surviving was harder than dying because you had to learn to live with other people's deaths. It had taken me a decade to figure that out and I still didn't have all of it. But I was a better grunt now than when we were invaded. It sucked that it took the destruction of the world to get me right in the head... well, almost right in the head.

PART TWO

> Revenge, lust, ambition, pride, and self-will are too often exalted as the gods of man's idolatry; while holiness, peace, contentment, and humility are viewed as unworthy of a serious thought.
>
> Charles Spurgeon

CHAPTER SEVENTEEN

MERLIN REJOINED US a different man. I think I'd been able to convince the survivors enough so they'd finally stopped blaming him. For them to change, it took the Yupik barely surviving an attack by savage aliens to set aside thousands of years of cultural indoctrination. But then again, hadn't that happened to all of us? I'd seen several tribe members go to him. I wasn't sure what was passed, but it resulted in nodding of the heads rather than shaking of the heads. He'd gone back to the longhouse to get his father's aangruyak, which had been in the family for more than two hundred years. The wood had hardened to an almost steel-like consistency. This lance, used to dispatch large marine animals, had an iron heel and whale ivory inlaid mid-shaft to give the hunter a better grip. Instead of the traditional steel tip, Merlin had replaced it with a Cray claw, making the weapon a wickedly savage combination of alien and ancient.

We'd finished transferring everything to the AC-

130 when he arrived. I looked up from where I'd been helping the crew chief of the new plane cinch down the alien bodies.

"You know you don't have to come with us, right?" I nodded towards the village. "You can stay and help them rebuild."

He shook his head. "I'm a hunter. I want to hunt."

"People hunt to eat. They hunt to survive. What we're doing isn't the hunting you're used to. We're not going to just hunt the enemy, we're going to track them down and destroy them."

"Then I want to be a part of it. I *need* to be a part of it."

A flash of worry swept through me. It had been my own inertia that had set Merlin on this path to revenge. The need for revenge was a powerful thing that required constant feeding and attention, and I wasn't sure if I needed someone on my team who had a different agenda. But then I thought about it. Wasn't everyone here fighting for revenge? Revenge for the loss of their homes, their loved ones, their way of life? What was done was done. We'd already proven we couldn't kick the aliens off the planet, so why were we still fighting? I tabled the question until I had more time to really think about it.

"If you travel with us, you are not alone. You're part of a team. Sometimes the team hunts. Sometimes the team doesn't. Is that clear, my brother?"

Merlin looked at me, cocking his head. "It is as you say. When you were on my hunts, I was the professional. I knew how to kill without being killed. Now on your hunts, you are the professional. I should pay attention to your lead."

I hoped that meant what I thought it did. I grinned.

"Cray don't taste half as good as the things you hunt."

Merlin made a face. "You've actually eaten them?"

I laughed. "No. I was just guessing."

Charlemagne broke in. "Taste like fishy chicken, but with the right combination of herbs and butter..." He brought two fingers to his lips and kissed them. "*Fantastique!*"

Both Merlin and I stared at the Frenchman, agog.

"You're not really serious," I said.

"How do you say... as a heart attack?" he replied. Then he added, "One of our *legionnaires* was a trained chef... Le Cordon Bleu. He made shoes *elegante*!"

I shook my head. "Not this guy."

Merlin mimicked me. "Not this guy, either."

I stuck my hand out to Merlin. "Then welcome to the squad, Merlin." Glancing once more at the village, I added, "It might be a long time before you get the chance to return."

"I understand. I've said my goodbyes. Now it's time for the long hunt."

"What about your sister?" I asked.

"She's going to be the new leader. She has the support of both Sam and George, as well as Black Hands Woman." He grunted. "While the rest of us were out hunting, she was at my father's side. She's going to do well."

"Then strap down your lance and we'll find you a place to store the rest of your gear."

Since he'd only brought a small duffel bag it wasn't going to be an issue. I held out my hand, but he made no move to hand it to me. "What is it?"

"I want to say something to the team first."

I gathered everyone around, then Merlin spoke.

"What you saw on the dock with the gasoline... that is a dead version of me." He took the time to look everyone in the eye to make sure that they understood. Then he pointed to his chest with a thumb. "This is the real version of me. The only version of me."

Earl and Pearl glanced at each other.

Charlemagne grinned.

I wasn't sure Merlin was done until he dropped his bag then found a seat. By his silence, I figured that was about all he was going to say on the matter. All righty then. I snatched up his bag and tossed it to Earl.

An hour later, we were underway.

The AC-130 was already seriously cramped because of the various ammo magazines necessary for the weapons. Unlike the sparse crew of the previous C-130, an AC-130 needs a lot of attention. I'd flown with the 160th Special Operations Aviation Regiment in Afghanistan and had seen firsthand how the flying tank operated. They usually had a pilot, co-pilot, navigator, fire control officer, electronic warfare officer (all officers), then a flight engineer, TV operator, infrared detection set operator, loadmaster, and four aerial gunners (all enlisted). With a compliment of thirteen personnel, working in the back of the Spectre was like having an infantry platoon work the line of a fast food restaurant in full battle rattle. You couldn't even move without rubbing up against someone else. Especially with a full complement of ammo.

Lucky or unlucky—that would depend on what we encountered on the way back—the Spectre had depleted all of its 105mm rounds, half of its Vulcan 20mm rounds, and a third of its 40mm Bofors rounds. Plus, they didn't have a full compliment of personnel. Evidently the end of the world manning requirement was less than half of pre-invasion. Still, with a pilot, co-pilot, loadmaster and three gunners, crampage was spectacular. Add the EXOs, the spidertank, and the remains, and it had been a challenge to fit everything into the smaller hold. In order to transport the Russian spidertank, they'd had to disassemble the 105mm Howitzer and use the gained space. Even then it was like trying to shove a Cadillac into a space the size of a Volkswagen. Earl and Pearl were forced to travel inside their EXOs just to alleviate crowding. I chose them because I knew they'd find use for the time, probably play some video game they'd illegally downloaded into the EXOs electronics suite. Charlemagne, Merlin and I had to sit on the remains and debris recovered from the trash site and hold on as best we could.

Luckily the first leg was short. We landed at Red Devil, Alaska and where a B2 Stealth Bomber was waiting for us. With its swept back wings, it was as sleek as any aircraft I'd ever seen. They offloaded the remains and the debris we'd brought back and stored it all in the aircraft's empty bomb bays, which alleviated a lot of room inside the Spectre. We wouldn't be doing the tango, but I wasn't sitting on someone else's lap, either.

A contingent of Alaskans manned a battery of .50 caliber machine guns. The runway ran northwest to southwest and on the southern perimeter I could see the remains of several Cray. With the warming of the climate they were coming farther north every day. One of them could bring down an aircraft or ground one if they came close enough. Their ability to EMP burst was as deadly to an aircraft as a tactical nuke. Even flying as we were, especially south, was a roll of the dice. Our only advantage was our ability to stand-off from the target and fire lethal rounds before they got within EMP range. We had to count on the pilots to keep us far enough away from large clouds of Cray and get us home safe. Based on my experience with the 160th Night Stalkers, I knew that we were in good hands. Even if we weren't, it wasn't as if I could fly the plane and do better. I just had to trust in the system.

The Stealth Bomber took off for Fort Irwin ahead of us. We took another fifteen minutes to top off our fuel. Once we began taxiing down the runway, the gunners manning the .50 cals began to leave their posts.

"What gives?" I asked the loadmaster, who was making last minute weight adjustments to balance the aircraft.

"No more fuel. We took it all. No more aircraft coming this way."

"So they're going home?"

The loadmaster, who couldn't have been older than twenty-one, grinned. "Place I'd like to be right now. Cabin in the woods, bear rug, roaring fire, good bottle of scotch. Oh, yeah."

"Sounds like you have a good plan. Got room for one more?"

"Sure do. Just close your eyes as you take off and we'll pretend together because I'm afraid it's as close as we'll ever come."

I nodded. "True that." But when we took off, I did as he told me, and for fifteen rumbling minutes, I was in a cabin in the woods, warmed on the outside by the fire and on the inside by good scotch. The world was still the world I knew and I'd never heard of the Cray.

We flew from Red Devil to Grand Prairie, British Columbia, then took off for the final leg. We went south, staying well east of Spokane, flying through Idaho above the Snake River Canyon. The only spot of trouble came when we skirted west of Salt Lake City. The pilot reported a cloud of Cray trying to intercept. The gunners leaped to the Vulcans. While one fired— the sound of the sky opening up a giant zipper—the other made sure that there were no jams and kept the gun cool. Shell casings flew like combat confetti, causing the three of us to shield our heads with our arms. Although we wore fatigue shirts, the hot brass still burned through the material, making us wince and groan. But no matter how much the brass hurt, the alternative wasn't any choice, so amidst our misery we laughed, cheering the crew as they laid down deadly hails of tungsten and carbine with incendiary effects produced by powdered zirconium. Meant to take down enemy aircraft, the rounds were deadly against Cray, and soon we were out of the danger zone.

It wasn't long after that we landed at Fort Irwin. Once the Spectre's ramp lowered, I was too busy preparing my squad to disembark to see who'd come aboard, but when I was tapped on the shoulder and I turned around, enough emotion went through me that I almost fainted.

The man I loved.

The man I hated.

The man I loved to hate and hated to love.

"Olivares," I managed. "I thought you were dead."

The left side of his face was burned horribly. The right side still held the knife scar. He flashed his switchblade smile. "Someone had to make sure you became a good NCO." He looked around the interior of the plane, then reached out and tugged at my long hair. "Not exactly in regulation."

I couldn't help but grin like an idiot. "Hadn't planned on going on any more missions. Thought I might retire to the country and become a proper gentleman."

Olivares sneered. "You know you're nowhere near a proper gentleman, right?"

"Not even if I hold my pinky up when I drink?'

He shook his head solemnly. "Not even then."

We'd never hugged, we'd never man kissed each other on the cheek. That wasn't the sort of relationship we had. But for a solid ten seconds we stared at each other, bonded battle brothers. We weren't friends but we were brothers in arms, compatriots, and there was no one else in the universe I'd trust more to have my back. And by the look in his eyes, he felt the same way.

For the first time in a very long time, I felt like I was at home.

They were watching, out there past men's knowing, where stars are drowning and whales ferry their vast souls through the black and seamless sea.

Cormac McCarthy,
Blood Meridian, or
The Evening Redness in the West

CHAPTER EIGHTEEN

"WHAT DO YOU mean they're human?" I asked, freshly shaved and washed and in a clean set of fatigues complete with the OMBRA Special Operations patch on the shoulder. My team was in our own special barracks and I'd been summoned to the conference room along with Olivares. My head felt more than a little heavy. Probably the result of all the beer we'd consumed last night.

"Just as I said." Malrimple had an abrupt East Coast way of speaking that sometimes seemed harried. "The remains you recovered from the crash site are undecidedly human, with few exceptions."

"Did you see how long one of the specimens was?" I should have said tall, but long was more suitable because I'd never seen it stand.

There was no love between the Chief Science Officer of OMBRA Special Operations and me. He'd been the one put in charge of HMID research and implementation. He'd been the one to make Michelle suffer. But looking at him now it was clear that something was wrong. He'd been a middle-aged man and overweight enough so that it looked like it bothered him. Now I'd guess his weight to be about one sixty—probably a hundred pound loss. His cheeks were sunken and his skin had a sickly gray pallor.

"Nine feet seven inches. The bone density test indicated that it had less than two thirds of the density of a normal human aged thirty."

"Then how could it stand?" Olivares asked, sitting across the conference table from me.

Malrimple shook his head. "It couldn't."

"That makes no sense," I said. Then I remembered some of my readings from Phase I of training. *Rendezvous with Rama*, *Ringworld*, not to mention *The Forever War*. Continued exposure to zero gravity could have deleterious effects on muscle mass, but more importantly bone density. Even the astronauts on the International Space Station found it difficult to walk after only six months in space. "Unless the body was never meant to stand."

Malrimple shook his head again. "I wasn't clear. It wasn't meant to stand in a gravity environment, especially one with Earth's gravity. This creature was meant to live and navigate in zero gravity. In fact, Dr. Wright and I surmise that it most likely lived its entire life in zero g and is the product of hundreds, if not thousands, of generations of living in zero g."

"Or possibly very low grav," Dr. Wright added. She had a wide forehead and symmetrical features. Her brown hair hung to just above her shoulders. She wore a white lab coat with her name stitched above the left breast pocket. "Such modifications would have to occur across generations, tens of thousands of years, if not hundreds of thousands. Think of the skin color of an African or an Asian, or the epicanthic folds Asians have around their eyes. These are ecophysiological evolutionary adaptations based on the environment from which they derived. Without gravity, the specimen's physiology wasn't constrained to the Earth norm."

"But what about the other specimen?" I asked. "He appeared to be—how to you call it—Earth normal."

"Neither specimen is from here," Malrimple said.

"And by here you mean—"

"Earth."

I couldn't help myself. "Holy Mary Mother of Fuck. Malrimple, am I going to have to jump across this table and strangle the information out of you or are you just going to brief us like you're supposed to?" My face raged white hot at the rationing of information. I didn't know why they just couldn't come out and brief us.

Olivares snorted. "Now there's the potty-mouth non-com I know and love. No pinky fingers there, I see."

Malrimple stared daggers at me.

I stared right back at him.

The moment stretched until it felt it was about to break.

Mr. Pink entered the room, followed by Captain Ohirra. Her wide grin shrank when she saw the tension at the conference table.

Mr. Pink—dressed in black shoes, black pants, and a black polo shirt with the OMBRA logo over the left breast pocket—looked up from the sheaf of papers he'd been carrying. "Sorry I was late. Did you start without me?"

Ohirra gave me a look like a mother silently urging her child to behave, but I ignored it.

Mr. Pink sat at the head of the table.

Ohirra, who was the ranking intelligence officer, sat to his left, across from Dr. Wright.

Olivares was sitting across from Malrimple.

I was sitting across from a red-haired young man in a lab coat who had yet to speak.

"So where were we?" Mr. Pink asked, seemingly unaware of the tension.

Malrimple looked at his hands.

I was about to say something when Dr. Wright said, "We were explaining our findings to your First Contact Team."

Olivares and I looked at each other and both mouthed the words *First Contact Team*.

"Yes, yes. Get on with it," Mr. Pink said, waving his hand.

I'd never seen him this harried. Something must be bothering the usually implacable leader of OMBRA.

Malrimple sighed, "Where was I?"

"You were explaining to us that neither specimen was from earth and yet they are both undecidedly human," I said.

"With few exceptions," Olivares added. "You left off at they were both decidedly human... with few exceptions."

I nodded. "Right. With few exceptions." I flashed a grin at Olivares, then stared flatly at Malrimple.

But it was the man across from me who spoke. "Ya'll can call me Reese. I'm not a doctor. The world blew up before my dissertation. But I am the only one around these parts with knowledge of proposed space travel and the effects thereof." He cleared his throat. "We measured the GCRs on both specimens. And while they are in the safe zone, they are much higher than the norm, indicating that the specimens had been subjected to an extra-Earth environment."

Grand Canadian Rail Road? "What exactly is a GCR?"

Reese shared a ready grin, showing overlarge front teeth. "Sorry about that. Galactic Cosmic Rays. From what we've been able to measure in our solar system, GCRs consist of 85% high energy protons, about 14% helium, and various other high energy nuclei, or HZE ions. GCRs represent the greatest risk to human space travel. The ionosphere protects Earth from the effects, but once in space, an unshielded human, over time, could get debilitating effects to the central nervous system. We've measured this radiation on all of our astronauts and are—were—still working on ways to properly shield a space craft."

"So if we go into space we get bombarded by radiation that could hurt us if we aren't shielded," I summarized. "Got it. And because of this, these specimens we brought back from the Arctic have a higher GCR reading than normal and therefore must be alien to Earth. Is that right?"

Reese nodded amiably.

"But what if the smaller specimen is from Earth and was captured by the other specimen and then was held as a prisoner? Did you see the circlet that was on its neck? Could Specimen B be the slave of Specimen A?"

Reese's smile fell. He glanced worriedly at Malrimple and Wright, who both looked suddenly concerned. I could almost see where their train of thought derailed. They'd been thinking all along that the tall alien humans were good, but what if they were here to enslave humanity?

Malrimple nodded, then shook his head. "We don't have the data for that, I'm afraid. Several of my team are trying to discern what the circlet is for, but as yet we can't even determine from what element it's made. With regards to the specimens, we ran DNA and found there's a .33% genetic difference between us and the tall specimen, and a .17% difference between us and the normal human-sized specimen," he said, using air quotes around *normal human-sized*.

"Doesn't sound like much," Olivares said.

Dr. Wright nodded. "It doesn't, right? But if you take into consideration that there's about a 0.1% genetic difference between everyone on the planet, those numbers seem astronomical. Those differences in percentages should be indicative of extraterrestrial origin."

My eyes narrowed. "So each of these specimens are human, but from different planets?" I thought of S.E.T.I, the search for extraterrestrial life, and realized that all of this time we'd been searching for ourselves.

"That's our presumption based on the facts at hand," Malrimple said.

I sat back in my chair. "So we're not alone out there."

"It might mean something more staggering," Reese said. He looked at Malrimple for permission to speak. The other man merely shrugged as he stared at his hands. Definitely not normal behavior for him. Something was definitely wrong. Dr Wright shook her head, but Reese was only looking to Malrimple. Not seeing any reason not to continue, Reese turned back to me and Olivares. "Ever hear of the Scopes Monkey Trial?"

We both shook our head. We were grunts. We hadn't heard of much we hadn't learned the hard way, or what little had filtered from our teachers to us, and certainly not a Scopes monkey.

"I'm from Dayton, Tennessee," he said, "so this has always hit home for me. It pitted William Jennings Bryan against the august Clarence Darrow in what would turn out to be a case to determine whether modern science— evolution—or the bible should be taught in state-funded schools. As a result, evolution was more broadly taught—not everywhere mind you, but more broadly. Then, in 1958, the National Defense Education Act was passed because the US feared they were falling behind in science to the Soviet Union. It mandated that evolution be taught as the unifying biological theory."

"Reese, please," Dr. Wright said.

But he wouldn't be stopped. He held up a fist. "Evolution." He held up another fist. "Creationism" Then he slammed them together several times as he said, "They've always been at odds with each other, fighting, scratching, clawing." Then he opened both fists. "But it seems like they were both wrong."

Dr. Wright hissed, "Reese!"

"There's a 1.6% genetic difference between us and the Chimpanzee. Chimpanzees and humans both share the same genetic difference from gorillas, which is 3.1%. Because of this, we've believed that we were both descended from apes and followed parallel evolutionary tracks. But there's always been a missing link—a supposed gap in our hominid evolution—you know, that thing we can hold up and show that this was the transitionary fossil."

"Adam Reese!"

Malrimple raised his hand. "What does it hurt? Let him finish, dear. This is exciting for him."

Dr. Wright sagged and bit back a response.

Reese nodded. "Remember that there is only a .33% genetic difference between us and the tall specimen and a .17% difference between us and the normal human-sized specimen. We are much closer to these human-like aliens than we are chimpanzees. It seems a stretch now that we're even related to chimpanzees." Reese's face grew serious. "Which means science and religion are both wrong. When it comes to planet Earth, *we* are the aliens."

My jaw hit the floor.

One man's 'magic' is another man's engineering.

Robert A. Heinlein

CHAPTER NINETEEN

"Now that you're up to speed with regard to the specimens, a lot has happened in the last twelve hours," Mr. Pink said. "But first let me take a moment to welcome one of us back into the fold." He glanced at me and grinned. "Welcome, Mason. Glad Ohirra could convince you to come back."

"If it had been anyone other than her, Mr. Pink," I said, relishing using the name I'd given him, "I'd still be in Savoonga."

"If you were still in Savoonga, you might be dead." His smile had taken on a menacing sheen.

"About that," I said. "If you'd told us about them, then we could have used the EXOs to protect the villagers."

Mr. Pink actually *tsked* before replying. "I reviewed the footage of the mission. It was a close thing getting there before the Russians. Had you stopped to save the villagers, our chance at getting to the debris field might have been limited."

And this was why I dislike Mr. Pink, OMBRA, and pretty much any military organization. I'd undergone an evolution since I'd first joined up. Back when I was a fresh-faced grunt and had to see the sky rain body parts, I'd been all about mission first and damn the consequences. But somewhere along the line—maybe it was the fifth or tenth or fifteenth soldier I'd lost—I'd changed into a people-first person, wondering what the effects of the mission might be on their lives. Probably because once the world had been invaded and we'd lost ninety percent of the population, people seemed a little more important than they had been.

"That debris field was the size of Denver," I said. "I'm sure there were plenty of dead alien specimens we could have grabbed."

"As it was, you lost one of your team. You might have lost more."

"Or we might have lost none." I sighed. "Listen, Pinkster. We can do this all day long. But I've spent the last few years dealing with your duplicity. When I was beneath the Hollywood Hive I saw things—the master shared things with me. Whether it meant to or not, I have no idea, but it showed me you." I pointed at Malrimple. "You were with the first crew to discover the alien HMID. You all stole the technology from the aliens and now they can listen in on our conversations just as we can listen in on theirs."

"We've dealt with that," Dr. Wright said.

"I'm not talking to you!"

Her eyes went wide and she jerked back.

I noticed that both Ohirra and Olivares were giving me the ugly face and I didn't care. Okay, yes, I did. I closed my eyes and counted to five. Then I shook my head and in a lower voice said, "I'm sorry. I didn't mean to yell." I turned to Mr. Pink.

"What is it you want from me, Mason?" he asked.

"I want for you to—I want for you to—" Fuck! I couldn't put it into words. I didn't know what I wanted him to do, but I just wanted not to keep finding things out after the fact. Then it hit me like an arrow through the temple. I stared for a moment without blinking. Why had I been trying to fight all of this time? After all, was I not a grunt? If there was one thing I knew it was that grunts were treated like mushrooms—kept in the dark and fed shit. I'd lived with it before, so why was I fighting it now?

Mr. Pink cleared his throat. "What is it you want, Mason?"

Because I'd had a false sense of control, that's why.

The moment of catharsis was utterly amazing. I felt a smile bloom on my face.

Part of the reason I'd fallen into the trap was because I'd associated some sort of hierarchical importance on being chosen by OMBRA and Mr. Pink. Sure, it had been the PTSD diagnosis in my med file that had originally drawn them, but there had to have been thousands out there like me. So the fact they chose me made me awesome. Except that it didn't. I could have been chosen because I was convenient. I could have been chosen by some algorithm. I could have been chosen because I was an asshole. To assign any importance to the fact I was chosen was a fool's errand, and evidently without knowing it I'd been hosting a fool's convention.

The other part was because of the way I'd been treated afterward. I'd been selected to be part of a recon squad. Then I'd been assigned, along with Olivares, to conduct the special mission beneath the Kilimanjaro Hive and destroy it. Then I'd been a trainer of young OMBRA minds. And then I'd been asked to lead another Hive destruction mission. It was like I was a special operator without being a special operator. But in truth, I was only a trumped-up lieutenant in a unit full of grunts leading a unit full of grunts, which meant I was...

A grunt.

"Dude, you're smiling like a madman," Olivares whispered as he leaned over. "Are you okay?"

I nodded, aware my grin was freaking people out.

Ohirra was looking at me like I had two heads.

Mr. Pink had such an expression of worry, I thought he might come over and comfort me or run the other way.

"Do you know what I want?" I asked, filling the silence, my smile unwavering. "I want you to treat me like the mission manager you want me to be."

Pink cocked his head.

"If you want to put me in charge of something, then let me be in charge. That means I need the most information I can have so I can make appropriate decisions. You're withholding information from me stops, or else bump me back down to sergeant and give me a foxhole."

Mr. Pink sighed and shook his head. "Some things are on a need to know."

My smile didn't waver, but I wasn't going to let him get away with that. "And I drop the bullshit flag on that. That's a personal foul. Fifteen yard penalty and start your play again. Just ask Olivares. When you're in charge of a mission, you require all the information so that you can not only execute the mission, but so you can keep your people alive. This has been true since Christ was a corporal and it will remain true long after we've turned into cosmic dust. Your problem, Mr. Pink, is that you've been working under false assumptions.

"You believe that had you told me about the hordes of Cray heading to Savoonga, I would have stayed and not gone on mission. Mission is always first. I learned that during my first body excavation detail in Kosovo. I've known and lived by that credo my entire career. What you don't take into account is that the first three Cray to attack might have made me presuppose there were more coming and these were the vanguard. What you didn't take into account was the idea I might have decided that the mission came first. But you'll never know.

"But let me tell you exactly how I would have reacted had you provided me the information I needed as your on-site mission manager. Mission doesn't always need to come first as long as the mission is accomplished. You see, I would have dispersed the tribe. I would have sent some of them into the ocean in kayaks. I would have sent some into their ice caves. And then I would have sent others south of the airport and into the land. I would have done this because I couldn't possibly stay. Mission dictated we move with all haste. But had I had that information, more than four hundred people would still be alive, and let me tell you, this planet can ill afford to lose any more humans, much less over four hundred, as a result of your micromanaging, specious need to control everything, including the information and intelligence you provide."

"Don't you think that's a little harsh?" asked Dr. Wright.

"Tell that to the four hundred who died."

She rolled her eyes, making me want to punch her, but I smiled instead.

Mr. Pink said, "That's some very comfortable hindsight you have."

"I would have done the same thing," Olivares said, sliding in for my defense. "What Mason said is SOP. If civilians are present and we have mission and hostilities are about to occur, we disperse and find shelter for the civilians as best we can, then go on mission." He shrugged. "Done it a hundred times."

If anything, his comments made me smile wider. I looked expectantly at Mr. Pink. If he wanted to treat me like a grunt, that was one thing. But if he wanted me to lead, that was another.

And to his credit, he seemed to understand. Mr. Pink looked from Malrimple to Ohirra to me. Then he nodded, made eye contact with me. Then he swallowed, and continued as if nothing had ever happened. Classic Mr. Pink.

"As you might have now surmised, Mason, we knew that there was an alien machine interface device (AMID) beneath the L.A. Hives. We just didn't know which one had it. Likewise, the hives in Vegas, Phoenix, Dallas, Cincinnati, and a host of other cities. We had a timed attack to disrupt communications and for the most part, we succeeded. 'Crealiac coms were significantly disrupted, as was their ability to monitor our activities. We used that time to reposition air assets and ground-based rockets."

"They're not monitoring us from space?" I asked. I didn't know alien invasion protocol, but if I was the head alien in charge, I'd have things in orbit to monitor.

"Evidently, it's not that kind of war," Mr. Pink said, his face pensive, his gaze darting to Malrimple, who was carefully examining his fingernails. Mr. Pink cleared his throat.

"Right," said Malrimple, looking up and taking stock

of where he was supposed to be in the conversation. "So one of our previous hypotheses was that we were some sort of logistical depot for an intergalactic war. Based on intercepts we've managed in the last six months from the Hypocrealiacs, as well as the hostile-to-them-actions taken by a new group of aliens, this hypothesis now has more credibility. Previously positioned station-keeping satellites that had provided the Hypocrealiacs with global communications capability have since been removed by the new aliens via unidentified means. We postulate that if the Hypocrealiacs had forces capable of stopping the destruction of the satellites, they'd have used them. That makes us believe that they don't have any of their actual military forces here..." He paused to catch his breath. "Jus—just the task-based organisms they sent to kill, dismantle, and terraform."

I glanced at Ohirra, who was staring at Malrimple with a pained look. Something was definitely wrong with him. By the way Dr. Wright was also staring at him, empathetic like a daughter might be to a dying father, I couldn't help jump to the conclusion of cancer. Thin. Sallow skin. Loss of hair. Trouble breathing. Damn. It was only a matter of time. I felt my heart soften for the man.

"What does that have to do with what Reese said?" I asked to fill the silence.

This time it was Ohirra who spoke. "Imagine, if you will, two warring intergalactic species. Let's say they've been fighting a battle across the galaxy for a million years. Clearly it's a war of attrition—whoever has the most territory and weapons wins. But the battle is spread so far across time and space that events are unfolding now which might make no difference on events that have unfolded before or in the future." Seeing my expression, she added, "Without some way to cross the vast distances between stars, time is more of an enemy than anything else. Generations could live and die aboard a ship before any contact is made."

"Unless there's FTL," Reese interjected.

Faster than light. Like *Star Trek*'s warp drive. Or wormholes. I'd read plenty about them in our Phase I training.

Ohirra nodded, flicking a gaze towards Reese. "We have to consider the possibility, but without data it's hard to include that in our postulate. Regardless, we're talking a war of logistics. On one hand you have an alien organism who is positioning planets to use by ridding each of its population, preparing it for exploitation, and saving it for a future resource. On the other, if what Reese has said is true, you have another alien organism who is leveraging the only thing it seems to have in quantity: people. Not that I'm a hundred percent believer in what Reese says, but if it's true, we were intended to be used at a later date but the Hypocrealiacs made it to our planet first."

My head was still spinning at the idea that there was no evolution and no God and no Jesus or any of the other things we were brought up to believe. The idea that we were forward deployed logistical material made by an unknown alien species but one who shared our DNA kind of pissed me off. No, not kind of... it *did* piss me off.

"This is very much like a Napoleonic War on an intergalactic scale," Ohirra summarized. "The winner and loser might very well be decided by who has the best access to resources, and we might just be those resources."

> God grant me the courage not to give up
> what I think is right even though I think it
> is hopeless.
>
> Chester W. Nimitz

CHAPTER TWENTY

I COULDN'T GET out of there fast enough. Most of the conclusions they'd come to were so disconcerting that my head was beginning to hurt. That said, I'd appreciated the air conditioning of the OMBRA HQ building. The temperature controlled rooms were more akin to Savoonga than the hundred degree day that slammed into me the moment I left the building. The sky was a white hot eye glaring down on me. Sand and dust blew everywhere. I'd thought Savoonga was desolate, but Fort Irwin, situated in Death Valley, was the very definition of desolate. I'd forgotten how dead center in the middle of nowhere it was. At least Savoonga had the ugly. The memory of the bull walruses bellowing gave me a moment of longing that was eventually destroyed by the whining after-burn of a jet taking off.

The briefers had gone on to explain the current state of OMBRA around the world. They'd detailed the odds OMBRA faced against the Chinese and the Russians, who'd established a loose alliance. I learned that the New United States of North America was growing rapidly, with people eager to run to a group of colors they'd revered prior to the invasion. Interestingly enough, much like when Dewhurst had broached the subject of patriotism to me right before he'd turned traitor to our cause, I didn't feel the swirling emotion I'd once felt, nor was I eager to reestablish the pride I'd so eagerly sought as a younger man racing to salute a flag. In fact, I didn't feel any affiliation to a country at all. I was a citizen of Earth, regardless of my nationality. I identified myself as a grunt, regardless of rank. And if push came to shove, I identified as a species, even if it was merely as grunt fodder for someone else's war. Scratch that. Now that Earth had been invaded, *my* war.

Coming to terms with the idea that the remains we'd brought back might be cousins and that we might not have originated on Earth was becoming easier to accept than I'd thought it would. A lot of it came from the reading and critical thinking we'd done during Phase I training. I tried to dredge some of it up, because once I shared what I'd just learned with my squad, they were going to have a ton of questions.

I found them in the EXO hanger that had been assigned to us, outfitting their battle suits with the latest and greatest. I'd been in this EXO hanger before and recognized the history decorating the walls. The hangar had once been used by a very special unit that prided itself on assaulting and taking the Tactical Operations Centers of all the various units visiting the National Training Center. Insignias and dates told the tale of who'd been the opposing forces from the 1970s on. This group had been called the Tarantulas for their ability to hide in the desert, then pop up and kill senior leaders when they least expected it. The crest was a black tarantula with knives at the end of every leg. I'd deployed out of this very hangar to destroy the Hollywood Hive and my team had worn that crest out of respect to the past.

I thought a moment about Sula and how we'd had to retrofit the EXO for her, as short as she was, so she could fully activate the arms and legs.

I remembered the eagerness of Malcom Macabre and the selflessness of the young man who'd been awarded two Soldier's Medals in a six month period, then had given his life so that Sula might live.

Ohirra had been part of the team on that mission and had kept me grounded and focused, even when I'd thought all was lost.

Then there was Rennie Stranz. We'd been at odds from the beginning because of his braggadocio, but he'd turned out to be the finest of soldiers, right up until the point where I'd sliced off his arm because the AMID master had control of my brain.

I hung my head for a moment as I breathed in the mixed aromas of grease and sweat and fuel. I never did find out what happened to Stranz. I marked it as one of my priorities. I'd done something terrible to him. Even if I hadn't been in control, he'd been my responsibility. I was reminded that Sula had survived my assault as well. I'd shot her in her faceplate. Thank God the rounds hadn't gone through.

I sighed. Was it any wonder I'd needed time away?

I nodded to the squad as I entered but made no move to stop them from what they were doing. One of the techs came up and briefed me. They'd improved the seals around the suit openings and installed a set of oxygen tanks for when the re-breather system was unable to function. They did this in order to provide the capability of operating under water. I wasn't sure who we'd be fighting underwater, but as long as the additions didn't hurt battery life or the ability to move and shoot, I was all for improvements.

Several techs were swarming around the spidertank like teenagers around a suped-up Corvette. Merlin sat in the cockpit, nodding as a tech began to run him through the diagnostics. Turns out that there was a Russian e-manual which had been downloaded and translated. As far as ordinance, the spidertank had a recessed modernized DSHK 1939 heavy machine gun. Called the *Dishka*, the machine gun fired 12.7 x 108mm rounds, which was slightly longer than the NATO .50 cal round. The *Dishka* was capable of destroying unarmored vehicles, penetrating lightly armored vehicles, and possibly destroying an EXO. There were four internal magazines of five hundred rounds each. The rate of fire was relatively low at six hundred rounds a minute, but fired in short controlled bursts, the *Dishka* could be devastating. Still, Merlin would need to conserve that ammunition because we didn't have any replacement ammo of that caliber.

The spidertank also had seven 9M133 Kornet missiles which could be deployed from a rear missile ramp. The Kornet was an anti-tank guided missile capable of destroying pretty much anything. Of interest, the techs had determined that each missile had a thermobaric payload, meaning its devastation was closer to a fuel air explosive than a standard ATGM round.

Then there was the acoustic disc. The techs were still scratching their heads over its capabilities, but it did appear to be a micronized version of the SRAD that the crew chief of the C-130 had initially postulated.

Without testing, there was really no way to know its limits.

Right now several techs were working to create a new blister to protect the driver. They were using a molybdenum steel alloy to create a metal replica of the original blister, then aligning a 360 degree camera mount to allow the driver to navigate and target. Although it looked like an ugly wart on the otherwise sleek spidertank, it would protect the operator far better than anything else we were capable of constructing.

Through it all, Merlin nodded and consulted with the techs. It was clear that he was in love with the machine. If I had my druthers, I'd let him deploy with us on our next mission. I'd have to see if I could sell that to higher, as long as we were going to be able to get a chance to practice.

I was about to pull Hero Squad aside and let them know about their new and snazzy patronage when Ohirra and Olivares came bouncing into the hanger.

"There you are," Ohirra said, a sly grin on her face. "You went running off right after the briefing and I wasn't sure where you'd gotten off to."

"Wanted to check on the squad and make sure they had everything they needed."

"It's good to see you in person," she said. Then her face turned serious. "Sorry about Nance."

"Yeah. Me, too." I remembered his story of avenging his mother and what he'd had to go through. "He was a good kid."

All three of us walked in silence, heading out of the hangar and back into the heat for privacy. We found ourselves pacing the fence line along the runway. Ohirra was to my left, Olivares to my right. I felt a sturdy bond between these two. We'd literally survived everything the universe had thrown at us since the beginning of the invasion. They were the closest thing to friends I had.

Finally I asked, "What happened to Sula and Stranz?"

"I've been waiting for you to ask that," Ohirra said. We walked a few more paces. "It took awhile to figure out that you weren't in control when you attacked us."

I spoke slowly, each word a land mine. "I was a miserable witness to the actions. I screamed on the inside for all I was worth. But in the end, I did kill the thing."

"And we realized that... eventually... but it was hard, especially for—"

"Stranz," I said, finishing.

"Yeah. Stranz."

"Is he all right? Did he make it back?"

She nodded as we continued walking. "He did. He was fitted with a prosthetic, but he doesn't like to wear it."

I tried to imagine losing an arm and just couldn't. "Can I see him, you think?"

Ohirra laughed.

"What's so funny?"

"You asked if you could see him," Olivares replied. "That's funny."

"Why is that so funny?"

"Because he's already on your team," he said.

My heart bounced. "He's what?"

"You heard me," Olivares said. "Stranz is on your team."

My mouth went dry. "Are you sure it's something he wants?"

"He requested it."

But why he would do such a thing? "Sula passed," Ohirra said suddenly.

"She what? She's dead?" I remembered Sula Ali and how bad ass she was for such a little young woman. Then I flashed to the moment where Malcom Macabre had taken the RPG round to save her. "How?"

"Appendicitis."

"But that's curable. That's an easy operation." Then I realized. Everything had been easy before the invasion. The Cray had killed her as surely as if they'd ripped her apart. "Did she suffer?"

Olivares shook his head. "By the time she got to medical, she was septic and out of it. The docs put her under. It was all they could do."

I hated the universe for killing Sula. She should have died in battle, not on a stainless steel table. Then I asked, "Malrimple has cancer, doesn't he?"

"Pancreatic," Ohirra said. "It's supposed to be very painful."

"And of course there's no cure," I said.

"There was a treatment. The NUSNA offered him treatment at Bethesda," she said, pronouncing the initials as *noosna*, meaning the New United States of North America.

"But he didn't take it." I concluded.

"He wanted to finish his work," Olivares said with a grim nod. "Gotta respect that. There was about a fifty percent chance he would have survived the treatment. He said fuck that and went back to work."

"How long does he have?" I asked.

Olivares harrumphed. "How long do any of us have?"

"Word that." We walked for about five more minutes before Olivares started laughing.

Both Ohirra and I glanced at him, trying to figure out what was so funny.

Olivares looked at me out of the corner of his eye. "Did you really call him Pinkster?"

I couldn't help my grin. "Yeah, I think I did."

"And all of that while smiling," Olivares said. "You looked like a maniac."

I chuckled. I'd felt like a maniac.

Ohirra joined in. "Man, I thought you were crazy there for a moment."

"I think I was." I grinned again. "Crazy. For a moment. But I'm better now."

"Good, because this is some trippy shit going on right now and everyone needs their heads on straight," Olivares said.

Trippy shit indeed.

We walked.

We talked.

We rehashed old times.

Then the first siren rang out and we were running back to our hangars and wondering what kind of intergalactic shit had just hit the fan.

> The only thing that makes battle psychologically tolerable is the brotherhood among soldiers. You need each other to get by.
>
> Sebastian Junger

CHAPTER TWENTY-ONE

I WAS HALFWAY back when a voice slammed into my head. To keep from falling, I went to one knee. Olivares and Ohirra did the same. Were they hearing the voice too?

Alert. Alert. Mission critical. Evacuate Fort Irwin immediately and achieve at least a thirty mile stand-off distance.

The message repeated itself over and over. The voice was familiar but it wasn't Thompson. Then I recognized it—HMID Salinas. The guy who'd cracked the Hypercrealiac language.

Olivares was the first to stand. He glared around, wide-eyed.

I got up next, feeling a little nauseous, Olivares helping me to my feet.

I looked at him. "You, too?"

He nodded and wiped the sheen of sweat off his face. "Most of us did. Not as bad a process as when you went through." He held the side of his head. "It has its uses. Like HMID alerts."

Ohirra joined us. "Are we really under attack?"

"Didn't your intel pick up anything?" Olivares asked.

She shook her head.

Now that I had my faculties back, I could think more clearly. I pointed to Ohirra. "Get back to HQ and find out what's going on." Then I pointed at Olivares. "You, come with me. Let's get the EXOs ready to move."

As we were running I asked, "Can we talk to each other like HMIDs talk to us?"

Olivares chuckled. "Dude, wake up. That's pure science fiction."

We passed a group running toward the flight line. Had everyone undergone the procedure? I remembered when I'd been infected and had no control over my body. Surely they'd created a better way to inoculate against the zombie spore. It had taken months for me to recover.

We ran into the hangar and were gratified to see it alive with activity.

Thompson, can you read me? I shouted inside my head. *Thompson are you there?*

Gimme a second, boss, came his harried voice, then he was gone.

I moved to my crew. Earl and Pearl were already in their EXOs. Charlemagne was helping the techs make the last few adjustments on the spidertank's cockpit blister. Three other EXOs stood beside the twins. I immediately recognized the face in the EXO on the left and went up to it.

"Stranz," I said.

"Morning Lieutenant." He smiled slightly, but his eyes were pure steel. I wondered what he really thought about me.

I grinned. "Morning. Glad to see you, especially after…" I glanced at his right arm. Although I couldn't see it inside the sleeve of the EXO, I knew where I'd sliced through it.

"Don't worry about it, L.T. Shit happens."

I nodded. I wasn't worried, but I was going to pay attention. "Who are your friends, Sergeant?"

"The galoot to my left is Cooper. Came from Chicago."

A wide African-American face stared at me from within the faceplate of the center EXO.

"Call me Coops," he said. "Corporal Coops."

To his right was another female, African-American also.

"And the other corporal is Francine Channing. Former Royal Marines."

"Lefttenant," she said, using the British pronunciation. "I go by Chance. Heard some bloody good stories about you."

I glanced at Stranz. "Don't believe them unless it's from this guy. He's one of the best."

Earl jumped in. "Know what's going on boss?"

I only got a moment, Mason. Let me give you the run down.

I held up a hand to my squad, turned to the wall, then put both hands over my ears so I could concentrate.

What's the scoop, Thompson?

Ever felt like you've been pushed toward doing things, that events had been predetermined?

You've just described the life of a grunt, Thompson. What's wrong? You HMIDs feeling down?

Something like that. I can't go completely into it, but know this. Everything all of us has done has been pre-planned by the aliens. They knew everything about every step, each step a gateway to a response. And once contact was made with the new alien species, the Hypercrealiacs instituted an Armageddon Protocol.

What the fuck is that? Whatever it was, it didn't sound good.

All concentrations of military forces are going to be bombarded from space. It's already begun. Elements in Russia and China have already been annihilated. Adjusting for the rotation of the Earth, you can anticipate the same for your location in just under seven hours.

When you say annihilated you mean—

Blown to smithereens. Fine red mist. Somehow the aliens are raining asteroids down onto the planet. You have to get OMBRA out of there or none of you will survive. Treat this as an extinction level event, Mason, and realize that there's a reason that the Hypercrealiacs suddenly decided to pay attention.

And why is that?

We think it's because for the first time since they invaded our planet they are actually afraid.

He signed off, leaving me with a maelstrom of thoughts. *Asteroids. Bombardment. The aliens afraid. Jesus wept.*

I spun and shouted. "Everyone, give me your undivided attention *now*."

Half the people in the hangar stopped what they were doing and looked curiously my way.

Stranz stepped forward and let five rounds rip through the ceiling. Dust fell with the silence.

I nodded my thanks, found a box and stood on it. "Listen up, grunts. OMBRA is about to be attacked in a big way. We have less than seven hours to get the hell away from here before asteroids come raining from the sky. We're not sure how far away we have to be, but I won't feel comfortable until we have at least a hundred miles between us and here. Everyone get in your EXOs. Load them with all the ammo they'll carry and charge them up. I want everyone ready to leave in six zero mikes."

I let the words sink in for a moment.

"Sergeant Stranz," I shouted.

"Yes sir, L.T."

"Make sure everyone does PMCS on their rattletrap EXOs and that they are ready to move when ordered."

"Roger, L.T."

I turned to Olivares, who was placing a magazine into the back of his EXO. "Let's suit up and go see what Mr. Pink needs."

Within moments we were running towards HQ in our EXOs. Mine was the larger white version OMBRA had augmented for northern recon. His was smaller by a third. Once painted red and black, it was now covered in deep scratches from Cray claws and dents from God knows what else.

We both had to duck to make it through the door of the HQ building. We took the stairs in leaps. When we rounded the corner to the second floor a woman screamed and dropped the box she'd been carrying. She recovered quickly once she realized who and what we were. She'd probably never seen an EXO this close. Most people never had because it meant bad shit was about to happen.

The conference room was empty and everyone had crowded into Pink's office. We entered into a cacophony of shouting. Angry insults were being hurled from the garrison commander at Malrimple.

"There's no way I'm letting my troops not evacuate their families. Those trucks belong to me and if I say I want to use them to save the women and children, then that's what we're going to do."

Malrimple tried to keep his voice even. "This is beyond chivalry. We need to keep the science team working."

The garrison commander glanced at the aide standing beside him. "This is so much bullshit." Malrimple sighed and looked to Mr. Pink for help. "It's the way it has to be."

"You're not getting my fucking trucks."

"Women and children aren't going to save the world. My science team is."

Mr. Pink stood behind his desk, looking shell shocked. He clearly wasn't up for this. Seeing him unable to respond was a first. He'd always been able to handle any situation.

Ohirra stood at his side. She gave me a pained look that seemed like it was meant to urge me to do something.

I took Stranz's example, but instead of shooting holes in the ceiling and possibly killing people on the third floor, I aimed at one of the filing cabinets, spun up my minigun, and fired three rounds into it. The room immediately fell silent, the only sound the whining of the barrels as they rolled to a stop.

"What's the issue?" I asked, aware that my speaker-delivered words were loud enough to make those in the room wince.

Mr. Pink was staring at me, his face still blank.

"Lieutenant, stand down," said the garrison commander. His name was Colonel Reynolds and was an all right sort. He just wanted to take care of his soldiers and their families.

I glanced at Malrimple, who looked to be one step into the grave. He was an all right sort, too. He just wanted to take care of his scientists.

"What's the issue?" I repeated.

"We've got this, Lieutenant." Colonel Reynolds put his hands on his hips, as if that would change my mind. He'd once bought me a drink in celebration of that Hero of the Mound nonsense. He'd been upset that he'd never been allowed to fight. He was a logistics officer, pure and simple. He'd seemed embarrassed that he'd never fired his weapon.

I guess we'd see how much he liked me now.

"Not sure why you want to cast Mr. Pink in the role of King Solomon," I said, "but if you want half of your soldiers and the women and children on Fort Irwin to be left behind along with half of the scientists, then you've achieved your wishes."

The colonel sputtered. "Wh-what are you talking about?"

"King Solomon. It's in the bible. Read it when you get the chance." I stepped forward, making everyone step back. "Listen, we have less than seven hours before the spot you're arguing on ceases to exist. You shouldn't be here. You should be out there." I jerked my hand towards the window.

"Listen, Mason," Malrimple began. "You and I have had our moments—"

I grinned and shook my head. "Oh, you have no idea."

"This is bullshit," said Reynolds, poking the chest of my EXO. "I'm not taking orders from a subordinate. Stand down, Lieutenant."

I didn't move.

Olivares stepped up and stood next to me. Although his EXO was smaller than mine, it was still head and shoulders taller than the garrison commander.

Reynolds stopped poking me and tried to stand tall enough to stare into my faceplate. "I said, stand down."

"I don't recognize your authority." I let that turd fall between us. As his face began to go red, I added, "Now what are you going to do?" I leaned in close. "This is the end of the fucking world, so at the very least you could figure out a way to work together." I marched over to the map on the wall. "Ohirra, how many trips could we make in the next six hours between Barstow and the Bicycle Lake Airfield here?"

She grinned slightly, then lowered her head as she did the math. "Given the number of C-130s at our disposal we could make four sorties of five aircraft. With one Spectre and the other four military variants we could transfer a total of 900 people in that period."

"But there's no airfield in Barstow!" Reynolds said.

"Then use the interstate or the desert. C-130s were made for combat takeoffs and landings. It can be done. Once the civilians reach Barstow, they can continue heading south. Meanwhile, military vehicles can be used to evacuate the remaining military and scientists south along this route and southeast across the desert."

Reynolds made a face like he'd just been forced to eat a shit pie. "So that's it, then."

I nodded. "Not unless you have a better plan."

"One problem with that," Malrimple said.

"Which is?"

"We're going to need some dedicated transportation for three HMIDs."

I shook my head. "Can't be done."

"Listen, Mason, I know you hate them, but they've been necessary to our continued existence. Without them we wouldn't have even known a threat existed."

I shook my head. "That's not the reason."

"Then what is?"

"Power. How long can they live without a consistent power supply?"

Malrimple stared at me, then his eyes lowered. "They can't. They need constant power."

"Will you be able to provide it to them?"

"If we use the HEMMETs, we can tie into one of the onboard generators."

"How many Dragon Wagons do you have?" I asked the Garrison Commander.

He stared at me but refused to answer.

"Seriously? You're going to act like a child about this? How many?"

He seemed as though he was about to speak, but shook his head instead. Thankfully his aide seemed to understand the significance of the moment, and he answered. "Three. We have three functioning HEMMETs. All are the LHS variant which will allow them to load and unload equipment up to eleven feet long and weighing ten tons."

I turned back to Malrimple. "Let's say you have three HEMMETs. Then what?"

"We were going to use the Railhead at Yermo. If we could transport them there, we have a flatbed which could help us move them to a safe distance. We'd planned to tap into one of the generators on the engine."

"How long would it take?"

Malrimple looked hopeful. "About five hours from start to tie-in on the train engine. Maybe less."

I thought about it. He said five hours, but that was probably an optimistic number. Yermo was too close to Fort Irwin. My guess was that anything within a hundred miles would be inside the range of the asteroids.

"What were you going to use the HEMMETs for?" I asked the aide.

"CONEXs with food and water. It's not enough to merely evacuate. We have to ensure survivability as well." He glanced at the commander, then back at me. "Know what I mean?"

I nodded. "Definitely. Proceed with your plans."

It took a few moments for Malrimple to realize I'd turned him down. He started to argue, then shook his head and left.

The room was silent for ten seconds, then Ohirra said, "Mason?"

"Yeah."

"Just wanted you to know that HMID Thompson was relocated from L.A. to Fort Irwin four months ago."

"I thought he was in Los Angeles."

"We needed to better protect him. Plus, now that we have—or had—the ability to tap into the Hypercrealiacs communication systems, we had no reason for him to be forward deployed. He could function here as well as anywhere."

"So he's one of the three." I closed my eyes. "Do you think he knows?"

I know, Ben.

I sighed. "Yup. He knows." To Ohirra I said, "Can you get the evacuations started and see if you can get Mr. Pink back to his bad old self?"

She nodded. "Can do. What are you going to do?"

"Visit an old friend." Then I added, "For the last time."

> Life is pleasant. Death is peaceful. It's the
> transition that's troublesome.
>
> Isaac Asimov

CHAPTER TWENTY-TWO

OLIVARES AND I consulted for a moment in the hallway. He wanted to take the squad to the main gates, where a refugee camp had been set up. They needed to know what was going on and that there wasn't going to be any help coming from the fort. The sooner they started to evacuate south the better. As it was, they'd clog up the roads. Luckily, we still had a few tanks that could make new roads for us, their tracks almost as good as a road grader. By then I hoped Mr. Pink would be back in the saddle.

But I had other business. Something I wasn't required to do, but something I felt needed to be done. And Thompson was none too happy with it.

Seriously, don't come.

Seriously. I'm coming.

But you need to save yourself, get the others ready to go.

My EXO can run forty-two miles an hour for eight hours. We're leaving at T-minus three hours. I have plenty of time.

Do you remember when we first met?

I do. You were a bright-eyed, wet-behind-the-ears kid who didn't know which end of the gun to shoot with.

Well, that changed in a hurry, he said. *Do you remember when you became Hero of the Mound?*

Of course I did. I was the hero and Thompson had been the goat. He'd frozen, then fallen to the ground, unable to come to terms with the idea that he needed to stand and fight. And then I'd come in and stood over him, protecting him, killing enough aliens so that they'd eventually piled around me, almost covering the both of us. The official story had been that Thompson had slipped and was unable to stand. The real story was never discussed.

I remember.

You truly were a hero that day and despite trying not to, you end up being a hero at everything you do. That's what I love about you.

My life is a constant exercise in two steps forward, one step back. I'm surprised I ever get anywhere.

I also love that you're humble.

Nah, I just don't like to talk about it.

Mason, if you care about me at all, then please don't come and see me.

I stopped running, then stepped to the side of the road to let a few trucks pass.

Thompson, it was my decision that sealed your fate. I at least need to look you in the eye.

Don't you get it? I have no eyes. I have no legs or arms. I'm not that bright-eyed wet-behind-the-ears kid. I'm a monster.

Don't you think that's a little harsh, kid?

I remember what you went through when you saw Michelle. Do you really want to go through that again? Do you really want to make me go through what Michelle went through?

But Michelle was different. She was my... then it dawned on me. There had been so many clues. Even before blowing the Hollywood Hive, Thompson had said to me, *My fear of you not liking me was greater than my fear of dying.* Then I'd gotten pissed at him and asked him whether he was capable of even feeling regular emotions like hatred, the desire for revenge, and love—the latter I'd asked because I wanted to be sure Michelle had felt what I'd thought she'd did. After the mind-jacking and his rescue of me by possessing the Cray, he'd asked, *Mason, do you remember when you asked if I was capable of love?* and I'd never responded. Finally he'd shown up as Olivares in my dream and asked me if I remembered the question I'd never answered. I hadn't then, but it all came back to me now. My God, how long had he felt like this?

I want you to remember who I was, not who I am, he said.

Even as enraged as he'd made me, I'd never stopped loving Thompson as a fellow soldier. But only as a soldier. I closed my eyes and pictured him cowering beneath me as I fought the Cray to save both of our lives. Damned kid. A lump grew in my chest as I thought about how alone he must have felt with the impossibility of reciprocation.

Thompson, I never knew.

Of course you didn't.

I opened my eyes and turned. I was close enough to see the building they used to house the HMIDs.

Okay then, I said.

Okay then what?

I'll respect your wish and not come.

Thank you.

No, Thompson. Thank you for your service. You found your niche. I wasn't always happy with how you did things, but they were always for the right reasons. You're more of a hero than any of us. You not only sacrificed your ability to live a life like a normal person, but you also sacrificed your body.

The silence in my head lasted a good twenty seconds. Then, *Thank you. Now go save yourselves and do what you do best.*

Which is?

Kill. Kill them all. Kill them until there's no more to be killed, then kill those who partnered with them. Kill, kill, and don't stop killing until there's not even a memory left of who they were.

I stared at the facility and flashed through our every engagement, from the first moment I laid eyes on the little drummer boy from the US Army Band until now. What a kid. What a damned good kid. I blinked away tears and then nodded. I replied with a single word, "WILCO."

Then I moved on.

I gaze-flicked to view Olivares's feed but was locked out. I then switched to Earl's. They were at the front gate. Evidently Olivares had just informed the thousands who were camping outside the fence about the threat. Fists shook as curses and epithets were hurled. Someone even threw rocks, which bounced harmlessly off the EXOs. Even more were terrified, hugging each other, staring fearfully towards the sky, as if it might rain down upon them at any moment. They hadn't been allowed into the camp because of resources. But it had soon become apparent that OMBRA couldn't have refugees dying on its doorstep, so they were provided with just enough subsistence to keep them alive. Now even that was gone.

I felt for them, but they needed to use this opportunity to save themselves.

"Hero Four, this is Hero Prime. Is Merlin with you?"

Earl turned to face the spidertank that stood behind them. The metal blister was in place giving the machine a menacing cyclopean appearance. I gaze-flicked to my squad directory and saw that his call sign had been added by the techs. I switched to a private line and asked, "How's it working, Merlin?"

"A little claustrophobic and jittery when it moves, but otherwise it's like being in a video game."

An image of Thompson interposed on my memory of Merlin—blonde hair, thin features, wide goofy smile. He waved at me and I realized that this was Thompson's way of saying goodbye. He'd put the image there. I didn't know what to do or say, so I shook the image away.

I cleared my throat before I asked Merlin, "Do you have full visual?"

"They have me wearing something called Oculus Rift. Headset used by gamers to put them in a virtual environment. Made me dizzy at first, but I think I got the hang of it." He paused. "Ben, are meteors really going to rain down from space?"

"It's what we're being told."

"My people have very traditional beliefs, you know? They'd see this as the end times... like it was something we did wrong and deserved."

"And is that what you think?" I asked.

He grunted, then said, "Part of me does. Can't help it. But another part of me knows that some damned aliens came and picked a fight with us. We've been losing so far, and just when it seems we can take it to them, they show us how strong they really are. Meteors? Damn."

I signed off, took one last look at the HMID facility, then spent the next ninety minutes assisting where I could. I was especially useful using my power-assisted strength to lift things into place. The first planes had already left, as had most of the trucks. It actually seemed as if everyone was going to get evacuated.

At least until the refugees attacked five trucks carrying women and children. The battle was short. Only the drivers had been armed. No one had thought about needing guards. Then the women and children were made to disembark and the refugees began firing on each other. Five trucks wouldn't make a dent in their numbers. Out of spite, those who couldn't get on the trucks turned their weapons on the tires. Now everyone was stuck out by Painted Rocks and Olivares was asking me to come help.

When I got there I saw what an unmitigated disaster it was. Where once it had been possible for some to escape, now it seemed as if none could. Olivares took Coops, Stranz and Chance to disarm the troublemakers while Ohirra and I assessed. Earl, Pearl and Charlemagne stood between the two groups, trying to ensure the safety of the women and children.

The refugees numbered in the thousands. I was trying to count them when I realized that there was an easier way. I gaze-flicked my HUD and had it provide me a full target profile on my surroundings. The targets were in two distinct groups. The group on the left representing the refugees numbered four thousand eight hundred and ninety. The group on my right numbered one hundred and sixty. One hundred and sixty wives, daughters and sons of the soldiers of OMBRA. Yet among the refugees there were also children. Using my HUD targeting software to distinguish by size, it showed me one thousand three hundred and fourteen targets below five foot five. Even with a twenty five percent error rate that number was extraordinary.

Then I remembered. I asked Ohirra, "I thought we'd established that the women and children were to take the C-130s and the scientists were to take the trucks."

"Mr. Pink countermanded."

"Of course he did. And did he give a reason?"

"He didn't."

"I wish he was here to see what he caused."

Ohirra paused, then said, "He's right over there."

I followed her gaze and noted a sleek red EXO racing towards us.

"Ah, so he got fitted for a suit. Isn't that special."

I noted that his EXO was the exact size of mine, which meant it was the newer model. I wondered what sort of modifications he had that we didn't.

"To answer your question, Lt. Mason," Mr. Pink said over coms, "we have to leave in thirty mikes. We have two birds waiting to take us."

My eyes narrowed. "Wait? Thirty minutes? That's not enough time to—"

"No, it's not." He waved a hand to the thousands clamoring for help. "And there's no way we can save them. There're just too many."

With the trucks destroyed, it would be almost impossible to save those still awaiting evacuation on the fort. We couldn't even get half to safety before the meteors hit. But as illogical as it seemed, I felt I had to do something. There must be a way to do it...

"What if we use our EXOs to carry flatbeds full of people? We can make good time, especially if they're loaded with women and children. With enough of us, the weight would be negligible."

"You don't understand, Mason. This is it. We have to go."

I glanced wildly at the refugees and the families of all the soldiers. We couldn't possibly leave them.

"Listen, Mr. Pink, we have to—"

He shouted, "It cannot be!" Pink positioned his EXO in front of me so he could look into my eyes. I saw the pain in them as he said, "The moment we received word of the bombardment, I knew they were dead. When you saw me, when that asshole Reynolds was trying to co-opt my equipment, I wasn't at my best. I just never thought this would be the 'Crealiacs next step. They'd ignored us. I'd come to feel comfortable in our position. The Cray couldn't reach us. The vine and the spore couldn't get to us. The 'Crealiacs seemed to have all but forgotten us. Everyone was just waiting for the other shoe to drop—the identification of the alien race they were fighting—and I never once posited that that shoe would be so damned big and devastating."

I understood everything he said and it made perfect sense, but I couldn't let go of the possibility. Even if we saved some. "But there must be a way."

"We have a window of time. A brief shot at surviving so that we can link up with the Kron. Yes, we've been in contact with the new race. They want us to do something for them."

Of course OMBRA had been in contact and I didn't know it. I'd expect nothing else.

"These people have to save themselves. There's nothing we can do."

Mr. Pink stepped away, then announced over the

command channel for all EXOs to form up on him. Hero Squad questioned the order on private coms to me, but I bid them follow the order. When everyone was formed up, I gestured to Mr. Pink for a moment. He nodded his assent.

I stepped forward, turned up my speaker volume to maximum, then addressed the crowd.

"We're going to fight them. We're going to kill them. We're going to make them pay."

As expected, my words were responded to with silence. They didn't care about the war. All they wanted to was to survive. "You have one chance to save yourself, and that is to run. Run like you've never run before. Run like the devil himself is after you." I pointed towards Barstow and put a growl into my voice. "But know this. I'd rather die a human than live a coward. You need to work together. The strong must help the weak. The big must help the small. Each human you leave behind is a stain on your soul and a mark that can't ever be removed. Now run. All of you. *Run!*"

They murmured amongst themselves, looking at each other, confused, angry, terrified.

I stepped forward and shouted. "Run. Now. *Go!*" Then I fired my minigun into the air.

And like a herd of gazelles on the Serengeti Plain, they ran. All of them. And by God, they were helping each other. My heart grew as I saw a man I'd seen shouting angry insults at the women and children grab two kids and carry them like sacks of grain. I wasn't sure if they were going to make it, chances were they would all die, but for that one moment, for that one precious moment in time, I was again proud of the human race.

I turned and rejoined the platoon.

"Not exactly a St. Cripsin's Day speech," Mr. Pink said.

"Been there. Done that. Got the T-shirt."

Then we, too, broke into a run, all of us, moving as swiftly as the slowest EXO towards the airfield, salvation, and some yet-to-be-defined revenge.

Do you remember the good old days when we thought aliens and UFOs were something funny? My father laughed at *My Favorite Martian* on television. I even laughed at Robbie the Robot in *Lost in Space*, although he wasn't really an alien. But Mork from Ork and Alf were. Do you think maybe this was intentional? Do you ever wonder if we really did have alien spaceships at Roswell and that we knew how terrible aliens were, but the governments of the world didn't want to scare us so they gave us funny aliens?

Conspiracy Theory Talk Radio,
Night Stalker Monologue #1819

CHAPTER TWENTY-THREE

TWELVE OF US loaded onto two C-130s whose holds had been cleared to make space for the EXOs, cases of ammunition, and parachutes. There was enough room for six of us per bird, but because of the spidertank, there was only five on my bird and seven on the second bird. I climbed into the first aircraft and was joined by Stranz, Earl, Pearl, Charlemagne, and Merlin. It was a tricky thing tying down the spidertank, but we just managed. The second aircraft held Coops, Chance, Ohirra, Olivares, Mr. Pink, and two other EXOs which my directory told me were Jackson and Liebl. They both wore the same gleaming red battle suits that Pink wore, so my guess was that they were some sort of protective detail. I tried to access their internal status matrix but was locked out. Interesting.

I sought a private channel with Mr. Pink. "Where are we going?" When I didn't receive an answer, I added, "I need to prepare my squad. To do that I need to know where we're headed and what we're going to do."

"Give me a minute."

I couldn't help roll my eyes. I'd had the rest of the squad plug in for charging, so I did the same. I keyed into our squad channel and listened for a moment. It was a good thing I did. Evidently Charlemagne was having a meltdown.

"I can't believe that there was nothing we could have done to help them," he said, his accent heavy with grief. "All those people. We have hours yet. We could've at least gotten some to safety, no?"

"And how would you choose?" Earl asked, his voice a dead monotone. "Would it be the children first? And then who? Would you choose the girls, or make it fifty-fifty boys and girls? What about races? Would you choose equal number of white and black and Hispanic and Asian? But if you did that, it would be discriminating against the whites because they make up more than seventy percent of the children, and by being fair, you fail to realize there's an ethnic and numerated division among the children that must be realized."

"Easy, kid," Stranz said.

Charlemagne sobbed for a moment, then asked, "Are you that desensitized, Obelix?" He used the kid's original call sign.

"I'm just being logical."

"Doesn't the fact that they're going to die make you feel anything?" Charlemagne pressed.

"The world is almost dead. The population is almost gone. People die all the time. And now you want me to feel bad for those folks? I don't even know who they are."

"Then what are you fighting for?" Stranz asked.

"Same thing everyone else is fighting for," Earl responded.

"Sex, drugs and rock and roll," Pearl added.

Silence.

I'd met soldiers like Earl and Pearl before. Their disassociation was a defense mechanism to keep them from going insane. What had she said earlier? *This planet's dead anyway. The problem is that no one has told it so it doesn't know to roll over.* I remembered their origin story. They'd been in Park City, Utah when the invasion hit. They'd been stuck and played nothing but video games until they'd been forced to leave because they'd run out of food.

"It's called emotional numbing," I said, breaking the silence. "It's a form of disassociation. It's a protective mechanism that keeps you from going bat shit crazy, Earl."

He sighed and said, "Whatev."

"No, it's cool. We all do what we've got to do. One of the reasons I bet the Pinkster instituted the new policy of tracking kills and giving personalized call signs was because it made reality into a first person shooter. With your targets separated from you by the EXO's heads up display, it was like you were playing a video game. It's called derealization and makes the events happening seem unreal."

"Then why'd you make us change?" Pearl challenged.

"Because it's important to be accountable for your actions."

"Even if it breaks something inside of us?" she asked.

"Who the hell made you a doctor?" Earl asked.

"Who the hell made you a doctor, *Lieutenant*," Stranz corrected.

"Yeah." Earl said. "That."

Like Earl, I hated being told what my problems were. But that wasn't going to keep me from telling him and everyone else who was listening. "It's not like I invented PTSD, but if there was a PTSD ranking system, I'd be Grand Master. Let's face it. You two were teenagers living the life all teenagers should have. Playing video games, hanging out with friends, going to the mall—"

"That is so 'eighties," Pearl countered. I could almost see her eyes roll. "No one went to malls anymore except old people doing laps. Everything was networked. All we had to do was choose which app to use and we could hook up with whomever we wanted, whenever we wanted."

"How's that working out for you now?" Stranz asked.

"The fact remains," I cut in, "that you didn't sign up to be a soldier. Stranz, myself, Charlemagne, we'd all come to terms in the middle of our basic training that one day we'd have to kill or be killed. It was a conscious decision."

"Hey, we didn't have to join OMBRA. It was *our* choice," Pearl said.

"Had you killed anyone up until then?" I asked.

We all waited for the answer. When it came, it surprised me. "Earl hadn't," she said.

"But you did?" I asked.

"It was nothing," she said in a small voice.

"It's never nothing," I said. "Every time you kill someone it means something."

"Yeah, like a fresh kill. A tick mark on the wall of success," Earl said.

"And I thought I was messed in the head," Stranz said.

"Break, break," Ohirra said across our coms. "Wheels up, then command briefing. Stand by."

The C-130 taxied, then took off. We weren't reaching altitude and seemed to level off at about five thousand feet. Ten minutes later, Mr. Pink began his brief.

"We're going to the Green River Launch Complex in Utah. It's roughly five hundred miles away. We'll be there in ninety minutes. All other EXOs have been dispersed and sent forward to Odessa. We twelve are to secure several Khron specimens and return them to Odessa."

"What's in Odessa?" I asked.

"A Khron beachhead. It's a rallying point. They're giving us the opportunity to fight for our planet."

"What do you mean by specimens?" Olivares asked.

"Evidently we've had Khron specimens since 1947. They want repatriation before they'll assist us."

"Wait. 1947?" Ohirra asked. "Are you telling me that we actually have aliens at Roswell?"

"It was before my time," Mr. Pink said. "The former United States government had in their possession a crashed ship and three dead aliens. They were aware of the Khron as an alien species but had no contact. The ship was a reconnaissance vehicle sent to keep track of human progress and industrialization. They were forbidden first contact with humanity and were merely to watch."

"Like the prime directive," Coops added. "You know, like in *Star Trek*."

"Oh, you mean that rule they always broke?" Chance asked.

"Can it," Olivares said over the net.

Mr. Pink continued, "All of this is new to me. HMID Salinas provided the information less than two hours ago. The Khron contacted us and asked us to get their missing... Khron."

"Why don't they do that themselves?" I asked. I'd seen how their spaceships moved when it had taken Nance and a spidertank.

"I don't know but I'll be sure to ask them when we get there," Mr. Pink answered.

"What's ROE?" Olivares asked, meaning Rules of Engagement—basically when we were allowed to shoot and at whom.

"As far as we know the facility is abandoned," Mr. Pink said. "If there are fungees or enemy combatants, then shoot first. Mason, I'm putting you in charge. Ohirra, you're with me."

"What about Jackson and Liebl?" I asked.

"They're with me as well."

"Fine. Stranz, you're in charge of Hero Team One. I'll be with you, as will Earl, Pearl, and Merlin. Charlemagne, you're with Hero Team Two. Olivares, if you would?"

"Roger. Team Two will be comprised of Coops, Chance, Charlemagne and myself. Call signs?"

"Let's not confuse things. We'll just use names."

"Roger."

What followed was forty minutes of verbally running everyone through battle drills, then mentally preparing for possible combat. By the time the pilots announced we were descending, I was actually hoping for action.

Conspiracy theorists of the world, believers in the hidden hands of the Rothschilds and the Masons and the Illuminati, we skeptics owe you an apology. You were right. The players may be a little different, but your basic premise is correct: The world is a rigged game.

Matt Taibbi

CHAPTER TWENTY-FOUR

THE C-130S LANDED without incident. As it turned out, the Green River Complex was an old launch site for Athena rockets, Pershing missiles, and ICBMs, which were fired to breach the atmosphere and then land at White Sands Missile Range in New Mexico for testing. The facility was nominally shut down in the mid-'seventies, but activity continued at its, until-now, secret underground facilities, evidently of the examining alien specimen variety. From the airfield it looked like an old army base, complete with the rounded roofed Quonset huts and old Cold War cement block buildings.

It was early afternoon with a few scattered clouds. A chain of mountains rose in the east. A small abandoned town surrounded the complex. My HUD didn't detect any activity, then again it couldn't see behind or inside any of the buildings.

"What do you think?" Olivares asked.

"You know the drill," I said.

"Is this really necessary?" Mr. Pink asked.

I could hear the edge in his voice. It was clear he wanted to press on. I didn't know anything about Jackson or Liebl. Their experience could range from US Army Ranger to Girl Scout. At the very least I expected them to keep Ohirra and Mr. Pink alive, which was what I'd told them.

"There's a way to go about things that keeps all of my heroes alive. Stranz, you familiar with FM 3.21-8?"

"Roger, sir. I got the field manual locked and cocked in my front brain housing group. Field Manual 3.21-8, The Infantry Rifle Platoon and Squad."

"Tell me about tactical maneuver, sergeant."

"'Tactical maneuver is the way in which infantry platoons and squads apply combat power'," he said, quoted verbatim from the FM. "'Its most basic definition is fire plus movement, and is the infantry's primary tactic when in close combat. Fire without movement is indecisive. Exposed movement without fire is potentially disastrous. Inherent in tactical maneuver is the concept of protection.'"

"So you're saying we should fire and move all the time?"

"All the time, sir?"

"Like now? We going to fire and move?"

"Negative. This isn't a tactical maneuver because we've yet to locate a target. This is a patrol."

I nodded, my chest filling with pride as I remembered my own sergeants drilling me on the manual. "So what exactly is the purpose of a patrol?" I asked.

Olivares responded instead of Stranz. "'A patrol is a detachment sent out by a larger unit to conduct a specific mission. Patrols operate semi-independently and return to the main body upon completion of their mission. Patrolling fulfills the infantry's primary function of finding the enemy to either engage him or report his disposition, location, and actions. Patrols act as both the eyes and ears of the larger unit and as a fist to deliver a sharp, devastating jab and then withdraw before the enemy can recover.'"

"That's good, man. Real good. Olivares, you're going to be the right fist and my squad will be the left fist." To Mr. Pink I added, "You four should stay with me but have a standoff of at least ten meters." I eyeballed Jackson and Liebl. "Do you two understand?"

Neither responded, which pissed me off, but before I could say anything, Ohirra spoke up.

"We got it, Mason. Let's Charlie Mike."

I nodded. The dramatic demonstration of infantry knowledge notwithstanding, the plan was for Olivares to take his squad and conduct a reconnaissance patrol to the right along a fixed route, while my squad would do the same on the left. Mr. Pink had provided us schematics of the base, along with a schematic of the central building that provided access to the UGF. The specimens were located seventeen stories down.

Olivares called me on a private channel. "Watch out for those two. Dirtbags make my hackles rise. They're blue falcons all the way."

I keyed to private and replied, "WILCO. Same to you."

We were exactly two kilometers from our target goal. Between us and the building were several Quonset huts. Each squad was going to use a wedge formation and conduct traveling overwatch, which meant we believed enemy contact to be possible, but not likely. The difference between bounding overwatch, where enemy contact was likely, was that we weren't stopping and observing before moving on, instead, we were going to be tactically walking. I'd ordered all EXOs to have their miniguns ready except for one per squad, who was to be ready to target possible enemies with the hydra rockets.

I deployed Merlin between both formations, to go right up the middle. I did that for two reasons. One, he had barely any experience using the spidertank, and two, I wanted both squads to be able to cover him if there actually was an enemy lying in wait.

The most dangerous area came at the very beginning where we had to cross the airfield, a highway, and breach the fence that still ran around the perimeter of the complex. It would put us out in the open for thirty seconds if we ran, or two minutes if we walked. The choice was easy. We were going to run.

"Merlin, are you ready?" I asked over the net.

"As I'll ever be."

"Okay then, let's move out."

Both squads broke into a jog.

Merlin moved the spidertank in a series of forward jerks which I supposed approximated a giant spider jog.

Mr. Pink and his command element let us make some distance, then jogged as well.

I lived for moments like this, where an enemy might be around any corner, waiting, ready and hoping to take you out before you take them out. Back before when the world was filled with Happy Meals, pepperoni pizzas delivered to your door, and honest-to-God paparazzi chasing movie stars like what they ate and where they shit was important. Back when knowing I could be shot by a sniper's bullet without even realizing it had been my greatest fear. For all of their juvenile flaws, the twins were right—the EXOs were like living in a video game. They made war easier to survive. Where before a sniper's bullet would've removed me from the land of the living, now it would only serve as a notification of distance and direction to a new target, all computed by the Heads Up Displays in our suits.

I scanned visually and electronically as I traveled across the space. Any movement would be immediately detected by my EXO. We were halfway across the intervening space when I got a red flash on my HUD.

"Squad advise left quadrant motion," I said as I kept moving.

My HUD flashed again and I brought my minigun around to fire just as a three point buck leaped from behind a building and bounded across a road and into the woods.

"Just Bambi's older brother," I said, returning my weapon forward.

The complex seemed completely abandoned. With the exception of the deer, I hadn't seen any birds or small animals. Certainly no people.

We crossed the road and reached the fence. We didn't have anything fancy to cut through it so we just reached out and ripped it down.

Then my HUD lit up with dozens of red highlights, showing incoming fire from several locations inside the complex. Earl went down. I gaze-flicked and toggled Pearl's hydra before she could toggle it herself and sent six rockets on a trajectory to where the rounds came from.

"Forward to the wall," I shouted over the net to my squad, pointing at a single story concrete block building.

I heard Olivares shouting the same and noted that they were under fire as well.

Merlin tore through the fence and raised his acoustic disc. His *Dishka* deployed from the hood and began to move back and forth, seeking targets.

I ran and slammed my back into the wall hard enough to make dust rain down. My HUD had plotted the trajectory and I peered around the corner to let my radar see what was there, but all I saw was a smoking ruin of a building. When I turned back around, Pearl and Stranz were helping Earl to the wall. I dialed up his vitals and they were at a hundred percent, but the right leg of his suit was shot. It looked as if the round had hit the knee joint.

To Stranz, I asked, "Is there any way you can fix his leg?"

"See what I can do." he answered.

Olivares was taking heavy fire. No one had been hit, but it seemed like it was only a matter of time. His squad had already fired several rockets, but to no avail. I dialed into his command channel and POV, and saw several distant shapes inside the complex that the HUD labeled UNK EXO—unknown exoskeleton.

"Ohirra, report," I said over the private channel.

"We've gone to ground. No one is hit. Who are they?"

"Don't know yet. Do you have any intel on other orgs having EXOs?"

"NUSNA has some prototypes, but nothing working."

"We'll see about that. Keep your head down."

The *Dishka* opened up, a slower but louder *TAT TAT TAT* than what our miniguns produced, but with a lot more power. I switched to Merlin's POV just in time to see something the size of a dog blown to high heaven.

"Merlin, what the hell was that?"

"Looked like a dog without a head."

I'd shoot something like that as well.

I dialed up the command channel and broadcast to all EXOs. "Enemy combatants include UGOs and EXOs of unknown origin. UGOs appear to be canine-sized with four legs and no head."

"Did he just say no head?" Earl asked in the clear.

"Stay off command net unless you have something to say," snapped Stranz.

I didn't notice it arrive. One moment there was nothing there, the next it was standing forty feet away. At first it seemed innocuous. A metal contraption on four legs about the size of a large dog. On its back was an oblong shape I couldn't identify. I couldn't even tell which was the front and which was the rear. Then it began to move, first by lowering itself about a foot. As it did, the legs bent in one direction and it began to stalk towards us. The legs were bent like a dog's, so the knees pointed backwards. I was mesmerized by it right up until the oblong shape on its back rose, resolved itself into a light machine gun, and began to fire.

I took three in the chest before I cranked my minigun in response. But even as I fired, it moved behind the corner of a building. I considered sending a snap of my video feed to everyone, but by the increased chatter on the command channel it became evident that they were now well aware of the new threat.

"We've got to move now," I said to Olivares. "We're sitting ducks."

"What's the plan?" he asked.

"Fire seems concentrated in your area. Increase your rates of fire and let us see if we can flank."

"Anytime you want to get froggy, then jump," he replied, voice tight.

I toggled Mr. Pink. "I need Liebl and Jackson OPCON to me now."

He paused as if he was about to argue, then said, "Roger."

I watched as the two immense red EXOs rose from a depression in the earth and sprinted in my direction.

"Stranz, is he mobile yet?"

"No doing, boss. They scored a one in a million shot. This EXO ain't moving without Third Shop repairs."

That wasn't good. I couldn't just leave him sitting here. I called Ohirra and let her know the situation. She promised to have his six as best she could.

To everyone else I said, "We're going to React to Ambush Far and flank the attackers. Watch out for UGOs. Formation is double column. Speed is optimum. Merlin, form up on Olivares and concentrate fire."

Pearl formed up beside me.

Liebl and Jackson behind us.

"Earl, if any targets pop on your HUD, send a rocket after them, but remember to give it time to arm."

He sent acknowledgement.

To the squad, I said, "Fire at anything that isn't us. Ready. Steady. Move!"

We broke into a synchronized run. I had my minigun ready on my right side and pulled my harmonic blade free on the left. I'd marked the route on a wire diagram and made it available as a popup on everyone's HUD. Three buildings forward, then left seven buildings should put us on the enemy's flank. The only question was what would we encounter before we got there?

That question received an immediate answer as another UGO appeared in front of us.

Stranz took it out with grazing fire from his minigun.

Liebl shouted, "On the roof," and opened fire, targeting something above us.

Jackson joined him.

A rocket whizzed past us as we crossed the space between buildings, taking out a UGO that appeared in front of us.

Pearl fired a volley of rounds and exploded another one in mid-air as it leaped from the roof of a two story building.

Before we got to the next space, I slowed and had everyone stop. A four count later, two missiles sped through the space we would have been in. They continued towards the airport and took out a hangar. I signaled for us to move again. We were able to make the far corner of the next building before anything else appeared.

I was peeking around the corner when three UGOs bounded towards us from our rear.

Liebl and Jackson opened fire, but instead of carrying a machine gun, these were carrying explosives. Suicidal, no-headed mechanical canines. The blast wave sent us all sprawling. My HUD sizzled but came back on. As I got to my feet, I checked vitals on my squad. All were still at a hundred percent and their suits were functioning. I was still locked out of Liebl's and Jackson's, but my visual told me everything I wanted to know. Jackson's faceplate was shattered and a six inch piece of metal jutted from his face. No need to check his vitals. Liebl, on the other hand, was still ambulatory. He was having trouble climbing to his feet. I stepped over and gave him a hand. The front of his EXO was covered in scorch marks, but he seemed otherwise okay.

"Let's not do that again," I said to the squad.

Then I peeked around the corner and targeted six UGOs. I sent the locations to Earl and ordered him to fire.

Six rockets arced up and down. Once the explosions died, I said, "On my mark, we move at full speed to point Bravo. Everyone ready?"

I got two nods and a thumbs up.

"Go!"

We turned the corner and sprinted forward, immediately encountering hostile action. Fire came from directly in front us. I took a few hits before both Stranz and I unloaded a hundred rounds on the position, silencing the oncoming fire. I heard the others firing as well. A UGF came at me from the left and I slashed at it with my harmonic blade. It danced aside, tumbled, then righted itself. Liebl managed to shoot it before it could get away.

We continued sprinting towards our objective, continuing to lay down a devastating rain of fire.

Then suddenly we were there. Point Bravo. Two automatic machine guns on sentry turrets lay smoking and wrecked behind a ruined pile of sandbags.

Rather than shoving them aside, I climbed over the top. "Form into fighting positions and be ready to move."

Pearl, Stranz and Liebl climbed over the bags and knelt, aiming their miniguns in four different directions. I ported into Ohirra's feed to see if Earl was okay.

"Olivares, we're in position. What's your status?"

"We lost Coops. Charlemagne was hit as well, but

he's still able to return fire. Those damned mechanical dogs have explosives!"

"Have you designated targets?"

"Roger, sending now."

A pop-up appeared in my HUD, showing me the locations of enemy fire. If we were able to get atop a three story building, we could have the high ground. Meanwhile, I sent the locations to Earl for targeting and decimation.

I plugged Point Charlie into the pop-up and sent it to the rest of the squad, then we made our move. We passed two buildings before we got to the three story I needed. The front doors were locked so I kicked them in. Stranz was the first one through and he led us up wide marble steps. The building was identified as Mission Headquarters and was probably where all the brass sat and shat. We made the third floor without incident.

After a moment, we found roof access. Stranz had just opened the access hatch when he was plucked bodily through it. The next thing I saw was him falling from the roof outside the window. I ran to it and watched as he plummeted to the ground. I checked his vitals but his EXO was offline.

"What the fuck did that?" Earl asked.

I stared at the roof access hatch which had closed. "I have no idea."

Water can flow or it can crash. Be water,
my friend.

Bruce Lee

CHAPTER TWENTY-FIVE

"Pearl, see if there's another access point to the roof."

She moved swiftly down the hall.

"Liebl, post at this access and advance on command."

"I'm not going up there," he said, his voice steady and even.

"It talks." I stepped forward and slammed my visor into his. "You will go up there on command." I locked eyes with him, daring him to do something. Finally, he averted his gaze. "Do I hear a WILCO?"

His eyes flicked back towards mine. Then he said, "WILCO," in a small voice.

I turned away from the blue falcon. I had little faith that he'd actually do it. But until that moment, we both had to pretend he would. I glared at the ceiling. What was up there? Was it an alien? Was it a Cray?

Pearl came running back. When I looked at her, she shook her head.

How were we going to make it to the roof? Going one by one up the ladder and through the hatch was suicide. We had to find another way up... find a way to distract whatever was on the roof.

Then I had an idea.

I told Pearl and Liebl my plan.

By the looks on their faces, I could tell they approved, especially Liebl.

I went to the end of the hall and found an office.

Pearl found an office opposite the roof access.

I counted to three on the command channel and we both opened fire at the ceiling. Cinders, chunks of wood, and drywall rained down on me. I kept firing until I could see sky.

"Now," I shouted.

Hopefully, Liebl was opening the hatch and standing beneath it ready to shoot anything that stuck its ugly face in his field of fire.

I stopped firing. While the six barrels spun to a stop, I pulled free my harmonic blade and hacked at the space above me until it made a hole big enough for me to climb through.

I sheathed the blade and announced, "Ready."

Liebl shouted, "Ready!"

But nothing from Pearl.

I shouted it again, as did Liebl. Still nothing.

"Pearl, status."

Then I heard what sounded like a gargle.

"Liebl, move!"

I reached up and pulled myself out of the office and onto the roof. I saw Liebl coming out of the hatch. But other than a complex control module powered by an almost silent generator on the other side of the roof, I didn't see anything.

I started to run over to where Pearl had made her hole when a great beast of an EXO pulled itself out of the hole to stand on the roof. It was definitely an EXO, but it wasn't Pearl's. It wasn't even close to being hers. This EXO was easily the biggest I'd ever seen. Twice as large as mine in both height and heft, it was gunmetal grey with only red, white and blue shoulder adornments in the shape of epaulettes. Unlike our suits, whose primary weapon was a built-in minigun with a retractable harness system, this EXO carried an M2 Browning .50 caliber machine gun like it was a child's toy. The cannon, an armament that was meant to be mounted on a tripod or on a vehicle, was this EXO's personal weapon and almost looked diminutive in its metallic hands. The .50 caliber round was more than three times longer than the 5.56 rounds used in my XM214 minigun and more than twice in diameter. I'm not sure my EXO could survive a single shot.

This super EXO was different in a lot of other ways, too. Instead of a bulletproof faceplate, the metal of the body carried upwards like a medieval knight's helm, leaving a thin slit covered with dark glass as its only way to see. Unshielded mechanical actuators were affixed to every joint, lending electronically-powered assistance to the human inside. A thick cable covered in metal skin ran from each side of the helm to the back. Wicked spikes protruded from the elbows, knees and feet.

I felt my anger erupt. Instead of working collectively to defeat an alien presence, the New United States of North America decided to put all of their design and ingenious effort into creating something that wouldn't stand up against the EMP effects of an alien, but was instead designed to wound, maim and murder humans. Like OMBRA had initially been before they became the de facto savior of the planet, NUSNA's selfish actions did more to erode their own humanity than any other action could.

As the super EXO began to bring the .50 cal to bear, I leaped high, firing as I did, sending a hundred rounds into the EXO's face. Half of my shots missed, but the other half hit, resulting in a scored and pitted view plate which I hoped would blind the damn thing. My barrel spun empty as another 500 round magazine was snapping into place.

I came down on the super EXO's .50 cal. My weight was more than it could take and it was forced to let go. As it dropped to the ground, I kicked at it. I'd barely managed to move it aside when I felt a comet punch me in the chest and I went flying. I hit the roof and skidded on my back all the way to the edge. I managed to stop before I plummeted over, my head dangling forty feet above the ground.

The super EXO reached down to pick up his machine gun. If he was able to fire it, I was a goner.

Then Liebl did something right. He employed his Hydra rocket system and let loose one of the 2.75 inch rockets. With two pounds of composite B4 high explosive traveling at 2,300 feet per second, it could take out a—

My heart sunk as it struck the front of the super EXO and shattered into a million pieces. The only effect it had on the super EXO was to knock it back a step.

The Hydra M433 variant had ten meter arming delay as a safety mechanism, making it as effective as a crossbow bolt.

But it did succeed in getting the super EXO's attention.

I took the moment to pull myself away from the roof edge and struggled to my feet.

Liebl redeployed his Hydra and brought out his minigun, but it took critical seconds and was long enough for the super EXO to stride across the roof and grab the gun before it could be brought up. Liebl grunted with effort over the command net as he used his left hand to help get the minigun pointed at his target. But he hadn't the strength. Suddenly the super EXO brought around its free hand and hammered the side of Liebl's head. He fell to a knee. The super EXO hammered the head again and Liebl went to the ground.

His vitals were steady but his blood pressure was thready. Knocked out cold.

I ran at the super EXO and caught it on the side right as it was turning. It didn't flinch and flung me off like I was a bug.

Damn, but this was one bad ass EXO.

I drew my harmonic blade, held it in a two handed grip and said, "My name is Inigo Montoya. You killed my sergeant, motherfucker, so prepare to die."

Then I swung.

It had enough sense to step back.

I swung again and it stepped back again.

I kept swinging, hoping I could herd it off the roof, but it must have sensed the danger and began to move to the right with each step. Still, it was heading towards the edge. Then I swung and before I could bring the blade back around, the super EXO threw a shoulder into me and pushed. I tried to find purchase with my feet, but the thing drove me across the roof. I tried to bring my blade around, but it caught my hand in its and wouldn't let it go.

I did the first thing that came to mind. I let go of the blade with my left hand, reached up and grabbed hold of the cable that came out of the left side of its helmet, and ripped it free.

The super EXO picked me up and slammed me to the ground.

I lay there, gasping, razorblade-wielding unicorns dancing before my eyes.

I glanced at my right hand and realized I'd somehow hung on to my blade.

The super EXO was trying without success to reattach the cable I'd pulled out.

I took a deep breath, then sat up and brought the blade around in an arc, intersecting the super EXO's knee. The vibrating metal of the blade bit in several inches but didn't sever the leg. Whatever material they'd used to harden the EXO was stronger than I expected.

Still, blood welled from the cut as soon as I pulled the blade free.

The super EXO took several steps backwards.

I got to my feet.

"Okay, let's try this again," I said. "My name is Benjamin Carter Mason. You killed my sergeant. Prepare to die."

I lunged towards him. This time, instead of swinging, I stabbed with my blade.

It reached out once to try and stop my weapon and got its hand pierced for its efforts.

I stabbed two more times and it ran at me. I tried to step to the side but couldn't get completely out of the way in time. It had also timed its move as I was pulling back the blade, so it easily pushed away as it spun, burying one of the elbow spikes in my left side.

I gasped at the white hot pain that shot through me. I tasted blood and copper in my mouth.

I tried to pull away, but I was impaled by the damned thing. That's when I knew I was going to die. I couldn't move and it wasn't about to let go and lose its advantage. All it had to do was wait until I lost enough blood, then finish me off. This wasn't the way it was supposed to go. This wasn't the way I was supposed to die, and certainly not at the hands of a fellow human.

I checked my vitals and saw them falling.

Then I felt the super EXO jerk.

The point of a harmonic blade thrust out of the visor window on its helm, coming within inches of piercing my own. I stared at the blood dripping off the tip of the vibrating blade, then watched as it was pulled back out.

When the super EXO fell, it took me with it, bringing me along on a new wave of pain.

I think I blacked out, because when I came to, Pearl was standing over me and the super EXO was nowhere to be seen.

Then the zombie version of Stranz walked up in his underwear, his face covered with blood, right arm missing, and I knew I was in a nightmare.

My question is, why are you coming in here and laying turds all over our yard? First you badmouth OMBRA. Where was the United States when OMBRA came to their door warning them? Where were you when the shit hit the fan? And coming in after the fact to try and measure the viability of one man's heroism against the threat of annihilation is something I'd expect from a sophomoric congressional aide, not from a military officer.

Lt. Olivares, speaking
to Maj Dewhurst about the
New United States of North America

CHAPTER TWENTY-SIX

Turns out I was still awake. Stranz had survived the fall but his suit hadn't, so all he had to wear were his Kevlar shorts and his toe shoes. For the first time I saw what I'd done to his arm. The lower part was removed right above the elbow. I pulled myself to a sitting position. What had happened?

"The battle is over is what happened," Olivares said over the command net. "Whatever you did up there shut down all the sentry guns and those strange mechanical dogs with bombs."

I glanced at Pearl, whose EXO showed scratches and

dents, as if she'd gone through a wash cycle with a box of razor blades. "When I fired on the roof, that beast was above me. Fell right on top of me. Wasn't sure if I was going to make it until you got on the roof and it went after you."

"What happened to it?" I said, wincing as pain shot through my side.

"Over the roof edge," Liebl said, offering me a hand up. He pulled me to my feet, then gave me my blade.

I resheathed it, and cried out as the movement sent what felt like foot-long shards of glass into my side. I checked my vitals and they weren't good. I was going to have to get out of this suit soon and see what the damage was.

"Looks like she was controlling the sentry guns and the mechanical canines using that contraption," Pearl said, pointing to the control panels I'd seen earlier. "Once I killed the bitch, I turned off the transmitter and everything just stopped."

"The gigantic thing I was fighting was a woman?"

Pearl shoved out her hip and gave me a look.

"What I meant was, that EXO was humongous."

"Well, she must have been a basketball player. Here." Pearl sent me a photo packet on the command channel. "I snapped this because I knew you wouldn't believe it."

I gaze-flicked the packet open and saw the face—or at least most of the face—of a woman. Blond hair shaved close to her scalp, pointed chin and high cheekbones. I'd have to guess the color of her eyes because that's where the blade had come out when Pearl had shoved it through.

"Olivares, report."

The reply came immediately. "We lost Coops. Charlemagne is wounded but functional."

"We lost Jackson, Stranz broke his suit as did Earl, and I just got my ass whooped by the biggest EXO you ever saw, plus I think I have a punctured spleen."

Totally ignoring my own predicament, Olivares asked, "How'd Stranz break his suit?"

"Let himself get thrown off a three story building by the same EXO that kicked my ass."

"Thought the EXOs were stronger than that."

"You can call the warranty in later, Olivares."

"And Earl?"

"Leg joint. Can't move. Everything safe down there?"

"Roger."

"Then let's get everyone together and get what we came here for."

I commanded Earl to abandon his suit and head in our direction.

I turned to Stranz. "You okay, sergeant?"

"Everything's a little fizzy, but I'll survive."

I noted his 82nd Airborne tattoo on the shoulder of the arm I'd sliced off.

"You always had that?"

He nodded. "You missed that one but I no longer have a tattoo of my girlfriend's name."

"What was her name?"

"Susan," he said, grinning behind the blood that was smeared across his face. He must have broken his nose. "There was an old school Sailor Jerry style picture of a mermaid on my forearm with her name beneath it"

"What was she like?"

"She wanted kids is what she was like, and all I wanted to do was deploy."

I'd led dozens of young men like Stranz. During their first deployment, they were terrified—jumping at every sound, twitching on patrols, eyes crazy with what they didn't know. Then they'd redeploy back to the land of women and easy days and they'd love it at first, relishing the freedom from the constant tension. But eventually boredom would overcome them. They'd get that far away stare and remember that they'd survived and how every day was a different challenge. They'd remember how close they got to their brothers in arms, relationships far closer than any other they'd had. Then they'd remember the tension, life balanced on the head of a grenade pin, so much fuller than playing video games. While *Call of Duty* was the methadone, actual combat was the heroine, and every last one of them wanted to mainline the freedom to fight for what they loved. They'd find a way to get back in the war, serve a tour of duty, and eventually return home again. Wash. Rinse. Repeat. And every time their enjoyment of the easy days would become less and less, until they couldn't stand the sight of their girls or their families or their home life, discovering that they were only truly alive when they were in combat.

"What do you think now, Stranz?"

He looked at me for a moment. "I think it might have been cool to have kids with her."

"Yeah, and I bet you would have made a good dad."

We made it down to the ground floor and were out the door. The more I walked, the harder it was to put one foot in front of the other. I was going to have to relinquish my EXO and have myself looked at before I passed out. I told Stranz to go get his right arm rig out of his EXO.

Earl showed up. Instead of the cocksure EXO driver he'd been, his face was sheet white and his eyes wouldn't stop moving. His arms were crossed over his chest like they could shield him from a stray round. He walked hunched as if he was afraid of being hit any second. Inside the suit he'd been a totally different person. Video Game Syndrome.

I ordered him to my side, then had his sister scavenge ammo from Stranz's downed EXO. While she scurried around the corner of the building, Ohirra and Mr. Pink came up. I stumbled and Ohirra caught me under my elbow.

"How bad is it?" she asked.

I shook my head. "Once we get inside, I'll see how bad it is."

"Was there only one of the EXOs?" she asked. "I followed the battle through your feed."

I glanced at Mr. Pink, who nodded. Evidently everyone had access to my feed.

I shook my head. "As far as we know. They could have stationed some inside. We won't know until we get there. Did you see that monster? It wasn't made to battle Cray. It was made to battle us."

She smiled grimly. "NUSNA has always had a personal agenda."

"They begrudge the fact that they turned down our help before the invasion," Mr. Pink said.

"You did ask them to pay you, though. It was a sort of blackmail," I explained.

"It was nothing of the sort. They weren't forced to do anything."

"By the way, what was it you asked for?" When he looked blankly at me, I added, "For OMBRA's assistance?"

"Alaska. After all, it was bought for $7.2 million. I figured the old USA could sell it to help us save the world, especially their cities."

"Why didn't they do it?"

"You know, I don't think it's because they didn't want to negotiate, they just didn't believe in the threat. They were so concerned with what women were doing with their bodies and who owned what guns that they just couldn't come to a consensus."

"And here we are," I said.

Stranz came back around, as did Pearl.

To him I said, "When we get inside, you're going to wear my suit. I want you to be able to do damage in case there's something we need damaged. Understand?"

"WILCO."

Olivares, Chance, and Charlemagne approached in loose formation. Charlemagne's left arm hung loose at his side.

Merlin walked behind them, no sign of his spidertank.

I looked to Charlemagne first. "What happened?"

"Explosion threw me into the side of a building," he said. "I think I broke it."

The wound might impede the function of the Hydra rocket deployment system, but it wouldn't affect anything else. He was walking wounded and could still fight. Good.

Then I turned to Merlin. "And you? Where'd you park your spidertank?"

Merlin's face was covered in soot and he walked with a slight limp. He used his father's aangruyak for support. "Afraid it won't be going anywhere anytime soon. One of those metal dogs blew up right beneath it."

I nodded. Too bad we lost the spidertank. The acoustic

disk would have definitely been a handy defense, but there was nothing to be done with it now.

"Did anyone do a sweep of the complex to see if there are any more lying in wait?"

Olivares stared at me, then cursed. "I was so glad the things we were fighting were suddenly turned off that I didn't check. My bad."

"Why don't you organize the EXOs and have them take a quick look. Don't want something trapping us. Meanwhile, Mr. Pink and I will stand here with our thumbs up our asses."

Olivares shot me a glare, then nodded. "I earned that one."

He rounded everyone up and sent out two teams. He led Charlemagne, Chance, and Merlin, while Ohirra led Pearl, and Liebl.

Stranz started to follow, and I called out to him. "What do you think you're doing?"

He stopped and turned, naked except for his Kevlar skivvies, one arm half gone. "What is it, sir?" he asked, like a kid stopped from joining the others.

"Don't you think you ought to sit this one out until we get you in my EXO?"

He grinned. "Nah, I don't need no EXO."

The kid was serious. I thought about telling him to stay put, but instead I said, "Go on then. Don't want you to miss any of the fun."

He turned to run, then stopped after a few steps. He rendered an awkward salute, then turned and ran again, looking like a child chasing after giant storm troopers.

Earl was still standing beside me and made no move to join Stranz. I spared Earl a quick look. The kid was almost hyperventilating. He was definitely shaking.

Mr. Pink didn't even seem to notice.

I stayed silent, mainly because I didn't have much to say. I was having a hard enough time trying to stand, so that's where my concentration was going. We had stopped in front of a building with a sign that said it was a dispensary. Entrance to the UGF was reported to be directly below. Personally, I was just hoping that they had something in there that would keep me from dying. At least, that was my first priority.

But it seemed that Mr. Pink needed to have a conversation.

"You know, I meant well when I recruited you," he said as if each word cost him a pint of blood. For whatever reason, Mr. Pink wanted to get sentimental.

"Doesn't make up for some of the shit you pulled with me," I said, not giving him a chance to sugarcoat things.

"No," he said. "I guess it doesn't."

But now that I had him alone, something was actually bothering me. "What happened to the people who owned the company?"

"You mean the heads of OMBRA?"

"Yeah, those guys who wanted to sell their services to the world. Those guys."

"They got killed shortly after the first wave. They were in a plane that was intercepted by a squadron of Cray. They attacked with an EMP burst and the plane crashed."

"Seriously?" I asked. "They all died?"

"Every last one of them."

"Why'd you keep on going?"

"I had military forces all over the world to control and a chance to defeat the aliens." He shrugged. "What else was there to do?"

I turned to look at him. "Well, son of a bitch."

"Excuse me?"

"You acted like a soldier instead of a businessman."

"I'm not exactly philanthropic."

"But you did the right thing for the right reason."

"I suppose," he said.

I felt light-headed and staggered.

He caught me, then leaned me against the side of the building.

My HUD flashed red.

Mr. Pink's must have too, because he turned to engage the target. I couldn't move, so I gaze-flicked into his feed and saw that it was one of the mechanical canines. This one had a square-shaped object strapped to its back.

Earl followed our gaze, screamed, then scrambled to get behind me.

"I got this one," Mr. Pink said, and began moving toward it.

"Just shoot the damn thing," I said.

"I will, I just want to… damn, I was right. These were part of DARPAs Big Dog program." He chuckled, then the machine leaped towards him and exploded.

When the teams finally returned, I was on the ground, holding Mr. Pink's body in my arms. The explosion had ripped through the entire front of his EXO and had turned his torso and pelvis into one long, red smudge. His surprised eyes were wide in his helmet, still so alive even in death.

> Above all things let us never forget that mankind constitutes one great brotherhood; all born to encounter suffering and sorrow, and therefore bound to sympathize with each other.
>
> Albert Pike

CHAPTER TWENTY-SEVEN

I NEVER SPENT any real time thinking about my parents. It's not that they were bad parents, it's just that they sort of gave up on parenting when I turned thirteen. I mean, who can blame them? My mother worked two jobs. My father worked ten hour days. They never saw me, and when they did, I was either in trouble or about to be in trouble. They called me a latchkey kid. Whatever. I was raised by the streets, fed dinner by my friend's parents, and found shelter by hanging out in convenience stores. When I was twelve, I saw my first fight—not a fight where two kids turtle up on the ground like in school, but a real one—in the parking lot of the 7-Eleven® when two winos from the Halfway House fought over a cigarette. I swear they would have killed themselves if it hadn't been for the Korean next door, who brought out a hose and wet them down like they were dogs. When I was thirteen, I saw my first death in that same parking lot when one of the 8th Street Angels flashed gang signs at a passing car filled with MS 13. Two months later, I saw my second dead body wash up on the rocks of Carbrillo Beach, and was sickened that so many of the families there with kids thought it was a cool thing to bring everyone over and look at the body.

My parents never knew I'd witnessed these things. I wasn't about to tell them. Not only would they figure out a way to limit my freedom, but it also might have made them feel bad about the way they were raising me. They worked so hard and were so tired all the time. Hell, the last thing I wanted was for them to have to deal with one more thing.

Things changed when I turned fifteen. We found out that my dad had been catting it with one of the other real estate agents. He told my mom he wanted a divorce, she told him to fuck off, and for the next year it was like two tired Dobermans trying to fight each other and asking me to be referee. My dad eventually left. I got one birthday card with a twenty dollar bill and a late Christmas present before he finally realized that he could still live his life and forget about me. My mother stopped working, went on welfare, and collected child support and alimony. I'd judge the quality of her day by how early she started drinking gin.

When I joined the Army, she barely noticed. I went through Basic Training at Fort Benning and then had follow-on Infantry Training. Then I went to Jump School. I'd gone from a teenage jerk to a certified red, white and blue teenage jerk, and I wanted to come home and visit. Thanksgiving was coming up and I sent her a letter asking her if I could. I'd sent it with the idea that I could turn her back into a mother. Evidently it worked. She read it, thought about what she'd turned into, became upset, then killed herself by tying a bag over her head and handcuffing her wrists to her feet.

Not exactly an image I want to keep remembering—the woman who gave birth to me, loved me, taught me how to ride a bike, then got so overwhelmed with life she gave up on everything. So drill sergeants became my parents instead. Then it was my platoon sergeants, and my sergeants major. Every unit I went to I'd get a new set of parents. Some were better than others. They were all tough as nails. They 'raised' me, teaching me things I never knew about other people, teaching me things I never knew about myself.

When I was promoted to sergeant, it started happening to me. I saw the looks in some of my soldiers' eyes, the adoration, the hero worship, the puppy dog *I will follow you into battle and the ends of the earth* look I must have given to my sergeants. And I took my role seriously. I led by example and did the right things, even when they were hard to do.

And then they started dying... those soldiers who were not only my subordinates, but my friends, my comrades, my confidants. Brian, Jim, Frank, Steve, Lashonne, Mike, Mike 2, Isaiah, Jesus, Todd, and Nathan died all across the face of the Middle East. Some died in my arms, like Mike, heart attack bringing him down, and some were shot through the face, like Lashonne, or blown into human confetti, like Jim, or caught in a fire like D'Ambrosio. Then there was Isaiah, who fell asleep under a track only to have it roll back over his face. Shoveling what was left of his head into the bag had been my responsibility.

Then came the invasion and I lost most of the world. McKenzie, fucking Jimmy McKenzie, the laughter to my horror. Later Michelle and Thompson. Malcolm, dead saving Sula's life from an RPG only so she could die of a fucking burst appendix months later.

I stared through tears at the man in my arms. My Steve Buscemi look alike. The singular asshole who had put me on this track and was absolutely responsible for me being here at this very moment, holding him, making me feel sorry for him, and absolutely pissed that I was. Even now I felt manipulated by him. Then again, maybe that's how parents operate. Maybe that's what they do best—getting a child to do something without them knowing he or she is actually doing it. Even Mr. Pink had been a father to me, a mother to me. In fact, he was maybe the best of them, because he gave me a chance to do things I'd never have been able to do had he not stopped me from killing myself.

I strained to remember what his first words to me had been.

What were they? Oh, yeah. Something that should have been in a movie. *This could be a beginning instead of an end, you know?* So dramatic, those words would have made Tony Scott proud. Then he'd unsuccessfully tried to get me not to kill myself. If it hadn't been for the net he'd strung below me, I wouldn't even be here to witness the end of what had turned out to be a great man. Instead, I'd be cloaked in the cold, oil-polluted waters of Los Angeles Harbor, my body home to schools of fish and Dungeness crab, unaware and unconcerned that we were being planet-jacked by drive-by aliens.

I felt a hand on my shoulder and looked up— Ohirra. Beside her stood Olivares. They'd been there at the beginning too, all of us locked in cells beneath the Wyoming plains in an old Strategic Air Command complex built back when the only enemy the world had was the threat of mutually assured destruction and an eternal nuclear winter. Then Olivares put his hand on my other shoulder. We were connected, the four of us, possibly by more than any four people in the history of the planet.

And now we were three.

But if there is any further injury, then you shall appoint as a penalty life for life, eye for eye, tooth for tooth, hand for hand, foot for foot, burn for burn, wound for wound, bruise for bruise.

Exodus 21:23-25

CHAPTER TWENTY-EIGHT

WHEN I WAS ready to stand, I found I couldn't. They helped me up and leaned me against the wall. I was so weak, I could barely hold myself up. They got Jackson's EXO and paired it with Mr. Pink's helmet for a full suit. Oliveras was about to give it to Stranz when I called him on private chat.

"Give it to Earl instead."

"Stranz is a better fighter, plus I trust him."

"Stranz can function fine outside the suit. Earl can barely breathe. The kid's terrified. We're going to lose him if we don't get him suited up."

"But I thought he was a crack fighter."

"He is when he's in his suit. Outside it, he's just a civilian, just a kid. He has Video Game Syndrome. As long as he can pretend it's not real, he can function."

Oliveras relented and gave the suit to Earl, who all but pissed himself climbing inside. Stranz looked a little hurt but didn't say anything. Instead he stood, holding his arm extender, looking around at all the huge EXOs.

"Okay, Wonder Twins," Olivares said. "Check the perimeter."

They checked the perimeter of the building, then Liebl climbed up on the roof.

"No access up here," he said.

"Can't see inside," Pearl said.

"We're going to have to breach then," Olivares said.

They broke into two teams. One took the back, the other took the front.

When they simultaneously breached, all hell broke loose. The open doors triggered sentry gun fire but Hero Squad was up for it. They kept the guns firing until they were out of ammo, then poured inside the building.

Outside and away from the action, I wondered off-handedly if one of the mechanical canines was going to rise and blow me to pieces. I hastily coded an app that tied my minigun into my HUD radar. Any movement that wasn't a friendly EXO would be targeted and fired upon.

Inside were two more of the super EXOs, but even as massive and dangerous as they were, they were no match for a complete team. Where I'd struggled to defeat one singlehandedly, the Super EXOs couldn't defend themselves against an organized attack.

I used alternating feeds to watch what was going on.

Olivares and Chance worked a high low maneuver, forcing the beast to choose its poison. It chose to block high and lost its legs as Chance hacked at them with the violence of the damned.

Ohirra forced the other super EXO into a corner and had it surrender. It slowly removed its suit. First the helmet, revealing the pock-marked face of a teenager. Then the rest came off, shoved into a pile for us to look at later.

I eased my way around the corner and into the dispensary as they removed his body armor.

"Name, rank and affiliation," Ohirra barked.

He was little more than a tall, rail thin kid. Had it been pre-invasion he'd be a star center for a high school basketball team somewhere. His dark hair was little more than a buzz cut. He wore Kevlar skivvies similar to ours, but instead of toe shoes, he wore some sort of metallic sock. His eyes were wide with worry.

"Name, rank, and affiliation," she repeated.

"Ss-Sam Sykes," he stuttered. "Lance Corporal, Armored Cavalry for N—New United States of North Am—American Armed Forces."

"That's a mouthful," Stranz said.

"You can say that again," Pearl said.

"That's a mouthful."

"How many more of you are there?" Ohirra asked.

"We have one four person squad and a platoon of raptors," he said, gaining enough confidence not to stutter.

"Those the mechanical canines?" Stranz asked.

"We call them raptors."

"Of course you do," Olivares said. He turned to Pearl, who was shielding her brother. "Hey, Wonder Twins. Go out and bring Mason inside. We don't need him wandering off anywhere. No telling what sort of trouble he'd find."

While they came and got me, Ohirra asked, "Where are reinforcements?"

The boy shook his head. "I don't know. Lieutenant Stanford was in charge of that."

"How would you communicate?" she asked.

"Don't know, that was Lieutenant—"

"Stanford." She licked her lips. "You mentioned that there were four persons in your squad. Who's the other one?"

He stared at the floor and was either unwilling or unable to answer.

"Who is the other member of your squad?" she repeated, nails in her voice.

But the kid continued to stare at the same spot on the floor. Then Stranz entered into it. He made eye contact with the young sergeant and got up close. It was laughable, actually. The kid was already tall enough to start on an NBA basketball team, and Stranz looked like a five year old talking to an adult. Still, the young man was unwavering in his courage, the complete opposite of Earl.

"Listen," Stranz said conspiratorially. "You really should answer. Last guy who pissed her off isn't with us anymore."

The kid flicked a look at Ohirra much like a dog might an onrushing car.

"She's a karate master, brother. Seven finger death punch and all that shit." Stranz knocked on the kid's sallow chest. "I kid you not. Her shit is real."

Sykes's eyes were wild.

Ohirra cleared her throat.

"Saxton," the kid said hurriedly. "Nick Saxton. He's out there waiting for our signal."

"What's the signal?" Stranz asked, now taking the lead.

"I don't know."

Stranz put his hands on his hips and shook his head. "Well, shit, Lance Corporal Sykes. You're just a huge fucking disappointment. There's a whole lot you don't know. Why should I even believe you? After all, you held out on us before."

"No really." Sykes' voice cracked. "I just don't want to be here."

"Shit, son. None of us want to be here." Stranz turned so that only we could see his face and beamed one of the biggest shit-eating grins I've seen in recent memory, then got serious again and turned back to Sykes. "Listen, you play your cards right and we'll treat you with respect. Now, how can we get in contact with Saxton?"

"He's on emergency channel two in my suit. I swear, that's all I know. We came here last minute. We didn't even bring rations." Then he nodded to the super EXO Chance and Olivares had killed. "And then he started to..."

"What?" Stranz asked.

Sykes clammed up.

"What did he do? Where is the staff?" He looked around. "Are there other people here?"

Sykes's eyes went wide again.

"What did you do?" Stranz asked, all serious, all mean.

Sykes actually started to cry. "I didn't do anything, I swear." He pointed to a door and sobbed, "They're in there."

Sykes looked at me. I nodded.

"Why don't you go and see what happened?"

Stranz had Merlin join him and both headed for the door. Meanwhile, Liebl and Olivares were clearing away both sentry guns and tossing them onto the body of the other super EXO. They righted an examining table. I slowly shrugged out of my EXO, every movement a jail house shank. As soon as I unclipped the front, blood poured out from where it had pooled.

Stranz and Merlin led a man and a woman in lab coats from the closet where they'd been held. The man, the doctor I presumed from the stethoscope around his neck, was in his fifties or sixties, bald, and a little overweight. His face was covered with bruises to the point where his right eye was almost entirely closed and his lips were puffed and bloody. The woman was in worse shape. Her head was down and her hair covered most of her face, but I could still see that it had been battered. She wore a lab coat as well, but hers was pulled about her shoulders like a shawl. It hung long enough to cover her naked torso and bottom, but not long enough to conceal purple bruises and smears of dried blood along the inside of her legs.

Upon seeing this, Olivares stormed over and threw the kid against the wall, pinning him there with an EXO fist around the neck. "What the fuck did you do?"

"I didn't do anything!"

"The hell you didn't," Olivares growled. "Look at her."

"I—I tried to—" He gagged as Olivares began to close his fist.

"The kid is telling the truth," the doctor said. He pointed to the dead man in the other super EXO. "It was that one."

Olivares released the boy, who fell like an empty sack to the ground, wheezing as he struggled to breathe.

"Help her," I said to Merlin.

He went to the woman, who jerked when he touched her arm. He tried to guide her to the side, but she began to shake. Urine flowed down one leg. Merlin gave me a pained look.

"Hold on a minute, sugar." Chance began to remove

her EXO. Within a moment, she was standing wearing nothing other than toe shoes and EXO skivvies. Her skin was caramel-colored. Her features were chiseled from what must have been thousands of hours in the gym. Her face was comely, even with close-cropped hair.

She trod lightly over the urine and placed both of her hands on the woman's upper arms, guiding her to the table. All the while Chance spoke in low soothing tones.

I was about to say something when darkness closed in and owned me.

WHEN NEXT I awoke, I was on the table and the doctor was talking to someone I couldn't see. He had tears in his eyes as he worked on me.

"... wanted to know where the aliens were. We couldn't tell them, of course. So he beat me first, then Nancy. I think he enjoyed raping her, even though it was meant to get me talking. She'd made me promise no matter what, not to tell him anything. She didn't want to be the reason to ruin the mission."

"'No matter what'," Chance repeated. "Rape definitely fell into that category."

"It took every ounce of will not to tell them."

"Doesn't matter if you had," Chance said. "He still would have finished. Makes me happy it was me who killed him." She stepped into my view so I could actually see her. "What was his name?" she asked.

"He called himself Picket." The doctor did something more then asked, "Why do you want to know?"

"I collect the names of those I hate." she said, her slash of a smile holding enough malice it could have been the twin to Olivares's.

I cleared my throat and managed to say, "Doctor?"

"Ah, the patient lives. Good." He nodded. "It means I'm doing my job well."

I noticed that a bag of blood was attached to my right arm.

"What's the score?" I asked.

"Twenty to nothing," he said. "Bases loaded and up comes Babe Ruth."

I grinned. I liked this guy.

"Looks like you nicked your spleen. Got that stapled and just closing you up now."

I noticed I didn't feel any pain. I also realized I felt strong... stronger than I should. "What'd you give me?"

"Local anesthetic so I could do what I needed to and a little blood."

"What's in the blood? Turbo fuel?"

"Something like that. It was harvested from one of our alien specimens and stored in our deep freeze."

"You put *alien* blood in me?"

He nodded but still concentrated on my side. "Indeed. They have the same DNA and this one was O Neg, so it's universal. This wound will probably heal in a matter of hours as well. Their blood has some type of nanites that do miraculous things. Their ability to clot is nothing short of incredible." He finally looked up. "All done. Now, I'm told it's you we have to thank for the rescue."

"Well, to tell the truth, we didn't come specifically to rescue you. It was just a byproduct of our mission."

"So you came to get the aliens, too," the doctor said.

"We're going to turn them over to their kind," I said. "They've asked for them. How's Nancy?"

His face grew serious. "Sedated. This was bad for her."

"Does she have any family?"

The doctor hesitated, then with his eyes lowered, he said, "She's my daughter."

"Oh." What was there to say? To watch your daughter get raped and do nothing had to have been the hardest thing he'd ever done. "Listen, doctor, is there anyone around here who can help? I'd take you all with us, but we'll be moving into a place that would make a hornet's nest look luxurious."

"We'll be fine. I've been on this mission since I got my medical license. Nancy is the same. We don't know anything else."

"So you stayed?"

He shrugged. "It's the mission. We considered the safekeeping of the specimens to be the most important job on the planet."

"As it turns out, it probably was." I felt constricted. I wanted to move. "Can I get up?"

"Once you take this in, yes," he said, gesturing at the bag of blood. Then he added, "And thank you, Lieutenant Mason."

I shook my head as I peered over to where Nancy lay on another righted examining table. "No thanks needed. The one thing we can't afford to lose is our humanity. There's a tenuous thread that connects everyone together that can't, or in this case, shouldn't be broken. Some people decide to take advantage of situations. Some people try and survive them. I wish you and your daughter the best of luck."

Stranz came over and stood by me. The doctor finished up and left us alone. "How're you doing, sir?"

"Did you really say that Ohirra knew the seven finger death punch?"

His frown turned into a grin. "You heard me?"

"Yeah, I heard. You did good, Stranz. Real good."

He blushed, then said, "We found the entrance to the underground complex."

"Can you get it open?" I asked.

"Given enough time, we could figure out a way to break it."

"How long would that take," I asked.

"A day? A week? Who knows?"

I turned to the doctor and stared.

He nodded without looking up. "I'll give you the combination. It'll be easier that way."

"I think so. Now why don't you go and take care of your daughter? We've got everything covered from here out."

He was halfway across the room when the earthquake hit.

Everyone in an EXO was able to stay on their feet, but those without one were hurled to the ground like dolls. I didn't even try to stand, instead turtling to protect myself from falling objects. Cabinets snapped open, emptying their contents onto the floor. Glass bottles and beakers shattered. Items on the counters bounced and twisted as the surface bucked. When the quake finally stopped, I realized it had only lasted ten seconds.

I made my way unsteadily to my feet.

Olivares and Chance were helping the doctor and his daughter up as Stranz righted an overturned table.

The place was a disaster.

Merlin began to pick things from the floor and place them back on the counters. He still needed his father's lance for balance.

"You know what that was, right?" Ohirra said to me.

"Fort Irwin?"

"My best guess," she said.

"But that's over five hundred miles away. How could we feel it here?"

She joined Merlin in putting things back the way they were. "If the meteorite was seventy-five meters it would deliver the equivalent of a hundred megatons worth of TNT. Such an impact would obliterate an area the size of Paris or Washington D.C. Each of them are roughly fifty square miles in size. What we felt here was merely a tickle compared to what happened at ground zero. My guess is it was a lot bigger than that, too."

I thought of all the men and women we had to leave behind. I thought of the refugees. I thought of Thompson. A lump formed in my throat as I realized that the 'Crealiac were raining these rocks all over the world. It wasn't just those at Fort Irwin, it was everywhere. To have that sort of power and to use it to hurl meteors at our planet made us seem so insignificant. Was there really any chance for us?

Revenge is an act of passion; vengeance of justice. Injuries are revenged; crimes are avenged.

Samuel Johnson

CHAPTER TWENTY-NINE

THE DOCTOR'S LAST name was Wilson but he said to call him Doctor Paul. Once we helped him and his daughter bring the dispensary into some semblance of order, he gave us the combination then told us that what we were looking for was on level seven. He said the other levels were abandoned, but we were free to look if we liked. Not that I wouldn't have wanted to, but we'd been at this location for too long already as it was. I was eager to get back on mission.

I ordered Olivares and Chance to join me. Once inside, we noted that the power had been turned off. Liebl and Earl were outside covering down, so I sent Stranz to find a way to turn the lights back on, which left Ohirra, Merlin and Pearl inside the dispensary; they were busy repairing my suit as best they could. Charlemagne's shoulder had been dislocated, but was now back in socket. I'd ordered him to take it easy, but I doubted he would. I led using the floodlights from the EXOs to illuminate the way. We bypassed the other levels, and on level seven a single door welcomed us at the bottom of the wide metal stairs. The door was locked from the outside.

It was an easy trick for Olivares to snap the lock off with his EXO fist. We opened the door to find a rather frail old man rubbing his eyes in surprise. The spotlights from two EXOs captured him in their beams. He was about five and a half feet tall and wore a rumpled blue jumpsuit. His skin was pale. A ring of hair rounded his otherwise bald head. Dark circles hugged bright intelligent eyes that he partially blocked with his liver-spotted right hand. He managed to grin as he said, "I thought you all had forgotten about me."

I have to admit this wasn't what I'd expected. I figured we were going for a few dead aliens, and now we had some random old guy to deal with.

What could I say? I shrugged. I guess since I couldn't figure out a strategy, I'd go with what was easiest—the truth. "I'm Lieutenant Ben Mason from OMBRA Special Ops. Is everything okay, sir?"

"Power went down three days ago," he said. "I've been locked down here in the dark since then."

"We're working to get the power reestablished."

On cue, the lights snapped on and equipment began to rumble in the background.

"Did you see Paul?" he asked.

"You mean Doctor Wilson?"

"That'd be him."

Now wouldn't be the time to bring up what had happened to him, and especially what had been done to his daughter. "He's doing fine."

"Why is it you're only wearing underwear?"

Good question. "I'm currently without an EXO. We're working to fix this."

"Quite unusual," he said.

I couldn't agree more. I had Olivares and Chance

spread out and search. I wanted to get back into the air as soon as possible. The room ahead of us was quite large. It had been sectioned off into five rooms with portable wall dividers. One area was a living room with a large flat screen television. One was a bedroom, another a kitchen, then a bathroom. Finally, there was a space that had been sectioned off along the entire back wall for storage.

Glasses and dishware had fallen out of the kitchen cabinets and broken on the floor. Food had spilled.

"You'll have to forgive me. I wasn't prepared for company." When I didn't respond, he asked, "What is it you're looking for?"

"We're here to get two alien specimens."

His eyes narrowed but his smile remained. "Specimens. Sounds like you're going to dissect them."

I shook my head. "Nothing of the sort."

"Then what are you going to do with them?"

"Sorry, sir. I can't divulge that information. It's on a need to know basis only."

Now his smile did falter. "Then I'm afraid I won't cooperate."

"Whatever you say, sir. Please stand aside."

The man did as he was told, watched what was going on for a few more seconds, then shook his head as he went and plopped down on the sofa, snapped on the television, and started watching an old episode of *Doctor Who*.

Chance and Olivares came out of the back room carrying a ten foot box. They set it by the door. "Found one of them, but nothing else is back there except old ration boxes, water, and a slew of technical manuals for some sort of aircraft I've never seen."

That didn't make any sense. Keene had said both of the aliens were down here. We'd found one, now where was the other? Under the bed?

"And you've checked everywhere?" I asked.

"There isn't much to this place," Chance said.

"Yeah, it's not like we can miss anything."

"False walls? False floors? Drop ceiling?" I was grasping at straws.

Chance shrugged. "If there is, we might never know."

We stared at each other for a moment, then all of us turned to watch the old man who was chuckling at the television. It couldn't possibly be. Or could it?

"Excuse me, sir, but what's your name?"

He ignored me and turned up the volume.

I glanced at Olivares and rolled my eyes. Then I walked over and gently took the remote from him. Thankfully, he didn't fight. I'd hate to have to get into it with an octogenarian. I turned off the television, then put the remote on the coffee table.

"Sir, I just need the proper way to address you. I'd like to ask you a few questions and I want to be polite about it. Now if you will, what's your name, sir?"

"They call me Alpha," he said, crossing his arms.

"Alpha what?"

"Just Alpha."

I doubted that was his name, but I'd tried. If he wanted to be called Alpha, then I'll call him Alpha. "Mr. Alpha, we're looking for two specimens. We found one but can't seem to find the other. If you'd help, then we could get out of your hair and let you get back to watching television."

He stared at me for a long moment, then got up and went to the bedroom. Maybe it was under the bed. But instead of leaning down, he went to a standup closet, grabbed a bag, and then strode purposefully towards the specimen box. He placed his bag on the ground, then sat down on top of it.

I glanced from Chance to Olivares, neither of whom seemed to know what was going on either.

"Mr. Alpha? What are you doing?"

He pointed to the box he was sitting on. "This is Bravo. He died in 1962 due to a compromised immune system." Then he pointed at his chest. "I am Alpha. We are your specimens."

You could have knocked me down with a feather.

"But you seem so... so..."

"Human? We're virtually the same species, you know. Whether you say Khron, Human, or Phenomnom, it doesn't really matter. We all came from the same seed. In fact, that's who we are. We are the seeded."

"Olivares, are you hearing this?"

I could see his narrowed eyes behind his faceplate. "Loud and clear."

"Have they arrived?" Alpha asked "Have my people arrived?"

I nodded. "And they want you."

Tears suddenly leaked from the corners of his eyes. "Damn, but it's been a long time."

Chance shook her head. "So you're the alien?"

He nodded. "I was a lot more fit when we were captured. More believable then, I supposed." He rubbed his balding head and his plump stomach. "Not as young as I once was."

"But you don't even have an accent," she said. Then she said, "Wait, does your kind even speak English?"

"No, dear. My kind doesn't speak English. But I

expect given seventy years of captivity you'd be able to speak the language of your captors pretty well."

"Jesus Holy Mary Mother of God," Olivares said, a tinge of fear in his voice as he crossed himself, finally realizing what was going on.

I was struck by the juxtaposition of a hardened Army lieutenant in a walking tank suit suddenly afraid of a little old man.

Alpha must have realized this and said, "Don't worry about me. There isn't any such thing as Klingons or Romulans and I'm certainly no Spock," he said, making pincer movements with his fingers.

"How do you know about *Star Trek*?" Chance asked.

"Not much to do here but watch your television. When we were first captured, you only had radio. Then finally television. It took years of your mind-numbing shows before you actually created something worth watching."

"What about *Lost In Space*?" I asked.

"Please, what a ridiculous show. We would have spaced the doctor after his first traitorous action and been done with it."

"But then there wouldn't have been a show," I countered.

"If life imitates art, then art should imitate life."

"Interesting. Sounds like you're a pragmatist," I said.

"It's how I could survive your poking and prodding all these years."

"Wait a minute... that had nothing to do with me. We're just soldiers."

He just gave me a look.

"How were you captured?" Chance asked.

"Engine failure. We were in the process of fixing it

when, how do you say it, we got rolled up on by the po po."

Chance snorted.

I laughed.

"So you were in one of the UFOs," Olivares said, finally managing not to sound afraid of the small man.

"Wasn't unidentified to me, sonny." Alpha followed this with a few words in an unidentifiable language.

I shook my head. "What is it you were doing here?"

"Waiting for the Umi. It goes like this. First comes reconnaissance. Once your infrastructure and grids are mapped, the Umi send in the hives with what you refer to as Cray."

"What do you call them?" I asked.

"When they came to my planet, we called them Othoids."

"How long ago was that?" Chance asked.

"In earth years, that would be about nine thousand years ago." He nodded. "Where was I... The Othoids come, then you develop a technology to fight them. I have to hand it to you. You came up with the EXOs faster than most of the other words that have been attacked."

"About that," I said, "Your reporting wouldn't have anything to do with that, now would it?"

"Do you mean did I provide significant data that would influence your ability to fight the invasion? That would have been against our regulations. I never would have done that." He paused for a moment, then added, "But I did take pride in the moment when Ripley blasted the alien out of the airlock. What an inspiring image, don't you think?" Without missing a beat, he added, "And then comes the terraforming, which is actually performed for two reasons. One, the water needs to reach a certain temperature so that the Umi can spawn, and two, metal needs to be harvested in the most expeditious manner to create lift vehicles to get the newly-spawned Umi off the planet. At that point, there's a lull that can last years, or decades, waiting for the water to become warmer. You aren't aware of this but the Umi have harvested hundreds of thousands of asteroids from your Oort cloud and have been firing them in to the Arctic to assist with the melting of the Polar Ice Cap.

"Normally we'd have already been in place because the watch station positioned in your solar system, which was waiting for these events to unfold, would have reported Phase I of the Umi conquest. However, since we were caught and there was no one to report, it wasn't until one of our automated beacons captured their movement into the system and sent the information back to the task force that we realized what was happening. By now the Khron have established several beach heads around the world and are preparing to launch attacks on the newly born Umi before they can be lifted from the planet. My guess is that's our next step. Am I right?"

We all nodded.

Chance asked, "Is it always like this with the 'Crealiacs...er... the Umi?"

"They're not particularly intelligent, but they have a way to control other species that supersedes genius. You experienced it with zombie spore. Its cross-species effects allow them control and direction of multiple alien species and to also direct them to do their bidding."

"So the Cray are infected as well?" I asked.

"To a different degree, yes."

Olivares interrupted. "Mason, Ohirra says everything is ready."

I nodded, picked up the old man alien's bag, and gestured towards the door, aware of what a turning point this was and how surreal it all was. "After you, Mr. Alpha."

"Alpha. Just Alpha," he said, then got up and walked out the door.

The language of friendship is not words but meanings.

Henry David Thoreau

CHAPTER THIRTY

ONCE WE REACHED the main level and Alpha saw Nancy and Doctor Paul, he rushed over to them. I couldn't hear everything they were saying, but I could hear Nancy calling him Uncle Alpha, which indicated how close they really were. After a few moments of learning what had happened, Alpha came over to us. One hand was balled into a fist. His frown would have made a lesser man cower.

"You didn't tell me everything," he growled.

"I figured you'd see for yourself."

He jabbed his fist toward Picket's body. "What they did was terrible."

"I agree," I said.

"Behavior like this is not worthy of saving."

"I agree to that as well. That is unacceptable behavior and isn't to be tolerated. None of my soldiers have ever, nor will they ever, act with such atrocity. My soldiers have character."

"That one seemed to have character," Alpha said pointing at Corporal Sykes.

I didn't know what I was going to do with Lance Corporal Sykes. I really didn't think I should leave him here. "But he's guilty by association. I'm sure they knew what kind of person Picket was. He joined them and he went on mission. Hell, he tortured them for three days. Basically the entire time you were downstairs without power. And Sykes did nothing to stop it."

"He could have been killed had he tried to do something," Alpha said.

"I would have died trying to stop it. The other man had to sleep or turn his back sometime."

"Indeed. Maybe your species is worth saving."

"Just as someone judged that your species were worth saving at one time or another."

He nodded but his frown didn't lesson.

"We need to get going," I said.

His frown finally fell as he stared with regret at Paul and Nancy. I realized that he'd been around them longer than anyone else in his life. For as close as they'd become, they might as well have been family. "Alpha, we need to go," I repeated

He turned to me, his face blank. Then he nodded. "You're right. Let me just go say goodbye."

I pulled my EXO from where it was leaning against the wall and climbed inside. Someone had patched the hole, but I doubted the integrity of the internal Faraday cage. Still, it would have to do. Once I was locked in and powered up, I contacted Liebl. "Report."

"Negative contact outside."

I called the pilots over the command net. "We'll be ready for wheels up in ten mikes."

I waited for a response but got nothing. I repeated myself, but still nothing.

"Liebl, do you have visual on the airfield?"

"Negative visuals. Do you want me to go check?"

"No. Stay on station."

I turned to those in the room. There was still another super EXO out there so I needed to be careful who I sent. It couldn't be Liebl. We needed someone to warn us if it was coming this way. Likewise, I couldn't send only one person. Whoever went needed backup.

"I'll go, sir."

I turned to Earl, who'd so recently been a cowering mess. "I don't think so, son."

"No, really, Lieutenant." He paused, seeming to realize how needy he sounded. Then he switched to private chat. "I know I was lousy out there. I really screwed up. I need this, sir."

"You definitely weren't yourself. What makes you think letting you go out there is a good idea?"

"I've proven myself over and over," he said. "This was just one time when I wasn't... wasn't... I don't know what I wasn't, but being in the suit makes all the difference."

"That suit doesn't make you invincible," I warned.

"I know. I just need to go out there and do something to make up for my actions."

I thought of Thompson and how he'd turtled up at the Battle of Kilimanjaro. I remembered others hiding and ducking while I fired and moved. Combat wasn't for everyone. It wasn't that I was suicidal anymore. I had a fine taste of life and a love for living. I was just proficient enough at infantry tactics to keep myself alive. I remembered having a drill sergeant back at Benning who preached battle drills. If you make them second nature, they would save your life. Earl had learned battle drills the easy way, but had been successful because he'd been protected by the firepower and armor of the EXO.

I'd learned my battle drills without the benefit of an EXO, so the EXO added to my portfolio of violence. Maybe it was just that he didn't have the ability to translate what he'd learned in his suit for use outside of his suit. It was clear he wanted to not only regain his own confidence, but mine as well.

Olivares requested private chat and I granted it.

"Don't do it."

"Don't do what?"

"Don't let your man Earl go on mission alone."

"I was going to send his sister with him."

"I guarantee you that if they get into combat he's going to do something stupid."

"But if I don't do it, we have no confidence in him."

Olivares paused before responding, then said, "You were right when you said Video Game Syndrome. He doesn't see what he's doing while in the suit as real. That means he's probably been taking chances he shouldn't normally take. Now, after he embarrassed himself, it's only going to be worse."

Not knowing I was also speaking with Olivares, Earl pleaded once more, "Lieutenant, seriously, I can do this."

"Olivares, thanks for your input," I said. Then I killed my private chat with Earl and broadcast on the command channel. "Earl and Pearl, go and recon the airfield and report back any evidence of enemy activity."

They both acknowledged and were out the door.

Olivares shook his head.

Ohirra wanted a private chat, but I declined. She tried twice more and twice more I declined.

While I waited for Earl to get into position, tracking his movement through his feed, I watched Alpha and his unexpected family say their goodbyes. The motions were a luxury. I'd never had a chance to say goodbye to anyone in my unit back in Afghanistan. Earl and Pearl had never been able to say goodbye to their friends because the invasion had come when they were on holiday. Everyone still alive on this rock was in the same position, and I watched as Ohirra and Pearl stared uncomfortably at the three pouring emotion into each other for the last time. Even Charlemagne watched, tears in his eyes, probably remembering family or friends he longed to have last words with. I considered getting their attention, turning them away to some task so they wouldn't have to watch, but I didn't. As painful as it was, I felt it was important for them to experience this, inculcate this, then use it as ammunition for the hours to come. No one knew what we were about to get into. Alpha was hardly the model for the aliens we were soon going to meet. And then what? To war? To space? Whatever it was, I was ready, and I wanted my Heroes to be ready as well.

Earl turned a corner and what remained of the airplanes came into view. Smoke curled from the smoking wrecks. I checked Earl's radar but there was no movement.

"Investigate," I ordered, and Earl and his sister began to jog in the direction of the air frames.

I began running through my options and realized I didn't have any. Unless it was on foot, I didn't know how we could possibly travel from here to Odessa. In fact, now that the aircraft were destroyed, we had no way to recharge, which had been my plan.

I sighed and tried to engage Ohirra in private chat, but she declined. I tried again, and she responded. "So now you want to talk to me."

"Sorry, I was tired of having my orders questioned. But I need you now because we have a more serious problem. Unless you know of a way to magically get us to Odessa, we're stuck."

I watched as she turned to gaze at Alpha. "What happened to his aircraft, I wonder?"

I remembered the silvery, donut-shaped craft I'd seen in the Arctic. Was it one of those? I imagined DARPA had been working on reverse engineering such a craft, so it was worth a shot.

I asked him.

"I haven't seen my Viper since we crashed."

"So it's not magically sitting in a hanger somewhere in this complex?"

He smiled wanly. "Not that I know of, sorry." Then he added, "But there might be another solution if we can find a way to transmit."

For whatever reason, we were on this mission because the Khron had asked us. If maybe we were able to provide proof of life, it was possible they might send aircraft our way. If we could find a way to contact them.

"Enemy contact," Olivares broke in. "The Wonder Twins are taking fire."

I switched to Earl's feed in time to see his sister take five rounds in the chest and go down.

I think that we all do heroic things, but hero is not a noun, it's a verb.

Robert Downey Jr.

CHAPTER THIRTY-ONE

"CHANCE AND OLIVARES, go go go!"

As they tore out the door, I watched from Earl's point of view as he skidded to a stop behind the fuselage of one of the C-130s. Both planes had their engines ripped from their cowling. The pilots and crew were heaped in a pile between the two aircraft. The flag of the New United States of North America was affixed to a pole that rose from the center of the pile. Behind this stood Saxton in the super EXO with the .50 cal machine gun balanced on the pile of bodies.

I checked Pearl's vitals. They weren't good. If she didn't get medical attention in the next few minutes, she'd be gone.

"Doc, do we have any more of that blood?" I shouted.

Wilson ran to a fridge and pulled out three bags. He handed these off to me along with a phlebotomist's set up. I took those and ran out the door. I gaze-flicked to split screen. The one on my left was my real time view, which would hopefully keep me from tripping and falling on my ass. The one on the right was Earl's. He was protected by the fuselage, but kept peeking out at the super EXO.

"Stay put, Earl. Help is on the way," I said, already breathing heavily from the run.

"I got this," he said.

"No—I said stay put."

"How's my sister?" he asked.

"She'll live," I said, hoping that it was so.

"Okay, then. Watch this."

He backed up, then ran from one plane to the other. Saxton was slow bringing the .50 cal to bear and missed with his shots, while Earl didn't miss, firing from his minigun as he crossed the twenty meters between the two planes. Most of the rounds found home in the bodies piled in front of Saxton, but at least a dozen hit the front of the super EXO, driving him back.

I noted that both Chance and Olivares had fired missiles, which were speeding towards the target.

Earl's current view didn't let me see, but in a few seconds, the super EXO known as Saxton was about to be dust.

I watched the missiles arching up, then down through my view. But before they could reach their target, they blew up in mid-air. Had they been set for an air burst? I contacted Olivares, but he was equally confused.

They fired again, and this time I was able to see through Earl's POV as Saxton raised a disc and pointed it towards the sky. Again the missiles blew up in mid-air. He had an acoustic disc! Had he taken it from the spidertank? What power source was it using?

While Saxton was using the disc, Earl took the opportunity to aim his minigun and fired, strafing the super EXOs helm with thirty plus rounds.

Saxton went down.

"Chance, Olivares—Saxton is down. I repeat, Saxton is down."

They ran around the front of the plane and were met with fire from a .50 cal sentry gun, forcing them to duck back around the fuselage.

Earl was climbing over the bodies when the super EXO stood again. Instead of the .50, it now held an immense blade, much like our own harmonic blades, but nearly twice the size.

Earl backed up and pulled his sister's blade from its sheath. Then he pulled his own. He approached Saxton and twirled both blades in a complicated pattern in front of him. The kid had sword skills, that was for certain.

I skidded to a stop at the rear of the same fuselage Chance and Olivares were behind. They began to climb over it as I ran to where Pearl lay in full view of the sword battle.

I gaze-flicked Earl's POV away and used only my own. I opened Pearl's suit and saw immediately that it was a waste of time—her chest had been torn apart by the huge rounds. Her organs were visible along with boney gristle from her sternum from where the rounds had plowed through it. A glimmer of life was left in her eyes. I put my hand on her face plate, then she was gone.

The EXO had been designed to protect the wearer from Cray claws and joint spikes. It had never been meant to protect the wearer from bullets. That it protected against small caliber ammunition was an accident of exceptional construction. But the .50 cal round was just too much; it seemed as though NUSNA had understood this and armed their own EXOs with the exact weapon necessary to fight OMBRA, something which made me hate them even more.

I left the bags of blood and the setup on the ground beside Pearl and rose.

Chance and Olivares had scrambled atop the plane and now crouched there. Olivares fired at where the sentry gun was and destroyed it, then he and Chance jumped down and got behind the super EXO who was closely engaged with Earl. Both Chance and Olivares pulled their blades, but held back.

I drew my blade and strode forward.

Earl had already gashed Saxton several times.

As far as I could tell, Saxton hadn't even scratched Earl.

I called to Earl to stand down and get beside me.

He gave Saxton another gash, then backed hastily away and stood at my side.

I used the PA system and said, "Saxton, surrender."

"Fuck you," he replied, using his own public address system. He held his sword in both hands and was heaving with exhaustion.

I stared at the bodies of the pilots and crew. What a waste.

"Why'd you kill them?"

"They were traitors. All of them. Just like you. Traitors."

"Traitors to what? NUSNA?" I asked.

"The New United States of North America. Say it right! The red, white and blue. George Washington. Thomas Jefferson. Pancho Villa. You are traitors to all of them. Thomas Paine said that he only regretted that he had but one life to give for his county. I feel the same way. You men and women of OMBRA are like roaches, feeding on the skin and eyelashes of a dying nation. Instead of standing apart, you could lay down your arms and join us. We'd welcome you back into the growing arms of the

New United States of North America. With you we'd be stronger."

"So you'd suddenly forgive that we were traitors?" I asked.

He lowered his voice and said, "You were traitors by circumstance. We know how they stole you away before The Turn. We know how they brainwashed you. Now you can return to your country and be loved again."

I shook my head. "You're insane, Saxton. There are no countries any more. There's us and there are the aliens. Why don't you join us so that we can have a unified front against the alien aggressors?"

"You can take my life, but you can't take my freedom," he said, something I'm sure came from that old Mel Gibson movie, *Braveheart*. "We have to have something to come back to. We need a government. We need a country. We need a foothold on tradition or we'll lose our entire culture."

It was becoming clear that his rabid patriotism made him unreasonable. Not that I expected him to switch sides, I just wanted as much information about his and NUSNA's intentions as possible. Still, I was sick of his diatribe. "You need to fucking surrender. Do you really think that as long as the 'Crealiacs are able to throw asteroids at Earth it's important to form a government? Or do you think maybe we should concentrate our efforts on trying to kick the aliens back to where they came from?"

Saxton's words were like sound bites he'd heard from someone else. "What culture? American culture?"

"Yes, American," he insisted. "And Mexican, and Canadian. We're more than united by borders, we're also united by the migration of Europeans to what was once called the New World. The New United States of North

America represents more than five hundred years of us trying to make this land a better place. We can't forget where we came from and who died. We need to remember them and honor them. One way is to have a country, the same country they fought for, only better, bigger, and stronger."

"Don't tell me about respecting the dead," I shot back. "I've led soldiers into battle all over the world. Their deaths always mean something. You don't need to create a country for that to happen."

"You tell that to all the dead you've made."

I didn't rise to the bait. "If you'd been a soldier, you'd know that we don't fight for objects. We fight for people. We fight for those soldiers beside us. We fight for our family. We fight for those we love. A country, a flag, a song... those are all just representative of those things we fight for. Symbols, all of them."

"Call it what you will. You OMBRA traitors are men and women without a country. You've decided that your company is more important than any country, any tradition, and any culture. Unlike us, you have no history. All you have is a capitalistic desire to steal land and keep it."

I remembered the negotiations Mr. Pink had had with Major Dewhurst about the translation data HMID Salinas created when he broke the 'Creliac language. OMBRA had audaciously tried to get NUSNA to trade Colorado, Utah, and Wyoming for the data, which was what had prompted Dewhurst to turn traitor and try and steal an EXO. As appalling as it was, I'd ignored it, using OMBRA as my own platform to fight aliens.

"I don't care a wit about capitalism," I said. "What I do care about is fighting the 'Creliacs."

Saxton laughed. "You don't get it. This is the new normal. We're conferring with the 'Creliacs. We have a partnership with them. They're offering to let us be alone if we help them defeat the Khron."

Now it was my turn to laugh. "Saxton, we *are* the Khron."

"What the hell are you talking about? We're not aliens. They are."

"Is that why you're here? To give the captured aliens to the 'Creliacs?"

"They're going to move on. They almost have what they want. Then we'll be able to rebuild. We'll start fresh and do it right this time."

Suddenly a scream of rage came from behind me. As I turned, Earl surged from where he'd been standing over his dead sister and pushed past me. He leaped into the air and spun. As he landed, both blades came down and swept through the side of Saxton's head.

Saxton fell to the ground, his brain sliding free to rest on the tarmac amidst dozens of empty .50 cal casings.

Just when I'd learned of a connection between NUSNMA and the 'Creliacs, Earl had learned of his sister's death. I'd have liked to have gotten more, but couldn't possibly begrudge him.

Earl kept hacking at the body for a full minute before he stopped.

When he did, he went back to his sister and knelt beside her.

"Look at this," Olivares said.

I climbed over the bodies and saw that the acoustic disc had been plugged into a black square about three feet on each side.

"What do you think it is?" I asked.

"It has to be some sort of power supply." Olivares pulled the cable from the disc. As he did, we noted that the surface of the square block was fluid. How it kept its shape was a complete mystery. "Whoa, did you see that?"

"Must have been how they kept their suits powered over the span of three days. We need to collect this and take it with us. At the very least, show it to Alpha. My guess is this is 'Creliac technology."

"Umi," Chance said. "That's what the Khron call them. Umi."

"Whatever. Chance, help me with Pearl's body, will you? And for the record, I don't want to lose any more of us."

My HUD fired a blue warning as it noted an inbound aircraft which it identified as an American MQ1-Predator. Its IFF signaled that it belonged to OMBRA. I realized it was trying to contact me and opened a coms channel... and was greeted by Thompson's voice saying *"If you are receiving this, then I am dead."* I wasn't ready for it, so I let the message download to my EXO. It was larger than I expected. I'd have to find out what it was later. For now, I helped carry Pearl back to the dispensary while Earl walked behind us.

An eye for an eye will only make the whole world blind.

Mahatma Gandhi

CHAPTER THIRTY-TWO

BACK INSIDE, WE all mourned Pearl. We removed her from the EXO and placed her on a table. Her unblemished face was visible above the blood-soaked sheet we'd used to cover her body. So many had fallen in the last few days, it was hard to imagine that any of us would survive what was to come... whatever that was.

Earl glared at Sykes, who stood still in the corner, fear plastering his face as if he knew retaliation was but moments away. But Olivares grabbed Earl and held him in place, whispering something to him I couldn't hear. Whatever it was, Earl finally tore himself out of Olivares's grasp and went into one of the examining rooms.

When we showed the strange, box-like object to Alpha, he said, "You're right, this is a power supply. And you said that some other humans had this?"

I nodded.

"We've seen this before. As we mass our forces against the Umi, they try and divide the inhabitants, weakening the forces that can be aligned against them."

"Does the strategy work?"

"If even one of the Umi offspring are able to leave the

planet, then we've failed. They can fold space and will have moved on to the next world without us being able to follow."

"When you say fold space, you mean what exactly?" I asked. I sort of knew what he was talking about, but I wanted to hear it explained. We'd read books about it in Phase I training, but damned if I could remember in which book the term was used.

"Your author Frank Herbert used it in his Dune series."

That was it!

"Yes, I read it," Alpha said. "Lovely books even if it does have those God-awful worms. So imagine that the shortest distance between two objects is a straight line, yes?" He looked for and found a pen and piece of paper. He drew a dot on each end of the paper, then drew a line between them. "Let's say that this is Earth and this is Jupiter. To get there with your level of technology would take months. But what if you were able to change your perspective of the universe? What if there were more than four dimensions... which there are. Now you can fold space." He folded the paper so that the dots were touching. "Now what took months is instantaneous."

"But can't you fold space, too? Isn't that how you got here?"

Alpha gave me an apologetic look. "What the Umi can do biologically, we can do technologically. Our problem is that we're not as precise in our navigation as the Umi. So I used the term *fold space* for the Umi. For us, for the collective we call the Khron, we actually crumple space." He unfolded the paper and crumpled it into a ball. "As you see, the two points are closer than they would be in a straight line. Just not as close as they would be if the paper were folded."

"So the Umi can do it naturally better?"

"It's why they have always been ahead of us."

"How long has this been going on?" I asked.

"This war has been going on for more sun cycles than you will believe. Like you, we believed that we sprung from the planet we were from, but we were seeded just as you were. The first bipedal human, as you would call them, came from a planet on the other side of what you refer to as the Milky Way. They looked much like you and I, but with various differences because of slight differences in gravity, climate, and visual and bolometric luminosity. This is all a haze in our history, so there's a lot of dramatic hand waving to make up for what we don't actually know. We know that a war broke out after the Umi came to their planet. We know that they couldn't defeat the Umi, but they did have the technology and the ability to send generation ships, seeking systems and stars similar to their own. These ships seeded every habitable planet they could find with DNA in an effort to not only hide their descendants, but to let them grow until they would be needed to help join the fight. Collectively we are called the Khron. We've been seeded and now are being harvested for use. What you did in between is of no matter to anyone."

I laughed hollowly. "Grunts on an intergalactic scale."

"I don't understand the reference," Alpha said. "But the hope is that you would have developed advanced social and technological systems so that when the Umi came, you'd be better able to fight. As you will see, not everyone is as advanced as you. The Reds were so constantly at war that they spent five hundred years in the industrial age and never advanced past coal and steam generation."

I waved my hand and changed the subject. "I collected two specimens from a crash site. One appeared to be a normal-sized human, but the other had features like they were stretched."

"They are descended from many of the older seeded and live their lives in zero or very low gravity. Over the generations, their bodies have adapted to the lack of gravity. They require mechanical assistance to maneuver in gravity wells. Many of them are ship drivers, preferring the darkness between systems. We have a name for them that translates to Thinnies."

"Where are you from?" Stranz asked.

"Ah, where is my home? I've never seen it, of course. It was destroyed so long ago. We called it *home*, just as you call your planet Earth. Simple names for something we took for granted, I suppose. Home was a little more than thirty-five light years from Earth. It's in your constellation Vela and is referred to by the embarrassingly unimaginative name of HD 85512 b."

"Thirty-five light years doesn't seem far," Stranz said.

Ohirra snorted. "You need to bone up on your science."

"But they can fold space, ma'am," Stranz countered.

"Our ships fold space at different levels depending on the ship and model. My ship, for instance, what you would call a Viper, is an intrasystem ship only and can fold space in units of up to five sectants. One sectant is equal to roughly sixty million of your miles. Which is a miniscule increment in the ever-expanding universe."

"But you could also travel three hundred million miles," I said.

"That's where it gets tricky. Remember the crumpling paper analogy I gave you? At one sectant the crumpled paper, or folded space, is very compact. But the more sectants we use, the looser the paper becomes. We could be off by millions of miles or we could hit our target exactly... or we could end up in the center of a planet."

I shook my head. "I can't imagine that's a good thing."

"Our ships are really meant for intrasystem travel only. It would literally take us forever to cross the distances between systems.

"Let me demonstrate. The speed of light is 186,282 miles per second, and a year has 31,556,926 seconds. So to figure out how far one light year is in miles, you just multiply the speed of light in miles times the length of a year in seconds. For those who can't do that in your head, that equals 5,880,000,000,000 miles. So if we were to fold space nineteen thousand six hundred times at max sectant, we'd be able to travel one light year. To travel to your nearest system, Alpha Centauri, multiply the number of folded space attempts by four."

"Then, of course, at max sectants you could be going in the completely opposite direction," Ohirra said.

"Maybe not the complete opposite direction, rather a deflection off the desired path. But it's clear you understand the concept," Alpha said.

I just realized something. "If that's the case, then how did you get here? Is there some huge Dreadnaught Class Battle Cruiser up there?" I asked, pointing towards the ceiling.

He smiled. "Ah, another *Star Trek* reference. Wonderful." But then he shook his head. "We don't have such things. We do have Revenant ships and Kaleidoscope ships, but mass and energy has always been our problem with increasing the distance for which we can fold space."

"Then how did you get here?" I asked. "Were you dropped off?"

"I was born in your system," Alpha told me. "I am a clone. Watchers identical to me have been in your system for over three thousand years. Bravo was a clone also. He was a Thinnie and the driver."

"And after all that, the only time you crashed was in 1947?" Ohirra asked.

"Oh no, we've crashed quite a few times. Some of us have even been worshipped as gods. But that ends when the new clone is prepared by the automated system and sent to recover us. I would have been recovered had my clone discovered where I was, but you Earthlings are very good at hiding things."

"How fast can the Umi fold space?" Ohirra asked.

"Your choice of verb is helpful. It takes a Viper on average six minutes to fold space and you know our distance limitations. An Umi, on the other hand, is capable of folding space every twenty-three seconds. Our only advantage is that their ability to travel distances limited to .36 sectants."

"So you can go farther but it takes you longer where they can fold quicker but can't go as far," I summarized.

"It makes chasing them very difficult. Knowing their destination is our only sure strategy."

Charlemagne shook his head. "And to think they traveled all this way just to have offspring, just so they can leave and do it all again. Do you even think they realize what they're doing?"

"Oh, they realize it all right," said Alpha. "They just don't care. And to be fair, the original Khron, those who seeded all of these worlds, didn't care as well. Sure, they wanted to ensure the continued existence of their species, but they certainly placed us in a position over which we have no control."

"How do they do it?" Stranz asked. When all eyes went to him, his face turned pink, "I mean, procreate. How are little Umis born?" He shook his head, now beet red. "I mean, you said we should be worried about them, so I figure the more we know the better, right?"

Alpha nodded. "Umis would be classified as asexual parasites. They procreate by a combination of fragmentation and endodyogeny. Phase one is when a piece of the Umi fragments. What's left of the original Umi withers and dies over time. Phase two is when this fragment produces two smaller daughter fragments, which then consume the original fragment. The thing is that they need your water to *do it*, as you say, but your water is too cold. Water in the breeding ground must be at a temperature of at least one hundred and seven degrees on your Fahrenheit scale to stimulate fragmentation and endodyogeny. Before the invasion, your highest noted water temperature was ninety degrees and that was in Indonesia."

"Wait a minute," Merlin said, jumping into the conversation for the first time. "What do these Umi look like?"

"At the end of their life cycle, when they are ready to give birth, they appear to be immense organisms. In space they can appear to be asteroids. In your oceans they could appear as islands. They can reach miles across."

Merlin looked at me. "The rising water, the melting ice, this was all part of it. You know who the Umi are, don't you?"

I stared at him for a moment, and then it hit me.

"The Leviathans," we said simultaneously.

"We saw some near the Arctic," I said. "Near where Merlin hails."

Alpha's eyes narrowed. "Not good. Things are progressing faster than I would have expected." Seeing our obvious desire for him to continue, he added, "If the Umi are in the frigid waters of the Arctic, then they've already spawned. No telling how long it will be until the offspring are ready to be transported to space. We need to find some way to move."

Then an idea struck me. Ten minutes later, I was outside and uploading a video we'd created of Alpha calling to the Predator for help in his own language. I duplicated the audio and set it in a broadcast loop on all frequencies so anyone monitoring would hear. Then I took command of the navigation controls and sent the UAV to Odessa, Texas. At this point, all we could do was wait.

Once we tested the efficacy of the strange bioblock with Pearl's broken EXO and determined that it did deliver power and didn't make the EXO explode, I had everyone jack their EXOs into it for full charge. For morale, I also urged them to get out and clean themselves up. I know that my suit smelled like a pair of gym socks, so I took the opportunity to refresh myself.

I was aware there was a message waiting for me, but I put it off for as long as I could. Finally, with nothing else to do after we'd redistributed all of the ammunition, I climbed back into my EXO and gaze-flicked play on the message. It was in two parts. One was an audio and the other was a video.

Mason, this is Thompson. If you're receiving this, then I am dead. I have one last bit of information to provide before the asteroid hits. The HMID network is officially gone. The 'Crealiacs used our neural connections to network their targets and used them to vector the asteroids. We should have seen this coming. This was definitely our fault. But one thing we were able to do was break into an encrypted message sent from the Chinese to NUSNA. Although the message itself was enigmatic, they intend on partnering forces to try to help defend against something that they refer to as the Spawn. Since they are in league with the 'Crealiac, the Cray are going to leave them alone. This may or may not be significant to you. I just want you to be aware. Now grab your popcorn, sit back, and watch what happens when a ninety meter asteroid impacts my forehead.

The message ended and the packet closed.

Reluctantly, I gaze-flicked play on the video. It must have come from the UAV because the perspective was moving away from Fort Irwin at high speed. I could just make out the shape of the cantonment area and the road leading from it past Painted Rocks to Barstow. After about five seconds, the asteroid entered the picture from the upper left and anticlimactically smashed into the center of the cantonment area. Dust and debris rose in a dark halo that spread outward at impossible speed, past the outer perimeter, sweeping across the open desert, past Painted Rocks, enveloping Barstow, then Yermo. All the while, the view got further and further away as the UAV traveled to my position.

I closed my eyes, not wanting to see anymore, but the impact and its terrible halo replayed in my mind. The more it played, the sicker I felt, until finally I had to run to the door and hurl myself outside. I tore my faceplate aside and vomited into the dirt.

We must be willing to let go of the life we have planned, so as to have the life that is waiting for us.

E. M. Forster

CHAPTER THIRTY-THREE

NIGHT FELL WITHOUT any contact. All we could do was feed ourselves and remain prepared to move. Charlemagne sat with Earl, talking in hushed tones. Olivares and Chance had their heads together. It was clear now that they'd become lovers while I'd been away. Ohirra sat alone, as did Stranz. Both kept their eye on Sykes. Liebl insisted he remain outside so I didn't bother replacing him. We just made sure he had food and his EXO was charged.

Merlin and I sat together on the front steps of the dispensary, staring into the night. Stars winked in the clear sky. I was well aware that I might never see this view again and was determined to take it in. From somewhere, a cricket chirruped.

"I was thinking about what you said to Black Hands Woman," Merlin said, breaking the silence. "About how it's disrespect to feel sorry for yourself when someone you love dies… how you should respect that they died so that you might live."

"Yeah," I didn't feel much like talking, but Merlin hardly ever spoke more than a sentence or two. In fact,

I'd been on hunting trips with him when he'd never said a single word. So when he did speak, it usually meant he needed to convey something important or come to an understanding. "What about it?"

"I don't think that's always true."

I glanced at him. "Okay. So tell me what you think."

"I think there are soldiers like you and Charlemagne who that applies to, but it doesn't apply to civilians... like the people of my village who were doing nothing but surviving, living life, when the Cray came and killed them. I think it's okay to mourn them. I don't think it's disrespect to feel sorry that you won't be around them that they won't be around you.

"I also think it's a matter of perspective," Merlin continued. "If you were to die saving me, I would mourn you. I would feel sorry for me that you weren't around because you enlightened my life. But I feel that way because I am a civilian. I am not a soldier. What you said about feeling sorry for yourself and disrespect applies to soldiers, people whose intent is to lay their lives on the line for others. Not civilians."

He was silent long enough that I knew he was expecting a reply. Without looking at him, I said, "You're probably right. I've been a soldier for so long I've forgotten what it's like to be a civilian. The fact is, we don't have time to feel sorry for ourselves in combat. When we do, it becomes debilitating... self-defeating. I've been under fire at times and been blinded with flashes of my squad mates dying over and over, crippled with convulsions and barely able to move. It's taken well over a decade for me to come to terms with it. You, on the other hand," I turned to him, "never intended to become a soldier. It wasn't until war came to you that you were forced to."

"I wasn't forced," he said. "I chose."

I flashed to my last re-enlistment two times ago, standing in a field beside the Pech River in Konar Province, Afghanistan. By re-enlisting in a war zone, my bonus was tax free. Not that I cared to spend the money; it was just something people did. The Pech River Valley was synecdoche for Afghanistan. It had previously been inhabited by Afghans who spoke the Dardic language Nangalami. They'd lived there for hundreds of years until Safi Pashtuns displaced them during the Soviet Occupation. And now, during the ISAF occupation, Taliban from Pakistan were trying to displace the Safi Pashtuns. I'd been attached to a platoon to protect the artillery guns at Camp Blessing. Instead of setting up a defense, we went on the offensive, constantly on patrol, checking villages for the presence of young men between the ages of sixteen and thirty-five, then interrogating them, especially if they were from out of town. We knew there was a house where they were storing weapons, but we weren't allowed to go near it because of a woman and her two children who lived there. Command was afraid they'd be killed if it was discovered that we knew about the weapons. Likewise, we couldn't just drop a bomb on the place or they might become collateral damage. Ultimately the Taliban positioned a sniper in the house to fire at us every time we left Camp Blessing and every time we returned. This went on for fifty-one days. Each day we'd request to return fire and each day it was denied. I hadn't been in charge then. I was just a corporal, but I remember Schmid getting shot, then a few days later Lee got it, then after that Sandburg took a round in the head. It ricocheted off his helmet, but it scrambled his brains. He began humming the Battle

Hymn of the Republic and wouldn't stop. Every waking moment Sandburg hummed that damned song that the Civil War rebels had called their anthem, and every day we were still getting shot at.

We became a jittery mess. We felt safer out in the valley than entering or leaving base. Finally our platoon sergeant couldn't take it any longer. He faked fire orders and sent a 155 artillery round into the center of the house. We got the sniper. The weapons cache blew to high heaven. We also killed the woman and her two kids. As much as I hated being fired at and as much as I hated the Taliban thumbing their nose at us about their weapons cache, I loathed the fact that the woman and her two children were dead. When I close my eyes I can still see the two boys, five and seven years old, kicking around a beaten old soccer ball in front of their mud hut while the mother sewed blankets out of old rags to be sold at the bazaar. The first time I woke up in a cold sweat was the first time I dreamed I was one of those kids and died in the explosion. I had that dream every night of that deployment, and it didn't go away until I'd redeployed and a doctor gave me Ambien.

I wasn't sure why I thought of that just now. I guess because the poor woman and her children were a lot like the people of Savoonga. They didn't choose war. War chose them.

"I've also been thinking about the origin story of the Khron," Merlin said. He hadn't noticed the cold sweat that had beaded on my face so I wiped it away. "It seems as if both the Umi and the Khron were always destined to meet. After all, they both required the same conditions within which to live. The problem was that for whatever reason they couldn't leave each other alone.

You have to wonder. Did the Umi arrive on that first home world with all these other species, the Cray, the spore, the Sirens? Or did the Khron continually attack them, necessitating the symbiosis of these species?"

"You mean, did we cause the problem to ourselves?" I summarized.

"Yes, and when I say ourselves, I mean the first Khron."

"You're suddenly very philosophical, Merlin," I said. "What's really going on?"

"I've come to realize some things."

"Go on."

"First, I am not a soldier." He shook his head. "I actually suck at it. Those mechanical dogs destroyed the spidertank you gave me. I should have been able to defeat them easily, but I was overwhelmed with sensory overload."

"That sort of stuff happens in battle."

"Does it happen to you?" he asked.

"Well, no, but I've been in combat off and on for the last fifteen years."

He stared at me firmly. "Because you're a soldier."

"Okay, I get it. What's the second thing?"

"Revenge isn't who I am. I'm angry for what happened to my people, but revenge isn't what I feel."

"What is it you feel?"

"This goes back to our beliefs. Do I believe this happened because I killed the Orca? Do I blame this on Raven? No, but I do believe there is a balancing in the universe that we cannot ken. Maybe we just don't understand it."

"So you're saying that the Cray are the universe's agents of action."

"I'm not sure what I'm saying, but I know in my heart," he said, pounding his chest, "that to fight against the universe is not the right way."

I didn't agree with Merlin at all, but then we didn't share the same belief systems. I couldn't count how many times I'd heard the phrase *It's God's will*, when I was growing up, usually when something bad happened to someone. *We can't begin to understand what God's plan is*, others said. This had always enraged me, especially when someone said it with regards to a dead or hurt child, or some travesty that could have been avoided. Half of the continent of Africa was filled with starving families, disease run amok, and child soldiers chopping off the arms of innocents—but it was God's will. This wasn't so different than what Merlin was saying. It was a struggle not to argue with him, but to ruin his belief system was to ruin the man.

"Anything else?" I asked.

"Yes, one more thing. There has to be someone left."

I yanked my head around and stared at him. "What do you mean?"

He waved a hand to the sky. "All the soldiers, all the fighting, all the Khron versus Umi eternal war. After all that leaves the planet, there has to be something left. There has to be people left to rebuild, to keep the story alive."

This was the sane version of what Saxton had been trying to say. It began to dawn on me where he was going.

"I think I'm going to go home," he said finally.

And there it was. "When?"

"Tomorrow morning."

"How do you plan on getting there? Utah is a hell of a long way from Prince Edward Island."

He shrugged. "I'll do it the old-fashioned way," he said. "I'll walk."

"All the way home?"

"Hopefully."

"But your leg..."

He shrugged, holding his father's aangruyak. "This will be my third leg. My father and his father before him will help get me home."

I sat and thought about it, and the more it rolled around in my mind, the better it felt. I'd felt an awkward responsibility for Merlin ever since I'd taken him from Savoonga. And he was right, he wasn't much of a soldier. If he stayed, it was more than likely he would die. We all might die for that matter. Did he realize this? Was that why he was doing this, out of self-preservation? Out of fear? But as soon as I asked myself those questions I also knew the answer didn't matter. Everyone has to come to terms with their own mortality and their own place in the universe. Ever since I'd first strapped on a tactical harness, I'd known I was made for combat. Merlin was made to lead. My guess was that his tribe was lost without him, or at the very least, would benefit from his return.

I held out a hand. "I wish you well, my brother."

He slapped aside my hand and grabbed me in a bear hug.

"You as well, brother."

He stood and turned to go back inside. "I'm going to tell the others. I owe them that much," he said.

I watched him depart, then returned my vigil to the sky. My heart was wide open and felt airy with anticipation. A battle was coming. The end game was near. I was itching to be a part of it. The very idea of the great unknown exited me. Everything that had transpired since the moment Mr. Pink had recruited us came down to this—everything in between had been merely steps to understand, to survive, and to prepare. Those of us who were left were the very best and it was going to take all of us to win the day... if there was a day to actually be won.

I sat like that until midnight, chilled by the night air, shivering on the steps. Only then, did I go back inside where I found a place to bed down. Once I warmed up, I fell asleep and dreamed of two boys playing soccer until the Umi came and changed their lives.

As we know, forgiveness of oneself is the hardest of all the forgivenesses.

Joan Baez

CHAPTER THIRTY-FOUR

THEY WOKE ME for breakfast at nine in the morning. I'd been using one blanket as a pillow and had the other wrapped around me. I stood, stretching, achy from the night on the floor. There was still no contact. I cleaned myself in the bathroom, then accepted a cup of coffee from Chance. We were all still in our skivvies, but the dispensary was warm enough that we weren't cold. To us, it was just another barracks room.

Merlin had acquired a backpack and a rifle, and was sitting and talking to the Doctor and his daughter. Earl stood beside them, listening, his eyes on the young woman. The bruising on her face was almost a black-purple, which told me it was two or three days old. Soon, it would turn green, then yellow. But that was on the surface. What Picket had done to her was etched into her soul.

Fucking humanity. Sometimes I hated who we were.

I stood, sipping my coffee, when Ohirra came up.

"What's our status?" I asked.

"Liebl's gone."

"How do you know?"

"EXO is outside, empty."

"He never was one of us, really. Probably doesn't want to do this next part."

She grinned. "I don't think any of us want to do this next part." She glanced at Alpha, who sat in a corner, his chin resting on steepled fingers. "But this is the end game. It's been played out before. We're just along for the ride." She turned to go, then remembered something. "Oh, Sykes wants to talk to you."

"Know what about?"

"He's a scared kid, Mason."

"Doesn't excuse what happened."

"I know. Still, he wants to talk."

I sighed, blew steam off the surface of my coffee, and took another sip. Drawing the blanket around my shoulders with one hand and carrying the mug in the other, I went into the examination room Stranz had placed Sykes in. He sat in a chair, his hands tied behind him. I regarded him.

His wide round eyes were pools of fear. His lip trembled. A trail of snot ran from one nostril. He'd been put in doctor's scrubs and they accentuated his almost frail features.

I put the coffee cup down on the sink, snatched a tissue from the dispenser, and wiped his nose. After throwing the tissue away, I retrieved my coffee, leaned against the sink and asked, "You wanted to see me?"

He nodded. "Wha—what's going to happen to me?"

"What do you think should happen to you?" I took a sip of coffee, relishing its hot bitterness. Whether it was in a Starbucks at Fort Bragg or a cup of instant java in a firebase, coffee was super food for any soldier. When Sykes didn't answer right away, I added, "Martial law is in effect. The local commander has jurisdiction over all civil and military crimes."

"Loc-local command—commander?" he asked, his high voice breaking.

"Which would be me, Lieutenant Ben Mason, Planet Earth."

"But I did—didn't do—"

"Anything to stop, Picket." I took a quick sip. "I know. That doesn't show very well for you. I'm going to have to weigh your inaction."

"But he would have killed me," he managed.

I shook my head. "You don't know that. You might have killed him. You might have found a way to get the upper hand, say when he was raping that poor girl and his back was to you." I pointed at him with my cup. "Then, maybe."

His eyes became haunted with the opportunities he'd missed through inaction, either out of fear or out of a strange voyeuristic need.

"Where are you from?" I asked.

"NUSNA."

"No, before the invasion Where did you live?"

"York, Pennsylvania. I lived with my uncle on the Susquehanna River."

"Was your uncle a good man?"

"I think so," he said.

"What happened to him?"

"He was shot by some marauders."

"Trying to steal your food?"

He nodded. "He died protecting me."

"What'd they do with you?"

He turned away and stared at the wall.

I'm just not surprised anymore at man's capacity to do harm. Still, I could see what happened like I'd been there, the same greedy disregard for humanity and insatiable need to be fulfilled that Picket had were probably a raging fire of desire in the eyes of the marauders. Still, I wanted the kid to face the memory.

"What'd they do to you?" I asked again.

"They didn't even take me into a bedroom," he said, his voice raw and low. "The whole time I stared at my uncle's face. His eyes were open and he was looking at me and—" He wiped a tear away. "It was like he was ashamed of me."

"He wasn't ashamed of you, son. He was dead. The dead have no emotions."

After a few moments, Sykes said, "I know that in here," he said, chin pointing toward his chest. "I just can't get it into my brain."

"We've all seen and done things that are terrible. You just have to realize which ones you can own and which ones you can't." I went to take a sip of the coffee, but it suddenly tasted too bitter. I poured it down the sink and placed the mug off to the side. "Let me ask you, did you want to stop Picket?"

"Desperately," he breathed.

I nodded and stood there for a good five minutes, watching him as he stared at the wall, life replaying over and over in the horror show of his mind. Finally, I grabbed my cup and turned to leave.

He looked up. "What are you going to do with me?"

I paused. "What is it you want me to do?"

"Part of me wants you to kill me. Then I can stop seeing it over and over. I can stop seeing my uncle's eyes."

"I think you'll live."

"What do you mean?"

"Living seems to be punishment enough. You've locked yourself in your own prison. I don't know how long the term will be, but eventually you'll find the key and let yourself out. Until then, it's your uncle's eyes."

I walked out of the room.

No one gets a free pass at the end of the world.

Ohirra was waiting for me when I came out. "So what'd he want?"

"To be forgiven. To forget."

"Did you help him?"

"A thing like that can't be helped. It needs to work itself out."

She nodded and turned to watch Chance and Olivares, who seemed to be sharing a joke. It gave me the opportunity to look at her, really look at her, not as a fellow officer but as a woman. It occurred to me that while I'd seen plenty of my fellow grunts hook up, I hadn't seen her with a man or a woman other than at official functions.

"What about you, Ohirra?" I asked.

"What about me?"

"You and I have known each other since the first time you kicked Olivares's ass on the mat. I had my thing with Michelle. Olivares has something cooking with Chance. But I've never seen you with anyone."

"What, you want me to find love at the end of the world?" She snickered. "It's not like I have much to choose from."

"It's just that, well…"

She put a hand on her and, with raised eyebrows, said, "What are you proposing?"

I cleared my throat. I could feel my face reddening. "No. I mean I would, but you're like a sister to me."

She punched me lightly in the chest. Then her face got serious. "You know I like girls, right?"

Now it was my turn to raise my eyebrows. "I had no idea, not that it is any of my business." This slender Japanese jujitsu master and former U.S. Marine was an anachronism. She'd never killed anyone in combat before the invasion and hadn't even seen enemy fire. But she had killed a family of five after one bad decision involving drinking and driving.

"You remember what I did?"

"I remember."

She sighed. "How could I be with someone when I deprived five people of their lives? A relationship was the last thing I cared about. It seemed ridiculous, really."

"Your drive, your need to be the best..."

"Is for them," she said, angrily swiping at a sudden tear in the corner of her eye.

"Listen, Ohirra, I didn't want to pick a scab. I just wanted to make sure you were good. So much happens so fast. I didn't want to forget about you." I grabbed her shoulder. "You and me were there at the beginning."

"And we're about to be to the end."

"What are you two whispering about?" Olivares asked, coming up on us. "You conspiring to leave me here?"

"You could stay if you wanted," I said.

He glanced at Chance and I could see him living a lifetime in his eyes, but it was someone else's life. "Nah. We weren't made for a house and a white fence. Three hots and a cot is what makes us happy." He turned his gaze back to us. "What is it you're really talking about? Why is little Ms. Badass crying?"

I gave him a genuine smile. "Just making sure little Ms. Badass is okay."

"Funny way to make sure she's okay. It usually

doesn't involve crying. Or have I been doing it wrong all this time?"

Ohirra wiped at her eyes. "I'm fine, you two. Just stay focused on the mission."

"Ohirra," I said, waiting for her to look at me.

"What?"

"I'm proud that you're by my side."

She punched me again in the chest. "Oh shut up." Then she walked away.

Olivares nodded to me and I nodded back, then he returned to where he'd been sitting with Chance. I wonder if she'd ever know that he'd been given the opportunity to stay. Would she have wanted it? Or was she the type to go out fighting like Ohirra?

Earl sidled up to me.

We'd buried his sister last night. Doctor Paul had pulled out a bottle of whiskey and let the boy have it. He didn't seem too worse for wear, but the circles under his eyes were dark enough I could fall into them.

"Mind if I have a word, sir?" he asked.

It seemed like everyone had something they needed to talk about. I nodded to him. "How are you feeling?"

"About the way someone feels when they lose a twin."

I remained silent, because there was absolutely nothing to say.

"We've been by each other's side since the invasion. The only time we weren't was during Phase I training, but even then she was in the cell next to mine. It's like cutting off a limb. It hurts," he said, pointing to his chest, "but it hurts in here."

"I never had any brothers or sisters."

"It wasn't all wine and roses. She could be such an asshole sometimes. But you know, she was my sister.

She was *my* asshole."

"I've had fellow soldiers I felt that way about," I said, looking at Olivares. "Probably not as intense a feeling, but something I can relate to what you're feeling."

"What is it we're going to do next?" he asked.

"Fight. Somehow we're going to link up with the Khron and fight the Umi."

"But why?" He licked his lips. "I mean, if they're just going to leave now and let us have the planet back, why not just sit back and wait?"

"It's the principle of it, Earl. We don't let strangers come into our house, piss on the furniture, fuck the family dog, and then leave without us doing something about it. We couldn't stop the Umi, but we can make them pay."

"So is that what this is about? Revenge?"

I eyed him for a long moment. This was the second person who didn't seem to believe revenge was a good enough reason to fight. "Maybe. Is that such a bad reason to fight?"

"You know Merlin is returning home," he said.

"I know. He asked to leave and I let him." I paused for a moment. "Is that what you want? To go with him?"

"Part of me does, but another part of me wants to get revenge, too."

"Conflicting feelings."

"What should I do, sir?"

"What would your sister say if you asked her the same thing?"

"I don't know."

"Would she want you to avenge her?"

"If she did, then it would be against NUSNA instead of the Umi or the Cray." He shook his head, looking lost. "I just don't know."

I put a hand on his shoulder. "Well, when you figure it out, you'll know."

I took a chair and slid it over to where Paul and Nancy were sitting with Merlin. "You guys going to go with Merlin?"

"We talked about it," Doc Paul said, "But we've lived all of our life here. This is our home."

"The town looks deserted," I said.

"There are still a few hardcore folks who want to tough it out. Been living on canned food, trout from the river, and wild game. They come by when they need fixing up. If I was to leave, they'd have no one." Then he pointed to the floor. "Plus, down there we have enough rations to feed a battalion for ten years. Even if we don't trade for fresh meat and vegetables, we'll have enough food and water to survive anything."

To Merlin, I said, "See you found a pack and a rifle."

Merlin grinned. "They have an entire armory down there, complete with clothes and equipment."

"That's good. No shortage of ammunition. How long do you think it will take you to get home?"

"It's about a thousand miles to Seattle. I thought once I hit the coast, I'd try and find a boat. If not, then it's another two thousand miles to Nome. By that point, I'll definitely need water transportation." As he spoke there was a light in his eyes that had been missing for some time.

"You look excited about going."

"I am excited. I was made to do this." Then his expression turned serious. "But what about you, brother? I don't want to let you down."

"You're not letting anyone down. You're what we're fighting for. The world might never be the same, but it will be our world, nonetheless."

"Thank you," came a small withered voice.

I turned to Nancy. It was the first time I'd heard her speak.

"No problem," I said.

"No, for everything. Not just..." She didn't finish.

I wanted to put my hand on her shoulder. I wanted to hold her hand. I wanted her body to understand that there were men she could trust, men who wouldn't do those things to her, but I knew if I did, she'd jerk away, her mind reliving moments I wanted her to forget.

"It's fine," I said softly. "There are more men like me out there than men like him," I said, not needing to explain who *he* was.

She stared at me with eyes as haunted as Sykes's.

I offered her a smile, then turned to her father. "Can I have a word?"

He nodded, patted his daughter's knee, then followed me to the other side of the room. Merlin watched us for a moment, then decided to join us. I did nothing to stop him.

"What is it?" Doctor Paul asked.

"The kid. Sykes."

The doctor's eyes narrowed. "What about him?"

"I don't know what to do with him. I'm not taking him with me."

"You shouldn't leave him here," Doctor Paul said. "He'll be a living reminder to my daughter of what happened."

"I realize that. I just don't know what to do." I paused, then added, "The same thing happened to him back in Pennsylvania. He was..." I didn't need to finish.

The doctor shook his head. "I feel bad for him, truly I do, both from a clinical and personal perspective. But that doesn't change my opinion."

"It wasn't meant to," I said. "I just wanted you to know."

"I'll take him with me," Merlin said.

We both turned to stare at him.

"Why would you do that?"

"If I want to start rebuilding the world, I should start now." He inclined his chin toward the room where Sykes was being held. "He's part of it."

As much as I appreciated Merlin's desire, I didn't know if I could trust the kid not to do something to my old friend. Then again, it was Merlin's choice and who was I to infringe upon it? I felt my shoulders sag. "If that's how you truly feel, then okay. Just don't think I intended for you to be his caretaker."

"I won't be his caretaker. But I will be his fellow traveler."

Doctor Paul shuffled off to find his daughter.

I was about to say something else to Merlin when Alpha suddenly got to his feet.

"They're here," he said.

PART THREE

The most exciting phrase to hear in science, the one that heralds new discoveries, is not 'Eureka!' but 'That's funny...'

Isaac Asimov

CHAPTER THIRTY-FIVE

WE ALL HURRIED into our EXOs, then went outside eager, to see who exactly was arriving. Even Paul and Nancy followed. But when we got outside all we saw was blue sky and mountains. We looked at each other, wondering what we were supposed to see.

"Where are they?" I asked.

"They're being a little dramatic." He nodded as if talking to himself, then turned to me. "Permission to contact you via neural link."

"Via neural... like in my head?"

"Yes. Like you had with your HMIDs."

I wasn't used to being asked. Normally Thompson or one of the other HMIDs would stomp around in my brain without a care in the world. "Okay. I guess it's fine."

Then...

You are commander of this force, came a computer-sounding voice.

I am Lieutenant Benjamin Carter Mason of OMBRA Special Forces Division. I have six EXOs that require transport as well as two of your own, one deceased.

We are Khron Semfled Fourteen.

To Alpha, I asked, "What's a semfled?"

"Military flight consisting of three Vipers."

*We have been assigned to transport you to Odessa
Base and to prepare you for follow on attack mission.*

Oh yippee. *Let's get on with it.*

"What's going on?" Olivares asked. "You talking to
someone? Thompson? Salinas?"

"Something like them," I said out loud.

"Switch view to thermal imaging," Ohirra said.
"There are three saucers to your twelve."

Before I could switch, three space craft appeared fifty
feet in front of us and about fifty feet off the ground.
They were the same as the one I'd previously seen. Donut
shaped and about the size of a house, their skin was
constantly moving in circles around the circumference
of the machine except for a section on the bottom.
Weapons bristled out of the top, while what looked like
sensors circled the base.

"Now that's cool. Cloaking device," Earl said.

"Ferrofluids," Alpha corrected as he beamed at the
space craft. "But does the same thing." He chuckled.
"Just love all the *Star Trek* references."

All three craft set down on the tarmac and were
temporarily lost from view.

I thought about dispersing my EXOs but I didn't want
to do anything that might precipitate violence, so I just
waited. It wasn't long before a single Khron rounded a
corner from the airfield. He looked a lot like Alpha. He
looked like... one of us.

Alpha stepped forward.

I noted that they were about the same height. In fact,
they could have been related, grandfather and grandson.
The newcomer wore a flat black jump suit with pockets

on the arms and legs. He wore the same black metal band around his neck as I'd seen in the Arctic. He carried a case with him.

"Greetings, 3962," the newcomer said in perfect American English, holding his hand open, palm up.

Alpha mimicked the move and said, "Greetings to you, 3964."

Then it hit me. They were both clones, only Alpha had been the one to age. I wondered vaguely what happened to 3963. Then the number hit me. It meant that there had been 3964 instances of a Khron watching the status of Earth. To think that far back in time was incredible. They'd been watching Earth before the first man wrote the first word in the first language. I suddenly felt incredibly insignificant.

The newcomer handed the case to Alpha, who then turned to me.

"You need to put these on," he said, opening the case. Inside were seven black metal bands identical to the one worn by 3964.

I remembered when we postulated that they were slave circlets like the thralls wore in *Star Trek* episode. Although the newcomer wore one, Alpha didn't.

"I don't know what those are," I said.

"Neural interceptor device. They have three functions once paired with an individual. They provide access to the Neural Net to those who had not been given the spore. They also translate all known Khron languages. And finally, but most importantly, they block Umi takeover."

"Only those three? Does it also keep track of us?"

"All connections to a planetside Neural Net are logged and geotagged."

"I don't think so," Olivares said. "Looks too much like a slave collar."

"I assure you that this is nothing of the sort. Your EXOs function as a moveable weapons platform, but are they not capable of providing command and control your location as well? This is a standard concept."

I wasn't at all thrilled with the idea of putting some strange alien tech around my neck, not that I wasn't a believer in all that Alpha had told us with regards to the Khron and the Umi.

"I don't think we'll be able to comply," I said.

Alpha's face grew serious. "But you have to. The Khron does not allow partner species to co-exist without the wearing of NIDs. The chance that Umi could be using you is too great. The consequences are too dire."

"Won't do it," I said.

The two clones conferred for a full minute. It was clear that Alpha was arguing on our behalf, but the other clone wouldn't be moved. Finally, Alpha turned back to me.

"Listen, Mason, there's just no other way. Every single human who is helping the Khron is wearing one."

"That argument isn't helping your position," I said. "That you've convinced everyone else to do something possibly detrimental to their health doesn't make it any more logical for me to do the same thing."

"If your primary concern is to protect someone against Umi takeover, then those who haven't been exposed to the spore need not wear it," Ohirra pointed out. "Neither Earl nor Chance have been exposed to the spore."

Alpha wiped a hand across his face and shook his head. "I did not anticipate this." He looked at me imploringly. "I know we don't really know each other so my word means very little, but this is not something we should be arguing about. The NID is meant to join Khron, to allow them to work together without fear of takeover. It's not something nefarious."

I got on private chat with Olivares and Ohirra. "So what do you think?"

"Everything he said makes sense," Ohirra said.

"I just don't like putting myself in a position to be controlled," Olivares said.

"I agree. It's too much like OMBRA," I said.

"And look where that got us," Olivares said.

"So this is where an irresistible force meets an immovable object," I said. "If we don't do it, we're out of the fight. If we do, then we're placing ourselves at the mercy of the Khron." I turned to look at Merlin and the doctor and his daughter. "I want to fight."

Ohirra said, "What if we wear them, but Chance and Earl don't. Think they'd go for that?"

To Alpha I said, "Okay, here's our plan. Those of us who were exposed to the spore will wear them. But the two who weren't, won't. We'll pass any and all information to them."

3964 said something to Alpha, and when Alpha turned I said, "If he wants to say something, why not just say it to us? I know he speaks our language."

3964 sighed. "How can we trust that you aren't deceiving us regarding who has been exposed to the spore and who hasn't?"

"The same way we're supposed to trust you that nothing nefarious is going on with the NIDs."

3964 stared at me for a cold minute. Then he nodded his head. "So be it."

We spent a few moments wrangling our helmets off to get the NIDs around our necks. They were small enough that we could wear them without interference. When I put mine on I felt an immediate connection to something broader, something bigger. I could hear what sounded like a constant buzz just on the edge of hearing. Then it grew louder and louder, becoming an almost painful static. Finally the static bled away and followed by the words, "NID Pairing Successful" in what sounded like a young woman's voice with an English accent.

I didn't feel any different. I hoped that I'd made the right decision.

"Can we go?" I asked Alpha, who was now also wearing an NID.

When he nodded, I turned around to say my goodbyes. I gave both Nancy and Paul a warm smile and thanked them for fixing me up. I told Merlin to be safe and that I'd try and come see him when everything was over. We weren't about to leave Leibl's armor behind, so Alpha climbed in and with a little guidance was operating it with ease. All of us marched to the tarmac where the three ships hovered just above the ground. Olivares and Chance were set to go on one. Ohirra and Charlemagne would go on the other, and Earl and I would travel in the third along with Alpha. Bravo's remains would be shipped in the first ship along with 3964.

Standing in front of the ships, I wondered how we were supposed to get inside. Then the side of the ship closest to us slid open and a ramp descended.

We started making our way aboard ship. I was halfway up the ramp when Earl stopped me.

"Sir, I'm not going."

I paused. "Did you figure out what your sister would have wanted you to do?"

"We'd never planned on being soldiers, you know. We were just kids."

"But you're soldiers now," I corrected.

"Not really. This was all just a game. The suits made us invincible, or so we thought. Strapping them on felt like a level-capped Pandaran Death Knight From *World of Warcraft's* Warlords of Draenor expansion set. There was nothing we couldn't fight. Then you made us stop being characters in our own first person shooters. You made us be us and kill being us. It became different. I was happy when I was playing Ender's game, but you made us responsible." He paused to breathe. "I just can't be responsible."

"Maybe that was my mistake, opening your eyes."

"No, I realize now that there are consequences. I've done some things I can't unsee, that I can't undo. But I wish I'd never done any of it."

"That's how we all feel."

"But you're soldiers," he said. "I'm no soldier. I'm just a kid playing at games, you said so yourself." He sighed. "My sister would have wanted me to go back to being a kid if I could. Now I have that chance. That chance for things to be normal once more."

"Things can never be normal, son."

"They'll be more normal with Merlin. Plus, he can't make the journey alone. He needs someone... someone like me."

I'd given him the opportunity to leave and wasn't about to take it back, but I had to ask, "So you feel no need to avenge her death?"

"No. No matter who I kill, no matter how many I kill, it won't bring her back. Revenge is a hollow panacea."

"Okay, son. You go do what needs to be done."

He went inside the spacecraft and slid out of his EXO, ran back down the ramp and across the tarmac. I had no doubt Merlin would appreciate the company, especially considering he was taking Sykes with him as well. That Earl was going too actually made me feel better.

Then I stepped into my very first UFO.

> Everything is theoretically impossible, until it is done.
>
> Robert A. Heinlein

CHAPTER THIRTY-SIX

THE INTERIOR WAS both more and less spacious than I'd imagined, probably because of the extra bulk from three EXOs. The area to the right of the door was filled with metal boxes stacked to the ceiling. The area to the left held a low slung couch. Alpha pressed a pad above the couch and it merged with the wall and disappeared, leaving a flat surface. Alpha had me press my back against the wall and I immediately felt it engage around my suit. I tried to pull away and found that while I could, it wasn't easy. Probably necessary to keep things in place. Alpha slid beside me, then got out of the EXO and left it parked. I exited my EXO then took a moment to park Earl's EXO as well.

Alpha invited me to the front where another low slung couch hugged the floor. Before it were a series of controls right out of something I'd seen in countless sci-fi movies, including a holographic display. They were at once familiar and not familiar, but I had no doubt that they controlled the craft. Sitting in a webbed cradle above this was another man, dressed similar to Alpha's clone. My guess was the pilot.

He turned to greet me. His mouth moved in a strange

manner and his words were unrecognizable, but in my brain I heard, *Welcome, Earthling,* and then he laughed.

I might have laughed as well, but I couldn't stop looking at his eyes, which were at least three times larger than my own. Add that he didn't have eyelids, but a nictating membrane like a snake. If it weren't for the eyes, he'd have looked completely human.

It spoke again. *It's not polite to stare.*

I coughed. "Uh, sorry. I just—I didn't—sorry." I averted my gaze and glanced at Alpha, who was smiling.

"Our pilot is from what you would call Epsilon Eridani, which is about ten and a half light years from here. His planet is remarkably like yours and mine, except it has a luminosity of less than thirty percent of your star, necessitating the evolutionary characteristic you see here."

He means to say I have bug eyes.

"I didn't mean anything of the sort," Alpha said.

You two need to strap into the crash couch so we can get moving.

Alpha reached down to the couch and pulled at it, stretching a piece around one hip and attaching it back to the couch above the opposite shoulder. Then he did the same on the other side, creating an X across his chest, affixing himself to the couch.

It took several tries, but I managed to do the same, all the while amazed at the stretch and stickiness of the unknown substance that made up the couch.

A sensation of movement suddenly made me dizzy as an oval view screen opened in front of me—correction, a display of some sort. I could just tell that it wasn't an actual port by the ever so slight out of focus edges. I tried to detect a spin but couldn't, so I asked Alpha about it.

"Why would you believe we're spinning?" he asked. Then he nodded. "Ahh, the movies. The Viper is not one of your flying saucers. It does not spin, although the ferrofluids on its outer surface give it that appearance."

"What's a ferrofluid?"

"The Viper has three layers of ferrofluid. The layer closest to the skin of the ship is a thick layer of magnetorheological fluid that can stiffened to a solid to protect the Viper from physical damage, such as meteorites and missiles. The middle layer is the thickest, and is a magnetic ionic fluid that actually provides the Viper's atmospheric propulsion. The top layer, the thinnest, is a ferrofluid made with reflective magnetic nanoparticles which can be tuned to pass light, etc. from one side of the craft to the other to give the ship the appearance of being transparent.

"Ferrofluids themselves use nanoparticles of magnetic material coated in a surfactant to prevent clumping and suspended in a viscous fluid. Magnetorheological fluids use larger particles and so are not permanently suspended in the oil, but give it the property of becoming almost solid in the presence of a strong magnetic field. Finally, Magnetic Ionic Fluids—the basic molecular structure of this fluid has a magnetic component, so the liquid itself responds to the magnetic field like a ferrofluid, not just the nanoparticles suspended in the liquid.

"Atmospheric propulsion is generated by a changing magnetic field that creates what you would call turbine blades of magnetic fluid that project from the skin and appear to move along it in a way to produce propulsion by pushing the air. For stability's sake, the fluid along the inner surface propels in the opposite direction of that on the outer surface. Both the inner and outer skins do this in opposite directions for stability reasons. We can adjust the blade patterns to gain and reduce speed."

My eyes were following our dizzying path on the display as Alpha gave the science lesson. I couldn't understand half of what he said. All I know is it had something to do with magnetic fluids that could be programmed and controlled, which was pretty astonishing. The crash couch hugged me in such a way that I could barely feel the turns and movement. The only way I could really tell anything was by watching the pilot, whose cradle moved left or right depending on the pitch of the ship.

"How fast are we going?" I asked.

"Two thousand miles an hour," the pilot said.

I could only imagine the string of sonic booms we were leaving behind. The speed was beyond comprehension.

"We will arrive at the destination in thirty-two minutes."

"Odessa, Texas?"

"Yes. That is our destination."

I was astonished at the speed. I watched the terrain race by below.

"What's your name?"

The pilot said, "Me?"

"Yes, please."

After a moment, he said, "You can call me Jarn."

"Jarn, can you tell me about what happened on your planet?"

"Before my time," was all he said, but I waited. After a minute he answered. "The Umi did much the same to your planet as they did to mine. The Home, as we called it, had about a quarter of the ocean water Earth has. On one hand that was a good thing, because far less Umi were being bred and the Khron responders were able to stop the Umi from leaving the planet. But on the other, The Home was twenty-five percent smaller than Earth and our population was far less, especially the survivors. We hadn't developed your level of technology either."

"Then how did you fight the Umi?"

"Fission bombs... slightly more powerful than you used on Japan."

World War II? That put their technology a good seventy years back. I never thought of other planets being invaded at different times, but of course it made sense. I could only imagine if the Cray had come three thousand years ago. We might never have known.

"So you found out where the Umi were going to be taken off planet?"

"No, we used the fission bombs on everything. Every Cray hive. Every Leviathan we came across. Every instance of the vine that carried the zombie spore. Everything."

"Everything?" And then it dawned on me what he was saying. Imagine if we'd nuclear-detonated every instance of every hive. Every single major urban area would be so irradiated it would be unlivable. I remembered studying something about a nuclear winter in school, as a possible result of the Cold War idea of mutually assured destruction. The temperature would drop and the sky would be covered with thick layers of ash for decades.

"So your planet..."

"We destroyed it. In destroying the invasion, we destroyed everything else. Less than five percent of our population survived and were removed from The Home. For us, The Home is dead."

"How long has it been since this happened?"

"Mine was the last planet the Umi attacked before Earth."

"So you don't have memories of The Home."

"I do. We all do. Those of us who survived still remember like it was yesterday."

Alpha answered for him. "Clones. All of us are clones."

"You mean there's not a real one amongst you?"

Alpha frowned. "I take umbrage at that. I'm as real as the Prime Version. The single exception is that I have had experiences that Prime has not."

I held out a hand. "Wait a moment. You are a clone and have the memories of the original person who was cloned? How is that possible?"

"Look at your HMIDs and the Umi's AMIDs. Once that level of technology is derived it's not so difficult to determine a method of downloading consciousness. Everything else after that is just quality control and efficiency."

"The distances in space are too vast," the pilot added, "for us to have anything close to families or social relationships. During the long chase, we live aboard our Kaleidoscope Ships with three versions of ourselves in varying degrees of age acceleration. When it's time for one of us to age out, we download additional memories to the stored consciousness, enabling the new version to know what has gone on from the inception of Prime to the most recent version."

"So your memory can span thousands of years."

"It does span thousands of years, but between final contact with the Umi and newest contact with the Umi, all versions are in stasis."

"So none of you were alive—by that I mean walking around, breathing and eating—until we were invaded?"

"We missed the invasion. My age in date began three months ago," the pilot said.

"And when this is all over, you're going to age out?"

"Some of us might elect to stay on Earth and live out a normal life, but that's after we download consciousness. Your world might still be habitable and many of the Khron would like to find a home again."

"And you? Jarn? What about you?"

"Your planet is intriguing. It takes the Home twenty-five hundred years to circle our sun, which means the ideas of seasons is a mythology to us. To live through the change of four seasons sounds like a miraculous concept. I might do that just to see snow fall."

I tried to imagine a year that was twenty-five hundred years long and couldn't. As if all the recorded time were encapsulated in a single cycle. The perspective that must give someone was incredible.

I laughed a little. I didn't mean to, but the observation I'd unintentionally made was too ironic not to.

"What is it?" Jarn asked.

"What's so funny?" Alpha asked.

"It's nothing," I said.

Alpha raised an eyebrow. "No, please tell us."

"Well, it's just ironic, you know?" I spoke slowly and carefully because I was feeling like Captain Obvious and I hated being that guy. "It's just that the Umi have succeeded in making you task made as well as purpose made. The Cray were made for a task. The Sirens were made for a task. The Spore was made for a task. Now you, their aggressor, the Khron—they have forced you to completely abandon your way of life in order to fight them. You don't even live anymore. All you do is create new versions of your old selves when it's time to fight, then kill the version of yourself when it's time to chase."

Both Jarn and Alpha were silent for a time. It was Jarn who broke the silence.

"Selected elements of your species will be invited to join the chase. If you survive what's coming, you can decide whether you want revenge, whether you want to stop the Umi once and for all, or whether you want to live a pastoral life on your own ruined planet."

I noticed that Alpha stared straight ahead and didn't say a thing.

"You make it sound so romantic," I murmured, realizing that I might soon be just like them.

None of us said another word until Odessa came into view. What I saw then made my jaw drop farther than anything else I'd ever seen.

Molon Labe.

King Leonidas of Sparta

CHAPTER THIRTY-SEVEN

AN IMMENSE SPACECRAFT perched in the middle of what used to be an oilfield, the derricks now dilapidated, metal remembrances of what used to drive the planet. Or at least I thought it was a spaceship—hundreds of meters high, it bristled with dozens of long, thin sharp objects. I wasn't sure if they were antenna or weapons or both. Narrow to the point of looking brittle, the ship squatted menacingly in the center of chaotic action. The air swarmed with Vipers coming and going. I could make out thousands of EXOs of various shapes and sizes on the ground. The vast majority were either older model OMBRA EXOs or my newer model. I even spotted the occasional EXO that was appreciably taller than even mine, but seemed to lack much of the bulk.

"It's a drop ship," said the pilot. "It was built en route to provide a logistics base for our weapons systems and to assist you Earthlings in obtaining the necessary war supplies you need to stop the Umi."

"You're going to fight alongside us, right?"

"Definitely," Alpha said. "But all the fights you've had before will be nothing compared to what's about to happen."

"Is the drop ship coming with us? Those look like serious weapons."

"It will never leave this spot. It was designed to ferry supplies from orbit to the planet's surface. Once in place, it becomes the base of operations. Five of these have landed on Earth. There's this one. There's one in Kursk, Russia; Sify, Congo; Haixi, China; and Primovera de Leste, Brazil. Each is designed to focus and attract friendly forces so that we can create an organized, aggressive, and focused force."

"Do we know where the Umi offspring have congregated?" I asked.

"We're following a large concentration in Sydney Harbor, and we're still searching. There may be more. Your planet has so much water we can't be sure."

Jarn landed the Viper.

Alpha stood. "Time for us to leave." He climbed into the EXO he'd worn.

I climbed into my own.

Then the wall slid aside and we descended the ramp.

It was absolute chaos at ground level, but it was my kind of chaos. EXOs ran in groups and as singletons back and forth across the space. Here and there an immense three meter tall EXO stalked ponderously. These were the much lauded *Thinnies* who required the EXOs not for combat but for sheer survival, the metal and silicon construct allowing their bodies to survive the gravity of our planet. Meanwhile Vipers flew unknown missions above us, sometimes disgorging other EXOs, sometimes uniformed soldiers.

I tracked down the rest of Hero Squad and sent them a message to form on me.

Ohirra and Stranz came first, followed by Olivares, Chance, and Charlemagne.

"This eez not ze Alamo," the former legionnaire said.

"No, it's not," I said. "This is Odessa. The middle of Texas nowhere. But as out of the way as it is, it's allowing us to prepare to defeat the Umi before they can scurry off."

Stranz nodded as he grinned, his gaze wandering across all the activity. "This is what I'm talking about."

Alpha was still standing with us.

"I have nowhere else to go. All the other functions are handled so I thought I might fight with you, if you don't mind."

I didn't mind, but I had to ask the team. They assented and we gave Alpha a brief welcome.

"Now what?" Olivares said.

I literally had no idea, but a moment later, I received a broadcast.

Move to Log Point Fourteen for retrofit.

A map packet downloaded, marking our target with a glowing red dot.

"Follow me," I said, breaking into a jog. "Looks like we're going to get retrofitted."

"What are they going to do, Alpha?" asked Stranz. "Give us laser beams for eyes?"

"Or pulse cannons for arms?" Chance added.

"I'm a watcher. I have no memory of fighting or of even wearing an EXO, so this is as new to me as it is to you."

We had to weave through several throngs of EXOs. I recognized some of the markings—Europe and Dallas. I also saw quite a few patches from the Kilimanjaro mission, and was glad to see that so many of my comrades in arms had survived to fight the end game. We finally came to Log Point Fourteen. An array of giant metal boxes akin to CONEXs were lined back to back, forming a field-expedient assembly line. I watched as an EXO marched into the first box where robotic arms removed the ammo packs and the suit's two main weapons systems. I held up a hand and walked to the other end. My squad watched me as I waited to see what would come out. It took about five minutes, but when the EXO finally appeared, it had an immense magazine attached to its back which fed into tubes that ran the length of the suit's arms. He had the named Franklin stenciled over his left chest like it was a uniform.

"What'd they do to you?" I asked the man in the suit.

"Flechette cannons. Five thousand rounds. Light as hell."

"Break it down Barney style," I said.

He gave me a look. "Hadn't heard that one in a while. You from Bragg?"

I shook my head. "173rd out of Vincenza."

Franklin held out a fist and we bumped. "Had a friend named Hammond in the 173rd."

"I knew old Chuck. Laziest sergeant I've ever met until it's time for mission, then he's aces."

Franklin laughed. "Sounds like him. Never liked to clean his clothes either."

"Smelled like old socks and vomit half the time."

"All the time."

We laughed as we reminisced about a guy we both knew. Such a small world. Then I sobered. "He hit an IED heading back home for R & R."

"Isn't that just stupid. Guy gets killed going home but

survives Taliban." Franklin shook his head. "Hamilton would have been good about now."

I nodded. "Aces."

"Anyway, breaking it down Barney style for you." He drew in a breath. "They're equipping us with five thousand moly-coated flechette rounds." He straightened out an arm and fired a single round into the ground. It disappeared in the dirt, but he used his metallic hands to dig it free. He held it up and I saw that it was the size of ball point pen but twice as thick. He handed it to me. "To fire you have to straighten your arms and gaze-flick firing sequence. You can fire one or both arms at the same time. A new nav packet allows me to assign priority targets and the EXO will do all the work for me. Rate of fire is five thousand rounds a minute, so conceivably you could empty it all out in one shot."

"How is it powered?"

He shrugged. "Alien battery. Also replaced the suit battery. Power meter now shows I have one-hundred and seventeen days of power."

"Holy smokes," I said.

"Right? So the EXO is now about twenty percent lighter, which you can really feel." He jogged in place and waved his arms above his head to demonstrate.

"What about the Hydra?"

"They say we don't need them. I heard that the Vipers have some kind of missile system they're going to use for close air support." He held up a hand and paused for a moment. "Shit, gotta go." He waved. "See you on the other side." He took off at a run.

I watched him for a moment, then went back and briefed my team.

We filed into the assembly line. First step was to remove our weapons systems. Then they added additional electronics to the back of the suit and directly into the back of the helmet. At one point I felt a tickle, but let it go. I was afraid to move. Something robotic and sharp might accidentally peel back my head if I did. Next came affixing of the flechette ammo pack, the firing tubes and the actuators. This was followed by more electronics, then the final stop was the removal and replacement of the battery. For seven brief moments I was locked without power and without air inside the EXO, much like I had been on the plains before Mount Kilimanjaro when I'd almost suffocated to death. But as the eighth second ticked, the EXO powered back up and I departed the assembly line leaner and meaner than when I'd entered.

The first one through, I stood and watched as each of my men and women went through the process. It almost felt like I was at one of L.A.'s hundreds of car washes, waiting for my car to show up so a fleet of low paid Mexicans could dry and shine it to get a tip, the only cash that allowed them to scrape by and feed their families. Back when there was an L.A.... and cars... and car washes... and families who barely scraped by.

I sighed and pushed the melancholy thoughts aside as Stranz appeared, flexing his arms, flechette barrels resting on the EXO skeleton just above each fist. By the time the others had made it through, I'd gotten a message to head towards another Log Point.

More messages flicked across my HUD about the necessity to contact Relocation Specialists prior to combat to ensure we had a place on outgoing vessels. Someone claiming to be an Information Tender sent me a packet with contact information and promised the ability to incentivize my ability to join the Chase. Yet another message offered to provide a Predictive Logic Solutions packet if I aligned myself with a group called the Greens. There was so much more going on behind the scenes than I could even know. When things slowed down, *if* they slowed down, I vowed to pigeon-hole Alpha and get to the bottom of things. The Greens? If there was one group, then there had to be more.

When we arrived, we were sprayed down with a liquid that covered the outsides of our EXOs with a noticeable but thin film which my HUD identified as ionic field dispersion spray. When I queried, I was informed that it would substantially reduce our signatures, allowing for greater stealth.

Finally we were assigned a rally point. I spotted it from a kilometer away, resting on the outskirts of the large circle of activity surrounding the drop ship. Before we joined the larger group, I took a moment to brief my squad.

"Gather round," I said, putting one knee on the dry dirt of central Texas. Above, the sky was an impossible blue with no clouds in sight. With the team now kneeling around me, I addressed them. "This could be it. I don't know if I'll be able to talk to you again once we join the larger group. TACON, OPCON and ADCON are all a mystery at this point."

"If you're going to get all smushy, we can skip this part," Olivares said.

"I'll take that under advisement, Francis," I said, revealing his first name.

Chance snickered.

"You mean, Frank," he said, his voice a timbre lower than it had been.

"No, I mean *Francis*, Francis." I cleared my voice. "Back to what I was going to say before Francis interrupted me." A packet arrived in my HUD. I opened it to see a picture of Olivares flipping the bird in a mirrored surface. I don't know when he took it, but the sentiment was clear. "Back atcha, Francis. And no, Stranz, this isn't going to be a St. Crispin's speech."

"Thank God," he said, probably remembering the speech I gave just prior to the mission where I removed his arm.

"We've been strung along and forcibly placed in the middle of a million year war between two species," I said. "Not only are we in the middle, we've been asked to be the grunts to end it once and for all. Us. Not Americans and the English, and not French, and not the Japanese. When I say us, I mean humans. Earthlings. We people of Earth who once thought we were the only sentient beings in the universe. Then the Umi came and intractably changed our minds. But we are not the first this has happened to. Everyone has seen *300*, right? The movie about King Leonidas and his three hundred loyal Spartans? During the Battle of Thermopylae in 480 BCE. Seven thousand Greeks were asked to hold off more than one hundred thousand Persians. The rear guard was a force of three hundred Spartans and they held the only road the Persians could get to. And let's face it, they knew the math. They saw how the strength of the enemy compared to their own. They knew they were going to die. But they didn't care. They fought. When asked to surrender by a representative of the Persian King Xerses, Leonidas said to them, *Molon Labe*. Anyone know what that means?"

"Come and take it," Stranz said. "My uncle had a

bumper sticker that said that. It came from the NRA. Said you want my guns, *Molon Labe*."

"Exactly. *Molon Labe*. Used by many people. Texas used it in their revolution. The National Rifle Association used it. Anyone who had anything they didn't want taken away used it as a daring insult. *Molon Labe* means come and take it but it's essentially the ancient Greek equivalent of *Fuck You, Eat Shit and Die,* and *Up Yours*. Texas never became a nation and Leonidas and his men were killed, but they shouted *Molon Labe* to the very end and died a proud representative of their peoples.

"So to you grunts I say, *Molon Labe*. This is our world until the end. *Molon Labe* our planet. When we fight and everything starts to seem hopeless, I want you to shout *Molon Labe*. When one of us dies, I want everyone to shout *Molon Labe*. I want each and every one of us to channel that ancient Spartan King Leonidas and every warrior in history who ever uttered the words *Molon Labe*. For as certain as this planet belonged to us, it also belonged to them, so their memory should be invoked.

"Remember, we were minding our own business, sitting out here in our lonely solar system, doing our own fine job of killing each other when the Umi decided to include us in their reproductive cycle. *Molon Labe* is a reason for fighting. *Molon Labe* is a reason for dying. *Molon Labe* is a reason for winning. So I want every one of you to go out there and take it to the enemy. You don't have to do it for me, you don't have to do it for yourselves, and you don't have to do it for good old King Leonidas. I want you to go out there and avenge the death of someone you loved, someone who deserved to live and not die at the hands of an alien fertility program.

"Olivares, who are you fighting for?"

"My sister, Louis and her three daughters, Gloria, Epifina, and Grace."

"*Molon Labe*," I said, clapping him on the shoulder. "Stranz, who are you fighting for?"

"My father, who taught me that being a soldier was the most honorable thing a man can do."

"*Molon Labe*, "I said again. "Chance, what about you?" I put my hand on her shoulder.

"Mr. Courtney Brown, who ran the tea shop on the corner across from my house and who would make fresh Madeleine cookies for me every day. He made them for ten years until he died, then put it in his will that I could have free Madeleines at the store for life as part of its condition of sale." A tear formed in her eye. "He did it because he said that if he'd had children, he imagined that they would have been exactly like me."

I laughed softly. "*Molon Labe* to Mr. Courtney Brown."

Everyone else repeated.

"And you, *mon frére,* Charlemagne. Who are you fighting for?"

He was so choked up he could barely speak. "I fight for the spirit of Jean Danjou. He was our Leonidas and fought with sixty-four legionnaires against the Mexican military in the Battle of Camarón." He put a hand on my shoulder just as I had mine on his and shouted, "*Molan Labe* to Jean Danjou! *Molon Labe*!"

"*Molon Labe* to Jean Danjou," we all repeated in unison.

"And you, Ohirra? For whom are you fighting?"

Her eyes were narrowed and her face hard. "Mr. and Mrs. Phillip and Susan Johnson and their three children, Betsy, Francy and Jacob, who were brutally mowed down and killed by a marine who'd too much to drink and was in too much of a hurry to care about anyone else but herself."

With my hand on her shoulder, I said simply, "*Molon Labe.*" Olivares knew the story but I doubted any of the others did. And now wasn't the time to tell them.

Finally, I put my hand on Alpha's shoulder, who was beaming at me with a strange, implacable smile. "And you Alpha, for whom do you fight?"

Pride filled his voice as he said, "I fight for the three thousand nine hundred and sixty-three other versions of myself who gave watch, because I can."

"For all the Alphas. *Molon Labe.*"

Everyone said, "*Molon Labe.*"

I stood and pulled Alpha to his feet. "Now let's go and take it to them. Let's go find the enemy and kill the Umi once and for all."

I started to put my hand out, when Stranz said, "Wait!"

"What is it?"

"L.T., you never told us who you were fighting for."

"Me? I fight for all of you."

"No, come on. That's a cop out. We all fight for each other, sure. But who did you love that you're fighting for?"

I thought of my time with Mother and how I'd insanely hooked up with one of my old girlfriends, Suzi. We'd dated for over a year back in the 2000s. But too many deployments had soured her on the idea of loving a soldier. Then came the invasion. She survived, but lost an arm and an eye. She also lost much of her sanity. She could barely function, yet she'd still recognized me. I thought I'd be able to fix her, to help her through the worst of it, but then she'd walked off one night and killed herself. Suzi Wanaka, the girl of my dreams, the only girl for a guy like me. Had she still been alive, I never would have gone to Savoonga and never met Merlin, and perhaps I wouldn't even be here.

"Are you going to answer?" Olivares asked, eyeing me with concern.

Suzi and I had seen *The Matrix* at Mann's Chinese Theater and had laughed at how tiny William Shatner's footprints were out front. Even her feet were larger than Shatner's. I pictured this version of her, laughing—war free, alien free and whole.

I nodded and cleared my throat. "I fight for Suzi Wanaka," I said. "*Molon Labe.*"

Everyone said, "*Molon Labe.*"

My chest was heavy and my heart was an anvil. Still, I put my hand out and everyone put their hands on mine. I could feel the weight of these grunts. *My* grunts. "*Molon Labe,*" I said.

They repeated it after me, then we all turned and headed towards the Rally Point. We were halfway there when a squadron of F-35s roared past above, dropping bombs and strafing all those on the ground.

> When your time comes to die, be not like those whose hearts are filled with fear of death, so that when their time comes they weep and pray for a little more time to live their lives over again in a different way. Sing your death song, and die like a hero going home.
>
> Tecumseh

CHAPTER THIRTY-EIGHT

EXPLOSIONS ROCKED THE Khron beachhead as twelve F-35 Lightnings hit their afterburners and shot into the sky. I watched in shock as six peeled one way and six peeled the other, clearly coming around for another sortie.

Fires burned where their GBU bombs had hit. EXOs lay dead and dying from the four-barrel 23mm Equalizer cannons. The drop ship still stood, but it was on fire in three places, and even as I watched, one of the tall antenna broke off, tilted slowly, then fell, impaling the earth with a sixty meter spike.

"What the fuck just happened?" Olivares said.

"NUSNA!" shouted Ohirra. "They're attacking."

I heard a rumble in the distance, which I immediately recognized as C-130s. A lot of them.

I searched the sky for the donut-shaped space craft of the Khron, but it was empty except for the returning F-35s.

"Alpha, where are the Vipers?"

"They were sent south to investigate an Umi sighting."

"All of them?"

He looked at me in horror.

The F-35s were coming back around.

"Hero Squad, follow me!"

I took off at a mad sprint perpendicular to the planes' attack run. All EXOs were being ordered to rendezvous at the drop ship, but that was the absolute wrong strategy. The last thing we needed was to put all of our forces into one small area and make it easier to attack. That's when I figured that coms had been hacked.

I got on the net and shouted, "Disregard order. Coms have been hacked. Do not rendezvous at drop ship. I repeat do not—" And then I was cut out of the net. *Son of a bitch*. But did that mean I'd lost coms with my EXOs? "Radio check all Heroes?"

Thankfully I got *Five by Five*s from all of them. So I couldn't communicate out, but I could still communicate with my Heroes.

"Alpha, you calling the Vipers back?"

"I can't be sure. I think I'm being jammed."

I gaze-flicked my radar but it was being jammed as well.

We'd put about two kilometers between us and the Khron beachhead when I had everyone pull up. We turned and watched as the twelve F-35s strafed the ground, each one twisting and turning to inflict the greatest damage with their Equalizer cannons.

"Shit, we got troops in the air," Stranz said, pointing east.

Dozens of C-130s shadowed the blue sky at five thousand feet. Hundreds of black dots began to empty out of them. I knew what that meant.

I looked around, but there was nothing but a few oil derricks on this wide, flat plain and that was the last place I wanted to hide. One or two rounds into one of them and we'd have geysers of flame shooting out of the ground. It looked like we'd have to make our stand here.

"Evasive action," Ohirra shouted. "F-35 headed our way."

"Spread out!" I ordered, bringing both my arms up. I locked out the elbows, initiating the actuator and aimed at the oncoming jet.

It fired as it came and I watched the 23mm rounds plow divots in the earth on a trail directly towards me.

I fired the flechettes, aiming for the right engine by locking a red target indicator over it. With almost no recoil, it was difficult to judge whether or not I was firing. If it hadn't been for the firing solution and constant target updates from my HUD, I never would have even known. The new electronics in the HUD controlled my arms and made microscopic adjustments that kept the flechettes on target. My eyes were wide with growing fear as the jet continued on its course, the bullets tearing up the earth towards me.

Then I was flying to my left as a great weight hit me.

When I bent my arms to stop my fall, I stopped firing. I hit the ground and rolled. Olivares rolled next to me. I watched in my HUD as the jet jerked to the left, then hit the ground erupting into a fireball. I covered my head as dirt and debris rained down.

Olivares was on his feet first. "What are you trying to do? Kill yourself?"

He helped me to my feet. "Just trying to shoot the damn thing down."

"Well, you managed to do that. Now what?"

I turned and began to run towards the crash. "On me!"

When we arrived I noted that there wasn't much left. About a third of the fuselage and most of a wing were the biggest pieces of the plane still intact. "Charlemagne and Chance, get this set up for protection."

"What are you planning?" Ohirra asked.

"Rorke's Drift until the Vipers return. It's all we can do."

"What's that?" Alpha asked.

"It was a battle in the Zulu War in South Africa," Stranz said. "One hundred and fifty Englishman against four thousand Zulus."

"That's right! Michael Caine played Bromhead," Alpha said excitedly. "I remember that movie very well. It was called *Zulu*."

"Eleven Victoria Crosses were awarded for the bravery of the soldiers there," Charlemagne added as he, with the help of Chance, heaved the wing into a position where it would serve as a wall for us to stand behind.

"Well, there's not going to be any Victoria Crosses here, nor will anyone make a movie out of it. Our job is to inflict as much damage as possible while surviving until the Vipers return." I shook my head. "I still can't believe that the damned Khron took all of them."

Chance and Charlemagne stood back as they finished. We essentially now had a V-shaped fighting position with the fuselage and a wing to protect us. Not that either would stand a continued assault of fifty caliber rounds, but it was far better than being out in the middle of nowhere with nothing but our *shwanzes* in our hands.

Ohirra opened fire from her position at the end of the fuselage.

I gaze-flicked into her POV and saw that several of the immense NUSNA EXOs were heading this way, with more landing. We seemed to be on the northern edge of the battlefront, which was fortunate. Anyone who'd heeded the fake call to rendezvous at the drop ship would get chopped up as NUSNA forces concentrated their fire there.

Near the drop ship everything was in frenzy. The jets had departed, but NUSNA EXOs were landing everywhere, firing from the air as they landed. Their fifty caliber rounds tore into Khron EXOs, laying them out in tens and twenties. Part of me wanted to run to their aid, but I knew that our best shot was to stay put.

My radar was still being blocked so I had no way to determine how many enemy EXOs there were. my best guess was about a thousand.

"I got two of them, but more are on the way." Ohirra said.

"There's no way for us to set up interlocking fields of fire because of the shape of our defensive position. So we'll play possum. Don't engage until they are five hundred meters out."

"Brilliant," Chance said. "It's the end of the world and I get to pretend to be a marsupial."

"What is this marsupial?" Charlemagne asked.

"Rodents with big eyes that carry their young in their pockets," Olivares said. "And this moment of zoology has been brought to you by Ex-Lax and the law firm of Dewy, Cheatem and Howe."

"Is he messing with me?" Charlemagne turned to me and spread his arms. "I cannot tell."

"Yes, he's messing with you, Frenchie," Chance said. "But he's also pretty accurate. That's what opossums are. Rodents with big eyes that carry their young in their pockets."

I watched as Charlemagne gave her a look like he knew she was lying but couldn't prove it.

"Chance, I want you and Charlemagne to cover the right. Stranz and Ohirra, continue covering the left."

"What about me?" Olivares asked.

"You and Alpha will stand by to reinforce as needed." I stared at the center of the V, wishing I had a way to fire over the shield wall, but it was too high. Then I saw the dead pilot. What I'd originally thought was red paint was actually his head pinned between metal struts.

"Four advancing towards our position," Stranz reported.

"Three more advancing towards our position," Chance added.

What I would've given to have my Hydra missiles back. "Let them advance to one hundred meters before engaging."

"But that will put them too close," Olivares countered.

"For whom? They might have a more powerful weapon, but we have a faster rate of fire." I shrugged. "The alternative is to let them come and try and defeat them hand-to-hand. I know we're lighter than they are, so perhaps that might be the best option, but I'm keeping that tactic in my pocket in case we run out of ammunition."

While I waited for the enemy to get closer, I thought of what went through the real Lieutenant Bromhead's mind when four thousand Zulus descended on his little outpost. All in all, Bromhead led the defense of the drift, killing nearly a thousand Zulus while experiencing barely twenty friendly casualties. Was he constantly strategizing, or did he merely stand and watch, hoping that his trained men could win the day? Of course, the Zulus carried spears and knives while the English enjoyed the superior technology of the rifle. We didn't have the same technological advantage with the NUSNA EXOs.

Or did we?

"Hey, Charlemagne?"

"Yes, sir, L.T."

"Did you know that a marsupial is a rodent with big eyes who carries its young in its pocket?"

"Oh no," he groaned. "Not you, too."

Chance laughed.

"Olivares, see if you can't carve out a firing port in the wing and the fuselage."

He stared at me for a moment, then nodded. He snapped his harmonic blade into his hand and went to work on the wing. The Stellite blade vibrated at ultrasonic frequencies, allowing it to cut through things a normal blade wouldn't even dent.

"Three hundred meters and closing," Ohirra said.

"Same here," Chance said.

While Olivares worked on the wing, I went to the fuselage. First I had to cut out a square of metal and electronics. I tossed that aside. Then I had to make the space large enough for one of us to fit our arm and shoulder into.

"Two hundred meters."

"Belay. Do not engage at one hundred meters."

Olivares said, "Are you serious?" but kept working on his firing port.

Pressing with every ounce of strength I had, I was able to push through the fuselage. Once through, I began to carve the hole. Then I stood back. It wasn't perfect, but it would do.

"Alpha, put your arm here and when I say fire, fire."

"But I can't see a target."

"Don't worry about it. Just follow orders."

"One hundred meters," Chance said, nervousness in her voice.

Olivares backed away. "Done," he said, sheathing his blade.

I nodded. "Attend the port. Everyone fire on my command. You two on each end, high low."

No one said anything. They didn't have to. I counted silently, then ordered, "Fire."

I drew my blade.

All six EXOs fired. Stranz and Ohirra fired high-low using their left arms on the left, while Charlemagne and Chance fired high-low using their right arms on the right. Olivares and Alpha fired from the center. I finally had interlocking fields of fire.

"Cease fire," I called.

All four EXOs on the edge of the position brought their arms back inside.

The fuselage shuddered with an impact.

A giant EXO came stumbling past Ohirra. It looked neither left nor right. It dragged a 50 cal in its left hand.

I surged towards it and brought my blade down on its neck. I hacked twice, and the head fell free. It stood for a moment, then toppled.

"Assess," I ordered.

"All down," Ohirra said.

"Anymore coming?"

"Negative," she said.

"Then stand fast."

"The Vipers are returning," Alpha said. "Inbound in five minutes."

I moved so I could see the drop ship. It looked as if there were two factions. The one nearest the ship was smaller but seemed to have successfully created defensive positions. The other faction, which I identified as NUSNA, had broken into two groups. One group was engaging the defenders, but the other had formed a circle and seemed to be doing nothing. I glanced back at the NUSNA EXO I'd beheaded, then glanced at its .50 cal.

Oh shit. Anti-aircraft. I wasn't sure what sort of shielding the Vipers had, but a concentration of .50 cal rounds couldn't be good. I gauged the distance. We could reach them in five minutes, the same time the Vipers would arrive. If only we still had our missiles.

"Heroes, on me!" I shouted, taking off at full speed towards the massed group of NUSNA EXOs.

All six fell in behind me. I told them my plan.

To Alpha, I asked, "What are the armaments on a Viper?"

He was already breathing heavily. I'd forgotten that he'd been in custody for more years than I'd been alive. If this wasn't the end game, I'd have benched him. "For planet-side the Viper can deploy a paralyzation strobe and plasma cannon."

"What kind of strobe? Paralyzation?"

"Light at different frequency..." He huffed and puffed. "Can cause Khron to be physically ill. Vomiting, screaming headaches." Heavy gulps of air. "Oh hell." Wheezing. "We use it as a non-lethal substitute. It works less well during daylight hours than at night."

We continued to run. I was barely out of breath because of the assistance provided by the suit. "And the cannon?"

Alpha replied, "I've never had to use it."

"But in theory?"

"In theory," he said, gasping, "it works very well."

"Is that all the information you have?"

"My Viper... didn't have... weaponry in... event... of... crash." Then after about thirty seconds he said, "We wanted... to limit... tech... nology... in... wrong hands."

"What about shielding?"

"Like in *Star Trek*?" he laughed, then started coughing. Chance had to grab his arm to keep him from falling on his face. Once he'd recovered, he said, "Nothing like that... ferro... ferro... fluid skin hardens."

"Well, we'll see how well they work against .50 caliber rounds."

We were almost to the point I'd judged we could halt and fire when an immense weapon on the drop ship began to fire.

We pulled up and stopped.

All of us except Alpha stopped and stared. Alpha bent over double and grasped his knees, chest heaving.

Whatever the weapon was, it made a sound like nothing I'd ever heard. The closest I could use for comparison would be a toilet plunger in an echo chamber. Backlit by the wide Texas sky, a ripple of air shot from the drop ship and onto the NUSNA EXOs closest to it. When it hit, it enveloped them and took them down. I didn't even see them move or struggle.

"What was that?" Ohirra asked.

Alpha stood, arms above his head, he said, "Plasma membrane. It's supposed to be used to cover Vipers during repairs, but it seems someone is using it as a weapon. Genius."

"What's it do?"

"Envelopes the target with an ionized radiation bubble."

"What effect will it have?" I asked as the cannon fired again. The bubble moved so slowly, I could easily track its progress with the same ultimate result.

"I expect it kills them."

Fire shifted from the ground to the drop ship as the NUSNA EXOs realized that there was now a new threat.

The first Vipers appeared on the horizon, moving like shooting stars towards our position.

With their arrival, the jamming stopped. The silence in my head was filled with the staticy chaos of battle—multiple nets overlapping, voices shouting, cursing, angry and confused. Along with access to netcoms came the return of my radar. My HUD came alive with red and blue icons, data streaming, interactives waiting for me to access. NUSNA had more than seven hundred EXOs, while blue forces had barely three hundred. I'd been certain we'd had more than a thousand before they arrived. Damned NUSNA had delivered one hell of a blow.

The grouped NUSNA EXOs began firing into the air, their combined salvo not seen since the first days of Bremen when Germany still had anti-aircraft weapons and had tried to defend their Nazi logistics center.

The first Viper they hit spun out of control, slamming into the ground.

The second Viper suffered the same fate.

I shook my head. Why were they flying into the maelstrom of lead?

Finally, the third took evasive action and began firing pulses from its plasma cannon into the grouped NUSNA EXOs.

Still more ionized radiation bubbles were fired into the crowd.

For the first time in ten minutes, it looked as if the tide might be turning.

Then I heard the gunfire close behind me and Olivares screaming.

Though I've belted you and flayed you,
By the livin' Gawd that made you, You're
a better man than I am, Gunga Din!
                                    Rudyard Kipling

CHAPTER THIRTY-NINE

OLIVARES LAY FACE first on the ground with Chance standing over him. Red bullet holes stitched a pattern of betrayal across his back. Chance hovered over him, both arms almost extended, smoke seeping from the barrels. Another inch would mean her firing again.

The momentary paralyzation of the squad was instantly replaced by activity as everyone moved. Stranz and Charlemagne grabbed at Chance, but she turned, locked both arms and fired. Stranz managed to duck, while Charlemagne fell hard to the ground as Chance's arm contacted the side of his head.

Stranz rolled to the ground and kicked her feet out from under her.

Chance fell hard to the side, folding her arms to allow her to catch much of her weight, but at least that meant she couldn't fire.

I grabbed Olivares's arms and pulled him away from the combat area. I quickly accessed his vitals through my HUD—not good. Then I saw another EXO on the ground—Alpha. His vitals were even worse. What the hell had Chance done? Friendly fire? I felt rage burn through my veins. I drew my blade.

Chance fired at Stranz, who dove out of the way, barely avoiding being holed.

I glanced at Charlemagne. He was down on the ground, but somehow his vitals were fine.

Chance surged to her feet in time to meet Stranz, who had gotten to his feet just as fast. He'd drawn his sword and brought it around in a wicked swing that sunk into Chance's left side. She twisted, almost tearing the blade out of Stranz's hands.

"Chance! Stop!" he shouted.

But Chance swung her sword, almost decapitating Stranz, who barely managed to dodge out of the way by stumbling to his left. Chance didn't let up. She ran towards him and swung again, and again Stranz managed to somehow get away from her.

"It's the Umi," Alpha said, coughing blood into his faceplate. "It's controlling her and all of the NUSNA fighters."

"But how?" I asked. "She'd never been exposed to the spore!"

"So she said," Olivares gasped as he rolled over. "Damn that lovely bitch!"

I was glad to see him still alive and vile, but was also still worried about him. His vitals weren't promising. Alpha's vitals weren't much better.

I selected the command switch to shut down her EXO but it didn't work. Just to see, I shut down Alpha's with a gaze-flick and was gratified and confused to see that it worked as he stopped in mid-step and fell. I snapped it back on, then prepared to wade in and forcibly stop Chance from killing the rest of my squad.

Behind me came several immense explosions.

I cringed but didn't dare look.

Ohirra moved towards Chance in a crouch. "Come here."

Chance brought her sword up and ran at Ohirra, who stood still, not doing anything to protect herself. I wanted to shout for her to move, but everything was happening so fast. One second Chance was bringing her blade down toward Ohirra's neck, the next Chance was flying through the air. Ohirra had used the woman's own impetus against her. When Chance hit the earth, her blade flew away. Ohirra was on Chance in a second, straddling her and wrenching at the EXO helmet. Chance brought up a knee, trying to dislodge Ohirra, but all it served to do was to make the Japanese-American angry.

"I'm done fucking around with you," she snarled, spinning to where both her EXO's feet were on Chance's chest. Ohirra tried to pull Chance's helmet out of its socket while simultaneously wrenching it against the bend. But the unintended consequence of the jujitsu move was to actuate Chance's arm cannon, which immediately began to fire. Ohirra jerked her head out of the way as 22mm rounds grazed her helm.

I saw at once that Ohirra had locked herself into an untenable, precarious position. If she let go, Chance could aim and fire. If she held on, Chance could still fire. Now Ohirra fought to keep Chance's arm from locking, forcing it to remain bent so her opponent couldn't fire.

More explosions came from behind me. I spared a glance and watched as the drop ship began to tip. It seemed to take forever to fall, but when it did, I felt the impact in the ground beneath my feet. I noticed Vipers swirling madly in the air, firing plasma cannons at targets along the ground.

More gunfire erupted from behind me.

I whirled to see Charlemagne with both arms locked and cocked, pointing at Chance. "Stop this craziness, Chance!" He fired again, bullets impacting the earth on either side of her head.

Was this what Stranz and the others had experienced when the Umi had taken me over... when I'd chopped off Stranz's arm? I remember being trapped inside my body, unable to stop, unable to control my own movement. Everything external was choreographed by the Umi while everything inside was me an unwilling audience to my own destructive ability. This must be how Chance felt at this moment. And Olivares... I knew they'd had a thing together and here she'd gone and shot him.

"Just shoot her in the head," Ohirra said. "I can't hold her forever."

Another great explosion, then Chance's body went slack.

Ohirra took the opportunity to adjust her position, spinning Chance onto her face and bending both of her opponent's arms behind her.

I noticed the quaking of Chance's shoulders. Then came a high keening sound.

"Ohirra, let her go," I said.

She gave me a sharp look. "But she's..." Then she looked at Chance and slowly released her.

Chance pushed herself over, bringing her hands to her face as if to cover them. But because she couldn't touch her face, she merely stared at her hands—and as I watched Olivares' vitals tick to zero—her murderous hands. My friend. My enemy. Dead after all this time and to think it was his lover who killed him. I felt a chasm open in my chest.

"I—I couldn't stop," Chance said between sobs. "The Umi was in control of me... like I was possessed." Then she shot to her knees and stared at Olivares's unmoving body. "Is he..."

"I'm afraid so, Chance." I looked at Ohirra, who had tears in the corners of her eyes.

Charlemagne helped Stranz to his feet, then both of them assisted Alpha.

"But you said you'd never been exposed to the spore," Ohirra said.

Chance shook her head, then ripped her helmet free. Her sharp cheekbones were red. Tears tracked across her skin. "I lied and I don't know why. Every time I wanted to tell someone I'd lied, I wasn't able."

"Somewhere along the line an Umi had her under control," Alpha said. "It's why we force everyone to wear the neural interceptor collars." He shook his head. "We should have made you all wear them."

Olivares and I had been so worried about becoming a slave species that we'd allowed Chance not to wear it. This was our fault. This was *my* fault.

"Don't do that," Ohirra said, approaching me and putting her hand on my shoulder.

"Don't do what?" I asked, knowing exactly what she was talking about.

"That thing you do when someone dies. You analyze it and immediately determine that it was your fault."

"But it was my fault."

"The buck stops here." She shook he head. "Right? I still stand by your decision. How could we be expected to blindly trust an alien species who comes up and says wear this and everything will be all right? We couldn't. That's the answer. Then bad shit happens and people die."

I laughed hollowly. "We should have that on a T-shirt. *Bad shit happens and people die.*"

"Is that what happened?" Stranz asked. "Was there an Umi here?"

"Probably brought with the NUSNA EXOs to help control them," Alpha said. "Jesus, but this hurts. Always wondered what getting shot would be like. Now I wished I'd never have known."

A Viper zoomed to our position. I waved it down and pointed to Alpha.

"A little help here, please."

Beware of false knowledge; it is more dangerous than ignorance.

George Bernard Shaw

CHAPTER FORTY

OLIVARES WAS DEAD, as were four hundred friendly force EXOs. All of the NUSNA EXOs were inoperable, their drivers dead or captured. The drop ship was destroyed. Five Vipers had been shot down. For all intents and purposes, the great Odessa Khron beach head was little more than a battlefield triage center. And to think that these geniuses were supposed to keep the Umi from leaving the planet? What a bunch of clowns. No wonder the Umi had always eluded them.

A meeting of all division leaders was called. I didn't know what that was, but I was certainly going to make the meeting. The idea that this *superior* alien species didn't know to place defenses around their beach head or obtain reconnaissance intelligence on possible enemy forces was indefensible.

While many of the surviving EXOs were cleaning up the area—stacking bodies, removing debris, setting up real triage to take care of the wounded and dying—the division leaders met in an area near the base of the now toppled drop ship. I was among probably two dozen other Earthling EXOs. Many were from various OMBRA units. I'd intentionally removed my helmet and let it hang on my waist, as had several of the others. I wanted them to recognize who the hell I was, so when it came time for recriminations, I could have the loudest voice. Most of the *division leaders* had chosen to keep their helmets on, signifying a total lack of trust. I could feel their wariness like ants crawling on my skin. They wanted to be prepared and ready in the event of anything. Normally I'd be with them, but I had a different agenda.

We all waited while the Khron got their act together. Two Thinnies in gravity support suits, the 3964 clone of Alpha, a big-eyed Eridani, and two black-skinned dwarfs wearing immense, bulbous goggles were conferring at the front. I couldn't help staring at the dwarves—as I'd called them. They couldn't be more than five feet tall and were impossibly stocky, like characters I'd seen in the *Lord of the Rings* movies.

I queried my neural interceptor device to see if I could learn more about them.

Earth annotated planet GC Gliese 667 Cc. 23.6 light years. Exceptionally hot resulting in Khron with increased levels of eumelanin occasioning a blackened skin appearance. Gliese 667 Cc Khron are short and stocky. Because of luminosity of 20% of Earth normal, Gliese 667 Cc Khron have wide luminous orbs much like the Earth haplorrhine primate tarsier. The pupils are fixed in the head so that they have to turn to see. The orbs give them the capacity to see in very low light including ultraviolet light. Note however Gliese 667 Cc Khron are unable to see colors. On Earth, Gliese 667 Cc Khron are forced to wear special goggles to keep from going blind. They are a warlike species whose—

I'd had enough. I only understood half of what it told me, but it explained their appearance.

An EXO with a Kilimanjaro sigil sauntered up to me. He still had his helmet on, but took it off when he approached. He wore a high and tight haircut. Although his face was scarred from burns, I could tell where it had once been handsome. Piercing blue eyes shone intelligently, cradled in worry lines.

"You're Mason," he said.

I nodded. "One and the same. And you? Did we fight together?"

"I was with Recon 10 at the Mound."

I jogged back through my memory. Wait, wasn't Recon 10 annihilated? Then I saw his scars. I guess a few did survive. "I remember," I said. "You guys had it bad."

"Wrong place, wrong time. We all had it bad." He was silent for a moment, then said, "Call me Casper."

I nodded. "You impressed yet?"

"With this soup sandwich? A platoon of Girl Scouts could have done a better job."

"No offense to the Girl Scouts," I said.

"Yeah, no offense to them."

Several other EXOs walked by, each making eye contact and nodding.

Good. I might get a chance to speak yet. I'd never cashed in on my Hero of the Mound status. If ever there was a time, it was now.

"Seen Pink lately?" Casper asked.

"Dead."

"Was it the Cray?"

"Nope. NUSNA."

A sigh. "We do more bad shit to ourselves than anything else."

"Makes you wonder if we should be allowed to continue... if we deserve it as a species."

He seemed to consider it, then said, "I'd agree, but I like good cigars, twenty-year old scotch, and medium rare steaks too much to just give it all up."

I thought about what I'd been through in the last five days and that sounded pretty wonderful. I couldn't argue with Casper. We all had our own destinies. I was glad he'd figured his out, because I was yet to decide.

Finally one of the Gliese Khron stepped forward and addressed the gathered EXOs. Our neural interceptor devices translated.

"*Sighting of Umi adolescents in southern Caribbean resulted in successful elimination of target sets. Mission success acknowledged. We are now preparing for mass attack at brood site in Sydney Harbor. We are downloading travel manifests and tables of organization and equipment to your neural interceptor devices. We anticipate Umi adolescents' movement off planet in T minus 36 hours based on reconnaissance conducted by Khron Vipers.*"

Khron 3964 stepped forward. "That will be all. Please return to your divisions and prepare for disembarkment. And remember, this is for you, this is for your planet."

We all stared. That was it? They could have done that through the NIDs. I could already hear the grumbling as it began.

Several Exos shouted questions from the front.

Beside me, Casper spat on the ground and shook his head. "Fucking unbelievable."

I thought there'd be more. I thought they'd have some explanation, but it seemed that none was forthcoming. I got the fact that we were grunts and the militant arm of effective battle planning, but in this case I had no confidence that any planning coming from the Khron would be effective. What was it I'd said to Mr. Pink? '*If you want to put me in charge of something, then let me be in charge. That means I need the most information I can have so I can make appropriate decisions. Your withholding information from me must stop, or bump me back down to sergeant and give me a foxhole.*' Sure. Treat me like a mushroom. Feed me shit and keep me in the dark. But it'd better be *good* shit.

I stepped forward, but instead of addressing the Khron, I addressed my fellow Earthlings.

I shouted to be heard. "Do you know who I am?"

There were more than a few nods on the angry faces. Their eyes flashed from me to the stage and back. I didn't flinch. Instead I tried to stand taller. "I'm Benjamin Carter Mason, formerly of the 173rd Airborne Brigade. Some have called me Hero of the Mound. I was there at Kilimanjaro and one of two who brought down the Hive. I did the same to the Hollywood Hive after I was the first to recover from the zombie spore."

I let that sink in for a moment.

Khron 3964 filled my silence. "*Please return to your divisions.*"

I ignored him. "I was there with Mr. Pink when he died." I saw many of the expressions change. "Yes, NUSNA EXOs killed him at our last location to recover some alien specimens we'd been keeping under wraps. I actually wish he was here. For all of his assholish bureaucracy, he'd have been the first one to call out these Khron and their farce of a war."

Those who hadn't been paying attention were finally interested.

Khron 3964 spoke again. "*Please, disperse. Please return to your divisions.*"

Without turning around, I said, "Shut the fuck up, you clone-fucking-incompetent-rear-echelon-motherfucker, I'm talking to my friends here."

This got me a few chuckles, along with more than a few worried glances towards the front.

This time it was the Gliese Khron who spoke. *"If you do not disperse, we will enforce behavioral protocol."*

And there it was. The reason they'd brought us all together. They knew we wouldn't take their shit, and they knew we'd question their authority, which is why they'd made sure we were all clustered in a small group away from our divisions... away from our forces.

Now I did turn. "What do you mean by behavioral protocol, you bug-eyed troll? 3964, can you explain this to us? Wasn't it you who told me that these NIDs were safe?"

The Khron clone looked uncomfortable and he stared at his feet.

The Gliese Khron stepped forward and the EXOs parted, allowing him to move through their line. He stopped ten feet away and pointed at me. I could see the very human rage I'd inculcated. *"You must be taught a lesson,"* he said as the NID translated.

"Oh yeah? Teach me, Obi-Wan Kenobi."

Pain suddenly stitched through my skull as if a thousand tendrils were electrocuting my brain from the inside out. I fell to one knee. My jaws were clenched. My eyes were closed. I forced myself to a standing position and lifted my right arm and extended it towards the Gliese Khron.

The pain suddenly shut off.

I gasped, then managed to say, "If you ever do that to me again I will kill you where you stand."

"Behavioral protocol is necessary for uncooperative Khron species who are unwilling to defend their planet."

"Unwilling to defend our planet?" I lowered my arm and looked around me. "Who the hell do you think you have here? A pack of Cub Scouts? We've been defending our planet from the beginning. Where the hell have you been? One step behind every step of the way while we've been at ground zero fighting the aliens." To the assembled EXOs, I said, "If he tries that again we commit to suicide protocol."

More than a few eyes widened. Begun with Strategic Air Command Nuclear Detonation Officers back during the Cold War, suicide protocol was used after detonation and allowed for each officer to simultaneously kill the other. We'd never had to do it during the Cold War, but it looked as if we might just have to do it now.

"What is this suicide protocol?" the Gliese Khron asked.

"Try that bullshit pain behavioral protocol and you'll see. You want us to fight the Umi? Then let us fight. But if you do that one more time, we'll make sure you have nothing to fight with. You see, all of my friends here understand and are dedicated to each other. Fuck the Earth. We fight for ourselves." I walked up to an EXO and put my arm around him. "This is my brother and I fight for *him*."

"Say it loud, brother," Casper called from the back.

"Many of my brothers here have live feeds open and are broadcasting everything back to the remaining EXOs. If you try and jam the feeds, our grunts will revolt. If you try and stop our recording, we'll revolt. And if you try and treat us as anything less than equals, we'll implement suicide protocol." I marched up to the bug-eyed troll.

"Savvy?"

This time the pain hit all of us.

I went back to one knee as spiders with razor-blade legs discoed through my brain. It took every effort but I managed to stand. Something I'd realized earlier was that by changing our weapon's systems to a straight arm actuator, they eliminated the ability for us to kill ourselves by shooting ourselves in the heads. But that didn't stop us from shooting someone else in the head. As I stood, I raised my arm and pointed it at the man I'd just called my brother. I could see the maddening pain in his eyes as he managed to do the same to me. I stared into the barrel, knowing that any second a flechette might pierce my skull, and I welcomed it. Out of the corner of my eye, I saw everyone else doing the same. Every EXO was engaged, promising immediate and permanent loss of any fighting force the Khron believed themselves to have.

The pain evaporated.

I gasped as I lowered my arm. I took three deep breaths, stepped forward and kicked the little fucker in the head.

He flew back, his goggles flying away and revealing red, bugged eyes. He didn't move after he hit the ground.

I roared with anger. "Did you not hear me? Did you not believe?" I pointed to Khron 3964. "You! Explain yourself."

He shook his head. "I don't have the knowledge. We have been watching Earth. We only know of Earth."

I shifted my finger to the Thinnies. "One of you Thinnies. Explain this behavioral protocol. Explain your *deceit*."

"*It is necessary. Sometimes species are unable to understand that there is a great plan in motion and that they are but parts.*"

Now I'd heard it all. Bullshit general speak.

"Don't give me that *We just don't understand the grand plan* speech. You'd better do better than that. Here's a straight question. Did you invoke behavioral protocol on the Eridani Khron?"

"Affirmative."

As I expected. "What about the Gliese Khron?"

"Affirmative."

"Has there been any Khron species who has not had the behavioral protocol used on them?"

After a moment, *"Negative."*

"So you've had to induce pain in every Khron species in order for you to get them to fight. Is that affirmative?"

"Affirmative."

"And why is that?"

"They questioned our tactics."

"And how are those tactics working so far?"

"We've achieved moderate success."

I laughed and crossed my arms. "Is that so? How long has this war gone on?"

This time silence.

"As I expected," I said, shaking my head and aware that I was on multiple feeds. There probably wasn't a single Khron on the planet who wasn't watching me. "We thought you Khron were superior because of your Dunkin' Donuts spaceships and your plasma cannons and your cool tech, but you're no better than any of us. In fact, I could argue that your behavior has demonstrated a serious lack of understanding of fundamental tactics. Why did you leave the drop ship unprotected?"

"We were advised of an adolescent Umi in the southern Caribbean."

"Advised how?"

"*Encrypted message intercept.*"

"That was convenient. So why take all the Vipers?"

"*We weren't sure what size force we'd encounter.*"

"And what size force did you encounter?"

"*The adolescent Umi was alone.*"

"What's that?"

"*The adolescent Umi was alone.*"

I rolled my eyes so hard I could almost see behind me.

"Yo, Casper."

"Yes, Mason."

"Can you explain to them what happened?"

"Easy peasy," Casper said, spitting in the dirt before stalking towards me. "Classic decoy. We already know that NUSNA is in league with the Umi. To lure away defensive forces, the Umi gave up something they knew you wanted—an adolescent Umi. They cut off the arm to save the body. They allowed you to kill it so that NUSNA could come and reduce your capacity to stop them from lifting the rest of the adolescents from the planet."

The silence was deafening.

I clapped Casper on the back, then asked, "Did any of you consider this?"

"*We did not.*"

I was about to ask why not, then it hit me. Clones required a memory download prior to activation or they'd only have the memories which were saved prior to the mission. That meant that unless a clone returned from a mission, the surviving versions would have no memory of what happened. They'd only know it was a failure. No lessons learned from the battlefield. No best practices to be added to TTPs. They wouldn't have learned a damned thing and wouldn't even realize that their tactics were a failure. And the Umi knew it!

I started laughing as I walked among the massed EXOs. I patted several on the back and shook a few hands. Some of them laughed with me. Others smiled. Even more eyed me warily, certain I'd gone off the deep end.

Finally I stopped. "Last question," I said. "How many Khron have successfully left a planet after combating the Umi?"

"None."

And there it was.

The reason for failure.

It was right in front of them the entire time, only they never knew it.

No matter how many people you kill, using a machine gun in battle is not a war crime because it does not cause unnecessary suffering; it simply performs its job horrifyingly well.

Sebastian Junger

CHAPTER FORTY-ONE

I EXPLAINED MY hypothesis to everyone. Once they understood, defeat supplanted any hope they might have had that we'd win the day. While the Umi had evolved in its strategy and tactics, the Khron had used the same tactics every time and failed. They were the classic child repeatedly touching the hot iron, only not knowing why his fingers were burning. Stop touching the fucking iron—stop using the same tactics—is what I explained.

Instead of continuing to piss in everyone's Wheaties, I let them know that there was still hope. "We have forces. We have willing fighters who will go into combat if we have a cohesive and effective strategy. We just need to come up with that strategy. Let me and a select group of Khron Earthlings sit down and mull over your plan and see where the strengths and weaknesses are. The good thing is that the Umi have every expectation that we'll fall into their traps just as you always have. What we have on our side now is that knowledge. We can capitalize on it."

I grabbed Casper, called in Ohirra, selected ten more OMBRA Khrons, then dismissed the rest. Everyone was ordered to get ready. I also requested that Alpha join us. His special healing nanites had him hale and healthy again. I had a special mission for him. We were linked into the Khron beach heads located in Sify, Congo, and Primovera de Leste, Brazil. They'd suffered similar losses because of attacks from UMI-coopted human forces. A former Congolese warlord was the first one to figure out the clone memory tangent, but he thought that I should be the voice of the group. As far as the beach heads in Russia and China, both were completely wiped out. We now had more or less a third of the force we'd envisioned using, so we had to treat each EXO and Viper like it was a rare commodity.

Once we began looking at what the Khron had planned, we were aghast—frontal assault followed by a rear assault. Three waves of failure, especially in the face of the Umi's brood ground defenses. We reviewed Viper feeds of the area and counted nine Cray hives surrounding Sydney Harbor, where more than a dozen Umi were preparing to be lifted into space. If each hive had a thousand Cray we'd be facing nine thousand Cray. Our total number of EXO fighters was nine hundred. Ten to one odds. Rorke's Drift all over again, except this time we were the attackers. Add to that there were Chinese and Russian anti-aircraft weapons bristling around the outer ring. We couldn't attack by land. We couldn't attack by sea. We'd have to attack by air. It seemed utterly hopeless.

Then Ohirra came up with an idea that might actually work, although it was about as desperate an attempt as anyone could imagine. We spent the next nine hours planning and synchronizing. The timing was going to be tight, but we had little choice. Once we finished, I went to my team and back-briefed them. They'd already eaten rations and had their helmets off and hanging at their sides. I ate as I spoke. It was only then that I discovered that not only had the division leaders around me enacted suicide protocol, but every friendly EXO on the planet had done the same after viewing the pain. Evidently the Khron had never encountered this before. That my actions had a planetary-wide acceptance was a little stunning. Too often I felt like I was just another dumb grunt. I guess even dumb grunts have their day.

Then I shared the video feed of Sydney Harbor with my team. The city itself had been destroyed by the damaging black vines that delivered the spores. I focused the feed on the nine hives.

"I've been inside and destroyed two of these hives before. It's not going to be pretty. Each hive has a queen that produces more and more Cray every day. She's the size of a tractor trailer and is the center of the hive universe. Without her, the hive ceases to exist. The only way we're going to stand a chance against such overwhelming odds is to take each one of them out."

"The problem is we can't get to them from beneath," Ohirra said, "Which is how Mason did it on both occasions."

"If we can't do it from beneath," Stranz asked, "then how are we going to… oh shit."

I nodded. "From the air."

Charlemagne didn't look convinced.

Chance was only half listening, staring out over the Texas plain. I was going to have to talk to her before we went on mission.

"But isn't it going to be crawling with Cray and anti-aircraft rounds?" Stranz asked.

"That it is," I said.

"Then how?"

I left the question hanging.

"I do not see how this thing is possible," Charlemagne finally said.

"Oh, it's possible all right. Our plan is far better than anything the Khron came up with." I focused the feed so that they could see the lines of humanity stretching from the hives on into Sydney and beyond, all the way into the country, down the M1 and across on the A4. Hundreds of thousands of people, men, women and children. Grandmothers and Grandfathers. Brothers and sisters. All standing in line waiting to be eaten, controlled and pacified by the Umi. Here and there bodies lay by the side of the road, starved, exhausted, dead. "When I was in L.A. the hive mother consumed eighty-four humans a day. In ten days, that's eight hundred and forty bodies. In a hundred days, that's eight thousand and four hundred bodies. That hive was barely active. These hives are a furious chaos of activity. They are preparing for attack. Current estimates are that each hive mother is consuming two hundred and twelve humans a day. That's nineteen hundred and eight citizens of our planet each day. In a week that equals thirteen thousand three hundred and fifty-six people consumed. In a month that's fifty seven thousand two hundred and forty people. While I've been talking, nine people have been eaten. If any of you've wondered what we're fighting for, look at them. Look at these people being eaten alive by some giant alien slug in the middle of an impregnable hive."

"But how?" Stranz pressed. "How are we going to do it?"

"Ohirra, you tell them." I got up and walked over to Chance. I patted her on the shoulder. "Let's take a walk," I said.

She glanced up, then climbed to her feet and followed me.

Small clusters of EXOs were doing the same thing we were doing—briefing the plan and having last words with their squads. As division leaders, we had little belief that we'd survive the battle. Mission first was the call of the day and all the leaders were making sure that everyone knew this was our one and only chance to get back at the Umi.

Several hundred Vipers were parked where the beach head had once been, while a dozen or so buzzed overhead, patrolling against another possible NUSNA attack.

After about a hundred meters I said, "I'm probably the only one you can talk to about this." When she didn't respond, I added, "After all, who else do we know who killed someone they loved?"

This stopped her in her tracks. By the cant of her head, I could tell she didn't believe me.

I nodded solemnly as the memory of Michelle and who she'd been and become washed through me with toxic finality. I didn't dare look at Chance as I said, "She was my girlfriend at the Mound, then she went and volunteered to be one of the first HMIDs. The only thing that remained her was her mind... mostly." Her crazed voice shouting

KILLMEKILLMEKILLMEKILLMEKILLME-
KILLMEKILLMEKILLMEKILLME

scorched me enough to make me wince. When I recovered, I glanced at Chance with eyes wounded from the memory. "She wanted me to kill her because she was ugly and couldn't stand being who she'd become." I hesitated, then simply said, "So I did what she wanted. I killed her." I wanted to laugh like a maniac, run in a circle, and hurl my clothes into the air. Anything... anything at all as long as I didn't have to remember those final moments. "It's not something I'm proud of," I said in a quiet voice.

"But she asked you to."

"Yes."

"Then you did as she wanted."

"It still doesn't help." I shook my head to get a little of the craziness out of my eyes.

Chance looked at me and chewed her lip. "She must have loved you terribly."

I laughed. "She did everything terribly." I sighed. "And me, as well."

"Francis and I were never that close, but we were working on it." She flipped her hand toward the ruined drop ship. "Even in the face of all this bloody bullocks." She shook her head. "Then I had to go off and shoot him in the back." She shook her head again. "And do you know what makes it worse?"

"What?" I asked.

She was about to speak when she stuttered, then threw her hands against her face and sobbed.

I reached out to touch her, but she pulled away. Not knowing what else to do, I just stood there.

After a few moments, she cursed and said, "Aren't you going to hold me?"

I stared at her, then put my arms around her. "Sorry," I whispered.

"It's okay. I don't know what I want." She pushed away from me and wiped her nose. "Know why I'm crying?

Because I was going to make a blasted joke about killing him, because that way it might be funny, right? But it's never going to be funny. It's never going to be anything. We're never going to be anything because I killed him."

I stared at her sternly. "Have you seen Stranz's arm?"

"I heard you did that." She grinned half-heartedly. "Was it because he didn't salute?" Then she rolled her eyes. "See? I did it again. I can't help it. Whenever I get scared, I joke. It's my defense mechanism." She took a deep breath. "Francis told me that an Umi took you over. How did it feel?"

"Awful. Terrible. Every bad word you can think of times a hundred million. I saw my body doing things over which I had no control. You know how it feels."

She looked away.

"You were used. Nothing more than a tool of the aliens we're trying to kill. If anything, it should piss you off and make you want to avenge Francis's death."

"It won't bring him back," she said.

"That's the thing about death. It's fucking permanent. There's nothing we can do to bring him or anyone else back. But remember, just as funerals aren't for the dead, revenge isn't for the dead either. Revenge is for the living and for some of us, we can't survive without it." I lowered my voice. "You see, revenge is a tool. Revenge is power. It gives us the opportunity to do something. Without revenge there's only helplessness."

She'd stared at me with wide eyes throughout my mini-speech. Then she nodded. "You're right. You are the only person who can talk to me about this."

"We're a very special elite club."

"Bloody damn great. Welcome to the Lover Killers Club."

I laugh softly. "Has a ring to it. Might get it tattooed on my ass when this is all over."

Now she laughed. "I'd like to see that when you do."

I clapped her on the shoulder. "Not in this lifetime."

I smiled, turned away, and walked back to the others, thoughts of Michelle and our one and only time together beneath the Kilimanjaro plains, the sound of the generator hiding the sounds of our lovemaking.

If the enemy is in range, so are you.

Unknown

CHAPTER FORTY-TWO

Seven hundred Vipers lifted off at the same time from three different locations on the planet. The three hundred and twelve located in Odessa carried four hundred EXOs. Only one Viper remained on the ground, to be flown by Alpha, his sole mission to watch. Despite his protestations, he wasn't to participate in the fight regardless of what happened. He was to watch and record, then if we failed, head into space and rendezvous with the orbiting Khron ships and provide them a comprehensive report of the battle. Only then would the Khron be able to mature their tactics and cease repeating the mistakes of the past.

Hero Squad, or what was left of it, was assigned to Khron semfled 8. Ohirra and I were in the first ship. Chance was in the second ship with Olivares's body. She'd insisted that she take him into battle and I didn't argue. Stranz and Charlemagne flew in the third ship. We stayed in our EXOs, locked to the walls on either side of the door, ready for combat when we arrived.

Through the NIDs we were able to project in our HUDs the various video feeds from Vipers on station. They'd remained undetected, using their ferrofluid skin to help render them invisible to the naked eye.

Thirteen adolescent UMI floated in the harbor. Although the fragmented offspring of the larger Umi—which still lived in Earth's oceans—were now bereft of their intelligence, each was roughly the size of a flattened house. Beneath each one had been detected a net made from some yet-to-be-determined material. Estimates were that these nets were ten to twenty meters beneath the surface. What their use was was still unknown, but some of the Thinnies had postulated they were some sort of transportation cradle. Because the Khron had never survived their battles with the Umi, they'd never been able to determine specifically how they got off this gravitational well and into space.

The Vipers on station had reported furious underwater activity by Umi-controlled humans, activity which had clearly been going on prior to the Khron's arrival, so whatever they were building was probably some sort of transportation system. Whether it was rockets or some other more advanced alien tech—or a combination— we didn't know. However, we did know that in the last twenty-four hours the activity had stilled and each Umi had had netting placed beneath it.

I marveled at the absolute transcendence of the Umi. They were almost god-like in their ability to transfer memory through procreation, maintaining knowledge that spanned epochs. Using client species to perform the functions they could not was ingenious. The spore which, had at first appeared to be nothing more than a way to control the survivors, had created automatons to perform functions necessary to move the Umi into space. Part of me wanted to watch and see what kind of science-fiction-brought-to-life tech the Umi had directed be built. But another part—the military part—wanted to destroy it before it even had a chance to rise.

And on the other side... the Khron. A technologically advanced collection of human-like species who'd been chasing the Umi across galaxies only to continually come up short at every last battle. Where the Umi had the advantage of memory, the Khron had the advantage of determination. They'd chased and fought, and chased and fought, only to finally arrive on Earth. When they'd tried to bully us into assisting, we'd stunned them by offering to kill ourselves instead. We were such an obstinate, stubborn, and bullheaded species. A sociologist would probably say something about how these traits were evolutionary developments that helped us survive, but I knew it was just an everyday grunt's *Take no shit* attitude. If the Khron had presented a worthwhile strategy, I might not have balked. But they didn't, and they couldn't, because they'd never succeeded and they'd never discovered why they hadn't.

And these were to be my people.

Well, at least now we had a chance.

The NID made an announcement. Phase One was about to go into effect. After much argument, I'd convinced the Khron to move one of their Kaleidoscope ships into low earth orbit above Sydney. We needed the ability to jam the Umi's control of the anti-aircraft forces around the harbor. In addition to over nine hundred spidertanks bristling with extra weaponry, the Russians had provided 290 ZSU-23-4s, seventeen state-of-the-art Tor Missile Platforms, four hundred towed ZU 23 anti-aircraft artillery pieces, and an unknown number of RPGs, ready to rip into any aircraft that might come near. I'd been told that the Vipers couldn't jam the Umi command signals alone, but with the help of one of their Kaleidoscope ships, they believed they could manage it. The problem was orbital decay. The Kaleidoscope ship could only stay on station for six minutes before it had to depart. Otherwise, the gravitational grip of Earth would be too much for it to overcome and the whole damned thing would come crashing down. Our hope was that with the Earthling Khron free of Umi control, they'd direct their weapons against the Cray. In fact, phases two and three depended upon it. Without a reduction in Cray, we'd never be able to get close enough to the Hives to do anything.

The argument was that the spore-infected who hadn't gone through the cure process were little more than zombies. I'd agreed, but then pointed out that zombies couldn't be employed building space ships, nor could they be employed to work complicated military mechanisms. My rationale was that the Umi must have certainly found some who'd been through the cure process, probably from China or Russia, then forced them to create the conditions necessary to cure many more. While spore-infected zombies might be fine for Cray Queen food, they had neither the will nor the dexterity to perform complicated tasks.

I absolutely believed in my hypothesis, but I was also aware that the fate of the world depended upon it.

Speeding towards Sydney at more than two thousand miles an hour, we watched through the feeds as the Kaleidoscope ship suddenly appeared as it lowered its orbit to an altitude of one hundred and sixty kilometers. I knew nothing about the ship, but it was immense. And it had to be. Alpha had mentioned to me that they repaired and created Vipers during the long galactic night between conflicts. Not quite a generation ship, but it had to house multiple versions of clones as well.

Now, at one hundred and sixty thousand kilometers, it was barely visible. That it was visible at all was impressive beyond anything I'd yet imagined. It was as like *Battlestar Galactica*, and *The Expanse* had created a lovechild spacecraft and named it Kaleidoscope.

Now, would the jamming work?

I set a timer in my HUD as I watched and waited.

Ten seconds ticked by.

Twenty seconds.

Thirty seconds. Still nothing.

Didn't they realize they only had six minutes?

At the fifty-three second mark, Chance called out. "There. Look on the M4."

Then I saw it. The long lines of the damned were disintegrating. The hundreds of thousands of spore-infected humans destined to be food suddenly had no guidance. Instead of waiting silently to be eaten, they began to move in all directions, spreading out, away from the hives, randomly moving into joyful chaos.

Suddenly the ground around the harbor opened up as thousands of tracer rounds and missiles shot to the sky, finding their targets by the hundreds. Cray began to fall, splashing dead into the waters of Sydney Harbor.

Ohirra and I cheered and we could hear cheering across the NID from every EXO as they, too, watched the feeds. That Phase one had worked gave everyone a tremendous surge of hope. We might just get through this yet.

More Cray surged from their Hives, until the sky was such a thick mass of black and gray we couldn't see the ground. Now for the other shoe to fall. Would they do what was natural to them? I waited and watched, realizing that I was holding my breath.

Then it happened. The Cray descended and began targeting their attackers. The mass of black, writhing Cray dropped from the sky and fell upon the battlements around the harbor. RPG rounds detonated at a hundred feet. I imagined that with such a thick contingent of Cray descending upon them they didn't even have to aim. For a moment there were two distinguishable sets of forces, then they came together as one.

All equipment that depended on electricity suddenly ceased to function, killed by the Cray's biogentic EMP blasts. Those which had a purely mechanical means to fire continued, but soon it was evident that it was a massacre. Calculations were pouring in that indicated nearly three thousand Cray had been killed, but that number paled to the estimate that all five thousand human defenders were now dying at the claws, spiked knees and elbows of the Cray.

I closed my eyes, remembering my own battles with the wretched aliens. The EXOs were created specifically to defeat them. Anyone without a suit was no more than a bag of blood waiting to be ripped open. It must have been terrible. For one foul moment I commiserated with my fellow Russian grunts. Then I dismissed them, their traitorousness disallowing any further empathy.

Phase two began in earnest as Vipers from three different directions flew past Sydney Harbor at two thousand miles an hour, firing plasma cannons at the now unprotected adolescent Umi. They made pass after pass as the Cray scrambled to return to their sentry duty. With each hit, we cheered. It was a glorious moment when seven plasma bolts hit one Umi and it erupted in gouts of flame. We managed to destroy five Umi before the Cray were redeployed and intercepted the bolts, killing themselves so that the Umi might live. The Vipers made two more passes, firing again and again, but the Cray had managed to create a blanket of protection in the clear morning sky.

"Get ready, Heroes," I shouted through my coms. "Ten seconds to show time!"

With all the Cray focused on protecting the Umi, they'd left the Hives unprotected.

Semfled 8 headed directly towards Hive Eight and hovered. The doors opened and we leaped out, grabbing at the edges of the Hive to keep from falling. Eight other Semfleds performed the same maneuver at the eight other Hives. I watched out of the corner of my eye as an EXO failed to grab hold and fell more than a hundred meters to his death.

"Inside!" I shouted, and we all scrambled into launch tubes.

"I'm doing this for you, Francis," I heard Chance whisper. He'd only come as far as the Hive. The Viper driver promised to later give him a burial at sea.

Charlemagne began to sing low and deep, *"Tiens, voilà du boudin, voilà du boudin, voilà du boudin. Pour les Alsaciens, les Suisses et les Lorrains. Pour les Belges, y en a plus, Pour les Belges, y en a plus, Ce sont des tireurs au cul."*

My HUD translated it from the French:

"Look, there's the pudding, that's the pudding, black pudding here

For Alsatians, Swiss and Lorraine,

For the Belgians, are over, for the Belgians are over,

They are shooters in the ass."

I couldn't help laugh along with Chance and Stranz as their own HUDs translated.

"What kind of song is that, Charlemagne?" I asked. "You singing about black pudding?"

"And what about the Belgians?" asked Stranz. "What did they ever do to you?"

"This is the song of Legionnaires," he said, his voice bright with optimism and the customary French accent. "It is the song of my people."

"And the pudding?" I asked.

"Is the things we carry."

"And the Belgians?" Stranz asked.

"Is the Legionnaires who do not fight."

"There's a song about it?" Stranz pressed. "Now that's weird."

"Easy, Stranz," I said. "It's his tradition. Sing it for us, Charlemagne. Sing us into battle."

And Charlemagne began to sing, his voice low, patriotic, and filled with emotion.

My HUD displayed the complete text of the song like some sort of opportunistic battlefield karaoke. I heard the others start to sing it haltingly along with Charlemagne. Once I joined in, even Ohirra lent us her regal tenor. I felt the fluttering of pride in my heart. This was what battle was like. This was why I'd always be a grunt. Even though death was my shadow, I still smiled, happy at last to be doing what I did best.

Killing aliens and breaking things.

The interior of the Hive was recognizable. The last time I'd been in a Hive had been in L.A. when I'd deposited a backpack nuke, then flown to safety on the back of a Thompson-controlled Cray. The time before that had been worse, Olivares and I coming up through the volcanic tunnels and blowing the hell out of the Queen and her offspring. That's where I'd gotten the idea. Without the Queen, the Cray ceased to function. Destroy the Queen, and we could destroy the Cray.

Phase three.

I pulled myself into the launch tube until I could see the central chamber of the hive.

We were a hundred meters up, so we had to climb down the inside face of the hive.

Charlemagne continued to lead us in the Legionnaire's march.

My back itched as I began to move down the inner face of the hive. My HUD was up and told me that there was activity below. In addition to the mother, there were between sixteen and thirty juvenile Cray. The numbers continued to fluctuate, which I couldn't understand. I was about halfway down when I noted several Cray launching from the Hive floor. I got a good place for my feet, held on with my left hand, then straightened my right, activating the flechette cannon and firing a twenty round burst at the oncoming Cray. Everyone else did the same, creating a wicked web of moly-coated flechettes that struck true, sending dead Cray back to the floor.

I continued climbing, hurrying before more launched at us, or worse, others came back inside, a situation which would put them above and below us. I was counting on the Umi's influence to be more powerful than the Queen's. We were about to find out.

I jumped the last five meters to the ground, absorbing the impact by dropping to a knee.

When I stood, it was with the four surviving members of Hero Squad.

The song ended and we were silent.

The Queen glowed and pulsed on the other side of

the chamber. She was moving, like an immense slug into a tunnel, probably to protect herself. Behind her were juvenile Cray, too young to have wings. They formed a protective line, bared their mouths at us and hissed, but didn't try to attack.

I raised both my arms and fired, as did the rest of Hero Squad, and it was like an old-fashioned firing squad. The Cray fell without a sound.

Then we stalked forward, firing at the retreating Hive Queen.

When we got closer, we grabbed our blades and began to hack at her. Her light began to dim as we cut and slashed. Soon we revealed a cluster of her unborn Cray. We hacked at those, too. We kept going until we were certain the Queen was dead—unmoving, dark and lightless.

Ohirra turned to me, an expression of concern on his face. "Either your plan was magnificent, or something's wrong."

I felt it as well.

"This was too easy," Stranz said.

I tried to communicate with the other squads, but the Hive was blocking coms.

"Let's get out of here and see what's going on," I said.

Ohirra climbed onto my shoulder and leaped for a handhold. Once she got it, she pulled the rest of us up. Soon we were moving upward. When we hit the first set of launch tubes, we made it easily out of the Hive. We stared towards the harbor and were shocked to see the Cray still in formation, flying and protecting the adolescent Umi. My HUD told me that there were more than six thousand of the savage aliens.

Even as I watched, a Viper flew too close and was hit

with an EMP. Its flight turned into a somersault, ending abruptly as it crashed into the Opera House.

One by one the other Semfleds checked in. The Queens of all nine hives had been killed. On the one hand, they wouldn't be eating any more humans. On the other, the Cray were still functioning. The Umi must have had total control over them. This was something completely unexpected.

I descended to the ground and began trotting towards the harbor, which was only two kilometers away.

"Come on, grunts. We got work to do."

They fell in line behind me.

I wasn't exactly sure what we'd be doing, but we had to do something. I was sure opportunity would rear its ugly head.

A man can be an artist... in anything, food, whatever. It depends on how good he is at it. Creasy's art is death. He's about to paint his masterpiece.

Christopher Walken in *Man On Fire*, directed by Tony Scott

CHAPTER FORTY-THREE

WE HADN'T GONE two hundred meters before spore-infected humans saw us and gave chase. I had no desire to kill any more humans, so I poured on the speed. Soon we were running, with an ever-increasing group of the infected running behind us. I ignored them, my mind working on a way to get the Cray out of the way so the Khron could get to the Umi.

Vipers zoomed above the Cray, moving fast enough and far enough away that the EMPs from the Cray couldn't affect them. But at those speeds they could only make a few shots per pass, and at that rate it would take forever to get through the shield.

I heard a rumbling coming from the harbor and increased my speed.

In front of us was a now useless Russian ZSU-23-4. An armored personnel carrier with four anti-aircraft guns, it would definitely be the tool we needed to help the Khron. But it was dead from an EMP blast. Beside it though, were two Bofors Guns, lifeless soldiers draped across them.

"Charlemagne and Stranz, get those things working."

Chance turned back to the oncoming spore-infected and opened fire.

The rumbling was growing louder and louder.

"How the hell do you work one of these?" Stanz asked, pushing a dead gunner from the seat and wedging himself into position.

"Ohirra, help Chance." I said and made my way to the guns. I found the crate of 40mm rounds, dragged it to Charlemagne's gun and loaded it.

I started to do the same with Stranz, but suddenly the water in a section of the harbor began to bubble and boil. I could only stare as four booster rockets emerged from the water, a corner of a net affixed to each rocket and lifting the adolescent Umi into the air. At least a thousand Cray protected the rising boosters from the sides, swirling and swooping and blocking all attempts from the Vipers to take down the rockets. Try as the Vipers might, they were unable to penetrate the wall of Cray flesh.

Would we fail here?

Would the first launched Umi make it into space?

Not if I had anything to do with it.

"Charlemagne!"

"I see it but I don't believe it."

"Shoot it!"

"Trying. *Merde*!" I watched as he furiously cranked the traverse to get a firing solution on the old gun. The insane juxtaposition of a cutting edge warrior in a combat exoskeleton firing a manual ackack gun that was designed to take down WW II aircraft wasn't lost on me, even if this was a newer version—probably circa 1990. He managed to get the gun around, then opened fire. The rate of fire couldn't be more than a hundred a minute, but I watched as two dozen of the Bofor's rounds struck a booster rocket from underneath the Cray shield and exploded it. The blast caused a cascade with the other rockets, destroying the Umi in a ball of flame. The whole mess fell onto another Umi, dragging both of them into the harbor's depths.

I cheered and smacked Charlemagne on the back. "You got it!"

He cheered as well and held up a hand with two fingers. "Non, *mon frère*. I got *deux!*"

"Uh, guys?" Stranz called.

I turned to see Ohirra and Chance creating a mound of dead that was growing in height and width by the second, their flechette cannons smoking with the continuous rate of fire.

"Uh, guys?" Stranz repeated.

"What is it?"

"Incoming!"

I jerked around and saw my red flashing HUD. Incoming, no shit! Seven hundred Cray were headed for our location. There was nowhere to hide. Nowhere to create a defensive position. We were truly and royally screwed. Then I saw the water.

"Come on, everyone," I screamed. "Into the water."

I ran.

From behind me, Stranz asked as he ran, "Are these waterproof?"

"We'll find out in a few seconds." I hit a wharf and ran onto it. The Cray were coming quick. It was going to be close. "Hurry!"

At the end of the wharf I dove. When I struck the water, I sank until my feet hit the bottom. My HUD relayed that I was in ten meters of water, and I could see sky glowing on the surface above. I checked vitals of everyone and saw that Charlemagne was offline. I switched to his feed view and saw a dizzying, tumbling view, but I couldn't figure out what was happening until the feed suddenly hit the ground and came to rest, a sideways view of the wharf we'd just leapt from. In front of the camera was the lower portion of a human in an EXO, ripped free from the upper.

You damned Frenchman.

"They got Charlemagne," I said.

The four of us stood staring up through the water. Several Cray tried to get to us, but once they hit the water, all we had to do was fire our flechettes and they went away.

Finally it was Ohirra who asked, "What now?"

Good question. Then my HUD did a strange thing—it identified something three hundred meters deeper into the harbor. I glanced back up at the surface. We couldn't go there, so we might as well check out what I'd found.

"Let's go," I said. "Ohirra, see if you can figure out what we're seeing... or rather, not seeing down here."

The going was slow. I was waiting for rockets to lift off again, but the Bofors had thrown off the Umi. They were probably wondering what to do next. I couldn't help think that the Umi might actually be scared, and it delighted me.

When we were halfway to our target, we identified the object. It was a rocket, probably affixed to an Umi on the water's surface.

"Come on! Let's kill ourselves an Umi." I poured on as much speed as I could with the water pushing against me. The bottom of the rocket was enclosed in some sort of immense domed chamber. I had no idea what it was for, but there were metal rungs built into it that allowed me to climb up to where I could get a grip on the booster rocket. A ridge ran up the first booster section and I used this to pull myself farther up. At one point I couldn't find a hold, so I made one using my blade. I don't know exactly what damage I'd done, but I didn't care. I kept going until I reached the huge bolt that the netting was affixed to. I grabbed onto the net and pulled myself onto it. The spaces between the netting were big enough to let me walk on it without falling through. The Umi rested in it like it was in a cradle. Its mass beneath the water was significant, measuring about ten meters.

From somewhere far away came a rumble. Another one launching. Thank God it wasn't this one. The surface of the water was ten meters away. I crouched, then launched myself, trying to grab the edge of the Umi. My fingers grazed it, but I couldn't find purchase and fell back. This time my foot surged through the netting, entangling me. It took a few moments, but I was finally able to disentangle myself.

Another attempt, and I had it. The Umi had a rubbery, slimy feel, like a barnacle.

I pulled myself out of the water in time to see three Vipers shooting towards the launching Umi. This one also had an impervious cloud of Cray, But the Khron had changed their tactics. Through my NID I was pleased to hear one of the pilots shouting, "*Tora! Tora! Tora!*" a Japanese code word meant to indicate surprise and taught to him by Ohirra. It had also been used by Kamikaze pilots who made suicidal runs at US Navy ships in the Pacific during World War II. The three

Vipers hit the Cray umbrella one after the other, spaced a hundred meters apart. The first knocked a hole in it, which was partially filled almost immediately. The second cleared the hole, and the third burst through the protective barrier. It obliterated the rockets, the shouts of "*Tora! Tora Tora!*" almost lost in the ensuing explosions which took out the Vipers as well.

The pilots had been afraid to die at first, but when I pointed out that they were clones so they weren't really dying, they couldn't argue with my logic. Even if they weren't, even if it took death to make a death, that's what needed to be done.

I pulled myself onto the surface of the Umi and stared at it. Up close it had a translucent appearance. I could see movement beneath its skin.

My HUD screamed warning and I saw Cray shooting down to get me.

I had no choice. I lowered myself back into the water and eased myself onto the net. I waited there until the others joined me, staring up at the surface, wondering if the Cray might come for me that way.

When we were all together, Ohirra asked, "What are you waiting for?"

"What do you mean?" I asked.

"The Umi. It's right here." She drew her blade and stabbed it. "Kill it."

The alien jerked as the blade went into it and a blue ichor seeped from the wound.

The rest of us pulled our blades and began to stab at it. Soon the water was clouded with Umi blood as it quivered and shook.

Then I almost lost my footing as the net shifted under me. I felt myself lift and realized that the rockets had fired. The water beneath me became hot as great gouts of flames superheated it. We began to rise.

"Jump!"

Stranz jumped, as did Chance.

Ohirra stayed with me.

We surfaced. I pulled myself up and onto the Umi, tried to stand but couldn't. An umbrella of Cray swirled above and around us, moving with such fury and chaos it was like seeing all the legions of hell taken to the air and merging into one terrible, demonic beast.

The Cray rose with the rockets. If any of them noticed us, we were dead. Hell, rising into space, we were dead already. I shouted, "Fuck this shit!" and shoved my blade into the Umi beneath me and began carving figure eights.

Beside me, Ohirra did the same.

The pressure became immense and soon we could do little beyond lay there, flattened. We'd have been crushed without the suits. Even with them, I could feel the incredible air pressure.

We were compressed, star-shaped against the Umi, riding it as it climbed higher and higher.

Suddenly the nature of the sound changed.

The Cray umbrella parted, revealing open sky above.

I could barely hear myself think. The rocket engines roared beneath us. I closed my eyes and felt my whole body shaking. I ground my teeth, afraid I'd shatter them.

The sound changed again, this time going higher in pitch.

This was it.

Why hadn't we jumped?

Maybe I thought this would be a fitting end.

Who was I kidding? I wasn't even thinking.

Then the engine noise disappeared entirely, replaced by silence. I felt lighter and realized I could move my legs and arms. I grabbed the hilt of the blade that was still in the Umi and opened my eyes to see the blackness of space before me. I managed to look over the side and saw that the net and the last booster had fallen away to Earth far, far below.

My God, but it was a long way down.

"You gonna give me a hand, spaceman?" Ohirra asked. "Or are you going to lay around all day?"

I glanced over to where she was on her knees, once more hacking at the Umi, her movements in slow motion.

"How can you tell if it's dead?" she asked. "Damned thing has more holes in it than the Grand Canyon."

I wrenched my blade free and began to carve out piece of it. I waged that if there was a major organ it would be in the creature's center to better protect it. "Here, dig here."

When the Umi stopped its upward movement, I was forced to stop hacking to keep myself from floating away. To stay in place I had to leave my blade in the Umi's flesh and hold onto the hilt.

Ohirra figured out the same thing and we hung there, wondering what to do next.

I checked my HUD and noted that we were one hundred and sixty five kilometers up. We'd achieved low earth orbit. I was now a bloody satellite.

Ben Mason to Earth. Come in, Earth. I began to hum that famous David Bowie song about Major Tom. Once I'd finished the song, stumbling over and making up many of the words, I sighed and stared at the numbers, which had stopped going up.

"Mason, we have a problem."

"You're just now realizing that?"

"We're out of air."

I felt the weakness come at me like a slugger with a baseball bat.

The suits had rebreathers which could recycle our own CO_2 if we had no breathable air outside. The scrubbers must have become overworked. It could even pull oxygen from water. But what it couldn't do was pull oxygen from space. My CO2 levels were rising quickly.

Then I noted that the altitude numbers were decreasing. We were down to one hundred and fifty eight thousand and falling. We'd reached low Earth orbit where the Umi could have escaped, but we'd killed it before it could. Now its weight and ours were bringing us back to Earth in a hyperquick orbit decay.

Oh shit.

We began falling faster and faster.

"Ohirra?"

She didn't respond.

"Ohirra?"

"Shut up and save your air."

"But—"

I did as I was told.

Our CO2 began to decrease as we dropped.

The Umi began to heat up beneath us and I had an image of the space shuttle coming back to Earth, flames firing from the nose in atmospheric re-entry. We weren't exactly aerodynamic. The flattened Umi was taking the entire heat load as we re-entered. I lay on it just as I had when we'd been rising. I watched my HUD and saw that my suit's temperature was already at one-hundred eighty-four degrees and climbing. It could survive five hundred degrees, but I didn't know what it would do to me, the wearer.

"Ohirra?"

"Yes, Mason."

"You're one hell of a grunt."

"Fuck you. It takes one to know one."

And then the Umi broke apart beneath us and we were truly flying.

I adjusted my angle of descent so that I was going feet first and watched my suit temperature rise to four hundred degrees in the blink of an eye. But then the temperature began to decrease as my speed dropped. I was at sixty thousand feet and falling. Now in the atmosphere, I was traveling much slower and didn't have the heating effects.

But then there was the problem of the ground.

Yeah.

That.

I'd reached terminal velocity and was plummeting feet first at a hundred and twenty miles an hour towards the earth.

"Mason, this is Alpha, stand by."

I blinked. Was I hearing things?

"Alpha, is that you?"

"Recovering Ohirra."

I watched my altitude decrease. I was now at thirty thousand feet and falling fast. If I was doing a HALO, about now would be when I activated my chute. But I didn't have a chute. Twenty thousand feet. I closed my eyes. This was going to be a really messy landing. Fifteen thousand feet.

Then I was no longer moving.

I opened my eyes and found that I was in the doughnut-hole of a Viper. I remembered when they'd recovered Nance's body and the spidertank from the Arctic that way. And now they had me, and Ohirra, both of us in some form of sticky stasis and at an altitude of a hundred and ninety feet.

Then Alpha lowered the Viper to a few meters above the ground and released the stasis field.

We fell to the ground, laughing.

Then I puked inside my helmet.

If you prick us, do we not bleed?
If you tickle us, do we not laugh?
If you poison us, do we not die?
And if you wrong us, shall we not revenge?
William Shakespeare,
The Merchant of Venice

CHAPTER FORTY-FOUR

"WHAT YOU'RE TALKING about is revenge, when it should be avenge."

I waved the comment away. "Words."

Ohirra's eyes narrowed. "Words are important, Mason. In this case each one is representative of a similar but different ideal. Avenge is applied when one is seeking retribution and justice. Revenge is much more personal, has less to deal with justice, and is more concerned with ameliorating one's personal feelings of being wronged."

After Alpha had let us down in Brazil, he'd taken us back to Sydney Harbor where the rest of the Khron were cleaning up after their victory. In the end, using the Vipers as their own weapons was what won the day. Once all the Umi were destroyed, the Cray fell from the sky. They didn't die right away, but I think that without their Queens or the Umi to guide them that there was probably little reason to live.

I'd already said goodbye to Stranz and Chance. With

Alpha's help, I'd also been able to say goodbye to Merlin and Earl, who were still on their way back and had refused the offer of a ride. Now it was just me and Ohirra. Alpha piloted the Viper and was waiting for me to get my farewells out of the way before we headed to space to track down more Umi.

"Avenge, revenge, both are interchangeable to me," I said.

"No, Mason. I want you to admit that this is personal."

"Of course it's personal, Ohirra. They came and fucked up the whole planet just so they could make babies. Of course I'm pissed. Shouldn't I be?"

"I didn't say you couldn't take it personally. It's just that when you do, when you're propelled by revenge, you don't tend to think straight. You want instantaneous gratification without considering the implications of your actions."

I stared at her. "How can I avenge the ruination of my planet," I said, using her preferred word, "if I don't join the chase and head into space with the rest of the Khron?"

"You're one man," she said. "Do you really think it will matter?"

"It's mattered so far, hasn't it?" I shook my head and exhaled. "I don't believe in God and I don't believe in fate," I said, flashing a weak smile. "Okay, I sort of believe in fate—the sort of fate where you're in the right place at the right time with the right training. Some call it luck. The Roman philosopher Seneca probably said it best. 'Luck is when preparation meets opportunity.' Sure, I'm one man. But I'm the one man who figured out why the Khron continued to fail. I'm one man who's spent a life preparing for this moment. I'm a human who wants goddamn revenge for what was done to his planet. And most of all, I'm a dumb grunt who wants to avenge the deaths of all of his fellow grunts at the hands of an alien species whose sole concern was promoting its continued existence regardless of the consequences." I paced back and forth, then stopped, whipping my head in her direction. "What I want to know, is that with all your combat skills and badassery, why are you staying and not going?"

She looked away. "That's a difficult question, predicating an even more difficult answer. You know my past. You know what I did that made Mr. Pink come after me."

Family of five dead in the road. Ohirra drunk and sobbing. Yeah, I remembered. I nodded.

"My culture isn't a revenge culture like Western ones are," she said. "We don't have a burning desire to react to every slight, every misspoken word, every effort that involves someone keeping us from being first in line. We don't spend every waking hour trying to make ourselves feel better by driving a little faster, being first in the queue, or having the biggest pickup truck." She laughed hollowly. "Want to know what my Japanese grandfather said about the iconic American pickup? He said that the bigger the truck, the smaller the man. For him, that single saying represented all of America. I don't believe in all-encompassing metaphors, but I see some logic in that. No, the Japanese don't generally believe in lynch mobs or getting back at someone. Buddha teaches us patience and the idea that retaliation isn't always the best choice."

"Turning the other cheek," I said.

"Right. Japanese turn the other cheek as a practice.

But that doesn't mean we're pushovers." She saw me not paying attention as I began wondering why we were even having this conversation. "No, listen. This is important to me. I identify as Japanese. It's part of my DNA and something I want you to understand. You see, although we turn the other cheek, we're also an honor and shame culture. My honor demands I be shamed for what I did, and I owe it to my honor to spend my life redeeming the shame... somehow, some way, however possible."

"You can redeem your shame by avenging all those who've died. Come with me."

She shook her head. "My shame is specific. Those five people. I bet you didn't know that I tracked down information and learned what and who they were, did you? Not just their names and ages. The husband was a doctor and his wife was a nurse. Think of all the people who died because I killed these two whose jobs were to save people."

"Then why'd you continue to be a grunt? That's like the opposite of what they were."

"I was going to quit. I'd already gotten my EMT certification and had two years of college. I was going to get out and see if I couldn't get into pre-med or nursing school."

I tried to imagine Ohirra in a doctor's or nurse's outfit but couldn't. She was one of the best grunts I'd ever had the privilege to fight with, and one-on-one she could take me down anytime she wanted.

"Know what happened? On the form it asked if I'd ever committed a felony and I had to check yes." She licked her lips. "After that there wasn't a college in America that would take me."

"I'm surprised the Marines didn't kick you out."

"Oh, they tried. You have no idea how hard we fought JAG. They'd been trying to kick me out of the Marines ever since I was sentenced, but I had a lawyer who was dropping the PTSD flag, saying I couldn't leave without proper counseling and treatment. The thing was, I didn't have PTSD before that. All I had was the drive to relieve my shame. All I had was this pervasive, ever-present guilt that filled my soul so much I couldn't think of anything else. But once they started talking about PTSD, once they began listing the symptoms, it struck me all at once."

PTSD for accidentally killing five people. I could see it. "So why do you think you didn't get PTSD right away?"

"I treated the dead as a problem instead of human beings. I treated them as the reason for my shame and something to be dealt with. Once I began to learn about them, about the children and what they liked and disliked—favorite TV shows and books, et cetera—then it hit me how I'd cheated them of long lives."

I sighed. "What are you getting at, Ohirra? You're losing me."

"How are you treating the dead, Mason? Are you treating them as humans? Do you know and care about them on a cellular level? Or are they your reason for avenging and revenging? You know what I think they are to you? Fuel for the vengeance engine you call a soul."

"Wow. Vengeance engine. Is that how you see me?" I asked.

"Sometimes, yeah. You're so focused, so intent on revenge. It's like a storm takes you over and sweeps all of us with you."

"You know, I used to be filled with guilt. I used to be powered by shame. You remember those times on mission in L.A. when I tuned out?"

"I remember."

"It was my shame boiling over. It was my guilt throwing its wet, clammy blanket over me." I shook my head. "I was totally fucked up. If it hadn't been the end of the world and the fact that my brain was already in tune with HMIDs so Thompson could backpack me into the hive, I never would have led grunts into combat. As it was, I relieved Stranz of his arm."

"That was the alien, not you," she said.

"Fine. It was the alien. But it was my body the alien took over. It was my hand that held the blade that severed the arm of one of the grunts trusted to my care. Don't you think I felt guilt about that? Don't you think I felt shame?"

She was silent for a moment, then said, "Yeah. I'm sure you felt those things."

"To use your words, they became fuel for my guilt engine. Mother helped me see that. My brother Merlin and his family helped me see that. Sometimes things just happen and they're beyond your control. There's no way you could have realized a single drink would have so impaired you. Likewise, those soldiers I led into battle who never made it out didn't die because of me. They died because they volunteered to fight. They died because someone else figured out that if an enemy walked in a specific spot, they could place a bomb there. They died doing what they loved." I prodded the side of my head hard with my right forefinger. "It took a long time for that to sink in."

"But I still killed them."

"Yes, you did. But drinking a single drink and driving while not knowing you were impaired is different than getting hammered and saying fuck all and then getting behind a wheel."

"Tell that to the judge."

"Ohirra, there aren't any more judges. There aren't any more lawyers. There's just you and me."

She stared at me long enough for her eyes to go bright as tears poured out of them and ran down her face. I went to her and wiped them away. She didn't move as her chest heaved and she sobbed. I put my arms around her, and after a few moments she hugged me back, pressing her face into my neck.

When she'd finally recovered enough to speak, she pushed herself away. "There's something I don't think you've considered."

"What's that?" I asked.

"If you leave Earth, you become Khron. You become a collective version of our species whose sole goal is to exact revenge. You can only be human if you stay. Human is an Earth term, Mason. Khron is a space term."

That was something I hadn't thought of. I'd taken for granted that I was human... an Earthling. I guess I'd still technically be that when I left, but then I'd also be Khron. Like OMBRA, it was something to which I hadn't intended to belong but seemed destined for. But there was a bottom line I'd left unspoken. Something that has driven me since I first ran the streets of San Pedro in fear of the Eight Street Angels.

"I admit that a lot of the reason I'm going to join the chase is for revenge. You got me, guilty as charged. But you know what runs through me a mile wide, what's always run through me? My hatred of bullies. I know it sounds trite, but the Umis are intergalactic bullies who need to be stopped. I want to be part of the group that rids the universe of them once and for all. It's a simple thing, really, especially now that we've actually won a battle. Do you know what they call someone who can't stand a bully? They call them human, because bullies of all sorts, no matter if they walk on two legs or fly between the stars, are as inhuman as anything can ever be."

"You're wrong about that," she said, pinning me with her eyes.

I felt my eyebrows quirk. "What do you mean?"

"You asked *What do they call someone who can't stand a bully?* Sure, human is a good answer, but not the best." She crossed her arms, wiped away a stray tear, and gave me a sideways smile. "What do they call someone who can't stand a bully and tries to protect those who are being bullied? Or keep someone from being bullied in the future? What do you call them?

"Why we call them heroes."

I shook my head. "That's not me. That's just a call sign I had everyone use to make them feel better."

She shook her head. "That's exactly what I'd expect a hero to say." She stepped back and started down the ramp to the ground. "Goodbye, Hero Prime," she said without looking back. Once she stepped onto the ground, she turned, and offered me a cock-eyed smile.

I waved, conflicting emotions roiling through me as I realized that I'd never see any of my fellow grunts again. "Goodbye," I said, to Ohirra and everyone else I was leaving behind. War zones where I'd laughed and cried. Beaches where I'd swam. Mountains I'd hiked.

Monuments I'd paid to see, only to cry when I saw them. And of course my grunts.

The word *Goodbye* seemed so insufficient. I was about to say something else when the door closed before me and I stood, staring at it and wondering if I'd made the right decision. I was afraid to turn because I knew that once I did, everything would be forever changed. I'd no longer be Benjamin Carter Mason. I'd be Mason 1—the original version who would be downloaded and studied and cloned for as long as there are Umi in the universe.

They'd made a new position for me. Battle Captain. Me and my future versions would maintain the strategic and tactical knowledge of all Umi-Khron conflicts. When next we met the Umi, it would be me again who would bring them down... a grunt from Earth, slogging endlessly across the galaxy, doing what I do best until the end of time.

Yeah. I could handle that.

I turned and became a spaceman.

Can you hear that, my fellow Earthlings? Can you feel it? It's quiet out there isn't it? I wonder if the aliens are gone. We've heard that there was a hell of a battle down near Sydney, but don't have any data to back it up. As soon as I find out, I'll let you know, but in the meantime, go outside and take a deep breath. It feels different, doesn't it? There's something in the air. I daresay it feels like hope.

Conspiracy Theory Talk Radio,
Night Stalker Monologue #1999

GLOSSARY OF TERMS

.357 Ruger Blackhawk: Large revolver.

9mm: Type of ammunition also used to refer to a type of weapon

AC-130: Weaponized version of C-130 also known as Spectre Gunship. Carries Vulcan cannon and 105mm howitzer.

Ack Ack: term for anti-aircraft popularized in World War II

AK-47: Former Soviet-era Russian-made machine gun which fires 7.62mm ammunition.

AN\PVS-7: single-tube binocular night vision goggles

AR-15: Former Soviet-era American-made machine gun which fires 5.56mm ammunition.

Ascocarp: The fruiting body of an ascomycete phylum fungus.

Belay: To stop or ignore, usually an order or command.

Bingo Fuel: Zero Fuel

Blue Falcon: Buddy Fucker

Bounding Overwatch: also known as leapfrogging or moving overwatch, is the military tactic of alternating movement of coordinated units to allow, if necessary, suppressive fire in support of offensive forward movement or defensive disengagement.

C-130: Airplane capable of taking airborne troops into combat. Can also take off and land with relatively short runways.

Call Sign: An alpha numerical unique identifier used in communications.

Caspers: White supremacist survivalists living in Rancho Cucamonga.

Charlie Mike: Continue Mission.

Chobham Armor: British designed armor named after the location of design, Chobham Common, Surrey, England. Made of special ceramics with a metal backing, this armor offers superior resistance against explosive rounds and kinetic weapons.

Claymore Mine: A directional anti-personal mine capable of delivering 700 steel ball bearings at 1200 mps.

CO2 scrubber: A device which absorbs carbon dioxide.

Cray: Initially an overarching term for all aliens, this term really only applies to the alien creatures who reside in the hives.

Cult of Mother: A survivalist group originally from Big Cieniga Spring with a leader who looks like Kathy Bates.

Devil's Thunder: Survivalist biker gang who control the I-15 corridor between Vegas and L.A.

Donghai-10: Chinese-made land-to-land cruise missile capable of delivering nuclear payloads.

DZ: Drop Zone is the location where airborne personnel and vehicles land.

Eleven Bang Bang: U.S. Army Military Occupational Specialty 11B (Infantry)

ELF: Extremely Low Frequency.

EMP: Electromagnetic Pulse.

Ethnobotanist: The scientific study of the relationships that exist between peoples and plants.

Evac: Evacuate.

EXO: Originally called the Electromagnetic Faraday Xeno-combat Suit, the EXO is an electro-mechanical exoskeleton with armor, targeting systems, and advanced weapons.

FOB: Forward Operating Base

FUBAR: Fucked Up Beyond All Recognition.

Fungee: Common term for those infected and wearing ascocarps.

Gaze Technology: Advanced technology that allows a computer to track the movements of the eyes and allows selection and operations of virtual command trees in head's up displays.

GEOINT: Geospatial intelligence.

GNA: The largest survivalist group in the L.A. area, led by a charismatic former TV star.

Grunt: The lowest life form in the military.

HALO: High Altitude Low Opening parachute operation.

Harmonic Blade: An electromagnetic Stellite-made sword mounted on the EXO which vibrates at ultrasonic frequencies, making it thousands of times more effective at slicing through armored opponents than a normal blade.

HK 416: Advanced rifle system based on the AR 15, typically used by assault and special operations forces.

HMID: Human Machine Interface Device.

HUD: Head's Up Display is a transparent display that presents data without requiring users to look away from their usual viewpoints.

HUMINT: Human-derived intelligence.

Hydra rocket: Adapted surface-to-air or surface-to-surface rocket fired from a pod mounted on the EXO.

Hypocrealiacs: The over-arching term for the aliens who have invaded Planet Earth

IMINT: Imagery intelligence.

infil\exfil: Get in\Get out.

JMPI: Jump Master Personnel Inspection.

Leupold Mark 4 CQ\T scope: State of the art rifle scope capable of providing night vision.

M-16: Vietnam-era and most common variant of the AR 15.

M-4: Modern variant of the AR 15.

M60A3: Vietnam-era main battle tank with 105mm main gun.

MAC-10: Compact sub-machine gun capable of firing .45 acp or 9mm.

MASH: Mobile Army Surgical Hospital.

Military Fatigues: Any uniform created for work or combat.

Mother: Leader of the Cult of Mother who has a striking resemblance to the actress Kathy Bates.

Mr. Pink: Recruiter for the OMBRA Corporation and commander of OMBRA Special Operations Command North America. Originally a nickname given by Ben Mason because of the man's resemblance to the actor Steve Buscemi, the name has stuck and is what Mr. Wilson uses instead of his own name.

MRE: Meals Ready to Eat are boxed and bagged rations used to feel troops in the field.

NAP: High-speed low altitude air travel following the contours of the Earth. Also called Nap of the Earth or NOE.

Needler: Alien variant which protects and pollinates the flowers on the black kudzu.

Net: A network of communication devices.

New Panthers: Benign survivalist group from Corona who merely want to be left alone.

NTC: National Training Center at Fort Irwin was the location where American military forces trained brigade on brigade combat operations.

NVD or Nods: Terms referring to Night Vision Devices.

OMBRA: Largest world-wide defense contractor before the alien invasion.

OPFOR: Opposing Forces.

Ophiocordycipitaceae: A family of parasitic fungi in the Ascomycota, class Sordariomycetes.

Overwatch: Units or elements of unit supporting each other during fire and maneuver.

P226: Semi-automatic pistol which fires 9mm ammunition.

P238: Very small semi-automatic pistol which fires 9mm ammunition or .45 ACP.

Prick-77: A man-packable, portable VHF FM combat-net radio transceiver used to provide short-range, two-way radiotelephone voice communication. Capable of communications operations up to thirty miles with booster.

PTSD: Post Traumatic Stress Disorder.

QRF: Quick Reaction Force.

Recon: Reconnaissance.

Retrans: Intermediate booster for FM signal to extend the range.

RPG: A class of weapon using rocket propelled grenades.

RTB: Return to Base.

Sirens: Alien variant which uses human brain-waves to establish alien to alien communication.

SNAFU: Situation Normal All Fucked Up.

SOCOM: Special Operations Command.

Spikers: Alien variant, usually in animals, with spikey ascocarps protruding from the skin.

T-80: Main Russian and Soviet battle tank.

UAV: Unmanned Ariel Vehicle.

VUAA1: Vanderbilt University Allosteric Agonist

Number One is a pesticide which renders the user invisible to certain species of insects and needlers because it causes sensory overload

W54: Manufactured in the United States in 1961, these were the smallest man-packable nuclear weapons devised.

WWWSD: What Would William Shatner Do.

Xenobotanist: The scientific study of the relationships that exist between extraterrestrial peoples and plants.

XM214: A weapon's system mounted on the EXO with a six-barreled rotating minigun fed from a backpack ammo supply through an ammo feed arm with 1500 rounds of 5.56mm ammunition.

ZSU 23-4: Former Soviet Union-produced self-propelled anti-aircraft weapons system.